The Novels of

The Parish of Hilby

by

Mrs Fairman Mann

Larks Press

First published in England by
Elliot Stock, Paternoster Row, London, 1883

This new edition published in November 2007 by
The Larks Press
Ordnance Farmhouse, Guist Bottom,
Dereham, Norfolk NR20 5PF
01328 829207

Printed by the Lanceni Press, Garrood Drive, Fakenham,
Norfolk. 01328 851578

British Library Cataloguing-in-Publication-Data
A catalogue record for this book is available from the British Library

A full catalogue of Larks Press books is available at
www.booksatlarkspress.co.uk

Front cover photograph by P. H. Emerson kindly supplied by
Norfolk County Council Library and Information Service
from the Picture Norfolk Archive

ISBN 978 1 904006 41 1

Introduction

'The dear old "Parish"', Mary Mann wrote in 1902 of her first novel. 'Ah, the pains and joys of the years fled since I wrote that – the only one I ever wrote without conscious or more or less painful effort'. She was 35 when *The Parish of Hilby* was published in 1883. It is a first-hand account of life in a typical small Norfolk village of the time. Mann's wit and her inventive command of language ensure that this book is a thoroughly good read and uniquely, certainly among female writers of the period, it describes an agricultural strike.

The name of the author on the title page is Mrs Fairman Mann – perhaps she assumed that this would be her only novel, and not as it turned out, the first of at least 39 to be published over the next 30 years or so. By the time the second one was published, the delightfully titled *Confessions of a Coward and a Coquette,* she had insisted that her own Christian name be used plus an 'E' for her second name Elisabeth. In 1901 she was to write, 'There is a reproduction of my old photo in "The Candid Friend" this week. I think it rather a cheek their calling me Mrs Fairman Mann. I chose for my literary work the name Mary E Mann.' By the beginning of the 20th century she had become very well known in literary circles.

In 1883 however she was a busy farmer's wife with four children between the ages of 5 and 11, a boy and three girls. It is amazing that she had found the time to write a novel. She wrote with a quill pen, sitting in her dining room, often with a child or two sitting on the arm of her chair. She herself admitted, 'I could not write at all if it were not for the servants', but she adds 'Yet so much of my time is taken up with organising them and their duties. People never dream that I require any privacy and I cannot bring myself to think that what I do is important enough to make a fuss about.' Yet somehow she does manage to find the time saying, 'I only know that I write because I must. It is out of the depths that we – that some of us, write.'

Moving to the country at the age of 23 in 1871 when she married Fairman Mann must have been a great shock to her. She'd been born and brought up in a wealthy middle class family in Norwich and was well educated and very well read. For the next ten years she was adjusting herself to village life and motherhood and the gradual realisation that it was becoming increasingly difficult to make a good living out of farming. 'When we first came here everything looked so promising!' Unbeknown to her though she was absorbing from all around her the very things that she could use as material for her writing. When Mann did start putting pen to paper she had a huge cast of characters and their rural life to draw on. She wrote: 'These simple folks that are born, grow up, grow old around us – every incident of their history is known to us; the slow working of their untilled minds, the toil and sorrows, the sins and foolishness and goodness of their lives.' A review of *The Parish of Hilby* published in *The Academy* magazine in

1883 says: 'The charm of this book consists in the admirable drawing of its characters. Like Jane Austen, the authoress is essentially a miniaturist; she delights in portraying fine shades, and she succeeds in producing portraits absolutely lifelike.' Another contemporary reviewer in *The Truth* calls the book: 'As perfect a picture of country life and manners as I have met with.'

Hilby is quite obviously based on the Mann's village of Shropham, near Attleborough in South Norfolk. It is a very clear picture of the rigid class system that was in place then. From the Squire to the Vicar, the tenant farmer to the most impoverished labourer, Mann depicts each one in accurate detail with humour and compassion and delightful irony. The story is about James Massey, new to the village, and like Fairman Mann at Manor Farm, a tenant farmer who has taken on the running of his late uncle's farm. The first people he meets are the Freemans, also tenant farmers although considerably lower down the social scale. There is an amusing description of his visit to their drawing room and the rather inept welcome that they give him. 'Mrs Freeman, removed from her proper regions, and debarred the discussion of her fowls and her servants, was not a fluent person, and she was quite ill at ease amid the 'glories' of her drawing room'. James Massey rightly suspects that this 'bower of bliss' as he thinks of it, must be the work of a Miss Freeman and sure enough she appears. 'Pollie Freeman was a pretty girl, he could see at a glance; under any circumstances she would have been pretty, in her best hat she was exceptionally killing'. Pollie has been for a year in London being 'finished'. 'Finished!' says Mr Freeman. 'I'm dashed if they didn't pretty well finish her. That year I reckon cost me a matter of a hundred pound, and they all but starved her! I can finish off my daughter in that fashion without paying a hundred pound for it, I fancy.' Of his 'fashionable daughter's uselessness and gentility he was naturally proud however.' Much of the characterisation and humour is contained in the dialogue and the Norfolk dialect, which with a rare skill Mann writes down so accurately.

Massey starts a gentle flirtation with Pollie who was 'a wee bit too plump. There was always that appalling threatening of a double chin above the lace at her throat; her waistband would assume that dreadful appearance of painfully cutting her in halves, and of losing itself in the operation.' She has a baby sister called Dollie - the name of Mann's own four year old. Mann does not pull any punches however. When Massey asks how many children there are altogether, Mrs Freeman replies: 'only three of 'em – two girls as you see, and a boy that's out on the farm. The two that came between him an' the little'un are dead.'

Pollie walks back through the wood with Massey to show him a short cut. She tells him that the wood will be a sheet of blue with 'wild hyacinths' in a few months. 'If you care for such things you will see the wood in spring – that is if Hilby hasn't killed you with dullness before then.' Mann herself found Shropham extremely dull a lot of the time, lacking the culture and intellectual stimulation she thrived on but she admits in a letter to her husband's nephew 'I have found beauty in this place.' Her writing and her ongoing correspondence with this nephew, Thomas Ordish, himself a writer and Shakespeare scholar, kept her mind active and he was of great practical help to her as she established herself as an author. She was later to write to him: 'The courage to write was largely fostered by you. It is as certain as anything that I should never have attempted to write, or do more than pester my friends with long letters if it had not been for you, my old friend and sympathiser, the champion of my poor powers and defender of all my scribblings.'

Pollie introduces more characters in this tight-knit social circle. Massey asks her if there are any other girls in the village. She replies: 'I am the single, solitary, blessed one. That's of course not counting the labourers' daughters. I am the only *girl,* but there is one young lady. I'm not to be mentioned in the same breath as her. I'm a tenant farmer's daughter, and she's sister-in-law to the parson – think of that! I'm a girl; she's a young *lady* if you please. To belong in the remotest degree to a parson, is supposed in this neighbourhood to give an advantage over every other class. Never mind if you can't pay your debts, never mind if you aren't quite honest, never mind if you've no more brains than a fool; you are, being a parson, or a parson's relation, select. I hate the race! – don't you?'

The young lady Pollie is referring to is Helen Smythe. Unfortunately for Pollie, James Massey only needs to take one look at Helen to be besotted. She is a beauty, though not 'fashionable' and her liberal views and ability to see the points of view of others, whatever their walk of life, reflects Mann's own personality. She lives at the Vicarage with her sister Anna who is married to the Vicar, Alfred Pearson. Mann had strong views on the clergy and did not suffer gladly those she considered to have double standards. She writes to Ordish: 'In a place like Dulditch (Shropham) you cannot dissociate the priest from the person, his precepts from his practise.'

Mr Pearson is fairly ineffectual, but harmless, and escapes the wrath of Mann's tongue if not her wit: 'He was a cipher in his own house, a nonentity in the parish.' Anna Pearson however is what Mann deprecatingly describes as goody-goody and is a wonderfully drawn character. 'Life was no difficulty to Mrs Pearson. People must do their duty that's all. What she looked on as her own duty was so exceedingly easy to herself that she never could understand or sympathize with the rest of mankind who seemed to shirk theirs. She was by no means an idle woman and always had some more or less unreasonable scheme on foot at which she slaved with all her energy. In the matter of the proper fulfilment of other people's duties she was most rigorous.' Her good deeds and particularly her fanaticism about Temperance have alienated her and her family from the whole village whom she is trying to convert. 'They love darkness rather than light, because their deeds are evil,' says Mrs Pearson. She does not seem to care about this alienation but her sister Helen says, 'I am tired of feeling that we have not a friend in the place, except among the very poor, for whose friendship we pay.' She continues; 'Anna what is to be done about that wretched Mrs Moore? Her husband has not had a stroke of work to do for the last fortnight and the children have not nearly enough to eat. She has another black eye.'

Anna asks if Helen took him a copy of *The Enlightener*, the paper for which Anna 'wrote her little heart stirring stories of conversion from drunkenness and poverty to sobriety and riches.' But Helen has not taken the paper to Moore. She feels it is too childish for him. 'I know it is very interesting dear, and fitted no doubt for a certain order of understanding, but Tom Moore when sober is an intelligent man, he really has thought and can talk.'

'*The Enlightener*, by the help of prayer has worked the cure of many thousands. I will go myself to see this dreadful person. I do not at all despair of being able to cope with him, in spite of his intelligence,' replies Anna. No wonder Pollie's nickname for this self appointed paragon of virtue is 'sour-krout.'

Tom Moore is responsible for encouraging the labourers to come out on strike on James Massey's farm. Agricultural strikes increasingly became a feature of late 19th century rural life as the agricultural depression took hold. Mary Mann saw the effects of the depression all around her and she and Fairman did what they could to help the poor in the village while they themselves were barely earning a living. Indeed another strong reason for Mann to begin her writing, and to write a romance that would sell, was the need to earn some money in order to supplement the family income. A series of disastrous harvests brought ruin to many farmers and terrible distress to the agricultural labourers who were struggling to feed and clothe their families on a meagre 11 shillings a week.

In his book *Rural England* published in 1902, Rider Haggard, a close neighbour of the Manns wrote: 'From 1879 onwards everything connected with agriculture had been going steadily downhill. What with the high rates and land taxes the outlook was very uncertain. Indeed short of the entire stoppage of the industry, things could scarcely have changed for the worse. Mr Disraeli refused to impose duties on imports from abroad and his commitment to Free Trade had disastrous results. Farmers had nothing to look forward to except ruin. Due to low wages and lack of prospects, the labouring classes began to desert the country for the towns, where they hope, often vainly, to better their prospects. Those left behind on the land must take their pittance of 11 shillings a week, or starve. Starve or shamefully take the hated road to the workhouse.'

Helen Smythe has taken pity on Tom Moore and his family and persuades Massey to give him work; 'by employing Moore you would be doing a great work of charity...putting bread into his children's mouths and raising a woman's soul from the depths of sluggish despair.' Massey does employ him although Massey's uncle had sacked and re-employed Moore at least twenty times before. Moore is considered a troublemaker, 'the worst lot in the village.' Mrs Freeman tells Massey: 'the men ye see always have an idea they're badly treated, and they're no hand at expressing themselves as a rule.

When they do get one amongst them clever enough to give tongue to it, they think his words are just gospel, and he can do what he like with the lot.'

The chapters concerning Helen's opinions and the description of the strike itself form the real 'meat' of this book. It is a fascinating insight into the delicate balance of the relationship between a master and his men at this particular moment in English rural history. Massey stands 'awhile to watch his beasts eating themselves into money in their stalls.' Helen tells him 'I have given up hoping to interest men of your class in the class you employ. If you went about as I do, heard what I hear, and saw the sights I sometimes see, you would not wonder that my sympathy goes so entirely with the labourer -' 'And consequently against the farmer,' interrupts Massey, 'our interests ought to be, and used to be identical. Why should not my men look on me as friend, as well as master? How much better was the state of things in such a district as this – say forty years ago! Servants had not learnt to rise against their masters in those good old times.' But Helen assures him that those 'good old times' were not good for the labourers. 'I could tell tales, that have made me thank God for this "union" you consider so iniquitous, and for having put into these men's slow minds a means of defence in their helplessness.' She tells him the tragic story of a baby who suffered terribly when her mother was forced to go out to work and neglect her. 'And but for this banding together of the men against their masters, and their starvation prices, such things would be going on now. You will think that I hold dangerous opinions, Mr Massey; I, however, keep them for the benefit of the farmer; I do not corrupt the labourer.' This is certainly Mann herself talking.

Massey would have liked to give his workers a rise, 'Thirteen shillings a week isn't much of a sum; queer work to live and bring up big families on that screw!' but he has made a pact with his fellow tenant farmer, Mr Freeman, that they won't give in. When he confronts Moore, the man is eloquent: 'Let my wife and children starve! What is it to you and the likes o' you, that murder women and child'en with cold and hunger, that grow rich while we that 'arn your money are dyin' for want, wi'our child'en's bellies going empty, that you may stuff and grow fat?'

As a result of the strike Massey is forced to work himself to get his hay in. Mann later put this idea to good use in her novel *The Patten Experiment* 1899 (also published by the Lark's Press) in which a middle class family try living on the eleven-shilling wage for a week.

The Parish of Hilby contains several very entertaining set pieces full of amusing detail and dialogue. The chapters 'High Tea at the Grange,' 'Dinner at the Vicarage,' 'The Village Concert' and 'Helen's Garden Party' are quite Dickensian in feel, involving several minor characters, notably Captain Back and the 'man about town' Arthur Gosling, a goose if ever there was one. Mann attended many similar events in Shropham and frequently helped to organise village entertainments. In the final scenes of this novel those readers who were looking for romance will have been satisfied! But the strength of the labourers' scenes lingers longer in the mind.

By 1906 when Mary Mann was a household name, Messrs Methuen issued new editions of her chief novels including this one. In it Mann is clearly honing her skills for the economy and power of her collection of short stories *The Fields of Dulditch,* based on these same Shropham characters. I am delighted to say that the Lark's Press is shortly preparing to republish all the Dulditch stories in one volume. The stories form the focus of Mary Mann's best writing, the seeds of which are sown here in *The Parish of Hilby.*

Patience Tomlinson
Stanhoe, Norfolk, 2007

Patience Tomlinson has created a one-woman show about the life and work of Mary E. Mann entitled 'A Tale That Is Told' which she has performed in many venues in and out of Norfolk. A frequent performer on BBC Radio3 and 4, she has broadcast several of Mary Mann's short stories and four of these are available on CD under the title *The Fields of Dulditch.* There are more recordings to follow, including an audio book of *Rose at Honeypot.*
email: patienceacts@aol.com

CHAPTER I

Some Parishioners

MR JAMES LAWRENCE MASSEY, new tenant of the Wood Farm, Hilby, leant over his garden-gate and smoked his pipe. It was but three o'clock of that late autumn afternoon, but he had already done a fair day's work, and was enjoying his rest with a clear conscience.

He had risen at six, had seen his men and horses go out to work, had tasted the first freshness of the fair morning, trampling over the unfamiliar fields, his dog at his heels, his pipe in his mouth; had returned, after a vast amount of tobacco consumed, to find that he had to wait for his breakfast, and that when it came he was in no better appetite than if he had just tumbled out of bed. He said to himself then that early rising was a swindle, and the boasted property of the first morning air a delusion. He repented of his excess of zeal, but not of his excess of pipes. He further reflected that his farm steward, whose place he had tried to fill that morning, not only knew more about his own work there than at present did his master, but that he was certainly more used to early rising, having been up with the earliest of the Wood Farm birds any time this forty years; and Mr Massey decided then and there, as he turned away from his eggs and bacon, that he would not attempt to usurp that steward's place any more in such presumptuous fashion.

Presently he had set himself to work to reduce the chaos reigning in his sitting-room into some degree of order. His housekeeper in charge of his goods and chattels had been sent forward a fortnight ago, but had apparently passed the time in a state of bewildered fussiness, during which refractory tables and chairs, wardrobes and bedsteads, had all but turned her brain, while the carpets, which refused to adjust themselves to the unfamiliar floors, had gone near to breaking her heart. 'I'm hanged if I know where to put my hand on any individual blessed thing that belongs to me,' her master had said to himself, looking round ruefully. So after breakfast he had pulled off his coat and gone to work with a will. He had unpacked the cases, carefully disposed in the most convenient position for stumbling in the hall, had hung up his few pictures, had disposed of his fewer ornaments, had stowed away his books; then, giving up as a bad job the effort to make his housekeeper understand his various applications to her for missing articles, he had, all unassisted, made voyages of discovery into districts hitherto but little explored, and had triumphantly rescued valuable property from many unlikely and dangerous positions. Altogether he was tolerably satisfied with his day's work, and as he now stood with his back to the little iron gate leading into the meadow, and placidly surveyed the house that from henceforth was to be his home, he had the pleasing consciousness that by his own efforts he had reduced to a habitable state his sitting- and bed-room, the two rooms important to his comfort, and that for the rest he need care very little.

He was no stranger to the house, although he had taken up his abode there but yesterday. His visits to his bachelor uncle, the last tenant of the Wood Farm, had indeed been but flying ones, and as infrequent as he dared to make them – the old gentleman being rather miserly and morose than hospitable and social in his habits; but full often in years gone by had he heard the history of the place from his father's lips. There, where the roof was covered with ivy, where the smokeless chimneys even were overgrown, was the big kitchen, unused now, where his own grandfather had eaten and smoked and snored with his men, none harder worked, and hardly one more untutored than himself. The rats held undisputed sway there now, and even promised to invade the smaller cosier kitchen, which the landlord had built, together with the bedroom and attic above it, when Jabez, James Massey's uncle, had taken the farm. It must have been very ugly, that excrescence on the house once, the young man thought, but time had toned down its incongruity, and the ivy had long ago overlooked the difference between the old bricks and the new.

In that room over the porch where the lattice-windows now stood open, his father and his father's brother had slept as boys. Full many a time had he had its position explained to him, and knew, with regard to that same window, how the two beds had stood, and that one of the boys had been hard to rouse in the morning, and that the other had risen with the lark. In that very room, too, it was that Jabez Massey, a few months ago, had died – poor lonely old man! with never a willing ear into which to pour tales of his boyhood's days, who if he had any memories of them, had locked them in his breast and brooded unsociably alone. That big bow-window on the other side of the door stood as witness of the only bit of romance which, so far as his nephew knew, had occurred in that barren life. It had been built on to the room, then called the parlour – but which James Massey had now appropriated for his dining-room – to please the fancy of a young woman who had promised to be his uncle's wife.

Something had gone wrong in this old love affair – no one knew exactly what; the young lady's property was deficient, or Jabez had not shown himself so liberal as was expected – the match was broken off. James Massey did not even know her name, if she still walked the earth, or if she were but dust; he only knew that the bow-window was a standing proof that she once existed, the thick stem of the vine trained over the brickwork a living witness of the years since the romance was new.

The garden, lying all in front of the picturesque old house, had a somewhat dreary aspect, as of a place that for years had been neither loved nor cared for. The drive and the wide gravel-sweep before the door were grass-grown and neglected, the bowling-green, surrounded on three sides by borders filled with overgrown shrubs and choked with decaying vegetation, was rank and untrimmed, the hedges were wild and straggling; but their present proprietor regarded everything with a lenient eye. The place would put on a different aspect under his care, he knew; and meanwhile every plant and shrub, almost every tree, had been planted by his own kith and kin – he had an affection for them all.

Presently he turned his back on the house and looked across the meadow, only divided from the garden by the iron railing against which he leaned. Here, in the summer evening, the youth of the village still pitched their wickets, and laughed and quarrelled and shouted over their game; here, long and long ago, had played and quarrelled and shouted his own father and his father's brother. Far away, over the lank dark winter's grass at the farther end of the meadow could be seen the narrow twisting river, too narrow and too shallow for any kind of navigation, but boasting now and again a hole looking 'likely' for a pike, and supposed by some ever-hopeful anglers to contain a vast quantity of fish, since so few were ever taken out of it. Very little, however, could be seen of this nameless stream from where Mr Massey stood, and cold and misty and uninviting that little looked to-day. Nearer at hand a dozen little bullocks stood deep in the wet grass, neither feeding nor taking good to themselves in any way on the raw afternoon, but looking, in placid expectation, to the gate at which in an hour's time they would emerge into the comfortable shelter of their yard, and to the unfailing consolation of their oil-cake. There was another gate in the pasture beside that at which the beasts looked with longing eyes, and over this gate a man was now seen to be climbing.

'And who is this?' asked James Massey of himself, looking on, 'and what may he be up to? Is he after stealing the bullocks? is he after driving them up? is he after buying them? He is something to do with bullocks, I'd swear, buy the cut of his trousers and by the way he carries his stick. No! He has ceased to contemplate the bullocks – he is making straight for me – he's grinning at me;' then, a happy light breaking upon him, 'he's a visitor!' This idea having occurred to him in time to call up a pleasant look upon his face, he raised his hat in answer to the other's unceremonious greeting, and pushing open the little swing-gate, admitted his unknown visitor with a smile of welcome.

'Good day to ye,' the stranger said, putting out a big hard hand, and holding Massey's for a moment in a loose and unsatisfactory grasp. He was a man of fifty or thereabout, and his large and heavy person was clothed in ill-made but well-worn garments; coat, waistcoat and trousers representing each some separate suit, of which the other members had perhaps fallen into decay. His very shabby hat, into which he crammed more of his head than is usual or becoming, shadowed a face which superficial observers were wont to call 'jolly' – it was fat and red and healthy-looking, telling of good living and of good hours, but there was no sign of joviality about it – certainly not in the small yet staring eyes, nor in the ugly unsmiling mouth. His lip was clean shaven, but his beard and whiskers, of a light brown colour, were luxuriant, not to say shaggy, entirely concealing the linen and handkerchief at his throat. In spite, however, of the unsmartness of his visitor's attire, Massey saw at a glance that the shabbiness was due to choice rather than necessity. He had lived too long among the agriculturists of that county not to know that dowdiness is with them no sign of poverty, but very often of the reverse, and that the humbleness of their aspect may not always with safety be received as a guarantee of the humility of their minds.

'I'm your nearest neighbour,' the stranger said now, by way of introduction, 'had to come round your way this noontime; thought I'd better look you up.'

'It's very good of you, I'm sure,' Mr Massey said. 'Let's see, if you're my nearest neighbour you must of course be...' he hesitated, being not at all clear in his own mind as to who his visitor must be.

'I belong to the Grange Farm, the other side of the wood,' the other said, jerking his head in the direction of some trees to be seen on the right of the house, and evidently considering the indication of his place of abode sufficient to proclaim his name to any civilized dweller on the globe.

'Then,' said Mr Massey, 'I think I have to thank you for many kind offices. My man appears to have been unconscionable in the amount of things he has borrowed, but we are of course in a terribly unsettled state for the present; and did he not tell me that you had been over the farm once or twice to see that things were going on all right in my absence? I am sure I am immensely obliged to you for –'

But the visitor interrupted him with a somewhat contemptuous sound that was more of a grunt than a laugh, for which perhaps it was intended.

'I'd no hand in all that,' he said. 'No; tha's Charles Selby, you may lay your life! He'd look after any man's business rather than his own, any day o' the week, and you can't please him better than to use up's things for him.'

'Well, really, that's very obliging of him, now,' Massey said, laughing; 'a man of that kind is a pleasing novelty, don't you think? Looked at from my point of view, just now, he is a decided acquisition.'

'I dare say!' the other assented. 'I fight shy of him myself – they that go a-lendin' come a-borrowin', I find. I make it a rule to do nayther. No; my name's Freeman, over to the Grange here. Selby's away right to th' other end o' the parish.'

'Then, Mr Freeman, pray come in,' the younger man said, beginning towards the house. 'We're in a state of commotion at present, as you will see, but I dare say we can find a chair and a glass of wine. It is really very good of you to have looked me up so soon. I hope that we shall be good neighbours.'

'Best to be friends, I s'pose,' Mr Freeman said, without enthusiasm, 'so the women said. No, I 'on't come in. I'm not one to waste much time in other folk's houses, and I'll be gettin' back agin. If you ha' nothin' better to do tho', you might walk along my way p'r'aps.'

And at length, after a little more talk, and many more vain efforts to get his visitor to enter his house, Mr Massey decided to avail himself of this invitation, and set out with his new friend.

He did not find him an amusing companion, nor a communicative one, and the weight of conversation during that half-mile walk fell on Massey's own shoulders; but he, who was of a friendly turn of mind and anxious to be on good terms with his neighbour, made gallant efforts to be entertaining, and started many subjects. He talked of the farm he had left to come to Hilby, and of his reasons for throwing it up; of the Wood Farm, and of how from quite his boyhood he had cherished a wish to live in the place in which his father had been born, and for which he, till his death, had maintained so much affection. He spoke of improvements he meant to make there, and asked advice about some new buildings he wanted to have erected. When they passed on to Mr Freeman's own land, he commended the excellent turnips over which they crossed, and said flattering things of the sheep they inspected in their fold. He did his best, but he did not seem to himself to make much progress; his listener encouraged him now and again with a grunt or a nod, or a muttered 'Dessay!' evidently his favourite ejaculation, but of words he was certainly embarrassingly sparing. A word or two, however, he did say about Mr Massey's uncle, 'old Jabez,' as he called him, and asked a question or so about the disposal of 'the old man's savings;' but the words were not very respectful to the dead, and grated on his companion's ears, and the questions were slightly impertinent and remained unanswered.

'Come in and see the women,' he said, when Massey would have shaken hands with him at his gate; and soon that gentleman, all unresisting, found himself ushered into the Grange drawing-room, and after a lapse of time (sufficient, perhaps, for the adjustment of a dress and the pinning on of a smarter cap) he had the happiness of being presented to Mrs Freeman.

'This is my wife,' said her husband, by way of one-sided introduction.

'I hope you're very well, sir,' the lady said, and put out a bony unbeautiful hand. 'Pray take a seat.'

When Mr Massey had dropped those stiff unresponsive fingers, had taken the indicated seat, had reported satisfactorily as to his health, and said a few deeply interesting words as to the state of the weather, he found that the conversation flagged somewhat. Looking at the angular form of the woman before him, sitting uncomfortably in a smart but most uneasy chair, her florid face surrounded by flaxen hair, arranged over pads in a happily long-exploded fashion, a very fashionable but unbecoming cap upon her head, he felt that she was being put at a disadvantage. Had she received him in less grandeur, had he come upon her unexpectedly in the kitchen, or the dairy even, how mutually entertaining might they not have been! He could have asked her advice about matters connected with his own housekeeping, and she would have questioned him on the management of his dairy. But the chill splendour of their surroundings seemed now to have frozen their tongues. In fact, Mrs Freeman, removed from her proper regions, and debarred the discussion of her fowls and of her servants, was not a fluent person, and she was quite as ill at ease amid the glories of her drawing-room as was her visitor himself.

Mr Freeman, after shuffling uneasily about the room for a minute or so, keeping his hat on his head, and offering no help to his wife in her social duties, suddenly withdrew, and busied himself, as Massey by various tokens was speedily aware, in the broaching of a bottle of wine. And now almost superhuman efforts in the cause of politeness failed to fix Mrs Freeman's attention on what was being said to her, while her husband could be heard calling for the servant, calling for a corkscrew, calling for wine-glasses.

Presently a young and evidently inexperienced handmaiden appeared at the door, and all but demolished the glasses on the tray she carried, by the vigour with which she 'bobbed' to the gentleman on the sofa. And at sight of those tottering glasses a look of annoyance flashed into her mistress's face, a ''tchick' of aggravation fell from her tongue.

'Whatever did you bring in *them* wine-glasses for?' she asked severely. 'Take 'em away – take 'em away! You know well enough they aren't the right glasses to bring in now.'

'Master didn't say as he wanted the best,' the unfortunate girl said, as she departed with the tray, her mistress following her from the room, and leaving Mr Massey to his own devices while she herself rearranged the waiter with the company glasses.

Left to himself, Mr Massey, with a little ill-suppressed chuckle of enjoyment, looked about him with a quick observant eye. As he looked he found much matter for surprise and speculation. This drawing-room at the Grange Farm was not at all the order of best room you could have anticipated as the sanctum of the Grange Farm mistress. This was a decided advance on the horsehair chairs ranged against the wall, the shining centre table, the coloured Scriptural prints, which the young man felt might have been expected of her. Here, the chairs were set about in admired confusion, the round table was pushed into a distant corner, while a perfect army of small, rickety tables, with little smart covers, arranged as traps to catch the unwary, lurked in every direction. There was a gorgeous but undecked épergne on the middle of the broad window-seat, and an array of specimenless specimen-glasses on the chimney-piece, while the fireplace, in spite of the chilliness of the atmosphere, was gorgeous in white muslin and gold.

'What a bower of bliss!' said Mr Massey to himself, grinding his head well into the crewel-worked chair-back against which he leant, for greater facility of observation. 'I don't believe,' his cogitations ran, 'that the wife of my uncommunicative friend here, with her bony fingers and her stiff back and her shrill voice, is equal to this really lavish display of decoration. There must be a Miss Freeman; and if so, why the deuce don't she show up?'

He was really interested in the question, having a certain weakness for the society of young unmarried females, or in other words being, as with sisterly frankness his own sister had often told him, somewhat of a fool about women.

For the present, however, only the parents of the assumed young lady 'showed up,' bearing the wine, at length decanted, and the glasses sacred to 'company.' Mrs Freeman's mind being now a little more at rest, she was able to give a less-divided attention to her guest, and a conversation, still far from brilliant, limped on. Her husband, meanwhile, still retaining his hat and his stolid demeanour, drank off some wine with celerity but appreciation; and Massey was beginning to think that he might be allowed to make his escape, when an interruption, which delayed him for awhile, occurred. A muffled tapping sounded low down on the drawing-room door, and an authoritative baby-voice demanded admittance.

'Open 'is door, somebody! Jus' open 'is door!'

'Tha's the young un,' Mr Freeman said, glancing at his wife – a smile on his heavy face.

'I wonder wheriver Pollie can be,' the lady of the house said, as she opened the door. 'She went out wi' the child. Run in, Dollie! run and speak to the gentleman.' Passing into the hall, she called aloud for her elder daughter. 'Pollie! Pollie! wheriver are you got to?' Then addressing the small housemaid, 'Run, find up Miss Pollie, and tell her she's wantin' in the drawin'-room,' she said.

The youngest Freeman, meanwhile, had gone over to her father, and was standing now between his legs, looking over from that safe refuge with much interest to Mr Massey.

'What a jolly little girl!' that gentleman said. 'Come over and give me a kiss, Dollie.'

But Dollie laughed, hanging her head, then hid her face in her father's beard. 'Dear Dollie won't,' she declared with decision. 'Dear Dollie don't like to kiss.'

'Dollie mustn't be rude,' her mother said reprovingly. 'Come here to me, there's a pretty one! and tell me where Pollie's got to.'

'Pollie's puttin' on her best hat,' said the youngster promptly. 'Dear Dollie not dot on my best hat.' This, while casting sidelong glances at Massey, who was making, with his walking-stick, friendly advances towards her fat legs.

Just as he had succeeded in hooking one of these baby members with the crook of his stick, and as 'dear Dollie,' finding her sturdy limbs fail her, was endeavouring to hold her position by lying on the flat of her back, and grasping her father's calves, the door opened and Miss Freeman appeared. Her mother, lost in her desire to see the effect on the visitor of Pollie in her new hat, was quite incapable of any introduction, and Mr Freeman was engaged in silently tickling his youngest born, lying at his feet. Mr Massey therefore arose and shook hands with the daughter of the house, without having been 'put a name to,' as he told himself afterwards with amusement. Pollie Freeman was a pretty girl, he could see at a glance; under any circumstances she would have been pretty, in her best hat she was exceptionally killing. It went on very much on one side, this hat, and was an expensive fabrication of lace and feathers procured from Gurton – the nearest town to Hilby, on last market-day. The hair, which only on one side showed beneath it, was of that red golden hue suggestive of old masters and strong soda, and by means of curling-tongs, or of innumerable papers, was twisted into hundreds of little curls over her already somewhat low forehead, and down to her pretty ear. Her eyes of light blue were darkened by lashes of many shades deeper than her hair, which lashes fairly swept a chubby soft cheek of enviable fairness. Indeed, Miss Freeman's one great point, besides that of being always deeply in the fashion, was this point of her faultless complexion. Her one great drawback (in her own mind at least) was that she was just a wee bit too plump. To do her credit, she had tried to obviate this defect with praiseworthy energy, by stays of surpassing tightness, by dresses in which she found it difficult to move, by copious draughts of vinegar, by abstention from sugar and potatoes; but alas, to no effect. The white, dimpled wrist still swelled perceptibly over the too tightly buttoned glove; there was always that appalling threatening of a double chin above the lace at her throat; her waist-belt would assume that dreadful appearance of painfully cutting her in halves, and of losing itself in the operation; and there were one or two friends of her mother's, more candid than ingratiating, who openly predicted that in the course of a few years Pollie would be as broad as she was long. This, it is true, was not saying very much, as her length was, to say the least, insignificant, in spite of her high-crowned hat and her high-heeled shoes.

Such as she was, however, Mr Massey regarded her with unconcealed admiration, and settled at once in his unsaintly mind that she would in all probability prove amusing. It may have been from the killing hat that he derived this impression, or from the conscious look in the blue eyes which seemed to seek his a good deal, or from the obtrusive fashion in which a certain short plump foot was displayed for his inspection on a bead-worked ottoman.

'Why, wheriver have you been, Pollie?' her mother asked. 'I thought you were niver goin' to bring the child home again.'

'I have only been into the village, ma. Did you think someone had run away with me? What a change that would have been, to be sure! Something for you all to talk about, too. And how do you like Hilby, Mr Massey?' This with a rather exaggerated air of self-possession, her mother listening in admiring wonder.

'Immensely!' declared Mr Massey politely; 'I am always finding something fresh to admire in it.' He was apparently admiring now, if one might judge from the direction of his glance – the smart bow-decked shoe of Miss Pollie Freeman.

'Ah, you'll tell a different tale before long,' the young lady said, from the depths of her great experience. 'Wait till you've lived through a winter here. That's the touch! 'Tisn't lively even in the summer, goodness knows! but you can get about, if you've a mind to, though there's nowhere to go and nothing to see. But in winter, with mud over the tops of your boots, and the darkness down upon you before you're hardly dressed to go outside, and with every evening a whole lifetime long – ugh! I never reckon that I live more than six months of the year, here.'

'But all that does not alarm me greatly,' Massey said, smiling; 'I have been used to those little drawbacks for pretty well all my life, you know. Hilby is not worse than other country places, surely?'

'Ah,' said Mrs Freeman, in her high shrill voice (she had a knack of discoursing as if each of her hearers was afflicted with deafness), 'Pollie likes London! That's where Pollie would live if she could have her way. She spent a year of her time there, besides visits every summer, and that have spoilt her.'

She spoke in an aggrieved tone, but was in reality highly proud of her daughter's predilection for town life.

'You spent a whole year in London?' Mr Massey asked, with polite interest.

'I finished there,' explained Pollie concisely.

Here Mr Freeman, who had been engaged till now with his younger daughter, tickling her fat ribs, pulling her shaggy locks, straightened his back, and for the moment neglected Dollie. He had heard a word which struck home.

'Finished!' he repeated, glancing contemptuously at his daughter, but addressing Mr Massey. 'Yes, I'm dashed if they didn't pretty well finish her! That year, I reckon, cost me a matter of a hundred pound, and they all but starved her! I'm dashed' (but he used a stronger expletive than 'dashed') 'if she weren't starved as near as a toucher! The missus there'll tell you the same tale – starved! And that's, as far as I know, all I got for my money. No more o' that for me. I can finish off my daughter i' that fashion without payin' a hundred pound for it, I fancy.' He was quite fierce about it, his small round eyes set up in his head.

His daughter turned a contemptuous glance upon him.

'Pa thinks only of the eating,' she said; 'his first question every holiday was, "What have they fed you on?" To feast is not the only thing one goes to school for, is it, Mr Massey?'

'If it were, one would suffer grievous disappointment,' said that gentleman, laughing; then, addressing Mr Freeman, 'My experience of young ladies, sir, is that what they have to eat is the very last thing about which they trouble.'

'Well, you've got up your plight again, haven't you, Pollie?' her father asked, knowing well that this fair plight of hers was, with the girl, a very sore point. In his slow way he enjoyed a cut now and then at his fashionable daughter, of whose uselessness and gentility he was nevertheless naturally proud.

A glance of silent scorn passed between mother and daughter at this ill-timed frivolity, and Massey, to hide a great inclination he had to laugh aloud, stooped down and entered upon a rivalry with Mr Freeman for the attention of little Dollie.

'What you doin'?' asked Dollie with pretended displeasure, but her face as bright as a sunbeam. 'Do away!' When, however, the suitor for her favour, feigning to take her at her word, drew himself away from her and began to talk to her sister, she apparently relented, crept silently up to him, and stood at his knee.

'Look at the little un,' said her father admiringly, drawing his wife's attention to the child. 'Ain't she a woman all over?'

'I'm afraid you're a bit of a coquette, Miss Dollie,' Massey said, lifting her in his arms. 'And where did you learn that business, I wonder?'

He put the little sturdy thing on his knee, and played with her bright hair, being a good-natured young fellow, and fond of children. But while he talked to her and responded satisfactorily to her calls upon his attention, his eyes, that were quick and intelligent, and sometimes bright with mirth, were watching the elder sister.

'How many brothers and sisters have you, Dollie?'

'Don't know,' said Dollie. 'Fifteen.' At which reply her father and mother laughed aloud.

'That is Dollie's one number,' said Pollie, in explanation. 'She is fifteen years old, and it's fifteen o'clock, and...'

'Pollie dot fifteen hats,' interrupted the little one, but was immediately abashed at the roar of laughter which the imparting of this confidence called forth. 'Dear Dollie feel shy,' she announced, and hid her head in James Massey's waistcoat.

'Fifteen of 'em,' said Mrs Freeman, recurring to Dollie's calculation. 'No, there's only three of 'em – two girls, as you see, and a boy that's out on the farm. A regular farmer he is too, never happy except he's on the land. The two that came between him and the little un are dead.'

'There's plenty to find food and clothes for now,' Mr Freeman said, in answer to the regretful sigh with which his wife concluded, and as he spoke he rose from his chair. 'You'll excuse me, sir,' addressing his visitor, 'but I have to get down to my low meadows and back b'fore tea-time. I must be goin'.'

Pollie turned red with anger, as Mr Massey jumped up and shook hands; she was always being called on to blush for the want of manners exhibited by 'pa.'

'Perhaps my way lies with yours?' Mr Massey asked, anxious to show that he was not offended.

But the master of the house shook his head, and jerked his thumb in the direction of the gold and white wallpaper.

'Your nearest way is over there,' he said, and with a nod took himself off.

'Did you come through the wood?' Pollie asked, as she also shook hands. 'No? Well then, mind you go back that way. It is prettier than the road, and shorter. You must always come here by the wood.'

'But how am I to find my way? You would not advise me to run the risk of being buried by redbreasts, would you?'

'Come, Pollie,' said Mrs Freeman, 'show Mr Massey as far as the little gate into the wood, then 'tis all straight before him. 'Tisn't such a very large wood, nor yet so far off, neither, that we shouldn't hear you call out if you was lost, sir. But Pollie'll show you the way in.'

'That is so kind, if it is not troubling Miss Freeman too much,' he said politely. 'Good-bye, my little Dollie, and will you not give me a kiss?'

'Dollie go too!' declared that young lady, and would not be dissuaded therefrom, but clung to Mr Massey's shoulder, and kicked rebelliously at his waistcoat when attempt was made to dislodge her.

'Let her go,' said her new friend. 'I will carry her.'

So the trio set out; passing through the neglected-looking Grange garden, through farm-yard, stack-yard, wood-yard – no neglect visible here – over the long, damp meadow grass, crossing a wooden bridge over a wide ditch, and stopping at the gate, all rickety and lichen-covered, opening into the wood.

CHAPTER II

The Wood

WHEN Miss Freeman had safely piloted Mr Massey to this picturesque but contemptible gate, which would only open far enough to admit of the squeezing in of one person at a time, and which refused to shut at all, she made no attempt to leave him, but having pushed through before him into the wood, looked up at him and smiled.

'It would never do to let you run any risk of losing yourself,' she said, by way of explanation. 'Gentlemen are so scarce in Hilby.'

'I'm rather glad of that,' he answered, struggling to force an entrance for himself and Dollie. 'Under those circumstances I hope and expect that you'll be particularly careful of me. What an exceedingly pretty place!'

'People say so,' she said indifferently, and followed his admiring gaze up to the gaunt bare branches of the trees, which met and interlaced across the green path down which they walked. 'Before the leaves fell you could scarcely see the sky above them. But if you care for such things you will see the wood in spring – that is, if Hilby hasn't killed you with dullness before then. The ground is one sheet of blue, then, with wild hyacinths; people come for miles around to see it. There is not much to look at now, that I see; and oh, how damp the leaves are!' She kicked them about as they lay brown and sodden on the ground.

'You'll spoil those pretty little shoes of yours,' he said warningly. Being an acute young man, he had divined that Miss Freeman made a point of her shoes.

'I'm afraid you've been used to girls that like compliments,' smiling.

'And I'm afraid you've been used to plenty of compliments,' sighing.

'Then of course I have been out of Hilby for them. Who do you think should pay me compliments here?'

'How in the world should I know? Look here – don't let us hurry. It is awfully pleasant here. Sit down on this fallen tree, and tell me something about yourself. Well, about Hilby then. Who are the people here, and what are they like? Now, Miss Dollie,' putting her out of his arms, 'run and play. Catch a butterfly, or pull a daisy, or –'

'Or run up a mountain,' suggested Pollie laughingly. 'Do you think that we have daisies and butterflies now, poor innocent! We shall have to teach you something of natural history, I think.'

'Will you teach me?' he asked.

He was leaning forward, and regarding his companion with what was intended for a sentimental air; but he was inwardly experiencing more amusement than tenderness, and there was an irrepressible twinkle in his quick grey eyes, and a flicker of a smile under his moustache. He was making good running, he thought, having a sufficiently light heart within his breast to still enjoy a 'bit of fun with a pretty girl,' despite his thirty years. It was evident that Miss Freeman also was not averse to a little easy love-making, and that Miss Freeman should have it was unquestionable.

She, on her part, was well pleased to look into that pleasant face of his without perplexing herself about its expression, and she had by this time decided that without being a handsome face (for Pollie Freeman had hard-and-fast ideas of her own about masculine beauty, and a straight nose, pale complexion, curling hair and dark eyes were indispensable features therein, all of which were unfortunately conspicuous by their absence here), without being a handsome face, it was one good to look at. The man's strong erect figure also met with her unqualified approbation, as did the cut of the rough suit which so well became it. Indeed, it is probable that this same well-fitting suit –whereof the coat-collar did not rise to the back of the head, nor did the trousers either 'ruck' at the calf or 'bag' at the knee – it is just probable that all this may have had more to do with the securing of Miss Freeman's approval than the possession of any charms of personal appearance might have had. She had had many lovers, had several still; it was, in fact, a commodity which from her babyhood the young lady had not lacked, but they had been of a rustic order. Their everyday apparel was of a different species of roughness to that of Mr Massey's, and their Sunday suits recommended themselves still less to the fastidious. There was nothing rustic about Mr Massey, unless it were a certain healthy out-of-door air which seemed to pervade him, and was certainly no drawback. There was something more of the soldier than the farmer in his carriage, Miss Freeman thought, and said to herself that some excitement had come into Hilby at last.

Her enemies had said of her, that Pollie Freeman was not particular. 'Give her a man,' they had said, or, in default of a man, 'give her a great big boy, and she would be content.' Certain it is that the astute young lady had a most decided preference for the sterner sex; and ought that fact to convey a hint of reproach? Is not that sex the more intellectual, the more consistent, the altogether truly admirable? Pollie was an admirer of mankind in general, it is at once freely allowed.

'But, there are men and men,' said the discerning young woman, and straightway smiled her wickedest, and looked her prettiest into those admiring grey eyes; while she inwardly congratulated herself on having put on her best hat for the occasion.

'Will you teach me?' he had asked, referring to his supposed deficiency in natural history. 'I will promise to be an apt pupil in anything you will teach.'

'I dare say!' she said with irony. 'You'd rather talk nonsense than learn sense any day in the week, I can see.'

'You are severe, Miss Freeman. Do you talk then, and tell me about Hilby, its inhabitants, manners and customs, exports, imports, fisheries, manufactures.'

'For gracious sake, stop! You'll make me feel as if I was at school again. And pray do sit up, Mr Massey. I shall get quite nervous if you keep on looking at me in that way; and then how can I tell you what you want to know?'

'Now, I should never have guessed that you were nervous,' he said slowly, without altering his position or removing his eyes from her face. 'And I do most sincerely hope that you are not going to be so cruel as to prohibit my looking at you.' A pause, during which Pollie blushed, but said nothing. 'I thought that pretty girls were made to be looked at.'

'They're rather scarce about here, whatever they're made for,' she said, laughing. 'I hope they aren't necessities with you, or you'll come off badly in this neighbourhood.'

'I don't believe that I shall have any cause to complain; but aren't there really any girls in Hilby?'

'I am the single, solitary, blessed one?' said Pollie, with emphasis; 'that's, of course, not counting the labourers' daughters. I am the only *girl*, but there is one young lady.'

'Ah! And who is that? You again?'

'Me? No! I'm not to be mentioned in the same breath with her. Mind what you're about, Mr Massey! I'm a tenant farmer's daughter, and she's sister-in-law to the parson, – think of that! I'm a girl, don't ye see – *the* girl, Pollie Freeman; she's a young lady, if you please – her Royal Highness Miss Smith!'

There was more than a little acrimony in the tone of Pollie's voice, and her hearer thought to himself it was just possible that pretty little Miss Freeman did not quite coincide with the parsonic idea of propriety.

'Go on, tell me about her,' he urged, being, however, far more amused with the girl at his side than interested in her subject. 'Let me hear more of this exalted young lady. By the way, is the being sister-in-law to the parson her only claim to superiority? It sounds feeble.'

'Ah, that's because you don't know! Have you a parson in your family? No, you needn't answer; I know you haven't; you're too agreeable. But to belong in the remotest degree to a parson, is supposed in this neighbourhood to give an advantage over every other class. Never mind if you can't pay your debts, never mind if you aren't quite honest, never mind if you've no more brains than a fool; you are, being a parson, or a parson's relation – select. I hate the race! – don't you?'

He laughed.

'I'm ready to hate them, if you think it's my duty so to do,' he said. 'I don't believe, however, that they're worse, as a class, than any other order of the community; the fact of the matter is, that I suppose they ought to be better. You'll think me unusually unfortunate, but I've really met with one or two favourable specimens in my time. Now about the young lady?'

'To begin with, she isn't so very young; she's in fact somewhat *passé*.'

Miss Freeman, it seemed, had been taught at that academy where she had 'finished' to pronounce this mournful word as 'passy.'

'She is supposed to be a beauty, you know,' she went on, 'but she is *passy* – decidedly *passy*.'

'That's bad for her! And what then is her age – thirty?'

'Well, getting that way.'

'Oh dear! And her name Smith – Miss Smith! To think that even at Hilby you must have Smith!'

'Yes, and the best of it is, she calls herself Smythe. It's downright affectation; her name is plain Smith, of course. I always call her so to her face; and do you – I know it riles her so!'

'I'm not anxious to get a chance of calling her anything.'

'Oh, she'll look you up soon enough; don't you imagine for a moment you're going to escape. She's the busybody of the parish, with always some new fad in her head, and fit to drive everyone crazy with it. Now 'tis one thing and now another, and always money wanted. Pa makes a rule of giving nothing to anything, and then he can't be wrong, he says. That's why we don't go down with the Vicarage people.'

'Then it is very clear to me that I shall not "go down" with them either. I have no sympathy with fads.'

'Your best plan is to show them at once what you mean. Make a stand!' said Pollie, quite eager and excited. 'Make a stand, and have done with them for ever!'

'And the others, the clergyman and his wife, are they obnoxious too?'

'They're hateful! You'll see. He, Mr Pearson, don't meddle; I give him that credit. Pa says he pockets his money, and that's all he cares about. Five or six hundred a year – fancy that! – just for getting into a pulpit twice a week, and prosing to mostly empty pews. He's only parson on Sundays though, and that's a mercy, I think, although there's many that complain of it; the rest of the week he muddles away on his few acres of glebe, and thinks he has the business of the nation on his back. Still, he is the best of them. I don't care what anyone says, and I shall always maintain that he is to be pitied with his women-kind. His wife is after Miss Smith's own sort, only worse – older, and more vinegary and faddy and mischief-making.'

'They must be a charming family!'

'Take my advice and steer clear of them! Not but what you'll be safe enough if you're friendly with us. They'll know you aren't on their side then.'

'I hope that I may be allowed to adopt that method of escape,' he said; 'it will be a very pleasant one. So much for the clerical element. Now, who else is there in Hilby? Tell me about them all.'

'Why, there's the Backs at the Hall (only tenants, you know; the owner – our landlord and yours – can't afford to live there). They're of a pretty good family, so people say; but there's none too much money, from all I can hear. They live at a great rate though, and give a little life to the place. There's an old paralytic father and a lot of stuck-up girls, and one stuck-up son, and one son who – well – isn't stuck up,' said Miss Freeman with a conscious look, remembering certain admiring glances and several friendly overtures to herward, made by Captain Archibald Back. 'You'll see them all at church on Sunday –that is, if you come in the morning. Do! The church is full in the afternoon, but there's no one a bit nice then. All the best people go in the morning. There's these Backs, and there's the Freemans – us, you know – and the Selbys, and…'

'Pardon my interrupting you,' he interposed hastily, 'but have you seen anything lately of the little girl – of Dollie?'

'Good gracious!' cried Miss Freeman, springing up and looking around. 'Where on earth is she? Dollie!'

'Which way is she likely to have gone?' he asked, slightly uneasy, and peering down various narrow over-arched paths. 'It will be a difficult matter to find her if she has strayed far. Dollie!'

'Which way does most mischief lie?' inquired Pollie meditatively; she knew the wood well, and was not in the least alarmed. 'That is the thing to consider. By the water, I should say, shouldn't you? Oh, it's not deep, there's no danger. Come along! This is the way.'

She ran off down one of the green paths, and Mr Massey observed that she did not make a very good hand of running. What with her small shoes and her high heels placed in the middle of the foot, and her dress tied tightly about her knees, it was a difficult exercise. Her breath, too, was soon exhausted, owing to the exceedingly ingirt condition of her waist, perhaps.

'Wait here, Miss Freeman,' he said, quickly overtaking her. 'I think I see the child. I will bring her back to you.'

Presently he was standing by a little shallow pool, which had formed itself in the hollow of the path. Impressions of Dollie's fat feet and legs were to be seen on the soft margin, and she herself had now, with much fearless enjoyment, set out to see how far she could walk into the water without being drowned.

'You young rascal!' Mr Massey cried, with great severity of tone. 'Come out directly!'

'Me won't,' said Dollie, with evident determination.

'Won't me? Me had better!' warningly.

'Do 'way! Dear Dollie paddlin'; dear Dollie *may* paddle.'

'But look at dear Dollie's gown all getting wet; and just think of her boots!' This with a regretful glance at his own feet, as the certainty grew upon him that he would have to ruin their appearance and destroy his own comfort by wading in after the little rebellious imp, plouncing defiantly a yard or so out of reach. There was no help for it. He looked back at Pollie Freeman, visible in the far distance, resting after her exertions on the trunk of a tree. 'I wish she'd come and risk her own life after her own flesh and blood,' he grumbled to himself, and then stooped and turned up his trousers and splashed into the muddy water after the delinquent, who screamed and kicked as he lifted her; and who, when on dry land, stoutly refused to walk to meet her sister.

'Her'll hit Dollie!' she cried, and hid her face against her deliverer's shoulder. 'Her'll hit dear Dollie krite hard!'

'Hush! No she won't,' poor Mr Massey said, and pressed the little head against his coat, for comfort, despite the unpleasing certainty that the contact of that small draggled person was not at all improving to his appearance.

'You little wretch!' Miss Freeman cried, as they reached her. 'Get you down this minute! Oh, Mr Massey, do set her down! she will ruin your coat.'

'But she won't be set down,' he explained, laughing somewhat ruefully. 'I have tried her twice, and the funniest thing happens. She gives way everywhere – the bones in these sturdy legs seem to dissolve, and she becomes a heap upon the grass. I suppose I had better carry her safely home now I've got her.'

So, laughing and talking, they trudged homeward again over the soft peaty soil, their feet sinking in soddened masses of decaying leaves, or catching in matted wreaths of briers and bramble; around and above them the intertwined bare arms of mighty trees. Presently Massey stopped.

'Who is this?' he asked. 'Look, don't you see, Miss Freeman? There is a lady stooping to gather ferns or something at the end of the walk. Now, Dollie, I rather think you and I'll cut and run; we aren't presentable objects.'

But it was too late. The lady had risen from her stooping posture and was coming straight towards them. She held in her hand some big branches of the tall brake fern, dyeing gloriously around in colours of yellow, crimson, and bronze.

'Oh, that is Miss Smith,' Pollie Freeman said, turning a little red. 'You can never be sure of her here. She's for ever poking about this wood. She has a craze for flowers and weeds – has names a mile long for them all at her tongue's end. Never mind! I shan't stop, however much she tries to make me.'

Mr Massey could not help being aware that this resolve was a thoroughly discreet one, as no indication of such intention was visible on the part of Miss Smythe. She came quietly on, a tall and graceful figure in a dark, plain dress, her fur-lined cloak thrown back over her shoulders, a big soft hat on her head. She bent her head gravely and a trifle distantly to Miss Freeman, and just glanced out of a pair of serious dark eyes at the man by Miss Freeman's side, with Dollie's little muddy feet rubbing against his waistcoat, and Dollie's curly head hiding against his neck.

'And so that is Miss Smythe?' he asked, in a low voice, when she had passed, and Pollie immediately remarked that he gave her name the proper pronunciation, and that the tone of his voice had changed a little.

'Well, what do you think of her?' she asked him eagerly.

But Mr Massey shirked the question.

'I wonder what she thought of me,' he said, with a laugh. 'Oh, Dollie, you have a very great deal to answer for.'

'I told you, you remember, that she was considered pretty,' Pollie said, as if anxious to justify herself for something. 'I suppose to some tastes she *is* pretty. Do you admire those tall thin women, Mr Massey?'

'Some day,' replied the cautious Mr Massey, 'I will tell you the kind of woman I admire, and perhaps she will be round and plump and rosy, like – like Dollie,' pinching a fat muddy leg of that now contented little body.

Then Miss Freeman, her doubts being set at rest, began to criticize the unfashionable cut of Miss Smythe's garments.

'Wasn't it right?' he asked, thinking of the supple figure, of the easy walk, of the careless grace.

'And the hat! What a hat!' Helen Smythe was always two seasons behind in her hats – had he noticed the hat?

No, he really had not paid much attention. Upon his life he did not understand such things. Miss Freeman would have to instruct him. But if the shape of the hat had escaped his notice, he could yet have told how gracefully it sat upon Miss Smythe's well-poised head, and how some waving brown hair blown up in pretty confusion showed well against the unfashionable verge.

Soon he had deposited little Dollie at her own garden-gate, and had taken farewell of her sister; and as he went through this latter ceremony with much impressiveness, his eyes were eloquent of the deepest admiration, and he contrived to put a good deal of tender meaning into his voice, so that Pollie, who never saw cause to doubt the genuineness of any sentiment favourable to herself, with whatever exaggeration it might be expressed, went in and divested herself of her best hat in a perfect flutter of delight.

Mr Massey, as he walked contentedly homeward, swinging his stick and whistling softly to himself, thought of his late companion with all the indulgence mankind displays towards the owner of a pretty face. 'She is a nice little thing,' he told himself complacently; and added, with a twinkle in his eye, that she would in all probability be 'some fun.'

'I shall like to get a good look at the parson's sister-in-law,' he was saying presently. 'I don't know that I have ever seen anything quite like that before.'

CHAPTER III

Helen and her Sister

MISS SMYTHE came into the unsmart, and indeed somewhat barren, Vicarage drawing-room, carrying her bundle of many-coloured brake in her hands. She was wont to return from her rambles with spoil after this kind – a trailing length of blackberry bramble whose crimson and dark brown leaves had caught her eye, a handful of scarlet berries, some rushes from the pit in Springmere field. The Vicarage was the more attractive from the arrangement of such daily trophies, and gained thereby a refined and at the same time home-like look, which it certainly would have otherwise missed. For its mistress was a person whose views were antagonistic to vulgar adornment, and there was never money enough to spare in the household to allow of artistic indulgence. Lace curtains were atrocious, and bad pictures were an offence. The faded green furniture was in better taste than the cheap bright cretonnes which might have concealed its shabbiness. One thing after another had been discarded by the severe judgment of Mrs Pearson, until the place would have been but a dreary waste, but for the manipulation of Helen. She contrived stands of plants in the barren tracts, and hung her trailing branches by the bare wall, while her canaries sang in some of the unshrouded windows, and her cat gave a more comfortable appearance to the somewhat inhospitable hearth.

Mrs Pearson was bending over her writing-table, which was drawn up to one of the windows to catch the last of the fading daylight. She was thus, the room being large, at a considerable distance from the fire dying on the hearth; but her occupation was of a too engrossing nature to allow her to compassionate herself for the chilliness from which she was suffering, or to permit her to remember that fires untended will, in course of time, go out. She was a woman of some thirty years of age, thin and spare as to figure, thin and sharp as to face, which yet was a pretty face. Her hair was lighter than Helen's, but with the same bewitching ripple, although brushed severely down, and fastened, with an entire absence of coquetry, in the sternest fashion behind her head; her complexion good, but – like her excellent resolutions and her virtues – fixed, whereas the delicate tinge of colour in Helen's paler cheek would seem to come and go with every thought; her eyes were light and round and steely, while those of her sister were dark and long of shape, with a seriousness and a sweetness in their gaze which made their expression very lovely. In the matter of her other features, Mrs Pearson might be said, perhaps, to have had the advantage; for her nose, although a thought too long, was severely straight, missing that little unclassical curve which made Helen's most prominent feature so pretty, and her mouth was smaller and well-shaped, if somewhat tight and prim-looking – but it lacked the expressiveness of the other sweet lips, which could form themselves into a smile of surpassing tenderness, or could curl with an easy touch of scorn.

There was about the two women that curious likeness in unlikeness to be seen in sisters. Their heads were set on long and graceful necks, but in Mrs Pearson's case the roundness of early youth had departed, and the skin was no longer delicately white and smooth. Their height was almost identical, and although Mrs Pearson was a good deal thinner than her sister, their figures were much of the same build. It was a somewhat notable fact that people who wished to be pleasant very often spoke to Mrs Pearson of her likeness to her sister, but that the resemblance was never commented on to Helen by these same amiably intentioned friends. Still the Vicar's wife was a pretty woman. Had she been a little less formal, a little less self-satisfied, a little more tolerant of the short-comings of less gifted mortals, she might have been called a very pretty woman, and Helen, her sister, was a very lovely girl.

'I have seen him,' she said now, standing before her sister, her ferns in her arms, a little mocking smile about her lips. She had a rather languid manner of speech that was yet quite natural to her, although it excited Miss Freeman's powers of mimicry, and her voice was refined and musical. 'I have seen him, Anna.'

Mrs Pearson pushed away her writing (she was of a literary taste, and contributed articles for a temperance publication called *The Enlightener,* a penny weekly paper which recorded the progression of the society, and contained accurate particulars of marvellous conversions to sobriety, or gave detailed accounts of the swift and unerring judgment overtaking those who still clung to alcohol).

'Well?' she questioned, 'what is he like?' There was no possibility of doubting to whom her sister had alluded. Mr Massey's advent had been a theme for general speculation since ever it had been known that the Wood Farm was to have a new tenant. There was only one 'him' of the slightest interest just now in the neighbourhood, and even Mrs Pearson was not above being slightly curious as to the manner of man 'he' might prove to be.

Helen turned away as she answered, and began sticking her brake ferns into a big and hideous vase which stood on the table.

'He was with Miss Freeman,' she said, and looked at her sister with a little gleam of amusement in her eyes.

'Already!' that lady ejaculated, and leaned back in her chair and regarded the girl as if her brief communication had been quite staggering in its importance.

'Yes, already! I came upon them in the wood, and they were evidently great friends. Pollie was very pleased and proud, and he was carrying the little girl and...'

'That will do,' interrupted Mrs Pearson, 'pray spare me further particulars. I can now judge of the style of person he is, and I am not surprised. But, Helen, what becomes of all your sanguine expectation? Some one to help us in the parish, to set a good example to the other farmers, to take an interest in your reading room, to beat up the due number of school children, to convert my drunkards –'

Helen smiled rather sadly, holding her head on one side to view the effect of the fern leaves in the jar.

'No, I did not quite expect all that,' she said, 'but I confess I did hope he might not be immediately prejudiced against us and all that we try to do. I thought, from what Alfred had heard of him, that there was ground for crediting him with sufficient discernment to perceive that we, at least, tried to do for the best in our situation; that there is no need for us to be unhesitatingly shunned on every occasion, or consistently thwarted in our harmless designs. I am tired of feeling that we have not a friend in the place, except among the very poor, for whose friendship we pay.'

'We have to do our duty,' Mrs Pearson answered; she was never troubled with doubts or misgivings as to the line of conduct to be pursued by anybody under any circumstances. Life was no difficulty to Mrs Pearson. People must do their duty, that was all. What she looked on as her own duty was so exceedingly easy to herself that she never could understand or sympathize with the rest of mankind, who seemed so generally to shirk theirs. She returned to her writing now as she spoke. 'We have to do our duty. If we do that and satisfy our own consciences, it signifies little what the mere mindless boors by whom we are surrounded think of us.'

Helen had finished her arrangement of leaves, and had sunk into a low chair by the window. She had taken off her unfashionable hat, and she swung it listlessly in her hand as she spoke.

'It is so foolish of me, I know,' she said, 'so dreadfully foolish, but I cannot help caring. It does, somehow, signify to me, in spite of my best philosophy. Whose fault was it, Anna, that you first happened to get wrong with everyone in the parish? I never can imagine how you came to be so terribly misunderstood. It cannot have been my doing, as I found matters so on my arrival. It cannot be Alfred. He is, one would think, a man after the farmers' own hearts, his pursuits are the same, and he certainly does not trouble them with learning, or offend them with new doctrines. It must be you and me after all, Anna. What is there about us? what is it that we do?'

'We are ladies,' said Mrs Pearson oracularly, and without looking up from her pen, 'ladies – gentlewomen, and they have no comprehension or appreciation of such.'

'But they must see that we, at least, mean well. We do nothing that ought to offend them, and yet how plainly they show us that they will have none of us. It is so disheartening to have them all set themselves against every project for their welfare.'

'They love darkness rather than light,' quoted Mrs Pearson serenely, 'because their deeds are evil.'

Miss Smythe was silent; she did not approve of her sister's habit of introducing scriptural quotations to clinch an argument.

'What a pity it is,' she began again presently, 'that that little Miss Freeman should have such odd manners! She is really very pretty, Anna, in spite of the exaggeration of her dress – very pretty! I was quite struck with her to-day; she looked pleased and a little excited – I had never noticed her prettiness so much before; but you should have seen the pert little nod which she gave me, and directly she had passed I heard her burst out laughing. I could not help being a little annoyed,' the girl said, the colour flashing into her face; 'I wonder what they laughed at, Anna.'

'I thought you were too well used to the insolence of that misguided little vulgarian to be surprised at any rudeness she might be guilty of. You make a great mistake about these people, Helen, a great mistake, in trying to propitiate them. I have always known that to be the wrong course. Keep them at a safe distance when possible, and above all things never let them guess that they have it in their power to wound you. I have seen you, more than once, trying to be civil to this insufferable little caricature, this Miss Freeman; you see the result.'

Helen took no notice of this rebuke. She was twisting her hat about in her hand, turning up the brim, turning it down, contemplating it in various aspects.

'I believed it was at my hat they laughed. It is not very handsome, is it?' She tossed it to the ground, and laughed herself. 'You may depend on it, it was the hat,' she said, 'and oh dear me, Anna! do not let us grudge them their laugh. We ought to rejoice that in such a world it takes so little to make some people happy.'

'Did the man laugh?' asked Mrs Pearson, as she blotted off a page of manuscript.

'The man? oh, I have no doubt that he laughed, but he had the grace not to do it so lustily. I should think he is rather a good-natured person. He was carrying that little child of theirs, and she was crying and covered with mud. I like him for that.' She rose and picked up her hat from the ground. 'Where's the child, Anna? Where's Perrie?'

'I don't know; I sent him outside; he was getting noisy upstairs. Do not bring him in here, Helen. I must finish this manuscript to-night.'

Mrs Pearson was, theoretically, a most excellent wife, mother, and housekeeper; she was enabled to prescribe minute and unimpeachable directions for the guidance of the parishioners in those offices, but it must be admitted that in her own person she decidedly fell short of her high standard. Mr Pearson had early learnt to dispense, even cheer-fully, with his wife's companionship, and little Perrie, their only child, had fallen quite naturally to his aunt Helen's care. Although Mrs Pearson burned to inculcate improved principles of cookery in the minds of the labourers' wives, her own knowledge of the subject was of the vaguest, as any guest at her table could not fail to see. She was, beside, a woman who scorned all accepted feminine occupations, who, for instance, was never seen to sew. It was whispered in the parish that before the advent of Miss Smythe, on the death of her father, to form part of the Rev. Pearson's household, that gentleman had been used to depend entirely on his own exertions for the safety of his buttons, and that he had established in a private drawer a repository of needles and thread, in whose uses stern necessity had rendered him expert. Still it must be understood that Mrs Pearson was by no means an idle woman; she always had some more or less unreasonable scheme on foot at which she slaved with all her energy, and that she ever failed in any of her natural and moral obligations was a notion that did not enter her head; while in the matter of the proper fulfilment of other people's duties, she was most rigorous. She now began to inquire into the disposal of her sister's time on that afternoon.

'What have you been doing? did you spend *all* your time in the wood?' she asked severely.

But Helen had not been idle, it seemed, and gave in a report of how she had been to the church to practise, and how she had taken her Bible-class at the school, and had made various visitations among the poor people.

'And, Anna, what is to be done about that wretched Mrs Moore? Her husband has not had a stroke of work to do for the last fortnight, she says; and the children have not nearly enough to eat. She has another black eye. Oh, dear!' with a heavy sigh.

'Did you take him the last week's *Enlightener*?' – the paper for which, as has been said, Mrs Pearson wrote her little heart-stirring stories of conversion from drunkenness and poverty to sobriety and riches.

'No,' Helen said slowly; 'I did not take it, Anna. I do wish we might persuade him to give up drink, but I do not believe it will be done so. Tom Moore is, when sober, an intelligent man. Have you ever talked to him, Anna? That all seems too – too childish for him. Oh, I know it is very interesting, dear, and fitted, no doubt, for a certain order of understanding, but Moore really has thought, and can talk, a – and – I don't think the good work is to be done so.'

'*The Enlightener*, by the help of prayer, has worked the care of many thousands,' said Mrs Pearson, seriously displeased at the implied depreciation. 'You trust too much to your own discrimination, Helen, and rely too entirely on your unaided power of persuasion. Your experience in such matters has, after all, been but slight in comparison with mine, and I am not totally deficient – I think I may say – in the gift of perspicuity. I will go myself to see this dreadful person. I do not at all despair of being enabled to cope with him, in spite of his intelligence.'

Helen maintained the silence which marked her disapprobation. Mrs Pearson was not a person to disagree with, her temper being so very short and so very sharp, and she herself so irritatingly conscious of her own infallibility.

'I will go and look for Perrie,' the girl said presently, rising from her seat. But when she had reached the door she stopped and turned.

'You never asked me what he was like – our new parishioner,' she said, and laughed her low and rather languid laugh. 'Aren't you dying to know?'

'I can wait until I see him,' said Mrs Pearson, with cutting indifference, and without looking up from her writing. But she was human after all, and – woman; and Helen still stood by the door, and presently, 'Well, what is he like?' she asked.

'Ah, I thought you'd be curious on the subject,' the other said mockingly, 'and so took particular notice of the man. You'll be glad to hear, Anna, that he is an improvement on her other admirers, and that Miss Freeman is justly proud of her last conquest;' and with this certainly meagre report Helen withdrew, and Mrs Pearson was obliged to be satisfied.

CHAPTER IV

High-Tea at The Grange

AN evening party is being given at the Grange, in honour of Mr James Massey. He has been for some weeks at Hilby now, and has made the acquaintance of his few neighbours. Being of a cordial and friendly disposition, he has welcomed with sincerity all friendly advances; but it is with the Freemans, owing either to their proximity, or to the superior attractions which their household can offer, that he alone shows signs of intimacy. His walks take him in the direction of the Grange nearly every morning; often he encounters Mr Freeman or his son, and drops in with them to drink a glass of beer in the 'study' (a name bestowed by Pollie on a little half-furnished room, where 'Pa' keeps his accounts, and where the labourers go in to receive their weekly wage, but where sign of 'study' is there none, unless it be in the encrusted pens stuck into a coagulated mass in the bottom of a dilapidated inkstand, or in the Webb's 'Farmers' Account Books,' surmounted by a 'Ready Reckoner,' which lie on the table); or he comes by invitation to smoke a pipe with Mr Freeman in these long winter evenings, when that gentleman, reclining in his arm-chair over the dining-room fire, is sleepy, and not too communicative, and his wife sits engrossed with the contents of her stocking-basket, the lamp, pulled dangerously close to her cap, shining on her red contented face; while Ted, the son and heir, sprawls his long legs and snores undisguisedly, and 'dear Dollie,' who should have been in bed hours ago, rolls sleepily about on the hearth-rug.

Pollie, however, always escapes the general drowsiness; and somehow those evenings are almost lively ones to the girl and Mr Massey, in spite of the torpor of their surroundings. All this is very pleasant and friendly, but there are certain laws of society which must be obeyed in Hilby as elsewhere; and Mrs Freeman and her daughter understand well the etiquette to be observed in such matters, and feel that until Mr Massey has been bidden to partake of a formal meal at their home, they will not have conscientiously fulfilled their duty towards their new neighbour.

Now, in a general way, when the Freemans entertained, the routine of the evening would be the simple one familiar to them through all their lives: a tea, with mountains of hot toast, cake, and ham; a few games of cards (the only amusement of which Mr Freeman approved), a very little music, an elaborate supper, and a final hour (during which their slow tongues would loosen in an amazing way) for the gentlemen over their grog and their long clay pipes, in the dining-room, and for the ladies, waxing cosy and confidential over the drawing-room fire, shuddering, as they drew closer to it, at the prospect of the long, cold homeward drive. This was all straight-forward and easy enough, Mrs Freeman thought, and did not trouble that it perhaps was not very lively; but Pollie had become ambitious of achieving grander things.

'I wish we could give a dinner!' she had said when the necessity for bidding the new-comer to a feast was first decided. 'He is used to dining in the evening, I know from Mrs Cobb, who goes up there on churning days to help. It seems so stupid to ask a man like that to *tea*. Why can't we have him to dinner?'

Mrs Freeman was aghast. 'And s'pose you ask him to dinner – I shall have to wait on him,' she had objected. 'You know well enough this new girl ain't to be trusted with nothing – and whatever *do* you think she should know about waitin'?'

'Oh, I could teach her that, fast enough,' Pollie had declared, with more apparent confidence than she really possessed, for the intricacies of the art were as a sealed book to her. 'I could soon put her up to all that – but I suppose it must not be thought of with pa; he'd be eating his pudding with his knife, and you never *can* get him to use a dinner-napkin. Pa'll never rise above anything he was born to; but he ought to think what a drawback all that vulgarity is to me.'

The behaviour of Mr Freeman was a frequently discussed matter on which both mother and daughter were well agreed, and in which they were also perfectly aware that no amendment was to be expected; it was an effectual stumbling-block in the way of the proposed dinner-party; and the idea, so entrancing to Pollie, with her advanced notions, had to be abandoned.

'We will have high-tea, then,' she had decided; 'high-tea, and no supper, and that will be as good as dinner, pretty well, and no formality.'

High-tea, therefore, it was to be, and of a most gorgeous and resplendent nature. Pollie had devoted her energies to the decking of the épergne, having driven into Gurton, the nearest town, for flowers for the occasion, and had made the drawing-room attractive with many specimen glasses, and a readjustment of the rickety tables; Mrs Freeman had passed two mornings in the kitchen, deep in the mysteries of pastry and of sweets, in the concocting of which she was a celebrated hand; Mr Freeman, by dint of much persuasion, had even been induced to broach for consumption in the evening his best port – not the second-best, which usually did service at the Freemans' at-homes – but the very best, that preserved for his particular solace, whose own charm was sufficient to enable the imbiber to dispense with those of society. All these preparations had been got over in good time, the other guests had long arrived, but as yet Mr Massey had not put in an appearance.

Much gloom has fallen on the expectant party, drawn up round the drawing-room fire, at the non-arrival of the most important member. Mr Selby, who farms under the same landlord, and who farms under him, too, is there, and the disposition to sleep, which always falls upon him when sitting in the warmth of the fire, after exposure to cold air, is upon him with gigantic force to-night. It is such a thoroughly well recognised fact that agriculture and he do not get on together, that he always shirks the prevalent topics of stock, mangolds, and manures, being sadly aware that his opinion is not held to carry weight. He is a man of gentle, deprecating manner, a favourite with everyone, an especial favourite, when no younger bachelor is by, with Miss Pollie. She regards him to-night with extremest ill-favour. What business has he to sit there with that unmeaning smile upon his face, to nod and yawn behind his hand, entailing upon every glancing that way the dreadful necessity of yawning too? Must they not seem a dull and stupid party to anyone coming in to-night – tonight of all nights in the year, when she would have had everything go briskly and well? Between watching sleepy Mr Selby and keeping her eye on her father, who examines his watch every half-minute, and persists in obtusely comparing it with the gilt and ormolu clock, in a glass case, on the mantelpiece, which clock has not, since its purchase, been known to go, she grows absent, and ceases to keep up her converse with Laura Wadman, the big, good-natured girl at her side, who has driven six long miles with her father, the little deaf, white-haired man, talking in a perfectly inaudible voice to Mrs Freeman, on the other side of the hearth, to be present at the introduction of a 'new neighbour'. Teddie Freeman, sitting in uncomfortable stiffness on the sofa beside old Miss Gay, his especial aversion and terror, loses, as time goes on, even the ever-present sense of his incurable shyness, and his all-pervading feeling of awkwardness and misery in his sister's fine room, in the aggravated pangs of hunger, from which he has been long suffering. Presently he rises, in obedience to a word from his father, and goes to the hall-door, peering into the darkness, listening in the stillness, for a sign of Mr Massey's approach. Every eye is on him as he re-enters and silently shakes his head. Teddie takes after his father in this, that he never wastes his breath where a nod of his head will do as well.

Tea was to have been at six – it is now nearly seven o'clock, and both Mrs Freeman and Pollie begin to feel the situation tragic. If only they had not arranged that unlucky 'high-tea,' they were both thinking; suppose he should miss his tea, there being no supper, what a terrible failure the whole thing would be!

'I suppose your friend ain't coming,' said Mr Freeman, at length to his wife, with masculine unfairness – there had been no hint of the young man having been specially the friend of Mrs Freeman until he fell into disgrace.

'He will come,' said Pollie, with pretended cheerfulness, and turned again to her chat with Laura Wadman.

'At any rate we 'on't wait any longer for him,' her father said, and rose from his chair. Up rose the Wadmans; up rose Mr Selby and the other guests;

up rose all but Pollie, who kept her place, and looked with angry eyes at her father.

'Of course we can't have tea without Mr Massey. Pa,' she said, 'it is absurd!'

'Anyhow, *I'll* have it,' said Mr Freeman, in his most dogged and least agreeable manner. 'All the rest of 'em,' with a comprehensive nod to his guests, 'can please theirselves.'

'Now,' said old Miss Gay in her fussy and mincing voice, 'now listen, all of you! What is o'clock? A quarter to seven – good, good! Now I propose that we wait until seven, giving him an hour's grace – you see – an hour's grace. I think he can have nothing to complain of if we give him an hour's grace.'

Now, although old Miss Gay was somewhat despised by her neighbours, being an old maid and being poor, yet in that she had always claimed to be a lady born, and in that she was on visiting terms with many of the better class houses in the neighbourhood, her voice, in a matter of etiquette, always carried weight, and the ladies of the party sat down again immediately, the male portion being conducted outside by Mr Freeman, to while away the stated time with their pipes in the darkness of the garden.

Mr Selby remained the sole representative of his sex; he, being a gossip-loving personage, was said to prefer ladies' society.

'Am I to go?' he asked of Pollie, his bald head held on one side, and a simper round his clean-shaven lip. Pollie, being cross, had rather curtly bidden him to please himself.

'Then I will please myself,' he remarked, and sunk again into his chair.

Now that the masculine element is removed, he is much less inclined to somnolence, and much more brisk and chatty. If his opinion be not of much value with regard to the root crop, and although, after his thirty years' experience, he may still show total ignorance of the value of a sheep or a bullock, he is yet of great authority in the matter of all village gossip, and knows a vast amount of the private history of most of the people whose names are familiar in Hilby. He discourses to-night on Mr Massey, of course – Jim Massey, he calls him; tells how much he was liked in the place he has left to take his uncle's farm, and gives fully his reasons for the change; mentions that he is a good shot and a capital judge of a horse, as was his father before him.

'Nice man his father – extreme nice man, easy, perhaps too easy for money-making. His wife was the business man, he had heard – shrewd woman – very shrewd, had money of her own, too; Jim Massey would be pretty well off some day, and even now he had a little property independent of his farm, which is what we want, Miss Freeman, in such times as these.'

'Oh, bother the times,' says Pollie crossly; 'I've heard nothing but that old tale ever since I was a baby. I'm too old to be frightened at the "times" now.'

Indeed, while Miss Pollie has her gowns and her little comforts and luxuries, she is not likely to trouble her pretty head as to their source. She is unusually satisfied with her appearance to-night, having managed to combine an air of festivity with one of domestic neatness by the adoption of a black velveteen gown possessing a train which would have reached across the drawing-room, had it not possessed an aggravating propensity for wabbling itself over and over and for twining itself around tables and chairs in a manner which renders locomotion unsafe. A large amount of cheap white lace disposed about her little person gives grace and gorgeousness, which does honour to the occasion; her yellow hair is clustered in a thousand curls about her head. After all, if her get-up be not, perhaps, in the best taste, she looks very pretty, and she knows this, and wants Mr Massey to know it too, and Mr Massey will not come. For the hour's grace at last is up. No further excuse can be invented, and the high-tea has to be eaten.

Mr Freeman, in high good-temper, displayed an alarming appetite himself, and encouraged the same in his friends, with a fiendish enjoyment of the dismay of his wife and daughter. The noble dish of cold turkey was sadly upset, the game-pie cut up, and its tit-bits picked out; the ham, which unfortunately fell to the bashful Teddie to carve, quickly lost the symmetry of its appearance; while the guests, as poor Mrs Freeman thought, seemed to take a cruel delight in the partial demolition of every sweet dish on the table.

It was not until nine o'clock that Mr Massey at length put in an appearance, coming so quietly, and at that time unexpectedly, upon the scene, that he was shaking hands with Mrs Freeman before that lady, engaged over an intricate hand of cards, had been aware of his arrival. After all, it seemed that he had not been to blame for the disappointment he had caused; he had sent a note by one of his men who passed the Grange on his way home to say that they must not expect him until late; the man had forgotten to leave the note – that was all. He quickly made his peace with the lady of the house, and passed on to shake hands with Mr Freeman, who permitted the salutation in silence, being a man who, in spite of his rubicund aspect, was the reverse of easy-tempered, and who would bear a grudge for a fancied slight until it grew to the dimensions of a real offence. He did not remove his pipe from his mouth (Pollie's utmost endeavour had failed to banish smoke from the drawing-room) as he nodded a surly greeting, and he unceremoniously interrupted Massey's expressions of regret for his tardy arrival by some remarks to his partner at whist about the game he was playing. The visitor, however, turned away from his host quite unimpressed by the coldness of his reception; he had seen enough of Mr Freeman to be well aware that his manners were eccentric, and he as yet knew the man so little that he would not have been surprised at any development. He took refuge with Miss Freeman, who had been singing on his entrance, and who, swung round on the music stool, had been watching her father's behaviour to his guest with no friendly eyes. She had been thinking beside, with quite a flutter at her heart, of how very well and how really – well, aristocratic, as she afterwards expressed it to Laura Wadman, Mr Massey looked. For that unfortunate young man, in the innocence of his heart, and the ignorance of the manners and customs of the Hilby natives which was such a drawback to him at this time, had put himself into his dress-coat. He could not tell the dimensions that the Freemans' 'party' was going to assume, but had imagined them to be formidable from the serious manner in which he had often lately heard the matter treated. He saw at once, however, that in the matter of his own apparel he had made a mistake, but he scarcely guessed at the heinousness of his offence.

Only Pollie could fathom the depth of her father's contempt, only she divine the uneasiness and feeling of oppression such a state of things was creating in her mother's mind, whose cheeks had at once assumed a deeper shade of scarlet; only she could translate the meaning of the half-suppressed titter which arose from the 'young table,' where the junior members of the party, assisted by Mr Selby, were engaged in the engrossing game of farthing nap, and where Teddie Freeman's hoarse whisper, to the effect that it was the getting into Massey's 'togs' which had cost him his tea, was met with that aggravating giggle which so offended Pollie's ears. She was enraged at it all, and felt the coarseness of such behaviour a personal injury; she so thoroughly approved of Mr Massey's appearance herself, and was conscious besides that it was in her – Pollie Freeman – to live up to dress-clothes every evening of her life. Was she not equal to, and eager for, any amount of high life? If only she were not doomed to be always dragged down and disgraced by her surroundings!

Massey sat down by the piano, and leant forward to look at the song in which Miss Freeman had been interrupted. 'Is that what you were singing? Pray go on. I have never heard you sing.'

But Pollie, who required a very great deal of persuasion at any time to induce her to show off her accomplishments, snatched the song from his gaze and flung it to the top of the piano. 'I don't want to sing,' she said; 'I'd rather talk. I can sing when I'm alone. Well, I wonder you troubled to come at all; we gave you up long ago.'

'Did *you* give me up?' inquired Mr Massey, with an emphasis that was quite tender on the 'you.' 'You, at least, might have been sure that I should come.'

But this sort of thing would not do to-night, as Pollie knew very well, however much she herself might appreciate the sentimental lowering of his voice, the flattering absorption in herself which Mr Massey had begun to show; she understood quite well that he was a person of too much interest to all present to allow of his being left to her exclusive entertainment now. She could see that while the young man spoke, even the whist-table received but a divided attention, while the Nap party listened with rapt and undisguised interest. She therefore spoke in a louder tone of voice, ignoring his last little speech.

'And pray, why didn't you come before, if one may ask?' she said. 'You don't give any account of yourself. What wonderful attractions had you to keep you at home?'

'The attraction was all here,' said Mr Massey, still in his softest tone of voice, and with eyes expressively fastened on Miss Freeman's face.

He was evidently not one of those dreadful young men, to whom Pollie was so sadly used, who had to be 'led on,' as she expressed it, and with whom you had to begin all over again, as it were, at every interview.

'Where you leave him, there you find him, and no trouble,' Pollie had said of him, and approved highly of the characteristic. But it would certainly have been better now if he could have been alive to the fact that all in the room were regarding him with gaping interest, and straining their ears to catch his low-toned words. He, however, sat contentedly with his back to them all, and put down the silence of the community to all-consuming devotion to their cards.

'I was so bothered at not being able to get away,' he went on. 'I was thinking about you all the time – fact! – and wondering if you missed me. Did you miss me? I vow you shall tell me before the evening is over. As if that confounded horse couldn't have picked on a more suitable occasion to make himself ill in!'

'Why, what horse was it?' 'What was the matter with it?' 'How did you leave it?' came at once in a confusion of voices from the whist-table, making Mr Massey jump guiltily at the unexpected chorus. He quickly faced round upon them, and saw that they had flung their cards upon the table in their interest. Mr Selby also had renounced the charms of 'Nap,' and drawn near, and the conversation at once became general. Mr Freeman alone remained apparently unconcerned, and slowly shuffled a pack of cards, with an elaborate air of glum indifference.

'Think of that!' his wife said to him, when Massey had explained the symptoms of the animal to the general satisfaction. 'You always do say, William, that there's more horses taken ill on that farm than on all th' others put together. My husband have thought 'tis the water, sir,' she remarked to Mr Massey. 'He think there must be something wrong in the water.'

'It was the water on this occasion certainly,' Massey said, 'for the fools let the horses go to the pit when they came home heated from work. It is odd, sir,' he went on, addressing his host, 'what a pleasure these fellows experience in the destruction of their master's property, and how eagerly they always anticipate the very worst that can happen. They made up their minds at once that the horse would die, and confined their efforts at assistance entirely to the consumption of beer.'

Mr Freeman made no further reply than to remove his pipe from his mouth for an instant, to shove out his under lip, after a fashion all his own, and to grunt.

'Do you think th' horse out of danger, sir?' Mrs Freeman inquired with extra interest, to atone for her husband's gruffness.

'Oh yes, I think he'll do now. Poor brute! he suffered horribly. We had to lash him with a whip to keep him moving about, you know.'

'How dreadful!' cried Miss Wadman and Miss Gay in a breath, putting up their hands to their ears.

'How horribly cruel of you, Mr Massey!' said Pollie, for the sake of saying something.

'It would have been crueller to let the poor brute lie still and die, don't you think?' he asked with a smile. 'But the subject is hardly a pleasant one for ladies. Let us change it.'

However, no theme of such thrilling interest was started again during that somewhat heavy evening.

'If you aren't for any more whist,' said Mr Freeman presently, flinging his carefully shuffled pack on to the table, 'we may as well put up the cards.'

'Have I been interrupting? Pray go on with your game,' Massey said good-humouredly, and resisted with great politeness old Miss Gay's entreaties for him to take her hand at the game.

'If you are coming,' said the host to her, in a voice that made the poor old lady start – she was mortally afraid of him, and he, on his side, put down all her little airs of superior breeding and her innocent affections as 'd—d humbug,' and held her in finest contempt – 'If you are coming – come!'

The Nap-table was broken up, and the conversation, such as it was, became general and vastly unentertaining, or so Mr Massey thought, and was conscious of a most distinct thankfulness to the fate which had prevented his earlier arrival. He did his best not to yawn over the scrapbooks, filled with pictures from fashion-plates and with Christmas cards, which were produced for his delectation; he tried his utmost to show the required interest in the family album, explained to him by Pollie, and in which her own face and figure were the prevailing attraction; which fact, indeed, made things easier for Mr Massey, the remainder of the representations being those apparently of people of whom it would have been too glaringly perfidious to say flattering things.

'I always have my portrait done twice a year when I go up to London,' Pollie said. 'My cousin Arthur takes me. He says you want to have a fresh photo with the least change of hair. He has quite a craze for having his own done, too. That's my cousin Arthur. No, not that black-looking man, with his eyes turned up; he's a great friend of mine though, and he isn't black a bit in reality. There, that's Arthur, that rather small gentleman with the hat on, and the riding-whip in his hand. Not that he knows anything about riding; London gentlemen don't, as a rule,' explained Pollie.

Under any other circumstances Massey would have begged to be entrusted with one of the many copies of his fair entertainer's face, but he did not feel himself equal to such a request under the existing position, with Miss Wadman's pale orbs watching his every action, with Teddie Freeman's eyes riveted on his face, with prosy Mr Selby plying him at every minute with information about people in whom he felt not the slightest interest. Better luck attended him later on, when he alone, of all the guests, was conducted under Pollie's escort to the dining-room, there to partake of the remnant of the high-tea. Besides his thankfulness at being thus released from the rest of the company, he, having neglected his dinner in anxiety about his horse, and having been feeling for some time in dire need of refreshment, was truly grateful for the fragments that remained to him. All his weariness, too, vanished instantly; he and Pollie, when left to their own devices, were quite at ease together, and never at a loss for a subject.

'You must not mind pa,' she said to him, in the course of conversation. 'He is a little bit put out with you now; but he will soon come round, if you take no notice. It's best not to pay much attention to pa.'

'Put out with me!' Massey ejaculated in unfeigned surprise, pausing in his occupation of inspecting the capabilities of the game-pie. 'Really! But what is it that I have done?'

'Oh, it is nothing,' she said reassuringly; 'but he was a little put out that you did not come earlier – thought it a slight, I suppose.'

'But –'

'There! I know all about it. Don't imagine that I find fault. You'll find you'll get used to pa and his ways in time. Don't seem to take any notice of them, that's all! Well, have you seen anything of the Vicarage people yet? You said something the other night about going there.'

He nodded at her over his plate of pie, his face suddenly alight with amusement.

'I have seen them,' he said.

'How – where?' leaning eagerly forward.

'He called, you know – the Vicar – and I had to return his call. I say! Mrs Pearson!' an expressive shudder. 'You did not half prepare me. Poor old Vicar!'

' "Sauerkraut" we call her,' cried Pollie, delighted. 'Does she not set your teeth on edge? She positively gives me the shivers. Did she present you with an *Enlightener*?'

'With a what?'

'An *Enlightener*. That's the paper she writes for. Didn't you know? She's clever enough, you know, if she wasn't such a fool, and she writes temperance tales for this trashy paper; and if she hears of anyone indulging in any drink stronger than the very weakest tea, she sends 'em one – oh, she sends them everywhere! Mr Selby, who likes his glass of wine very well, as you can see by his nose – Mr Selby has one every week. And pa had one too, for a time; but he sent them back again, unopened, and that put a stop to it. I once tried to read some of Mother Pearson's tales to Dollie, but she is much too advanced for that sort of rubbish, and would not listen. Well, when you called – tell me about it – did you see Ellen?'

'Did I see whom?' he asked, looking with an appearance of great innocence in her face.

'Ellen – Ellen Smith.'

'I thought her name was Helen; they called her Helen. Oh, yes; I saw her.'

It was in quite an indifferent tone that this fact was mentioned. It would never have betrayed that on the occasion under discussion Mr Massey had seen nothing but Helen – that he had hardly even thought of anything else, since.

'Well?' inquired Miss Freeman breathlessly.

'Well?' repeated Mr Massey, with that look of innocence on his face.

'What do you think of her? Now, is she so very wonderful after all?'

'What do you mean by "wonderful"? that is the question. She is wonderfully self-possessed for a girl, and wonderfully indifferent, apparently, to what goes on around her.'

'Oh, I know that way of hers! That's all put on. The Smiths are as high as high, you know. There was a grandfather, a baronet, or something, and scarcely anyone is good enough for them. As for farmers, they are dirt beneath their feet. Fancy her beginning already to treat you in that fashion!' There was satisfaction as well as indignation in Miss Freeman's tone.

'Oh, I don't complain,' Mr Massey said, in a tone of mildest resignation, 'I don't complain. So long as you will treat me with kindness, Miss Freeman, I am more than content.'

How could poor Pollie guess that as he looked, with a gaze that might have been one of admiration, at her pretty plump face, her little yellow curls, her tight black velvet, he was really seeing, in his mind's eye, such a widely different form? The comfortable dining-room, with its crowded table, was less present to him, just then, than a certain chill comfortless room – the Vicarage drawing-room, bleak and barren – empty of occupants too, save for the presence of one woman in a low chair by the fire. What a feeling of discomfort and strangeness had been upon him as he entered; but the woman had risen from her chair and come forward with a courteous, unembarrassed greeting, and lo! the room was transformed, the very atmosphere pervaded with beauty. Mr Pearson and his wife had quickly appeared upon the scene, and Helen Smythe had borne no part in the conversation which ensued, but Massey had never for an instant lost the consciousness of her presence; and although he had in reality performed all that Mrs Pearson, who preferred the sound of her own voice, required of him in the way of conversation, he was unable, on reflection, to remember one word that he had said, and was horribly inclined to believe that he had been, for the time being, dumb. 'What a dolt and fool she must have thought me!' he had told himself a hundred times, and then a hundred times more had failed to find solace in the probability that she had not thought about him at all. His reminiscences of that visit were far from being all pleasant; for although there had been something of infinite attraction in the careless grace of the girl, although the serious smile with which she greeted him had seemed to him marvellously sweet, there was still something about her – her coolness and her indifference and her calm superiority – which had piqued and almost angered him. He pushed his plate away from him impatiently now as he thought of it.

'Do have some more pie,' said Pollie, with anxious solicitude, 'do! What, not if I find you a dear little titbit? Well then, what will you have? An apricot puff? Yes, now! I am so fond of apricot jam, aren't you? Well then,' sighing, 'if you won't eat any more, we must go back to the others. We are here for you to eat, and if you won't eat, why, we must not be here.'

'Why in the world not? Who's to prevent it?'

'Oh, pa and ma wouldn't like it, and old Miss Gay is such a gossip, and Eliza and Mr Selby would lead me such a life about it.'

'Then pass the apricot puffs, by all means,' he said with a laugh, 'I am equal to any amount of them under the circumstances. But stay; do *you* wish to go back?' with a sudden change to gravity and sentiment. 'Am I, perhaps, keeping you from greater enjoyment?'

'Oh no,' very low and bashfully.

'Do you know, Miss Freeman,' pushing away his plate and looking across at her with much solemnity; 'do you know that I have been hearing something very dreadful about you – something that has shocked and surprised me very much?'

'About me?'

'About you. They tell me,' here he gave a tremendous sigh; 'they tell me that you are a – flirt!'

'Now who could tell you that?' cried Pollie, with outward indignation. In reality this was a title she had been a little ambitious to bear. 'Oh, the spite that I meet with in this place! I insist on knowing who it was that told you, Mr Massey. I have a right to know, although I am quite certain that you know me too well to believe it. Now, do you believe such a horrid insinuation – do you think that I look in the least little bit like a flirt?'

The blue eyes lowered as she asked the question, but not before a wicked flash from out them had shot into his.

'Do you believe it?' she asked again in a whisper. 'Do you think I am a flirt?'

'I think you are a very dear little girl,' he said. And pushing back his chair, he rose, and walked round the table to her.

Pollie's heart beat quickly, but at this most inopportune moment the drawing-room door was heard to open, and in an instant more the whole of the Freeman family, attended by their guests, had broken up the thrilling *tête-à-tête*.

CHAPTER V

Dinner at the Vicarage

SOON after the celebration of the festival in honour of Mr Massey, the Freemans received their annual invitation to partake of the Vicarage hospitality. Ever since Pollie had been promoted to the honour of taking her mother's place on these occasions, and to the privilege of supporting her father through several hours of martyrdom, which yet (by reason of long-established custom, or through some dim notion that this yearly sacrifice proved him an undoubted member of that Church whose privileges he accepted in no other way), he never dreamed of shirking – ever since this felicity had been accorded her, Pollie had been wont loudly to declare that the 'Vicarage evening' was the dullest and least satisfactory of her year.

'Never a creature but old Selby to meet us! We're not good enough for the Pearsons' friends,' she would cry indignantly, thinking with longing of that family of Backs of Hilby Hall, whose acquaintance she would dearly have liked to make. 'We're not good enough for their friends, but we are, to my thinking, a vast deal too good for their dinners.'

And, indeed, it was a tolerably well-known fact that the Vicarage dinners were none of the best. On this occasion, however, the young lady secretly looked forward with more than usual satisfaction to the event, knowing quite well that a, to her thinking, more interesting person than Mr Selby would also be of the party.

To do the Vicar justice, he would fain have imparted a more festive tone to the entertainment; but festivity and Mrs Pearson were as incompatible as fire and water. Life was something more to her, she thought, than a mere attention to the requirements of the body; her mind had won a triumph over the material part of her, and creature-comforts she despised. She did not even deign to notice that on this evening, when her guests were expected, the lamp burnt but dimly, and that the air of the drawing-room was as chill as the charity she herself administered.

'Aren't we going to have a better light than this?' her husband asked querulously, from his position on the hearth, where he was endeavouring to attract some warmth to the back view of his portly person.

The Vicar was a man of forty years of age, tall and stoutly built, with a universal redness of complexion, a fat large face, a heavy double chin, a small upturned nose, quite out of character with the rest of his face, and a pair of dull and inexpressive eyes. He cultivated a scanty crop of whiskers, but no beard; and the long light hair brushed over a high and narrow forehead was very lank and thin. He had, too, big flat feet, upon which he walked in a very clumsy and whole-footed way, while his hands were also big and red as his face. It is altogether pretty certain that, deprived of his clerical garb, he would have been taken for anything in the world rather than for a gentleman. What he was, and how he looked, however, were matters of trifling import to his wife, too absorbed in herself and her crotchets to waste time or thought on him. So it had come to pass that, a cypher in his own house, a nonentity in the parish, Mr Pearson, all unconsciously to them both, had been taken under the protection of his sister-in-law, who cared for and defended him, as was her habit with the neglected or the weak. She tried to stir the fire into a blaze now, in response to his complaint, and the lamp into better behaviour.

'It does look rather dismal, certainly,' she said. 'Anna, don't you think we might have in some wax candles just for to-night? No? Then we must leave the illumination to our guests – we shall soon have some shining lights among us.' She smiled as she sank again into her chair, and was at once taken to task for her levity in the tone of pompous disapprobation which Mr Pearson so often used to her, in spite of her championship.

'It is not good taste in you, Helen,' he said, 'to laugh at people who are about to enjoy our hospitality. However – um – um – inferior to ourselves they may be, they are at least used to warm and well-lit rooms, remember.'

'Oh dear!' cried the girl, in some distress. 'How can you call it laughing at them, Alfred? Of course I meant nothing unkind; and did I ever hint at their being inferior to me? Is it not a constant endeavour of mine to win the people from some of their prejudices against us all? It is unfair to say such words to me, of all people.'

In truth, to do Helen Smythe justice, she was the only one of them who exerted herself in any measure to do honour to the occasion, and when the light at length burnt more cheerfully, and the fire blazed up, the bleakness of the drawing-room was seen to be relieved by greenhouse plants and delicate ferns, and the dining-table had been made beautiful in the same way by her tasteful hands.

The dinner was much such a one as she had unconcernedly assisted at many times at her sister's table, but never before had she been so observant of the various eccentricities consequent on Mrs Pearson's manner of housekeeping; never, too, had her surroundings appeared to her so blank, and dull, and hopelessly depressing. It was a slight incident she noticed, as they first sat down, which engendered this critical spirit. It was nothing more than a little telegraphic communication from Pollie Freeman to Mr Massey, to the effect that he was to eschew the soup. Miss Smythe had happened to look up at the sound of the affected cough which had likewise compelled the young man's attention, and had understood, as he did, the glance in the direction of the soup-tureen, and the frown and shake of the head. The worst of it had been that Mr Massey had caught her eye and seen the intelligence in it, and must have noticed the angry crimsoning of her face; and yet this was not the very worst. The very worst was that he would take the soup after all; and did not Helen know from sad experience that the concoction justified Pollie's warning, being lukewarm, and tasteless, and greasy? Both she herself and wise little Pollie, who had remorselessly declined soup on her own account, watched his progress through that dreadful plateful. He ate it manfully, to the very last drop, the other guests unceremoniously dropping their spoons after the first two or three mouthfuls. It was a relief to Mr Massey himself when he had finished; and as he looked involuntarily across at Miss Freeman, and met her wicked smile, and noted her little contemptuous shrug at what she deemed his obtuseness, he heaved a sigh of satisfaction, as at an unpleasant duty well performed.

Helen, as a rule a pleasant talker and an appreciative listener, was quite overcome by this commencement; and instead of giving her attention to Mr Selby, against whom she sat, and who was rather a favourite of hers, she employed herself in anxiously going over in her mind the courses to follow, and in imagining what was likely to be the manner of the failure of each. She had been so used to Mr Pearson's complaint that his food was ill-cooked – chill where it ought to have been hot, and tepid where it should have been cold – that it had long ceased to make any impression on her; but to-night the flabby overboiled cod-fish, the bleeding leg of mutton, the sauces that had been made and the sauces that had been forgotten, filled her with dismay. She was for ever imagining those terrible glances of intelligence between the two young people, although she would look no more to catch them, and her blood tingled with anger and vexation.

And why, oh, why must her sister pick upon to-night, of all nights in the year, to promulgate her scheme for teaching the labourers' wives to cook? The titter which came from Pollie Freeman was speedily converted into a cough behind her smart lace handkerchief, but Helen knew too well that it had been a titter; and the alacrity with which Mr Massey (no one else speaking) seconded his hostess's views was an insult, for was he not wanting dreadfully to laugh the while? When the dreary evening should be over, and he and that most objectionable girl were together once more, how he would laugh! Could one not imagine the vulgar jesting, the hideous comparing of notes? Helen looked quite fiercely into the grave attentive face turned towards her sister, and almost hated the young man for the sparkle of fun she saw in his eyes.

'We do not sit over our wine, Massey, but perhaps you will like to have a cigar,' Mr Pearson said, as the ladies left the room.

Mr Massey was holding the door open for them to pass, and Helen heard Pollie's whispered entreaty to him not to stay long, as she passed out behind her.

'I cannot talk to that little thing to-night,' Miss Smythe said to herself. 'She is really so – so vulgar. I have tried to like her, but I cannot. I must leave her to Anna.'

Anna, however, quickly and without ceremony lapsed into silence, and Helen took up the burden of her duty once more; talking to her guest but languidly, and with little interest, as that young lady was quick to see. Pollie, unsupported in the presence of these two ladies, was quite on her good behaviour, and even humble in her demeanour. She looked at the albums with pretended interest, and turned over the books, magazines, and photographs which Helen reached her with commendable docility. But all the time she was storing in her memory little incidents of speech and action to reproduce for Mr Massey and her home-circle by-and-by. In a pause of the conversation she even practised a certain curve of the lip which Miss Smythe's mouth had worn just now. Pollie had been questioned as to her literary tastes, and had unhesitatingly declared that Ouida's books were the only ones she cared to read. 'Are they?' Helen had said with unconscious expressiveness, and 'Are they?' drawled Pollie to herself with imitative languor, caricaturing the disdainful curl of the beautiful lip. 'Oh my goodness, what women!' she was saying to herself presently, holding at the same time a view of a cathedral in her hand, and listening with apparent interest, while the two sisters held forth to her and to each other on the beauties of the architecture.

'What a dreadful girl she is!' Helen was on her part thinking, the while. 'How can I talk to her? – she does not even understand what I am saying. We have not two ideas in common. She kills me with weariness!'

Then, in desperation, she had gone to the piano, and had taken refuge there, playing softly to herself. Pollie meanwhile clung to her 'views' in silence, and Mrs Pearson, leaning back in her chair, in forced and unwelcome idleness, occupied herself, as Pollie falsely thought, in making an inventory of her person and belongings.

'She knows, to a yard, how much lace I have on my dress, and she counted every button,' the young lady declared delightedly, as she walked home.

But in truth, Mrs Pearson could not have described a single article of her apparel. She regarded the girl as a whole, and disapproved of her without reservation; thought what a horror it would be to have to live continually with a creature so far opposed to all ideas of refinement and good taste, and then forgot all about her, and with her eyes still unconsciously fixed on Miss Freeman, turned her thoughts to the only subject of any real interest to her – her hobby for the time being.

Presently the bad half-hour was over, and the gentlemen were in the room – Mr Pearson rubicund and cheery, from the effect of his cigar and coffee; Mr Freeman even more than usually awkward, heavy and sullen; Mr Selby with an exaggerated air of cheerful wide-awakeness, which his quick-coming yawnings and blinkings speedily belied; Mr Massey very eager and alert, making his way at once to the piano, from which Helen rose at his approach.

'Won't you sing, Miss Smythe?' he asked.

'Not to-night,' she answered, with quiet politeness of tone, but without glancing in his direction.

'You do sing, I know, for I hear your voice in church.'

Of this observation she took no notice.

'Perhaps Miss Freeman will sing,' she said.

Now, to hear Miss Freeman sing was not at all what Mr Massey desired, having already had that pleasure on several occasions. He attempted no further remonstrance, however, but sat himself down with a somewhat discomfited feeling.

'I suppose she means to snub me,' he said to himself. 'Certainly little Pollie is right – she is a most discouraging person to get on with; but what a face!'

While Miss Freeman was struggling through her song, in a pretty but untutored voice, to an accompaniment very loud and frequently faulty, Mr Massey took the opportunity of observing this same unconscious face with a good deal of interest. Apparently the air of languor, at which Pollie laughed, and the touch of disdain about the beautiful mouth, were not thoroughly distasteful to him. Pollie's song, which had been a little something concerning an ivy leaf, delivered with much energy and spirit, came to an end, and the two girls stood together for a minute, looking at some music which one of them held. The Vicar was deep in some wonderful sporting anecdote, of which he himself had been the hero – he generally was the hero of his own tales, by the way – but Mr Massey gave him but mechanical attention, as he watched the girls at the piano. Helen Smythe, who looked a lady – more than a lady, a gentlewoman – in whatever position she might be placed, looked to-night, by the side of pretty, smart Pollie, a princess!

'Were you aware, Mr Massey, that such a thing was possible?' the Vicar was asking, and Massey, pulling himself together, and quite in the dark as to the subject of the inquiry, pledged himself to its possibility.

'What the dickens was it?' he asked afterwards, as they walked homeward. 'I believe I was dreaming – what was it that he was prosing about?'

Said Pollie, 'He was relating that favourite tale of a hare that he saw run up a tree, and you said that it was not at all astonishing – that they often did it.'

However, much had to be gone through before they had that homeward walk, which one of them thought so much the pleasantest part of the evening. A whist-table was inaugurated, principally for the delectation of Mr Freeman, who was known to approve of whist, and who now, seated on the least comfortable chair in the room, which he had insisted, with some mistaken idea of politeness, on taking, was looking a picture of unalloyed misery in his shiny black frock-coat, with his big red hands, unshaded by any vestige of wristbands, lying on his shiny black legs.

'Oh, I don't know about that,' he said, with a slow drawing down of the corners of his mouth, in answer to Miss Smythe's remark that Mr Freeman would like a rubber. 'I don't wish you to make any difference for me, ma'am'; and he showed a coy reluctance when, the card-table being prepared and pushed forward, he was called upon to join.

He certainly was not the easiest style of person to entertain, and Massey, regarding him as he sat at length in his place at the table, his back well up, his head down, and that ugly lower lip of his pushed out, thought to himself that he was not too pleasant to look at either, and in the chivalry of his nature he almost wished that he had himself taken him for his partner, and so saved Miss Smythe the unenviable office of sitting opposite to and playing with him.

Pollie, who, as a matter of duty, had declined to make one in the game, lest it might be imagined by chance that she was in any way amused thereby, sat and overlooked Mr Selby's hand, and ostentatiously yawned and weariedly sighed in a manner very distracting to the peace of mind of one of the players; and being a sharp little person, and having been used to cards from her infancy, she was enabled to make comments on that same person's anything but perfect play, with much inward delight and many outward expressions of annoyance.

'Why,' she would cry, 'you have trumped pa's best card, Miss Smythe!' or, 'There! you should have given pa credit for that.'

'I'm so sorry,' Helen would say, 'but I really do not understand the game, you see. It does not much signify, does it?'

Then Pollie would give a superior smile, and say that there wasn't much interest in a game like that; that it did not signify as it would if they were playing for money. 'We always play for money everywhere else we go. I dare say pa won't mind for to-night.'

Here Helen would triumphantly trump a thirteenth card, or commit some equally unpardonable sin, and Mr Freeman, pushing out his nether lip, and glancing to his daughter for sympathy, would remark that he 'shouldn't care to be playing for money now, for certain.'

Mr Massey, looking on at all this, while he ostensibly listened to the display of Mrs Pearson's conversational powers, now in full swing for his benefit, did not feel too pleased with, or proud of, his friends.

'The man is no better than one of his own hogs,' he thought angrily, watching the colour flush Miss Smythe's delicate face.

'Oh, do wait one minute,' she said, hesitating over her cards, and half drawing one, then another. 'I cannot remember if that knave is the best card.'

'Oh, *don't* you know?' Pollie cried, emphatically anxious. 'I *wish* I might tell you! Do think, Miss Smythe'; and Miss Smythe, glancing distressedly from the perplexing cards in search of inspiration, looked straight into Mr Massey's sympathetic grey eyes, intently observant of her. In an instant he had left Mrs Pearson, in the very midst of a description of the working of a coffee-tavern which she proposed to start in the village, and about which he had professed great interest, had gone over to the whist-table, and drawn a chair up to Miss Smythe's side.

'That was simply the rudest behaviour I have ever witnessed,' commented Mrs Pearson inwardly.

'Will you let me offer you my valuable advice, Miss Smythe?' he said eagerly. 'Two heads are better than one, they say.'

And so it came to pass that Miss Smythe made no more mistakes that night.

'Won't you take the cards?' she asked him more than once. 'Please do take them.'

But he found his position close behind Miss Smythe's chair too pleasant a one to give it up so readily. She was as proud as Lucifer, he knew, and as cold as ice, he divined; and altogether would undoubtedly be, as Pollie had said, a dreadful person to spend one's life with. But this was not a question of his life, and she was very beautiful, and there was a certain foolish pleasure which he experienced in watching that white hand of hers flutter uncertainly about the cards, always awaiting his direction; and once or twice, he pretending to be inattentive or engrossed with other matters, she leant back in her chair, bringing her dark head very close to his, and held the cards for inspection before his face. At such moments he even felt that the 'Vicarage evening' had not been quite purgatorial after all.

'Of course they've won,' said Pollie to Mr Selby, with acrimony. 'They ought to win – three against two. It is hardly fair to Mr Selby and Mr Pearson, pa,' she said, turning to her parent. 'You are three against two, you know.'

Mr Freeman slowly shuffled the cards, and licked one thumb preparatory to re-dealing. 'I wish only what is fair,' he said; 'don't let anyone be ill-convenienced for me.'

'I think you must not advise Helen, Mr Massey,' said the Vicar weightily: 'hardly fair – hardly fair. Let the game take its chance.'

Mr Massey said a word about 'the game' under his breath, which would have profaned the Vicarage drawing-room, and continued to inspect Helen's cards.

'You had better leave me to my own erratic courses, Mr Massey,' she said. 'But – oh, do look at this hand! Mr Freeman, I really cannot play it: one trump – only one; and see, not one single court card!' In spite of Massey's restraining hand, she spread the thirteen doleful-looking cards face upward on the table.

'Oh, Miss Smythe!' cried Pollie, in a tone of shocked remonstrance.

'Helen!' thundered the Vicar; 'Helen! what are you thinking of?'

'Pick 'em up – pick 'em up,' said kindly Mr Selby, commencing to shuffle them together.

But Mr Freeman threw his own cards (an especially promising lot) on the top of them, and noisily pushed back his chair. 'That isn't whist,' he said with angry contempt, and the game was over.

'I have done something dreadful now, have I not?' asked Helen, looking to Mr Selby.

'Not a bit of it,' Massey answered for him, reaching past her to gather up the cards. 'You did quite right, of course. When you want to get the game over, have a disagreeable partner, or a bad hand, it is always best to throw your cards down – so.' And with this valuable piece of advice Miss Smythe's whist for that year concluded.

CHAPTER VI

The Meet

'DO you know that the hounds meet to-morrow at Bracknell Wood? I want you to take me there, Ted,' said Pollie Freeman one evening to her brother, picking upon an occasion when her father had gone to his 'study' for his nightly confabulation with his steward. It was only on periods of state that the smart drawing-room came into requisition; the family was at its ease now in the more comfortable dining-room – Miss Pollie in an easy-chair, next the fire and opposite that recently vacated by her father; her mother by the table, with the lamp drawn close to her head, intent on the restoration of a bundle of dilapidated stockings; 'Dear Dollie' perched in a tall chair by her mother's side, piling up reels abstracted from the work-basket.

'And how come you to find out about the hounds?' Mrs Freeman asked. 'Your father put the paper out o' the way, so you mightn't see.'

'I wonder pa don't make a prisoner of me at once,' said Pollie bitterly. ''Tis sure to be wrong if I want to go outside the door.'

'Well, he don't like meets,' explained her mother, intently examining the long stocking-leg she was pulling over her hand. 'He say the pony always come home knocked up, and it unsettle the boy; and women ha' no call to be at such places. I don't know there's much harm in it myself, but I don't see what pleasure you find there, nayther.'

''Tis better than at home, at any rate,' said Pollie. So many things were 'better than home' to her, who was ever possessed with a craving for excitement which all the gaieties of the world would not have satisfied, and which her present narrow uneventful life fretted into a perpetual unrest. Ted, staring, sleepily content, into the fire, his long thin legs stretched out in tired enjoyment, looked up slowly at the mention of his name.

'How should it unsettle me?' he asked of his mother, in his hoarse cracked voice. 'I don't want to go, 'tisn't that, but how d'ye mean?' There was not much fear of unsettling him, apparently; a more stolid, less excitable youth it would have been hard to find.

'Pa is afraid,' said Pollie, answering for her mother, 'that you should see how other young men do, and should pluck up a spirit, and want to do the same. I would too, if I were in your place – that I would! You are old enough now. Why shouldn't you have your hunter, and take your pleasure like the others? Pa can afford it very well. Why don't you stand up for yourself and do it, Ted? Are you to be a drudge and a clodhopper all your life long to please pa?'

Ted, quite unmoved by this eloquence, wrinkled up one side of his face into a wink at her, and calmly turned back to the fire. 'Listen to her!' he croaked derisively. 'Listen to her, mother!'

'Yes, and she've no business to say such things,' said the mother, with some heat. 'You ought to be ashamed, Pollie, putting such notions into the boy's head. And why is it that your father can afford such goings-on – if he can afford 'em, I'm sure I don't know – but by doing without the very things you want the boy to run into? If your father had kept his hunter, and done his horse-racing and his betting, where do you think we should have been now? But he have been a man that have worked, and I ha' been a woman that have saved, and so we ha' managed to keep afloat, while men around us, that you'd have the boy copy, ha' sunk. People that 'ud ha' done better mindin' their own business have twitted us wi' bein' extravagant wi' you, and ha' said that we kep' an extravagant table, but 'tisn't the buying of a few dresses for a girl, nor the puttin' her to a decent school – no, nor the broachin' of a bottle o' good wine now and then, that'll ruin a man. Let them that say so look to their huntin' and their bettin' and their unlimited loo –'

'Massey's got a splendid hunter,' croaked Ted, interrupting his mother's flow of words, and again executing that arduous wink at his sister.

'And why not?' demanded Mrs Freeman warmly. 'Why not? Massey's a young man, according as they tell me, not dependent on his business, as Ted there will be, nor dependent, like him, on his father; but with property of his own, and – a very different case!'

'Dear Dollie like Maffy,' said that little one, piling up her cottons with chubby hands. 'He bring dear Dollie fweeties.'

'And Dollie is a naughty girl to ask him for sweeties, and mother oughtn't to let you do it. You'll drive me to-morrow, Ted? we must start by ten o'clock.'

'Oh, I daresay,' said Ted ironically, and with his ridiculous chuckle.

'Dear Dollie go with you, Teddie,' cried the child, knocking down her reels and clambering from her chair.

'Dollie had better go to bed, mother,' said Pollie, her hand on the bell. ''Tis long past her time.'

'Dear Dollie won't!' screamed that young lady, with sudden violence. 'Beastly ole Pollie! Dollie hate you!'

When Mr Freeman entered the room a minute later, his younger daughter, screaming and kicking, was in process of being carried off. She bent her little body back from the servant, and stretched out two appealing arms to him. He took her at once from the girl, and hugged the child with rough tenderness to his breast.

'She shall stop wi' her father,' he said. 'Father 'on't let his little girl go to bed.'

'That is how the child is spoilt,' said Pollie, with as much virtuous severity as if Dollie had been the first child spoilt in that family.

'I don't yike Pollie,' the little sister sobbed confidentially to her father, as she lay in his arms.

In spite of her father's black looks, in spite of her mother's tongue, Pollie and Ted Freeman, in their little car, formed part of the assembly at Bracknell Wood next morning. The weather proved fair and propitious; the meet was large, and Pollie, looking round on the many vehicles drawn up to witness the start, was perhaps justified in some feeling of dissatisfaction at what she would have called her own 'turn-out' – the mud-splashed, jolting car; the small pony, sound in wind and limb, but shaggy as to coat and shabby as to harness; the stolid, honest boy at her side, his hat well over his big ears, his coat-cuffs almost concealing his knuckles. Ted had suffered so much in his growing-time through insufficiency of covering for his arms and his ankles, that the one idea now steadily clung to by him was to have his sleeves and his trousers of a sufficient length to hide those bony and obtrusive members. Poor youth! he had not been finished off in Nature's best manner – the raw material for a young man was there, but she had declined to model it after any approved fashion; his tailor, too, in this case had apparently been unequal to 'making the man.' He looked now, with no outward show of any sort of feeling, at the people about him, and made no attempt to converse with his sister.

Two or three young men, sons of neighbouring farmers, came up to speak to pretty little Miss Freeman, and Pollie was always anxious to hold these rattling youths up to the boy as models; but he would receive all her admonitions in unmoved silence, or would wrinkle up one side of his stiff, red face into an untranslatable wink, which may have meant a great deal and was certainly unanswerable.

'Here's your Vicar's old shandrydan, Miss Freeman,' one of the friendly young fellows said to her presently. He was coaxing his horse's neck and leaning down to speak to her – a good-looking young man enough, well mounted and irreproachably 'got up' – altogether a creditable acquaintance for the occasion, felt Pollie, whose ears were not acute enough to mark his indifferent English, nor her critical powers sufficiently developed to enable her to take exception to his rustic coarseness of manner. 'By George! what a turn-out it is!' he went on, his eyes on the somewhat mournful-looking Vicarage equipage. 'I'm hanged if I wouldn't go without a coat to my back rather than go about with that beastly old hearse rattling after me. Look at that infernal old screw in the shafts, too! Ain't it a shockin' sight?'

'I'm sure they're all of a piece,' said Pollie contemptuously, glancing at the waggonette. 'I don't know which is the shabbiest and the mustiest – the Vicar himself, or his old manservant, his old horse, his old carriage, or his old sister-in-law in her shabby old hat and jacket. They are all much of a muchness, I think.'

The young man laughed, looking across at the 'old sister-in-law,' who having recognised Miss Freeman, was in the act of executing a little smile and bow.

'Come,' he said, 'you're rather hard on the young woman. I've heard people call her a beauty, and I'm hanged if she is a bad-looking girl. A little bit too much of the saint about her – flesh and blood's more in my line, I confess; but –'

At this moment the butt-end of Teddie's driving-whip was driven with some force into Pollie's side; it was his method of compelling her attention.

'Look, there's Massey,' he said, his face showing unusual signs of animation; and he forthwith gave himself up to uninterrupted contemplation of that gentleman and his horse both of whom had happened to awaken a spark of animation in that slow nature.

There came a light into Pollie's blue eyes and a flush to her face that made her unusually pretty for a moment, and her little vain, selfish heart beat quickly. The young man who had hitherto engaged her attention took advantage of her temporary abstraction to move off, and Miss Freeman was at liberty to watch uninterruptedly the object of the intensest interest (outside her own little personal vanities and comforts) she had yet known. He was a young man any girl might be proud of, Pollie thought, noticing with a pleased eye how well he sat his horse and how thoroughly at ease he looked; and although he was neither so good-looking nor so extensively 'got up' as the young farmer who had just left her, she instinctively felt a difference and a superiority which she could not have defined.

Mr Massey had made few acquaintances in the neighbourhood yet, and Pollie noticed, as he slowly moved his horse about among the different groups, that in many instances people observed the new-comer and asked each other who he was.

'Teddie, let us drive across and speak to Mr Massey,' the girl said; but the boy declined, with much wisdom.

'We're all right here,' he said; 'he'll see us as soon as he wants.'

But it seemed to impatient Pollie that he would never see them. He had ridden up to the Vicarage waggonette, and was being talked to loudly and energetically by the Vicar on the driving-seat, and now and again answered in languid, musical monosyllables by the sister-in-law, sitting with the little son and heir of the Pearsons in the body of the carriage. Presently this child, a little pale morsel of five or thereabout, stretched forth a timid but eager hand, and tried to stroke the shining neck of Mr Massey's horse, and that obliging gentleman instantly reined the animal close up to the carriage, that the boy, held by his auntie, might reach it.

'Have you a pony, my little man?' was asked. And upon the boy saying shyly 'No,' Pollie, listening with all her ears, heard a promise made to him to be taken for a ride one day on Mr Massey's horse.

'Would you – would Mrs Pearson be afraid to trust him to me?' he asked of Miss Smythe, and asked as anxiously as though he were begging a favour for himself.

'It would be troubling you too much,' said the languid voice; but noticing a sudden drooping of the child's head, and a babyish trembling of the mouth, his auntie apparently awoke to some interest in the matter. 'What do you say, Perrie?' she asked tenderly of him; 'should you like to go?' and a swift flush of colour over Perrie's pathetic face, and an eager brightening of his eyes, answered. 'Some day when the summer comes again you shall go,' she said, kissing him. And Massey, putting out his hand, patted the outstretched baby one:

'We will not wait till the summer, will we, Perrie?' he said.

'He must be a young man who is really fond of children,' Helen said afterwards to her sister, thinking of this, and recalling her first sight of him with mud-bedraggled little Dollie in his arms. 'He seemed quite anxious, you know, that Perrie should go.'

And now, to Pollie, impatiently watching, a welcome diversion was created by the arrival on the scene of a strong force of those Backs from Hilby Hall in whom she took such a strong interest. There was quite a cavalcade of them, some on horseback, some in a handsome barouche, while two of the fastest of the girls, boyish-looking young females, sitting very straight and square, drove themselves in a little light yellow cart. These all exchanged greetings with the Vicarage party, and two of the young men riding up to the waggonette, Massey withdrew, and in turning away at length encountered Pollie's anxious blue eyes fixed on him. Pollie was not, however, regarding him with such undivided attention that she failed to observe the curiosity with which the fast Miss Backs in the cart inspected him, and she was likewise fully aware that those young ladies' brothers were looking in Massey's direction, and speaking of him to Helen Smythe.

Massey's face lit up with a smile as he caught sight of Pollie's smart figure in the muddy car.

'Do you mean to say,' he asked, bending down to her, 'that you have been so near to me all this time, and that I did not know it?'

'I began to think you did not want to see us,' said Pollie, a little offence in her tone. 'You managed to see everyone else first.'

'You did not really think that, I know. I looked about for you when I first came up, and I have not seen a creature to speak to but the Pearsons. Tell me who the people are, Miss Freeman – you always know everyone. Those young ladies, now, in deer-stalkers and greatcoats, who are looking at you with so much interest, who are they?'

(The young ladies in question were in reality looking at Mr Massey, as he saw quite well.)

'Oh, the Backs!'

'And those two men by the Vicarage waggonette, who may they be?'

'More Backs,' said Pollie. 'They are only just home for Christmas, you know; that's why you have not seen them before.'

'But I really was not anxious to see them. And they are great friends of the Pearsons', I suppose?'

'Oh dear, yes. Ellen quite wakes up when they are at Hilby. I fancy she would not mind being Mrs Captain Archibald Back; but Captain Archie himself don't see it. How do you like the look of him? – he is *so* handsome! No, not the one talking to Ellen Smith; the one by himself, looking over this way.'

Pollie blushed very becomingly as she directed attention to this handsome young man staring with a good deal of boldness straight into her face; and Mr Massey quietly moved his horse a step or two, so as effectually to screen his view. Pollie's heart swelled within her as she witnessed this manœuvre. She was very proud thus to monopolize the attention of the man who, being a stranger, attracted, unconsciously to himself, so much notice. She was particularly pleased that the Vicarage waggonette should stand alongside the Freemans' car, and that Helen Smythe should be a witness of Mr Massey's devotion. As a matter of fact, Miss Smythe did not, after one look, glance in their direction; being so fully and placidly convinced of the devotion, she thought it more charitable to turn her eyes elsewhere. Pollie, however, was not left to an undisturbed enjoyment of her triumph. All too soon, Mr Selby ambled up on his cob, and gently insinuated himself into the conversation. And then the handsome young Back rode forward.

'How do, Selby?' he said, with a careless nod. 'Not going with us, surely?' Then he turned to Massey. 'I think you are a neighbour of mine, Mr Massey,' he said. 'Should have given you a call, but I've been so confoundedly busy since we came back. Glad to see that you are a hunting man. That's a nice animal of yours.'

Pollie grew delightfully excited as she heard the two men talk of the probable day's run, and of their hunters. It was a great deal to her that her friend should thus be sought out by the great people of her world; it was more that the man who had always bestowed on her glances of open admiration should thus be brought nearer.

Then the deer-cart had rattled up, and all was confusion. Lord Barnett, the Master of the Hounds, in a stained pink coat, and with a battered hat crushed on to the top of his handsome old head, galloped up, and shouted and swore, and demeaned himself generally after his demented habit on such occasions.

'Good-bye,' Massey whispered, bending down to the girl. 'I'll come in this evening to tell your father where we find. May I come?'

'Of course you may, and mind you do.'

'Good-bye. Glad you brought your sister, Ted; take care of her, old man'; and he was off, and all the fun was over for Pollie.

A small flavour of excitement lingered for an hour or so, during which they pursued the hunt by road and lane, catching now and then a sight of some straggling horsemen, or hearing in the far distance the music of the hounds. The Freemans tore along, in company with several other vehicles, galloping recklessly over highways, jolting painfully down rutty short-cuts and narrow by-paths, until Teddie, taking a sudden and judicious turn, lost sight of his companions and lost scent of the hunt, and Pollie was at last regretfully compelled to allow him to drive the tired but plucky little pony homeward.

CHAPTER VII

A Village Concert

THE Hilby annual amateur concert is held to-night in the village schoolroom. The proceeds are to go, as usual, to augment the fund for the purchase of an organ, to supersede the old harmonium on which Helen Smythe plays Sunday after Sunday in church. This scheme, it must be said, does not meet with much support from the more influential parishioners, and it is a lamentable fact that the 'Hilby Organ Fund' is in much the same condition in which it was started five years ago by the donation of ten pounds, made by one of Mr Pearson's college friends. Mr Freeman had suggested, more than once, that the sum would be more sensibly expended in the purchasing of sermons for the Vicar. Mrs Freeman had a natural dislike to 'cotton,' as she said, to the fancies of 'those two women,' and did not 'hold' beside with too much singing and 'musicking' in church. Even James Massey, who did not trouble as a rule to interest himself in parish matters, thought to himself that it would be a pity to lose the sight of Helen at the harmonium. He could watch her comfortably from his seat, and the organ was to be in a different place, where the player would be hidden.

'Make all your minds easy,' Polly would say gaily; 'there is never the slightest chance of our getting an organ. The concert never brings in more than three pounds at a time and most of that goes in expenses. Organs are not likely to pour in on us at this rate.'

But the greater part of the audience who fill the concert room, trouble themselves vastly little about the ultimate destination of the threepence they pay at the door; they are simply bent on their own amusement, and boast no ulterior object whatever. Having cleaned themselves up to an unusual state of polish, they stump into the room in large bodies, and keep up an undercurrent of whispering, giggling, and scraping of heavy boots on the gritty boards throughout the performance, which accompaniment is changed now and again to a mighty storm of applause produced by the clapping of stiff horny hands. The two or three rows of shilling seats are filled by farmers' wives and daughters, who have in many instances driven several miles to get there – amusement of any kind being rare in the neighbourhood, and the Hilby concerts popular. The Hall party, mustered in strong force, are conspicuous by their chatter and their laughter and by the fact that they alone of the assembly, with the exception of the performers, are in evening dress. These last, ranged along at the back of the little platform, do their best to look at their ease in their exalted position, and now and then exchange shy smiles with their relatives and friends in the body of the room. The organist from the neighbouring market town officiates at the piano, occasionally introducing one of his popular comic songs, considered by many to be the gems of the evening.

The entertainment is half over when James Massey puts in an appearance, coming in from the cold and darkness, half dazzled, into the close little room, made brilliant by a multiplicity of mal-odorous lamps hung amid green boughs and flags on the walls. He is not consciously musical in his taste, and has purposely lingered over his dinner and his pipe, in spite of Miss Freeman's commands to him to be early.

'Your song comes in in the second part, you say? Be sure that I shall be in time to hear you sing,' he had assured her, and had candidly added that if he should happen to miss a great part of the remainder of the performance, he should not look upon it as matter for regret.

The Gurton organist was in the midst of one of those telling songs of his when Mr Massey entered, and there being no vacant seat, he stood near the door, rubbing his light great coat against the yellow flaky walls, and listening with no high appreciation of the singer's talent. Indeed before the conclusion of the song he had conceived a most unmerited hatred for the poor man who, as has been said, had a way of rendering his ditties that had become immensely popular with his audience. He had not much of a voice, it is true, but he contrived to compensate for this deficiency by a redundancy of dramatic action; he had, too, a habit, which never failed to please, of taking his audience into his confidence, as it were, lifting his shoulders at them, wrinkling his face at them, whispering, and even winking, where his desire was to be particularly impressive after a fashion, which Massey found irritating in the extreme. When the song and the inevitable encore were over, and the applause had somewhat subsided, Mr Pearson, who also was not musical, and who tried to relieve the fatigue of his mind by an attention to the arrangement of seats, and who had been making frantic, futile gestures to the newcomer since his entrance, now arose and called to him by name.

Massey looked round, startled, to find every eye in the room suddenly upon him, and the vicar wildly beckoning him with a chair.

'Come over here, here is a seat, Massey,' he called.

Massey accordingly had to leave the pleasant obscurity of his position, and bearing away a considerable portion of the wall-plaster on his rough great coat, to betake himself to the aristocratic neighbourhood of the front row, where he sat himself down on the outskirt of the vicarage party.

The next song in the programme happened to be Miss Freeman's, and Massey had only time to discover that Miss Smythe was immediately on his left hand, and was wishing him 'Good evening' with her usual languid indifference, and that her sister was bending her head in frigid salutation from the extreme end of the same bench, when some slight expression of welcome on the part of the audience told that Miss Freeman had come forth to sing.

She was attired in that killing costume of velvet and cream lace in which we have seen her on a former occasion, and her whole appearance was found fascinating in the extreme by a great many of those present. The little thing was slightly nervous, and the music shook visibly in the plump white mittened hands. Miss Smythe, quietly enjoying the situation, fancied that her neighbour was nervous too, for after one quick glance in Pollie's direction, he had looked no more, but had commenced to study the programme in his hand with the closest application. She watched him with the corner of her eye, as he pulled his moustache, frowning heavily at the paper in his hand, and she smiled to herself, enjoying the well-known signs of the love story she had discovered.

It was a song, popular at the moment, which Miss Freeman sang, and despite her rather moderate quality of voice, and a little flatness and a good deal of affectation, she apparently gave universal satisfaction, and received a rapturous burst of applause at the end of the song, and a great cry of 'ong-core, ong-core' from one masculine pair of lungs somewhere in the distance. In answer to this appeal, Miss Pollie, being sought by the gentleman at the piano, and once more led to the front, was pleased to substitute 'Barney

O'Hea,' evidently an old favourite of the audience, and with this, sung with a good deal of roguery and spirit, she made the success of the evening.

After this, 'Hush thee, my Babie' having been delivered by the choir in a manner to awaken the drowsiest infant that ever was drugged, a big young man in a dress-coat and large rucky white gloves, came forward and executed a comic song, the burden of which was to the effect that he 'couldn't keep still.' By way of illustration, he jumped and floundered about the little platform in his huge patent boots, in a manner to inspire the liveliest apprehension as to its power of supporting him.

'How a man can willingly make of himself such an ass!' Massey said to himself, regarding the big young man with contemptuous wonder, as he shouted the refrain, 'Oh I can't keep still! I can't keep still!' and thumped and jumped with his great carcase. The more the creaking boards were punished, the more the audience roared with delight. A musical little gurgle sounded at Massey's side – even Helen Smythe was laughing. She stopped as she met Mr Massey's eye wonderingly regarding her.

'I am afraid you are not amused,' she said, a suspicion of raillery in her tone; 'or is it that you do not care for music?'

'I don't know much about it, I suppose,' he answered. 'My sister is down on me always, if I venture to express an opinion. I'm bound to like the wrong things, she says. But this is not music, is it? It is simply a pitiable exhibition, and don't you think it a pity that people should encourage this poor fellow to make such a beast of himself? It is very cruel of you to laugh, you are inciting him to go through the degrading performance again.'

'I am glad to laugh when I can,' she said with a sigh. 'And you – if you are so superior to our innocent mirth – why did you come?'

'I came to hear one song,' he said, looking at her with some intentness. 'I would have gone much further to hear it. I know that it will repay me for my present sufferings.'

'I suppose he means that it *has* repaid him,' said Miss Smythe to herself as she leant back, and directed her gaze once more to the leaping countryman. 'It is perhaps a good thing that he is not musical, for Miss Freeman really was so dreadfully out of tune to-night.'

'Now why was not music made an extra in this lad's schooling?' asked Massey presently of his neighbour, a poor little boy with shining face and much oiled hair having commenced to torture himself and the public by a solo on the pianoforte. 'Poor little beggar! Heaven grant he may not break down utterly. Think how that unfortunate lad's holidays have been ruined, and the peace of his young mind utterly destroyed by looking forward to this fatal evening.'

'Never mind! Do clap him!' Helen said, with a sigh of relief as the juvenile performance came to an end. 'That last chord was quite correct – it was indeed – and there is no applause. Mr Massey, pray do clap him, poor little fellow!'

'Are you quite sure he won't do it over again if I do?' he asked, bringing his strong hands together at her bidding.

'Oh, please go on,' she entreated. 'How cruel of everyone not to applaud! His mother, who is just behind, thinks so much of his music.'

'She will think much of me after this,' Massey said, vigorously clapping; 'and the rest of the audience will think I am mad. I will, of course, clap the palms of my hands if you wish it, only tell me when to leave off.'

'That will do,' she said, smiling, and she rose from her chair. 'I am going to inflict my song upon you now, Mr Massey.'

'It was for your song that I came,' he said simply, as she moved away.

There was none of the applause that had greeted Miss Freeman's appearance, when Helen mounted the platform. Pollie's style was much better appreciated, and Pollie herself more admired, it seemed. 'Miss Smythe's song was ill-chosen,' was said afterwards, and it was also said that she herself had 'no life in her,' that she looked as cold as ice, and stood as though she had been carved in marble.

'Pity that woman is not made of flesh and blood!' Massey overheard one of the young Backs say to his sister. 'She has a perfect face!'

'She looks like a saint,' said Miss Back contemptuously, evidently being of opinion that the approach to that appearance was the one of all others to be regarded with horror.

Massey never forgot the sight of that girl whom they were all so coldly criticising, as she stood before him; he never ceased to remember the words that she sang. Whenever he heard them in the after-time, there would arise before him the vision of that 'perfect face' as he saw it now, with its look of purity and calm, which some called 'cold,' and some dismissed as 'saintlike,' but which had come to be to him a symbol of the loveliest soul which dwelt within.

Miss Freeman and her friends in the background were touching heads and whispering over her dress. Massey heard a great deal about it afterwards, and was told that it was quaint and unstylish, and after a fashion not approved in Hilby. He only knew that it was something light in hue and texture, that it fell gracefully about her graceful form, that it seemed to him a fitting garment for her beauty, and that it harmonised perfectly with the pure pale face and the rippling dark hair.

> 'Pray the good God to keep thee
> As pure and fair as now,'

sang the sweet voice solemnly, as though it had been, indeed, a prayer – and looking at her beauty, at the soft eyes raised above the head of the people whom she had, for the moment, forgotten, at the light of goodness and innocence about the lovely head, James Massey, although not a specially devout person, felt something of an echo to that prayer in his breast.

He had been thoroughly absorbed in his own thoughts and had forgotten to applaud at the finish of the song; among the rest, but very slight signs of appreciation were shown; before Helen had seated herself all sound of it had died away. She did not return to her old seat but went and sat down on the platform by Pollie Freeman during the rest of the entertainment which was now nearly over.

'She told me my song was a success,' Pollie said, afterwards. 'And I knew that without any telling, and I could not return the compliment.'

Miss Smythe had talked beside of different persons present, and said that they all appeared to have been pleased with the evening, 'except Mr Massey,' with a smile. 'I am afraid we have all rather victimised him.'

To this Pollie had volunteered the information that that gentleman was not musical, and that she herself had had some trouble to induce him to come, and she farther confessed that it had been for his convenience she had postponed her song until the 'second part,' in order that he should not be compelled to sit through so much to hear it.

'Ah, yes, I know what his attraction had been,' Helen said, smiling kindly at the girl; but in her heart she felt some contempt for the man and his insincerity, remembering a word he had said to herself but now.

'He is mistaken enough to imagine that what pleases Miss Pollie Freeman pleases me, I suppose,' she thought. 'How terrible it is to have to do with a man who is not at heart a gentleman! When once that kind of person imagines himself at liberty to pay compliments to one – he becomes unbearable and must be shunned.'

It was for this reason that a request she had intended making to Mr Massey himself, she preferred to Miss Freeman instead. 'Besides she no doubt has influence with him,' she thought, 'if she can only be persuaded to use it for good.'

'Miss Freeman,' she began accordingly, when they, among the rest of the singers, had retired to the little sitting room of the schoolmistress – converted into a cloak room for the occasion – to put on their hats, 'I want you to do me a great favour, will you?'

'I don't know that I can,' said Pollie, instantly on the defensive. Parsons and their people were always asking favours, according to the Freeman creed.

'You can, I feel sure, if you only will. It is about that unfortunate man Moore. You know he is – his wife and children are – so terribly poor. How they have contrived to live through the winter I do not know! I want him to have another chance. Will you speak to Mr Massey about him?'

'How do you mean speak to him, Miss Smythe?'

'I know that you have influence with him – will you ask him to give Moore one more trial? You remember that he used to work on that farm before Mr Massey came, and since he was turned off, he has acquired bad habits – very bad, of course – and his wife and children nearly starve.'

'And so they always did, Miss Smythe, and he had got his bad habits long before old Massey turned him off. No!' with a decided shake of the little be-curled head, 'I am quite sure Mr Massey would not think of such a thing, I assure you it would be useless for me to ask.' She was mollified somewhat by the implication of her influence with Mr Massey, but she would not for that forego her right to be disagreeable, she was not going to forget her fixed resolve to thwart the 'parson's sister' and to cross that lady's assumed intention of 'coming over her' of which Pollie had often spoken.

'Nevertheless, do ask him – will you? Do, Pollie! It is just to give him one chance more. Think how we may all want that one chance in the days to come. And the children they have done no harm, at least. Mr Massey will do as you wish him, I know,' (feeling instinctively that the girl's vanity was easier to touch than her compassion), 'ask him to do this!'

'Oh, I can mention it to him,' Pollie said with importance, 'but I can't hold out any hopes to you, I really can't, Miss Smythe.'

The Vicarage people and the Freeman party were the last to leave the schoolroom, and they started at length like so many glow-worms – each carrying his own light – most of the lamps dispersed about the room belonging to those two families.

'It has gone off very well I think, ma'am,' said Mrs Freeman to Mrs Pearson, as they stood together at the schoolroom door, while their respective husbands counted up the proceeds of the evening.

'Oh, yes! the people seemed amused. Something will have to be done another year to introduce a better class of music. Their taste wants educating woefully.'

'Three pounds fifteen,' called out the vicar as the result of his investigation, 'about the same as last year, Freeman. Wonderful how well these concerts seem to be appreciated.'

'It's a wonderful lot o' trouble for a wonderful little money,' Mr Freeman said, grumpily; 'now then, Pollie! are you going to carry one of these lamps?'

'Coming! Oh, Mr Massey, do come and get me this one from the bracket, I cannot reach it even on a chair.'

'Immediately!' called Mr Massey, who was at the moment performing a similar service for Miss Smythe. 'Good night,' he said to her then, putting out his hand and looking into her face surrounded by the white woolly shawl she had thrown over her head, 'good night, and I thank you for your song.'

When the Vicarage party passed the people from the Grange soon after, on their way home, it was observed by the former that Miss Freeman and Mr Massey had dropped considerably behind the others. Pollie, who was tired after her exertions, was hanging on the young man's arm, and he was carrying her lamp.

'What! is that going to be a case?' the Vicar asked of his womankind, having peered at the couple as he passed.

'A decided case,' said Helen, laughing. 'Mr Massey is evidently deeply in love, and Pollie is not likely to be difficult.'

'Dear me!' said Mrs Pearson. 'If it be so, I think it much to be regretted.'

'Regretted! why?' asked her sister, in a tone of surprise. 'It seems to me a most natural and fitting arrangement. I knew how it would be from the first time I saw them together. She is so pretty – yes, really! I know that you don't admire her, but that does not alter the fact. And he is most susceptible. It was sure to happen. Why should you regret it?'

'Perhaps the expression was too strong,' Mrs Pearson said, in her superior tone. 'My interest in the matter is not very lively, I confess. It appeared to me undesirable that she should settle in this parish, that is all. You know that the girl is no favourite of mine.'

'She won't improve Massey,' the Vicar said, turning his head to look for the light of the lamp, moving so slowly on behind. He was the most interested of the three in the subject under discussion. But that he dreaded his wife's scorn of such vulgar curiosity, he would have waited at his own gate to see that lagging couple pass. 'There is a great want of reverence about that girl,' he went on, as they walked up the tree-shadowed drive. 'Now, there is nothing encroaching about Massey. He knows his place, and what's due to – hum – to people. I had great hopes of Massey.'

This was great praise from the Vicar, who was not weakly given to speaking good things of the absent. He was, however, in the habit of spending some hours of every day at the Wood Farm – enjoying Massey's cigarettes, indulging in sundry glasses of weak whisky and water (prohibited at home), in his new parishioner's snug and homelike room. The hospitality he received at the hands of his other neighbours had been for years rather formal and heartless; Massey had not lost a genial tone in his words of welcome yet.

Supper was over at the Grange, but the family were still sitting round the table, when Pollie broached the subject of Helen's request to her.

'A likely tale!' Mrs Freeman said, with hot indignation. 'What'll the woman run her head at next? To have that feller, the worst feller in the whole parish, upsettin' things again.'

'Ah!' ejaculated Mr Freeman, his eyes glancing approbation on his wife. He gave sundry contemptuous grunts over his long clay pipe, being less than ever inclined for speech with its soothing stem between his lips.

'Do you say that she told you to ask me?' Massey inquired. 'Why could she not have asked me herself?'

Pollie laughed and blushed. 'I suppose she looks on you as our friend,' she said; 'and I daresay she thought I was going to persuade you. I was straight enough about it, whatever she thought, and told her the whole thing was out of the question.'

'Did you tell her so? Why is it out of the question?' He was moving a half-filled tumbler round and round on the table, and minutely studying its course. 'Why is it out of the question?' he repeated, without looking up.

There was a moment's pause of blank amazement, then Mrs Freeman looked at her husband.

'Mr Massey know nothing about the man,' she said apologetically. 'No one have told him as yet.'

'He worked for my uncle for years, did he not?' Massey enquired.

'Ay, and was turned off twenty times, and begged back twenty times,' Mr Freeman said, removing the pipe from his mouth, and staring at Massey with quite an excited look in his pale orbs. 'The worst lot in the village, he is! We never had no peace while he was among th' others.'

'The men, ye see, Mr Massey, always have an idea they're badly treated, and they're no hand at expressin' theirselves, as a rule. When they do get one amongst 'em clever enough to give tongue to it, they think his words are just gospel, and he can do what he like with the lot.'

'And 'tain't only your men, mind,' her husband explained; ''tis *my* men – all our men! A meddlin' fool!'

Massey looked up rather quickly.

'Do you mean that I am a meddling fool?' he asked, 'or the man, or – or – Miss Smythe?'

Pollie saw the flash of anger in his eyes, and sprang up from the table.

'What's the use of all the bother about the man?' she asked lightly. 'Turn round to the fire, and let's be comfortable. Of course Mr Massey 'on't take the man, pa; no one ever thought he'd take him, not even Helen Smythe in her heart. I shall tell her to get Mrs Pearson to send him some of her *Enlighteners* to convert him first, for he is a terrible drunkard!'

'I'm afraid, altogether, he is what must be called an unpromising lot,' Massey said, rising from his chair. 'No, thanks, I won't stop longer to-night. You are tired, I know, Miss Freeman, and the music seems to have made me stupid. Good-night, sir' – putting out his hand to his host.

Mr Freeman eyed him somewhat distrustfully, as he made his adieus to the wife and daughter. As the young man reached the door, he pulled his pipe from his lips.

'You are not thinking of taking on that blackguard – eh, Massey?'

Massey turned, his hand on the door.

'Well, yes, I think I shall give him a trial,' he said, calmly regarding the elder man. He waited quietly for the space of half a minute after the electrifying remark, then 'Good-night again,' he nodded, and was gone, leaving the group of Freemans staring in each other's faces in the blankest dismay.

CHAPTER VIII

Some of Miss Smythe's Opinions

AS Mr Massey walked over his fields the next morning, talked with the shepherd on the condition of his flock, or stood awhile to watch his beasts industriously eat themselves into money in their stalls, he thought a great deal about these few words which had taken place over night.

'I suppose I shall get wrong with the Freemans now,' he thought, 'and I daresay, after all, that that surly beggar was right, and that I shall be a fool for my pains – not that that'll be any particularly new experience – and I'll do it in spite of fifty thousand Freemans if she – if I wish. I wonder why the dickens she couldn't have asked me herself? What queer creatures woman are to deal with! There is no telling what that pert little person said to her. And what is it that makes Miss Pollie so spiteful in that quarter, I should like to know? If she would not ask me – at least she shall thank me,' he finally decided. 'If I am to make myself a bugbear to the rest of the parish, I will have something of compensation there, at any rate.'

And so, when he had gone through his usual business on the farm, he bent his steps towards the Vicarage, determined to exact some reward for his magnanimity. He could not shut his eyes to the fact that this reward would, in all probability, be a most meagre one; he should see her for a minute, and she would, perhaps, look pleased, and would say a word of thanks in a voice that thrilled him, although it was so calm and cold, and then would vanish from his sight, in the unsatisfactory manner habitual to her, he thought. She seemed to have a knack of vanishing, apparently, for on most of the occasions on which he had presented himself at the Vicarage, being taken in, as a rule, on one excuse or another by the Vicar, who liked to hold communion with a friendly soul, she had disappeared after a few minutes, leaving him to the perils of a conversation with Mrs Pearson, or to the weariness of the Vicar's companionship. Once or twice, even, he had missed her altogether. The remembrance of those dreary occasions filled his soul with forebodings now, as to what might probably be his approaching fate, as he walked along that winter's afternoon, seeing nothing of the wintry landscape, taking no heed of the muddy country roads.

His luck favoured him apparently, on this occasion, for on entering the drawing-room he found only Helen there – Helen and the little pale boy who was the only 'hope' of the Pearsons.

It was getting dusk within doors, and she was sitting on the hearthrug to catch the light of the fire on the book she was reading to the child, who was lying his little length before her, his head in her lap. She rose up quickly to receive the visitor, and the fairy tales fell to her feet. Little Perrie scrambled up and sat down primly in a big arm-chair, from whence he regarded his aunt and Mr Massey by turns as they spoke.

'Mr Pearson is in his library,' Miss Smythe said, as she gave her hand, thinking at the same time what a mortification it was that the servant had not possessed the sense to show the visitor into that shabby sanctum – library by virtue of one scantily filled book-case, whose meagre shelves were seldom disturbed by their proprietor, who spent most of his indoor hours in their presence over his letters – he was a great correspondent – and his newspaper, of which he read every word.

'Pray do not disturb Mr Pearson!' Massey said, with eager politeness.

'And my sister, I am sorry to say, is unwell. She has had to keep her room all day – she suffers so horribly from neuralgia, in this cold, damp weather.'

'That is very bad,' the young man said, in a tone of much sympathy; but looking across to the fire-lit face opposite to him, he was conscious of feeling less sorrow than he ought to have done for the solitary sufferer upstairs. 'She is right to keep her room,' he went on with hearty approbation; 'the air is terribly raw to-day. You are wise to sit indoors over the fire, Miss Smythe.'

'Oh, I have been out. I am not a neuralgic subject, happily, and do not fear the weather. Run, Perrie, and tell papa Mr Massey is here.'

The child slipped obediently from his chair; but Massey stretched out an arm and caught him as he was passing.

'Do not, pray, disturb Mr Pearson,' he said again. 'It was you that I wished to see to-day.' He drew the child to his knee. 'Are you the little man that is to ride my horse for me one day?' he asked, and turned the little pale face up with his hand.

The child smiled shyly, brightening, and looking at his aunt.

'He has often talked about the horse,' she said. 'Where's your tongue, Perrie? Can't you speak to Mr Massey? He sees so few strangers, that he is shy with them,' she explained, looking at her visitor. 'He is quite a chatterbox with me. You are fond of children, are you not?'

'Well, yes. I have never thought particularly about it, but I suppose I am fond of children – I was going to say I was fond of all dumb things,' he said with a laugh, 'but that would be an insult, eh Perrie? You aren't quite dumb, are you, although you won't talk to me?'

'I don't know,' whispered Perrie, with a shy glance into his questioner's face, and a smile about his lips.

He did not altogether dislike this dangerous new experience of sitting in the embrace of a big strong man.

Said his aunt, laughing, 'It is time you set your doubts on the subject at rest. Tell Mr Massey what I have been reading to you about.'

'About a girl who – who struck matches and – and made fires for pictures to come.'

'Dear me! But that was very imprudent of the girl. And what happened next?'

'She died.'

'I should think so! There was a very wholesome moral to that tale, Perrie. That must be a dangerous book, Miss Smythe.'

'Hans Christian Andersen?' she asked, smiling as she picked it up from the floor, 'have you never read it? Oh, you should! The tales are delightful. I enjoy them as much as Perrie.'

'I will certainly read it,' he said, 'if you will lend me the book.'

'It is all about fairies, and little boys, and – and tin soldiers,' explained Perrie, waxing courageous and looking into Massey's face, who smiled to himself as he answered the child, and encouraged him to dilate on the wonders of the book. 'Now I wonder,' he thought, 'what wicked little Pollie Freeman would say to my having pledged myself to read a fairy-tale book?'

Meanwhile, Helen, who had a great tenderness for the child, and loved to see him petted, helped him in his small efforts to talk to the stranger, but all the time she was thinking impatiently 'why does he not say what he has to say and go?'

'I wanted to see you about the man Moore,' he began at length. 'You wish me to take him on again, do you not.'

'I should like him to have another trial,' she said, speaking with animation. 'Do you not think it a terrible thing that he should not have another chance?'

'I do not know about that,' Massey said, who was not desirous of having his clement intentions with regard to the man put down to any but the right reason. He was not at all inclined to pose as philanthropist. 'I don't know about that. I think from all I hear that he is a thoroughly bad specimen, and I greatly fear that what I am going to do cannot be reckoned as an act of wisdom. However, if it will give you any pleasure I am glad to risk all that.'

'But I cannot allow you to run any such risk simply on my account,' she said proudly. 'It is very good natured of you, but really *my* pleasure in the matter is the very last thing I should wish to have considered. It is for the man's redemption – soul and body – that I am anxious; not' – disdainfully – 'for my pleasure! Of course if you think the allowing of this wretched creature – living for months in enforced idleness – to work for the money he could earn, if you think the putting of bread into his children's mouths, and the raising of a woman's soul from a depth of sluggish despair into which it has sunk, if you think the doing of this at all detrimental to yourself, I could not for a moment expect you to do it. I asked Miss Freeman to point out to you, that by employing Moore you would be doing, quite easily, a great work of charity; I certainly did not comprehend that you could at the same time be running any risk to yourself.'

That pretty, flexible lip of Miss Smythe's was expressive of the liveliest scorn as she said this, but Mr Massey, whose organization was not a highly sensitive one, was thinking far more of the beauty of the disdainful face than of the contemptuous speech. The room had grown almost dark since his entrance, and no lights had been brought in, but the firelight showed him distinctly the pale, proud face, and played on the fair, ringless hands clasped on her dark dress. In looking at her, and thinking certain thoughts of his own about her, he forgot to answer.

'Will you tell me,' she asked presently, still in that slightly scornful tone, 'why it is such a dangerous undertaking to befriend – no, scarcely to befriend – but to treat this man with common justice?'

'I am going to take him on, you know, Miss Smythe – if he burnt down all my stacks, caused my best friends to turn their backs on me, and turned me adrift a homeless wanderer, I should still take him; but there really are reasons,' smiling at her, 'which justify me in thinking it is not wise. To begin with, is he not a drunkard? – and –'

'Ah! you can set your mind at rest about that if you take him!' the girl interrupted eagerly.

'Of course I shall take him.'

'He has promised me that if I get him work to do, he will take the pledge!'

'That is well!' Massey said. 'If you can get him to do that, and if you can get him to keep it. I don't believe much in the system, myself. That form of madness is bound to break out again in an unfortunate victim, such as that. They say, beside – Mr Freeman tells me – that he is a dissatisfied fellow, a revolutionist, upsetting his fellow-labourers, and creating an ill-feeling. He is a great "union" man, too, is he not?'

'I suppose he is, and what man in his position is not? and can you blame him? Oh, I daresay what I am saying sounds heretical and dangerous to you, but I never can help seeing that there are two sides to every question, and you will forgive me for saying that you – that farmers generally, limit themselves strictly to one view.'

'We look out for ourselves as well as we can, I admit,' said Massey, hugging the child on his knee, and much admiring his lecture. 'But then so we had need, don't you think?'

'Yes, oh yes! I do not expect you to see things as I do. I have given up hoping to interest men of your class in the class you employ. I have tried – tried hard with – with the other farmers, and I understand quite well that I am laughed at, and – and have done no good. Mr Massey, if you went about as I do, heard the tales I hear, and saw the sights I sometimes see, you would not wonder that my sympathy goes so entirely with the labourer –'

'And consequently against the farmer,' he interrupted. 'But, Miss Smythe, that is where the whole thing is wrong, and who is to blame for it but the men themselves? Our interests ought to be, and used to be identical; why need the men who depend on us for bread and life, why need they regard us as their enemies – just victims to supply them with all they want, to be cheated, maligned, detested? Why, for instance, should not my men look on me as friend, as well as master? How much better was the state of things in such a district as this – say forty years ago! Servants had not learnt to rise against their masters in those good old times –'

'Oh, those good old times!' she interrupted, her eyes shining, her manner almost eager, there was no languor in her voice now. 'Those good old times, when you had the chance of making friends of your servants, and when you treated them worse – far worse than the beasts they tended for you! Hear the old people talk of those times, when their interests were identical, as you say, with yours, and when you ground them to the dust and crushed them, soul and body. Have you ever thought of what a happy period those halcyon days must have been for them? – for a man, for instance, earning his eight shillings a-week, with a houseful of little children, and bread at famine prices. Mr Massey, I could tell tales, which I have heard, that have made me thank God for this "union," you consider so iniquitous, and for having put into these men's slow minds a means of defence in their helplessness, a way to help themselves, as you abused your trust, and would not help them.'

'Things were not so bad as they tell you, I hope, Miss Smythe; they earned more money than that. You must remember that the women then were not above working too, and –'

'Yes; and how did they work? Picture to yourself a woman – perhaps delicate and unfit for hard work – certainly ill-clad and half-starved – going into the fields in all weathers to do work unsuited for any but strong men – and all for what? for the munificent sum, say of sixpence a-day; leaving her baby, perhaps, shut up at home to long hours of hunger, neglect and misery! Have you seen that poor woman who lives at one of the "low cottages" on your farm? Ask her what she thinks of the good old times! She was a weakly baby that wanted nursing and care, but her mother was daily away earning this fine sum of money on your uncle's farm, and the child had to take her chance, crawling about, and finally walking about on little weak, distorted legs. They could not, of course, afford to buy boots that such as she should have worn on her poor deformed feet; and so, when she was old enough to go to the school which some one had started in the parish, she went barefoot! And I have heard the older people say that many and many a time they have tracked her course there or back, by the bleeding of her wretched little feet. Well, she has been a cripple ever since, as you see her now – a terrible cripple too, for she is in constant suffering. Oh, I could tell you of many a case as sad as that.'

'Pray, do not,' he said very gently; for he saw the tears in her eyes.

'And but for this banding of the men together against their masters, and their starvation prices, such things would be going on now. Do I not know that your labourers' wages are extorted from you, that you grudge and grumble over every shilling? And you wonder that the men turned against you at last; you resent their, in some measure, having certainly got the best of you!' here she paused a moment, and her voice had resumed its somewhat languid tone as she said, 'You will think that I hold dangerous opinions, Mr Massey; I, however, keep them for the benefit of the farmer; I do not corrupt the labourer.'

'I only think you very good,' he said; and thought that he would like to say how sweet and beautiful he also thought her. 'Very good to feel so much interest in them. I am bound to confess, even at the peril of still farther disgusting you with my hardness of heart, that they do not, as a race, recommend themselves greatly to my sympathy. They appear to me, for the most part, an ungrateful, ungracious, discontented set of people; some of them are lazy by nature, the rest are lazy by intention, and none of them earn their money! I assure you, Miss Smythe, there is a very great deal to be said on our side of the question.'

However, Miss Smythe had apparently had enough of the discussion, and would not prolong it.

'Your men are what you have made them,' she said lightly, and spoke of other things.

Mr Massey knew that now he was expected to take his leave, but he still stayed on. Presently the Vicar appeared on the scene, and had a great deal to say on the subject of a hare, which it appeared he had only that very evening taken out of a snare, set in the most barefaced manner in one of his own fences.

The Vicar's sporting tales and poaching grievances were the subject of many rough jokes in the village, and Massey listened with great interest to the present narrative; while Helen, who had rung for tea, at her brother-in-law's request, poured out some, and Perrie, having fallen asleep in the young man's arms, herself carried his cup across to him.

'Dear little Perrie!' she said, looking down at the child. 'Look at him, Alfred. Is he not pretty when he is asleep?' and she moved the loose hair from his closed eyes with a light, caressing touch, as the little head lay on happy James Massey's breast.

Certainly none of them much missed poor Mrs Pearson, lying upstairs in raging pain. They were very cosy and friendly, one of them thought, encouraging with a word now and then the Vicar's prosy talk, and hanging on the few sentences which dropped from the lady's lips, or watching her when silent with never flagging interest.

When decency would permit him to stay no longer, he put the child gently and skilfully from his arms without awaking him, laid his lips on the little pale brow where Helen's fingers had strayed, and went out regretfully from the semi-darkened room that was no longer shabby and barren to him, but gorgeous with beauty and alive with happiness.

CHAPTER IX

Mr Massey Gathers some Snowdrops

THE next morning found Mr Massey bending his steps in the direction of John Moore's cottage.

'If I am to make a fool of myself, I may as well get it over,' he said to himself, 'and set the poor devil's mind at rest.'

It is but charitable to hope that this Christian spirit had more to do in directing his steps than had the pleasant elation which possessed his breast at the thought that he had it in his power to do something to please Helen Smythe.

His nearest way lay through the wood, and as he walked down the path, brown with dead wet leaves, and tangled with naked boughs of briar and bramble, he saw with no surprise, for was she not constantly in his thoughts this morning, but with a quickened throbbing of his pulse – Helen Smythe.

She was but just entering from the other end of the wood the path which he had three parts traversed. Had they ever so greatly wished to avoid a meeting it would have been impossible, but he welcomed the sight of her as though his eyes had wearied in watching for her appearing, and she was just indifferent as to whether the man advancing to meet her were Mr Massey or one of Mr Massey's men, whose way home, for the most part, lay through the wood.

'Were you going to Moore's?' she asked, as she gave him her hand. 'I have just come from there. The wife is so overcome, Mr Massey, at the prospect of better times for them all, and he himself is ready to promise anything.'

'That is well,' Massey said, smiling, and turned, somewhat to her surprise, to retrace his steps by her side. 'Promises are very satisfactory things – sometimes. Yes, I was just going to arrange with him about coming in the morning.'

'He will be so pleased,' she said. 'It is kind of you not to keep him in suspense.'

But she wondered to herself why he did not proceed to fulfil his generous intention, instead of doing which he sauntered by her side, putting back the dead fern and bramble with his stick, now and again stooping to remove a fallen branch from her path. He had made all necessary inquiries for Mrs Pearson and the neuralgia, had asked after Perrie with much interest, and had even extended his politeness so far as to make investigation twice over into the state of the Vicar's health – the Vicar, who had never had a day's illness in his life! But after this it did not seem that he could, conversationally, advance much farther. Miss Smythe was disinclined for talk that morning, or perhaps did not quite approve of the enforced companionship. With a remembrance of her enthusiasm of last night, he tried to get her back to the subject at which she had kindled. But it would not do; she was not, apparently, a creature to be 'trotted out' for any moment's amusement. The silence and the restraint were becoming, he felt, awkward, when she suddenly stopped by a fallen tree, and began to stir the dead leaves around it with her foot.

'There are generally the earliest snowdrops to be found here,' she said, by way of explanation. 'I thought perhaps – yes, here are some! I came through the wood to-day on purpose for this.'

'Let me get them for you,' he said eagerly; 'the ground is too wet for you – look here, perfectly sodden.' And in spite of Helen's protestations (who lost half the delight of her first snowdrops in not gathering them for herself), down he went on his devoted knees, and after much groping about and scattering of the decaying leaves, he succeeded in collecting about half a dozen little short-stalked, unopened specimens, which he put into her hand. This was not the worst for Helen, for, having now discovered this plan of interesting and delaying her, he did not readily abandon it, but persisted in searching under heaps of leaves, and around roots of trees, in all likely and unlikely places, in spite of her now laughing assurances that all such search was useless.

'It is only in that one place, really, Mr Massey. Oh, pray do not trouble! In a week or so I shall find a great quantity under that one tree, and I have these to-day to tell me that the spring is really coming at last.'

'You often walk here in the spring?'

'Yes, the wood is lovely then. People come from all around to see it. There is a perfect carpet of flowers – cowslips, primroses, hyacinths, orchises, anemones – but perhaps you do not care for flowers.'

'You care for them very much?'

'Yes.'

'And why should it be taken for granted that I do not?'

'I said "perhaps." I wished to give you the benefit of the doubt. But I have noticed that farmers, as a rule, are indifferent about such profitless vegetation. You do not often see their gardens nicely kept, for example. I suppose it is only natural. What you have to grow – wheat and turnips, and so on – are matters of such terrible earnest to you that cultivation for the mere purpose of beauty, I daresay, appears childish. Is it not so?'

'It is easy to see that your opinion of us is not very high, Miss Smythe. I have noticed once or twice such a scornful emphasis on that word "farmer." What have we done, as a body, to offend you? It is something more serious than the neglect of floriculture, surely?'

'Oh, you are mistaken,' she said, flushing and turning her eyes to his face. To accuse her of prejudice, which was very strong in her, was always to touch Miss Smythe in a tender place. 'I hope you are not in earnest in saying that I have given such an impression. I daresay I have spoken thoughtlessly once or twice; but pray believe that I am not unjust or uncharitable in my thoughts.'

'I am quite sure,' he said simply, 'that your thoughts are only wise and good. And I do not mind your disapproval a bit – I mean, of course, I mind it a very great deal – but I shouldn't – shouldn't mind it a bit (I am not expressing myself gracefully this morning) if you would talk to me about it. About the garden. Now, I suppose you do not know the garden at my place – the Wood Farm. Have you ever been in there?'

'Oh, yes; in your uncle's time, often. He did not care much for it, nor for what grew there, and it was – well – rather wild then. Once I found courage to ask him – he was rather an alarming old man, I don't know I dared – to let me gather some violets – they perfectly overran the place – and he was very gracious to me, and said that I was to have anything that I liked from there, and at any time. There are all sorts of sweet old-fashioned flowers, half hidden and overgrown with weeds. I used often to go for them.'

'And will you come now?' Massey asked, with unmistakable eagerness. 'Will you, Miss Smythe? It would make me very – it would give me great pleasure if you would.'

She laughed, and the colour came a little to her cheek.

'Thank you,' she said; 'but I fear there is not much to gather yet.'

'But next week – next month – when is the right time? Will you come sometimes then? I am not going to neglect my garden after the fashion you disapprove. Don't you think it is capable of looking pretty well? I shall put some men in soon, and get it put to rights. Now will you come some day before then to give me advice about what to do with the place, and to tell me about these old-fashioned flowers you say you like – which they are, and where they grow, that I may be sure to have them saved. When will you come? Perhaps Mr Pearson' (with a sudden happy remembrance of the proprieties) 'would bring you one day.'

Helen waived this part of the subject.

'I am glad you think of getting the garden into better order,' she said evasively. 'It is really a sin to neglect a place so pretty. A garden is always such a source of amusement too; it will amply repay you for any trouble.'

'I shall be more than repaid,' he said, 'if you will sometimes come to gather my flowers.'

Miss Smythe did not quite approve of such persistent harping on the string of his wish to please her. It sounded, she began to think, as if the foolish man were trying to flirt with her, a thing which no one – no one had tried yet! Her face was too pure and too cold, and her manner too reserved and proud to encourage such frivolities. What Pollie Freeman had said of her was true to a certain extent – men were afraid of her. She had not, therefore, despite her three-and-twenty years, and her undeniably lovely face, had her due experience in the dangerous and fascinating art, and she feared to draw too hasty conclusions. Surely a man in Mr Massey's condition of life would not venture to insult her – Helen Smythe – by an attempt at a vulgar flirtation! But there was a certain something in his manner which she had not noticed before, and for which she could not satisfactorily account; and he had contracted a disagreeable habit of allowing his eyes to dwell on his companion's face with a persistency and an earnestness of regard anything but reassuring.

They had reached the end of the path by now, and Helen stopped at the little gate giving out from the wood on to the meadow she had still to cross before she could gain the road, and held out her hand.

'I hope you have not relinquished your purpose of seeing the man Moore this morning?' she said. 'If you will set his mind at rest at once, it will be doubly kind of you.'

'Of course I will see him.'

'Then, good-morning, Mr Massey.'

He was holding her hand in his.'

'You have not yet told me if you will come to gather my flowers, Miss Smythe.'

She pulled her hand free with a very decided movement, and he saw her face flush angrily red as she moved a step nearer to the gate.

'It is hardly a thing of sufficient importance to make such a point of,' she said contemptuously. 'I really do not think I can pledge myself to gather your flowers.'

Massey began to see that he had in his own language 'made a mess of it' over that morning's walk; he had bungled matters horribly, and had lost rather than gained ground in the favour he had begun so seriously to covet. He was not, however, a man to be easily discouraged, nor one to collapse under a feminine snub. He stepped in front of her, and laid his hand on the latch of the gate as though to open it for her, and then he turned to her again.

'I will go back and see Moore now at once,' he said, 'and I'll do my best to keep him straight. Is there anything else you want to have done that I can do? Tell me if there is. I have heard you complain that you get hindrance instead of help from us in your work. I daresay it is true. We are a selfish race and like to have our men well under us, and to get as much work as we can out of them for as little money – we are like that, I daresay – I know that I am; but I will never be against anything you wish. Show me what you wish to have done, and I will do it. If you would give me leave, I should like to be on your side always! Will you give me something to do for you? Is there anyone else you want to find work for? I will –'

But Miss Smythe interrupted him with some hurry in her voice; she was too unused to such fervour to be unmoved, and her face was quite pale.

'If you want to do works of charity,' she said, 'there are plenty to your hand, Mr Massey – plenty! But you must do them for another motive. It would be wrong to undertake them for such an unworthy one as that.'

'But then you see that would be my motive – and that only. I have no taste for philanthropy myself, nor do I believe in the sudden conversion of drunkards to total abstinence, and poor people do not greatly commend themselves to me solely on account of their poverty, – I am thoroughly unregenerate in such matters – but I have a very strong desire that you should think well of me – that you should think of me at all, even, would be something. Will you let this understanding be between us, that in everything I am on your side – and that when you want a thing done you will come to me? Whatever it is, however difficult or against my own ideas, you may be sure that I would do it gladly – for you! Will you agree to so much?'

'No,' she said at once, 'I think not. I should be pleased of course if you would try to do what is useful and good for its own sake, but it would not please me at all that you should do it for mine. And – may I trouble you to open the gate, Mr Massey?'

'You mean that?'

'Certainly!'

'That I am not to try to please you? Perhaps you also mean that it would be useless for me to try?'

'You really must excuse me!' she said with irritation; 'I do not care to answer such questions – the matter altogether does not appear to me to be worth discussion. And – and I think I had better say at once that this style of conversation is extremely distasteful to me, and – and I think that you have made a mistake. Will you now allow me to pass, if you please?'

'I think you are wrong to be angry,' Massey said, as he slowly moved to push open the gate. 'What I have said, and more that I should like to have said, may not, unfortunately, be acceptable to you – so much the worse for me – but there should have been no offence in it. I fear, if you were not very badly prejudiced, you could have found no offence.'

CHAPTER X

By the River

AS Helen Smythe walked homeward with a flushed face and a quickened step, her mind was so far confused by this interview, that she could not quite determine whether to be more angry or amused with what had befallen her.

'Mr Massey, too evidently considers himself a lady-killer,' she thought. 'Now Miss Pollie Freeman, now Helen Smythe! And I had formed a better opinion of him, I was even beginning to think he would be thrown away on poor little Pollie, and to pity him somewhat for his blind admiration of her! After all it is she that ought to be pitied, for if there be one order of man on this earth to be despised above all other, it is surely the universal-lover order. What had he seen in me to let him dare to make me those would-be pretty speeches. Would I pluck his flowers?' (here Miss Smythe indulged in an irrepressible laugh). 'No, I won't! If I know it I will never touch his flowers – pah!' and suddenly bethinking her of the hand which had gathered the two or three sickly snowdrops which she held, she flung them contemptuously from her into the hedge. But presently, being tender-hearted, she called to mind compunctiously that snowdrops *were* snowdrops even although the too familiar farmer had gathered them, and she went back repentant, and picked them with difficulty from the hedge. 'I will give them to Perrie,' she said to herself, 'and will tell him who it was that plucked them; that will recommend them to Perrie, although it has the reverse effect on me.'

After that she fell to wishing that she had some one to whom she could relate her morning's adventure. How ludicrous it had been, and how unpleasant! If Anna had but been possessed of a congenial spirit how she would have enjoyed to unburden her mind to her! But this was out of the question with Mrs Pearson. She would certainly fail to see the fun of the situation, being as devoid of the sense of humour as her own husband, and Helen knew that her wrath would be quite disproportionate to the occasion. 'She would forbid him the house, or something equally dreadful,' the girl said, 'and that is not worth the while. I think that I can manage Mr Massey myself.' And then she determined how slight should be her communication with that gentleman for the future, and how few should be his opportunities for repeating his mistake of this morning.

But in the confined village life which these people lived there was little chance of any direct avoidance of one member by another passing unnoticed. Mr Massey did not discontinue his visits to the Vicarage because of Miss Smythe's secret desire to see little of him; and Helen, spite of the foolish pride which had been part of her education, and the shyness which for a time made his presence unpleasant to her, was in reality too sweet-natured and too gentle-hearted to maintain a sustained coldness towards one with whom she was constantly brought in contact, was too much of a lady, beside, to give any but a gracious welcome to a visitor at her sister's house. Therefore it came to pass that as time went on; as the snowdrops grew white about the fallen tree in Hilby Wood, and then gave place to sweeter if not fairer spring flowers; as the dry branches began to burst into leaf, and the birds to be heard among the blossoming hedgerows; as the meadows through which Massey walked grew yellow with cowslips about his feet, and the wood in which Helen loitered and little Dollie played became a paradise of sweetness and beauty – Mr Massey came to know Miss Smythe much better than in the cold winter months when their meetings had been but rare, to know her better and to find her farther off! He would not have dreamt now of asking her to take interest in his garden – he would no longer have dared to hint to her that he would like to please her. She was so near to him that his hand was nearly sure to touch hers once in the course of the long spring day – she was so far off that she might have been the north star in distance, and un-attainableness, and beauty.

But if she was far off, some one else was close at hand; some one who was never cold, nor proud, nor shy; some one whom Mr Massey saw daily, hourly almost, and was always glad to see; some one, blossoming at this season of the year, like the hedgerows, into the daintiest clothing of palest blue, and pink, and white; some one with always a smile upon her face for him whenever he came in sight – whether in her own drawing-room, whither the two would now all unquestioned adjourn on most of his visits, holding pleasant *tête-à-têtes* among the crewel-work, while Pollie, now and again, played a few notes on the piano, by way of compliment to the sagacity of the elders, who were supposed to be imagining it was for the enjoyment of music that they repaired there; or in the pleasant fields, where it happened that she so frequently crossed his path; or in the wood, where Dollie would accompany her, and would play, unthought of, among the flowers, while the man and the girl laughed and talked; or even in Mr Massey's garden, where she, at least, had not been too proud to take an interest in his flowers.

After all, though the wisdom of such unrestricted intercourse might have been doubted, and though Mrs Pearson was shocked at what she called the 'shamelessness' of the girl's conduct, and though the Vicar, who was the biggest gossip of the village, had always some fresh tale of the movements of this interesting couple, how harmless it all was! What innocent nonsense it was they talked! What a little everyday comedy they played! Massey sometimes cursed to himself the idle tongues that would interfere.

'If it please us, what is it to anyone else?' he would ask himself. 'The girl's society is not at all likely to hurt me; and as for herself, it is precious little danger that Pollie runs of being in love with anything more than her own face, and her own way, and her own hats and gowns. If the old fool of a mother lets her run about after me, surely no one else wants to trouble.'

But in spite of these arguments he would sometimes have an uneasy feeling that the state of things was too pleasant to be either safe or right. Those spring days, when there was no more hunting, and when his gun was pretty well at a standstill, would have been dull to him without this companionship, and he did not often scruple to encourage Pollie in her strollings among the meadows he was likely to cross, and if for long she failed to come he would grow uneasy, and would presently go to seek her.

She was sitting with him one evening by the side of the little river which ran through his farm. It is but a poor apology for a river, being narrow and shallow, often choked with weeds, and always unnavigable; but it winds away amid the meadows in a zigzag and picturesque fashion, while in the summer the banks are bright with forget-me-nots, yellow irises, and other water-loving flowers; and near where the two are sitting now, some old distorted willows lean down to look at themselves in its shallow waters.

Massey had walked down to look at some colts which were feeding on these 'low meadows,' and having satisfied himself that they were correct in number and satisfactory in condition, he had suggested that they should rest for a while at the river's side.

Pollie was tired, the day having been unusually warm for the time of year, and she being, unless under strong excitement, or for some sufficiently attractive object, but an indifferent walker – as a rule wearing boots that hurt her feet, and skirts that impeded every step. She was tired and unusually silent, sitting there – a little incongruous figure – in a new spring costume, truly fashionable as to colour and build, with a hat to match, contrived so as to show most of the yellow curls over her forehead, but not to protect her eyes from the glare of the sun, illuminating the river now with a dazzling glow before he sank to rest.

'I think the water makes you feel hotter than ever when the sun is on it like this,' she said, with some impatience. 'My eyes quite smart with looking at it.'

'Do they?' he asked compassionately, just lifting his head to regard her from under his tilted hat. 'We'll be off in a minute. Poor little girl! She is tired. I shouldn't have brought her so far.'

Miss Freeman did not hasten to protest that he had not brought her, but that she had come of her own accord, as would have been truthful as well as generous, but she sighed rather crossly as she stared at the shining water.

Massey looked away from her again, lying on his elbow at her side, and idly pulled up bits of grass and lumps of mould and flung them into the river.

'I rather like this,' he said presently. 'Do you know that I am fond of the water in any form? It is hard that I should be doomed to pass my life on the banks of such a stream as this, eh! When I was a little chap I remember I was a great fisherman. My father used to take care of me, and instruct me in the art. When I look back to that time, I'm hanged if I don't seem to have been *always* fishing with him! I never see a river, even such a bit as this – I never catch a distant whiff of it even, without thinking of him.'

Miss Freeman looked down with some surprise at the man at her side. His face was hidden; she could see nothing but an inexpressive light rough suit and a hat tilted forward to shade eyes that were just then unusually soft and tender. His voice had taken a tone that was unknown to her, and which she could not understand. Was it really for his father's memory, that accent of affection and regret?

'Fancy a man being like that!' Pollie thought, perplexed. Why, fathers were not things to grow sentimental over, certainly. It might be different, it is true, with a father who was dead, she reflected. People never need know what he was like then; and one would not always be feeling ashamed of him, or dreading his anger. She did not want her own father to die, of course; but she could not help seeing how much smoother things would go at home without him.

'Has he been dead long, your father?' she asked, trying to bring a sympathetic tone into her voice.

'Oh, years,' he answered, 'years! He died when I was a lad of eighteen. Poor old man! I don't believe I think much of him now, unless I catch sight of a bit of water now and then.'

'It's like Mrs Pearson,' Pollie said flippantly. 'Cold water makes me think of her and her teetotal lecturing, always. You have never told me anything about your people. Your mother is alive, isn't she?'

'Oh yes, she's alive.'

'I knew that, because I heard some one say you'd come into some property when she died.'

'Oh, you heard that, did you?'

'It's true, isn't it?'

'And, pray, who is it who talks of my affairs to you?'

'Heaps of people! They never talk to me of anything else; but Mr Selby is the only one that really knows, and he says – what I now told you.'

'He does – does he? Benevolent old Selby! He wants to improve my credit.'

'But it's true, isn't it?' the girl persisted.

She was anxious for a straightforward answer on this point, her father being accustomed to pooh-pooh the accounts of the length of Mr Massey's purse – but then, as Pollie always observed, no one ever had any money, according to Mr Freeman's impression.

'He said, Mr Selby did, that there are only two of you – you and your sister – and that the property will be divided between you.'

Massey laughed.

'Upon my word!' he said, 'I am very much obliged to Mr Selby. Very much obliged to him indeed!'

'I don't know why you should laugh,' Pollie said severely, 'or why you should be ashamed of saying outright if it is true.'

'Ashamed!' he said – 'ashamed! a tenant-farmer in the present day with – what did you call it? – property? Old Selby ought to take me round the country in a show!'

'Then I suppose you mean it's not true. Isn't it true?'

Mr Massey left off idly plucking at the grass beside him, and changed his position that he might look into his companion's face.

'Would it make any difference to you, Pollie, whether it were true or not – to your friendship for me?'

A pause of a moment.

'I suppose it wouldn't,' said Pollie then, with some uncertainty of tone.

'Then what's the use of talking about it?' he asked, rolling himself back into his original position on the grass.

'It's a mistake of old Selby's after all,' Pollie thought, not too well pleased. 'And pa was right.'

For a person to have money in hand, or in prospect, and not to be glad to have it well understood of him, was an unimagined possibility in Miss Freeman's simple mind.

'A little mercenary wretch!' said Massey to himself. 'Who would have thought it of her?' But he smiled indulgently as he said it, and Miss Freeman did not sink much in his estimation. It was little but her pretty face and the amusement she afforded him which recommended her to his regard; about her moral qualities, it is to be feared, he interested himself mighty little.

'It is true that you have a sister, I suppose?' she asked presently. 'You are not going to deny that.'

'I have a sister, I admit.'

'And what is she like?'

'Now, how in the world am I to tell you that?'

'Well, who is she like? You can tell me so much.'

'That I cannot. She isn't like you, one bit,' looking with open admiration into her face; 'not half so pretty.'

'Is she like Ellen Smith, then?'

Mr Massey struggled into a sitting posture, and cut a swish with his stick at a swarm of gnats dancing above the river.

'No, she isn't,' he said curtly. 'What in the world made you think of her?'

'Perhaps because I know you admire her.'

'Come, I say; you are making some rather wild statements this afternoon. First, that I am a person of property; and then, that I – what is it that has come to you to-day? About my sister – let's see. She's a kind of a medium in everything; neither pretty, nor plain, nor dark, nor light, nor fat, nor thin; neither –'

'How old is she?'

'Two years younger than I am. There's a sum for you.'

'As much as that? Twenty-eight?' In a highly disparaging tone. 'Then she is going to be an old maid, I suppose?'

'Well, no, I fancy not. She tells me she is to be married in a couple of months.'

'Married! To whom?'

'Now what's the use of my telling you his name! To a parson fellow that has always been hunting her up.'

'A parson!' In a tone of much surprise. 'Is she really, though? Have you ever told the Pearsons that?'

'The Pearsons? Why on earth should I tell the Pearsons?'

'Oh, I don't know; only they think no one so good as themselves.'

Mr Massey only stared at her in reply to this apparently irrelevant remark, and Pollie presently proceeded to say with candour:

'I know I shouldn't like her.'

'My sister? I hope you will. She is coming down to me before she marries. You will find she is all right.'

'She isn't my sort, I'll warrant,' said Pollie, with conviction. 'You might manage to have her while I'm up in London, if you must have her. She isn't my sort, or she wouldn't marry a parson; and of course it's true, after all, that you must be well off – you and she – or no parson would want to marry her.'

'What a shrewd young woman you are!' Massey said, tossing a pebble into the water. 'I'm quite afraid of you. Did you pick up that deep knowledge of the world from experience now, or is it the result of study?' But although he laughed, he would not pursue the subject. 'What was that you were saying just now about going to London?' he asked. 'You are not going to London?'

'Indeed, then, I am; I always go every year. Father has a married sister living there, you know, and her son, my cousin Arthur, comes down always in summer for his holiday, and takes me back for mine.'

'The deuce he does! He won't take you back this year, at any rate.'

'And pray why not?'

'Because you will stay here with me. Of course you will. What in the world do you suppose I should do without you now?'

He laughed a little as he asked this foolish question, but he was half serious, too; he had become so used to the companionship of the girl that he did think it would be a not exactly light matter for him to miss it. Pollie was very pleased. Was he going to be serious at last? Was the offer that everyone had been foretelling for weeks really coming? She said in a voice that shook a little:

'I suppose you must learn to do without me, Mr Massey. Perhaps it is time you began.'

'You surely don't mean that, Pollie?' he said, and slipped an arm about her waist – not quite for the first time – and drew her closer to him. 'You are a particularly cruel and heartless girl; but you can't mean that! What am I to do in this hole of a place without you – tell me that? You'll promise not to go and leave me, Pollie?'

'I think, perhaps, it's time I left you,' said Pollie, her rather shrill voice still a little tremulous. 'You are just like all the rest of the men, dreadfully selfish; I suppose you care only for yourself. What do you think now would be said to me if I were seen by either father or Teddie, sitting with you like this?' (Massey loosened his arm a little, but the girl only leant the closer.) 'Of course you never trouble your head about what I go through to be so constantly with you as I am. I can tell you it has been no light thing for me at home!'

This was quite news to her companion, and would have been rather alarming news, but that he in no way believed it. He had noticed no anxiety on the father's part to guard his daughter from him; and he was shrewd enough to know that the mother connived at their meetings. For the rest, imagine Teddie concerning himself with the delicacies of love-making! Beside all this, Mr Massey was perfectly well aware that Pollie had had flirtations before, and had come safely out of them.

'What is your father afraid of – if it is your father?' he asked. 'He might know that I would take care of you, eh?'

Pollie gave a sigh.

'Perhaps he thinks that you take care of me too much,' she said.

She herself had small objection, it seemed, to being cared for in such fashion – Massey's arm about her waist, and her cheek rubbing against his coat – it was all delightful to Pollie, but it was not quite perfect. Why did he go so far without going farther? Did he mean anything, or did he not? Lookers-on were much surer of Mr Massey's intentions than was the girl herself. She half divined, although she had never admitted the possibility to herself, that his devotion to her was but a mock devotion after all, and meant nothing more than the idle passing of a young man's time. The girl's friends, however, were not given to subtle analysis, and were satisfied that the quite open attention she received could mean only that one thing, which Miss Freeman, if she were not quite so sanguine of obtaining, did certainly most ardently desire.

'How could I care for you too much?' he asked lightly, in answer to her last observation. 'That would not be possible, eh, Pollie?'

He leant his head to look in her face, and laughed with unmistakable carelessness; at which Pollie, with a dreadful feeling of disappointment and discouragement, a bewildering mixture of sorrow and anger, began to cry.

'You are wicked to laugh about what is so serious! I do not believe you care for me at all,' she said, with childish petulance.

At sight of her tears James Massey, being not a whit less soft-hearted, nor a degree less of a fool where pretty women are concerned, than other honest young men of his age, lost his head completely, and forgot all his wise precautions in a sudden rush of protecting tenderness.

'My dear!' he whispered, at once contrite and tender. 'My dear!' and he pressed her wet cheek yet closer to his coat with a strong and gentle hand.

'You do not care for me!' Pollie repeated, tearful still, although so nearly triumphant. 'If you cared you could not laugh at me. It is all pretence. You do not care a bit!'

'Laugh at you!' he repeated, quite shocked at such an accusation, although he had been guilty of the act many and many a time. 'Oh, my dear little girl, do not say such things to me – do not! I cannot bear to see you cry. You know that I care for you – of course I do – you know I love you, my poor little silly girl! For heaven's sake do not cry any more!'

But Pollie, having begun to cry, was at some trouble to leave off, although, as she fully believed, the triumph of her life was now come. Massey's hand on her cheek was wet with her tears.

'Don't you know that I love you?' he whispered, his head bent down, his lips on that wonderful yellow hair of hers. 'Tell me, Pollie.'

'Ye – yes,' she sobbed; 'I know that now.'

'And you are not angry with me – are you?'

'No.'

'And – and you don't love me, I suppose?' he went on, with a kiss on the too amber curls, having now quite delivered himself over to destruction. But while he waited for an answer, Pollie still struggling with her successful emotion, some instinct of self-preservation, some warning sense of having gone too far and being on the very brink of peril, returned to him. 'No, no! of course you don't,' he said hurriedly, stopping the words on her lips. 'I know that you do not, and I was a fool, and worse than a fool to ask you. Forgive me, my dear!' Then pressing her with sudden fervour to his side, he abruptly withdrew the support of his arm from her waist, and to her most intense surprise arose swiftly to his feet. Then, she looking up at him in blankest astonishment, he put his hat straight on his head, stretched his arms, stamped his feet.

'I am cramped,' he said, 'cramped and stupid. We have been sitting there too long, Pollie. Come along!' He held out his hands to help her to rise. 'Forgive me for being such an idiot,' he said, keeping her hands for a moment in his. 'You must never tell me I don't care for you again, you see,' in a lighter tone. 'It's dangerous!'

The girl walked by his side for some distance in silent but most bitter disappointment – resentment too she was feeling, and humiliation. She knew only too well that he must have been sure of what were the words on her lips which he had so summarily checked. She grew full of helpless rage as she walked over the meadow, away from the river, stumbling over the unequal ground, for once unmindful of how wet her smart boots were getting on the rough marshy soil. Massey, regarding her face with much apprehension, addressed to her several remarks to which she vouchsafed no answer. Was she going to quarrel with him outright he wondered? and was not fool enough to fail to see that this would be the safer course. 'It has been a near thing,' he told himself, and could not get to feel contented with the manner of his escape.

There was, however, a persistence about Miss Freeman, and a want of sensitiveness, of which he must have known, but which he had quite omitted from his calculations. 'Pollie never lost anything for the want of asking,' her mother had often said of her in fond admiration – she was not going to relinquish this game yet.

The still short spring evening was closing in as they reached the Grange gate; the dew had been falling heavily, and Pollie's pretty new dress was all draggled from the damp grass, the yellow curls were loosened about her face, the smart feather on her hat sticking about, straight and damaged. For once she was unconscious and careless of it all.

'Good-night,' Massey said to her, putting out a doubtful hand. The lamp was lit and shining in the sitting room, the other windows were growing dark and gloomy in the spring twilight. Pollie just glanced at them, and then turned to her companion.

'Wait one minute. I want to speak to you just one word before I go in,' she said. 'You – you asked me a question to-night, which I did not answer at once because – well, because it was such a serious question, and so – so unexpected that I could not make up my mind there and then. But I have been thinking of it all the way home, and I know now – now – what I shall answer.'

Massey interrupted her, hurriedly. 'You were right not to answer,' he said; 'it was a question I had no right to ask, and I do not ask you for an answer. Dear, say good-night to me and run in.'

'Wait,' she said, 'you shall not go so. You – you said that you loved me, James Massey; why should I be ashamed to say as much to you?' He was leaning on the gate, and she moved closer and put her hand into his. 'I do love you,' she said, 'I am not ashamed.'

'My dear!' he whispered, greatly perplexed, but still grateful, and even, for the moment, exultant. What could he do but press the plump little hand which had crept into his? He did press it, and then, embarrassed and undecided, passed his other hand over it, smoothing and coaxing it in an irresolute way. Then, seeing her eyes anxiously regarding him in the half light, he scattered all his prudent, ungenerous scruples to the wind, and taking her suddenly into his arms he kissed her, once more whispered 'Good-night,' and left her.

CHAPTER XI

The Nightingale's Song

MASSEY walked slowly homeward, giving himself plenty of time for reflection. He was a good deal embarrassed, but just a little bit elated too – man-like – at what had taken place. He felt some contrition for his share in the catastrophe –

'I have been a fool,' he acknowledged, 'and have gone too far' – but also some amusement at the remembrance of how Pollie had borne her part. 'There has been enough of it – we must make a finish,' he decided, cutting at some wayside nettles with his stick, and the decision was not arrived at without a little pain. She had made things pleasant to him, this little flirting girl; the days, he knew, would be dull and barren without her. For all that, he did not hesitate as to how it must end. The kind of thing which had taken place to-night must never be repeated, he knew: he did not mean to marry the girl, and so that he must not kiss the girl was an incontrovertible fact which no casuistry must subvert. It was useless to remember that it was the girl who had put up her face to be kissed, the girl who almost insisted on having love made to her – it must not be done. 'I must make her understand it somehow,' he said, with an impatient sigh – 'God knows how.'

He walked along, his head bent meditatively, mechanically swinging the stick in his hand, the meadow grass damp about his feet. What a lovely night it was! How calm and pleasant! A young moon rising over the dark trees of the wood, a bird singing loud and sweet –'the music of the moon' – and here, close at hand, the church and the sound of the old harmonium, skilfully touched, stealing through the evening air. He stopped and leant over the church wall to listen – many a time lately he had listened there to the same sound. She had a fancy for haunting the church in the half-dusk, Miss Smythe – for touching the harmonium into solemnity in keeping with the place and hour.

Massey leant there – thoughts of Pollie clean gone from his mind – his arms laid on the low stone wall, his stick idly swaying amid the long grass of the graveyard. Presently the music ceased; he still waited, his heart beating quicker now; and Miss Smythe came out of the little chancel-door, and had closed and locked it behind her, before she caught sight of the figure beyond the wall.

'Good-evening,' she called to him as he raised his hat; then, having hesitated for a moment, picked her way towards him among the graves, until only the wall divided them. 'You are enjoying this lovely evening,' she said, giving her hand in her usual calm and, perhaps, too self-possessed manner.

'I have been listening to your music; I often hear you in the dusk hour.'

'Indeed!' in a tone of surprise, quite unmixed with pleasure. 'My sister scolds me for being so late with my practice; perhaps that is one reason – so perverse is human nature – which makes me choose this time. But somehow the church always seems a grander, more solemn place at nightfall; and the music – You are not fond of music, Mr Massey?'

'Am I not? I don't know. I am no judge of it, if you mean that. But I have thought lately that there is something very wonderful in it, as I hear it in this place; it has seemed to me that nothing could be grander or more beautiful. Perhaps the evening hour and the church lend it a solemnity, and – and these,' he pointed to the graves before him with his stick. 'Anyhow, I have decided that music, to be appreciated, should be heard under such conditions. You did not sing to-night. I liked that thing you sang last night. But you are standing in the long grass, and there is a heavy dew.' He went forward and opened the gate for her; for the short distance to her home, her way was the same as Mr Massey's, and they walked on slowly side by side.

'How the birds sing to-night!' she said presently. 'I never remember the nightingales so glorious as this year. Do you know, I have an especial one who sings all night long outside my window.'

'Have you? So have I. I wish I hadn't.'

'Oh, really?' half-stopping, and looking with a shocked expression into his face. 'Is it possible that you do not like to hear them sing?'

'I like them well enough in proper places and at convenient seasons. Listen to this fellow for a moment,' pausing, and pointing up vaguely to a darkening tree, in which a little unseen bird was loudly and impetuously singing out his soul. 'Just stay one moment and hear what he has to say,' the young man pleaded. They were by the Vicarage gate now, and the bird was singing noisily in the plantation that bordered the road. Massey leant with his back to the gate, listening with apparently rapt attention; presently Helen, gazing into the tops of the fir-trees, came and stood at his side. 'Is that the bird that sings to you at night, do you think?' he asked.

'I don't know,' still peering into the tree. 'I wonder if it is!' A pause, during which Massey's gaze dropped from the unsatisfactory tree to the moonlit face beside him. 'And you are not grateful to the nightingale which sings for you?' she said presently.

'I am not?' – vaguely. 'I beg your pardon?'

'You said one sang to you at night, and –'

'And keeps me awake.'

'Oh, so does mine; I like it.'

'I don't. I go to bed to sleep, and – and I *can't* sleep,' with an angry sigh.

'But if my bird keeps me awake, he gives me beautiful thoughts and a feeling of happiness, and –'

'Mine doesn't, then – bad luck to him! He makes me think of the dreariest things in the world: of things I have failed in, and things I have sinned in, and things – things I want – want with my whole heart, and shall never attain to! He is a perfect beast of a bird – mine!'

Silence for a minute. What a song that nightingale sang to-night, and what a night for a nightingale to sing in!

'I know that feeling you mean,' presently she said. 'Anything that is very beautiful – grand music or the peaceful moonlight, or even, as you say, the song of a bird in the quiet night-time – will give it. It is a kind of half-painful longing, a sort of uneasy craving for we know not what. Everyone has experienced that feeling – I myself have it, oh, very often! But I think it a good feeling to have. Don't you think it is a proof of – well, of our having been made for better things?'

'I don't know about that,' he said. 'I don't believe the feeling that I have does me any good; and I know quite well what it is that I crave for. I want no nightingale to remind me of that.'

There was a tone of impatient sadness in his voice; and Helen, who had a sort of natural attraction for the disappointed and the sorrowful, stood silent for a minute, pondering what soothing words she might say, the moonlight shining on her pure upturned face – so very pure and so very fair in that light, that it wore almost an unearthly look.

'I have been hearing something of you to-day,' Massey said, regarding with untiring interest that glorified face.

'Of me?' with but half-aroused interest; it was not of herself she cared to speak just then.

'Of you. I have enjoyed the privilege of a lengthy interview with an intelligent old lady of the name of Harper.'

'Old Happy Harper?' smiling. 'That was very good-natured of you; but as you already do not approve of the poor as a class, I fear your prejudices are not likely to be removed by that individual specimen. I'm afraid she is not a good old woman, Mr Massey; and I do hope you did not give her money, because she will surely spend it in tobacco or gin.'

'Gin?' he said, laughing. 'She called it "tea" to me. And does she really smoke? I shall go in and have a pipe with her sometimes. She is altogether the most intellectual and interesting woman I have ever met.'

She laughed.

'There is no accounting for taste. I am bound to admit that, for my own part, I find her a horror; she is a discanting, deceitful old body – all her sons drink, and her daughters –'

An abrupt and expressive pause.

'And this from you?' he said, with mock reproach. 'You should have heard her speak of you.'

'Do not listen to her – pray do not believe her! She has said dreadful things of other people – of my sister even! She would say dreadful things of me if she thought that you would like to hear them.'

The moonlight was bright enough to show the faint blush which came to Helen's cheek as the awkwardness of the speech struck her.

'It is not true, then,' he said, in a lower voice – 'it is not true that her son would have been sent to prison as a poacher but for your intercession with my uncle? It is not true that for three weeks you went down to her hovel, night and morning, to dress the burns of her wretched little grandchild, because its own mother dared not touch it? It is not true that you still pay for the support of this miserable little mortal, not fortunate enough to enjoy legal claims on the parish? These things are not true?'

Helen left gazing at the home of the untiring songster, and silently began to move homeward. The tone of Massey's voice, as he asked his questions, touched her somewhat; deeply was she conscious that his interest in herself must have been made very patent to cunning old Happy before she would have troubled to mention any of those benefits received.

'All this must have been very wearisome to you, I fear,' she said weakly, knowing in her heart how little wearisome it had been. 'What evil fate drove you to that cottage? Mr Massey, if you want to bestow your charity profitably –'

'But I don't believe I do,' he interrupted; 'and it wasn't charity that took me there, but dilapidations. Old Happy's roof has begun to tumble about her head.'

'Oh, pray see to that! All those cottages are in such terrible repair.'

'They are. I shall see to this one, at any rate. But that was not all she told me.'

'Indeed! I hope her other communications were equally edifying.'

'They were very solemn. She has had a vision of Heaven – did you know that? – can describe in the most realistic way the minute details of a four hours' sojourn there. She believes in this, too. I really do not think there is hypocrisy here; she *imagines* she had this vision – that she saw –'

'Oh, spare me, please!' Helen cried, with a shudder. 'I have heard it so often, and I think it so wicked! It is all the most terrible blasphemy. I know what she says she saw – what she *dreamt* – quite well.'

'I was not going to shock you,' he said; 'I was only going to tell you of the angels – do you remember the angels? – "ringes of 'em," she said, "all blowin' on brass trumpets, all like Miss Helen in the face, and all dressed in light blue gowns, like Miss Helen was at the Cottage Flower Show last year."'

'Oh, I have heard it all,' Helen said, with a little angry laugh. 'It is all so frightfully ignorant and impious!'

'Why? I do not see it so at all. How is a poor old soul like that, who has seen no statues and no pictures, to form an orthodox idea of an angel? In the absence, do you see, of these aids to the imagination, she simply picks upon the most beautiful thing she knows, and shapes her angels accordingly. I have a high opinion of the talents of Mrs Happy Harper; I think her a very clever, as well as a deeply religious woman. It was watching your face, just now, looking upward in the moonlight, which made me think of Happy and her vision,' he added, with a sigh.

She began to speak hurriedly.

'I do not care to continue the subject, nor do I wish to destroy your illusions,' she said; 'but I must just tell you that the Backs – the girls from the Hall – who had heard of this trance (it was dignified by that name) of Happy's, and who are always anxious to get fun anyhow, went down and questioned the old woman about it. I am bound to say she stuck to the account of me, and my blue dress, and the feathers in my hat; but when they pressed her about angels of the opposite sex (there were "ringes" of them, too), she explained that they also "blew on brass trumpets, that they were dressed in red coats and top-boots, and looked for all the world like Mr Tom and Mr Archie (the girls' brothers) when they go a-huntin'."'

'Ah, she descended a little bit too much to detail there,' he admitted, laughing; 'but she is a clever old lady, for all that. Hark! the nightingale is still singing. I wish I knew if it were the one that sings for you?'

CHAPTER XII

Pollie has her Way

WHEN James Massey awoke the next morning, he at once formed a virtuous resolution not to run into temptation any more on that day. He would not approach the Freemans' dwelling, he would keep his feet from paths where Pollie was likely to tread. He considered himself to be thus deciding for her interest as well as his own. He did not want to be 'into a mess,' as he unpoetically expressed it, for his own part, and certainly he did not want to behave badly to the girl. It was true that Pollie herself did most of the love-making, but Massey was not a man to be ungenerous to women, and even to himself did not make that charge.

'She is a nice little thing,' he said to himself, 'and an affectionate little thing, and perhaps she would marry me if I asked her. I'm deucedly afraid she thinks I shall ask her; I've got to make it clear to her that I shan't, and I'm hanged if it's a pleasant business to do.'

In some such way he cogitated over his after-breakfast pipe, leaning over the light iron railing which divided his garden from the meadow. Above him a big apple-tree just bursting into blossom, the morning air sweet with the scent of it; before him the emerald meadow, his blood-red herd standing deep in the dewy grass; beyond, the glint of the river, whose windings he and Miss Freeman had followed yesterday. He turned away from the sight of it with some impatience, and glanced to where in the near distance the tower of the church showed among the elms. He kept his eyes on it as he leant there puffing at his pipe, and the expression of his face changed. Miss Freeman and her embarrassing affection were all forgotten, the church – unregenerate though he was – was a sign and symbol to him, just then, of sweeter possibilities by far.

'It will all be of no use,' he said to himself presently, with a sigh. 'I think there is not a doubt but that it will be of no use; but for all that, I mean to have a good try.'

With which darkly mysterious remark he gave over dreaming for that time, looked at his watch, knocked the ashes from his pipe, fetched his stick from the house, unloosed his dogs from their kennels, and prepared to start on his morning's walk.

His way led him through the spacious kitchen garden, and he stopped here to speak to a man putting in some seeds.

'Get on, Solomon,' he said. 'The ducks'll be ready before the peas at this rate.'

Solomon did not look up at this remark, nor were his movements in any degree quickened. Had his face been capable of any expression, it would probably have shown contempt for his words; as it was, there was nothing in his blank countenance to give offence, at any rate.

Massey stood a moment watching the man's stiff deliberate movements.

'We ought to get some fruit this year,' he said; 'plenty of blossom here,' touching the buds on a neighbouring espalier.

Solomon slowly lifted his stiff old back, and looked in his master's face. In a few hours perhaps that last remark may penetrate his brain, and he may probably be in a position to give his views as to the state of the fruit crop by the time Massey has forgotten the subject. His intellect was required for quite another matter now.

'The young 'ooman from yonder ha' bin,' he said, drawing the back of a shaking hand across his mouth. 'She's lookin' for you somewheres about.'

'Do you mean Miss Freeman?' Mr Massey asked, with a quick feeling of discomfort. 'Where is she? How long ago was she here?'

'She's somewheres hereabout,' Solomon repeated, beginning to get himself on to his knees again; and Massey, looking round, at once caught sight of a light skirt among some currant-bushes at the farther end of the garden. She had seen him from the moment of his entrance, and was waiting till he should have finished his talk with Solomon.

Mr Massey's step was slower than usual as he went towards her, and although he smiled a welcome he was not too well pleased.

'What a fool the girl must be to come here alone,' he said to himself, and perhaps Pollie caught an expression on his face she had not been used to see there, for there was something of apology in her tone.

'I was obliged to come,' she said, as they shook hands. 'I wanted to see you before you went out.'

'Is it something you want me to do for you at Gurton?' he asked, having been used to execute various commissions for her on his frequent visits to that town.

'No, it is not that,' she said. 'It's about – But I want to speak to you alone. There is something I have to tell you.'

Massey smiled down at her as she stood among the currant-bushes.

'Well, say on. Solomon – have you the pleasure of Solomon's acquaintance? – could not hear you at this distance, and would not be a whit the wiser if he did.'

But Pollie turned and led the way out of the garden into the orchard beyond, where she stood among the cowslip-strewn grass, the branches of an apple tree, just breaking into blossom, above her head.

'You have not forgotten what you said to me last night?' she asked, her eyes fixed on his face, an unusual nervousness in her manner.

Massey saw at once that something serious was coming.

'What did I say to you?' he asked. 'I'm afraid I say a good many foolish things. I can't be expected to remember them all.'

'You would hardly forget that you told me you loved me,' she said, a breathlessness as of deep anxiety upon her; 'that you asked me if I loved you? At least you have not forgotten my answer?'

What could he reply but that he certainly could never forget that? But there was no exultation in his tone, and he attempted no endearment, standing before her, his stick run through his elbows at his back, looking far more careless and at ease than he felt.

She held his eye with her own, and there was an excitement about her manner such as he had never seen before.

'You do not regret it?' she went on. 'You are not ashamed of having said you loved me? You aren't sorry that I love you?'

'My dear!' he expostulated, but got no further. 'Great heavens! what a kettle of fish this is going to be!' was his mental ejaculation.

'Because – I hope you will not be angry with me – you did not say it was to be a secret – I had to tell my father.'

'To tell your father!' he repeated, startled. 'To tell him what?'

'That we' – she hesitated, dropped her eyes from his face, and turned away her head – 'that we are engaged.'

For a moment Massey stood silent – stunned, while the apple-trees with their pink buds seemed to be chasing each other round the orchard. Then a feeling of rage came to clear his bewilderment, and the instinct of self-preservation forced him to collect his wits.

'I'm hanged if I'm caught like that, young lady,' he said to himself, and swore a wicked word or so by way of emphasis. Aloud, 'Engaged!' he repeated, with an unsteady laugh; 'it is hardly such a solemn matter as that, Pollie. I'm not at all the sort of fellow for you to enter into an arrangement of that kind with. I'm not a bit of a marrying man, you see; and if I were, you'd be sick of me in less than a month.'

'I'll run all risk of that,' she said; 'I am not afraid. As for marrying, we don't want to talk of that for years to come.'

This was a relief, at any rate, for Massey had already begun to feel the toils of matrimony closing round him as he stood there.

'You had better let me hear what has taken place between you and your father,' he said, in his coldest tone. 'What induced you, I wonder, to put things in such an uncomfortable position for us all? Of course I shall have to explain matters to him. He will blame you as well as me. It is a devil of a scrape for both of us.'

'But why need you speak to my father? It would be horrid for you, and my father does not expect it. Do not.'

'But surely he will expect it, if you have really told him that we are – what you now said. I must tell him that it is a mistake, that – that I am not fit to be your husband, nor – nor likely to make you happy.' He hesitated over the words, feeling how unreal and perhaps heartless they were. 'I hate to have to say such things to you, Pollie,' he went on with some compunction, seeing that her face, half turned from him now, was pale, and that her lip quivered. 'I feel like a cad and a beast, but what can I do? My dear, let us stop before we go too far. I have been foolish – madly foolish to – to be fond of you, and to make you think that you are, or could be, fond of me. It has all been a mistake – all –on your part, child, and the whole of the fault has been on mine. Don't you feel, can't you see, that I am the last man in the world that such a girl as you should dream of marrying? The very last!' He repeated this the more emphatically, as he would have found it difficult in the extreme to explain his meaning less vaguely. 'You must forgive me, Pollie, you must know that I would not for worlds willingly cause you trouble; I should like to be kicked if I have really made you unhappy, you, who have been such a dear little friendly soul and so pretty and so kind! Come, don't turn away from me – I can't have it. You do not fear any unpleasantness with your father? I will take all the blame on my own shoulders, of course I will; and shall take, as quietly as I may be able, all the hard things he will probably say to me. You shall take no harm there.'

'How can you help it?' she cried, angry but tearful. 'I told him and mother we were engaged, and you – you' (with choking sobs) 'are going to tell them 'twas a lie of mine. How can you make that pleasant?'

'Well – oh, for heaven's sake, don't cry, Polly! If you'll only be reasonable and listen for one moment, you'll see there's nothing to cry about. I can stand anything but that! Now do be quiet, and hear what I have to say.' He laid his hand kindly on her shoulder, but she shrank angrily from him, and sank down upon the orchard grass, covering her face. 'Now what I shall say to your father will be this – it will be simple enough –' here he paused to groan inwardly over the difficulty of the task. 'I shall say that I – well, lost my head for a moment – and said more than I had any right to do, and that you were taken by surprise, and – and lost your head too, don't you know, or words to that effect; but that on reflection I – we – that is – you saw, quite saw that you had been mistaken, and that – that – that it was a mistake, in fact,' said Massey, quite aware of his own lameness and tameness. 'There, what is easier than that? Don't you be afraid, Pollie! It will be all right, my dear.' He knelt down beside her as he spoke, and watched her distress with a great deal of concern. His anger had all evaporated; he was overpowered now by shame and disgust at the part he had to play, and was penetrated with the intensest pity for the girl. 'Let us be friends, my little girl! You are not very angry with me?' he pleaded.

At the softened sound of his voice Pollie's grief grew deeper; she rocked her body to and fro as she sat in the grass, and he saw the tears drop through her fingers. How easy it would be for him to comfort her, the young man knew too well; he had but to put out an arm and draw her to him, and the sobs would cease – and his liberty be gone! 'At least, tell me what it is that so distresses you, Pollie?' he asked, when he had watched her grief in helpless misery for some time. 'Is there something beyond your fear of your father? I did not know till now that you held him in such awe. Can it be this – this idea which you had not thought of till last night, and which you will forget to-morrow?'

'Why do you talk to me such rubbish as that?' she broke out, uncovering her face and turning angrily upon him. 'What is the use in pretending it is only a little thing? How dare you call it an idea! You – you have taken the trouble to put the "idea" into other heads as well as mine, as you'll find to your cost. Haven't you singled me out since ever you came here, and paid me all sorts of attention, and set everybody talking and saying – saying what it ought to mean? And father has been angry with me – times, because of your being always after me – but could I help it?' cried Pollie unfairly. 'How was I to know it was all to end in nothing – how was I to know? And last night father was in a rage because I had stayed out so long (mother had said I was with you), and he stood at the window looking out for me, and he saw – he saw what you did –'

'And what was that?' asked Massey miserably.

'He saw you take me in your arms and k-k-kiss me!' sobbed Pollie, with a fresh outburst of grief; 'and when I came in I thought he would have struck me, he looked at me so white and so fierce. I was frightened – I was! and I thought you had meant what you had said. How should I know – oh, how should I know it was lies? – and I cried out to him that I had done no wrong – that we were engaged. And now, will you tell me what is to become of me? You do not know what he is when he is angry – he will turn me from his house; and what is to become of me? Tell me that – what is to become of me?'

Massey leant forward and took her hands.

'Pollie,' he said solemnly, 'I promise you – do you hear? – I promise you that it will be all right. Can't you trust me, you poor little child? At the worst, do you see, it is but the unpleasantness of a time – of a moment; while if I allowed you to enter upon that arrangement with me it must be for always, and you would be miserable. My dear, if I were foolish enough – wicked enough – to hold you to what you have said, if I were really to allow you to marry me, you can form no conception of how infernally miserable you would be.'

'Marry!' she said contemptuously; 'who talked of being married? I do not want to be married!'

'Then, my dear girl,' he asked, intensely relieved, 'what is it that you do want?'

'I want you to promise not to make any fuss with my father. James Massey, promise me not to go to him! Why should you? You know how little given to words he is – he will not speak to you about it. Why should you insist on putting me into such a plight as that? I think I shall die if you do – die of shame and misery! Whatever have I done to you that you should be so cruel?'

'Then what would you have us do?' he asked, perplexed.

'I would have us go on as we are, as we always have been. What difference need there be?'

'Nonsense!' he cried irritably. 'That is all absurd, Pollie! You'd find there'd have to be a difference, and a very considerable difference, if we were supposed to have entered into an engagement to marry each other. Immediately that fact became known we should have all the world about our ears – every prying fool within ten miles of us would imagine he had a right to meddle.'

'But we needn't let them meddle,' she said eagerly; 'they need never hear of it, even. It will concern no one but just you and me, and we shall understand each other – there is no fear but that I shall understand,' bitterly.

'My dear girl, now don't you know that you are talking nonsense, sheer nonsense! I'd bet a crown that this thing, if it is not stopped at once, is all over the neighbourhood by to-morrow morning! Do people wait to talk of only what concerns themselves? Our business is everyone's business, and would be in everyone's mouth. For my part, I do not care' (an untruth, Mr Massey, for you cared very much); 'but I will not allow your name to – that kind of thing, when it comes to nothing, is bad for a girl, don't you see?'

Pollie was not so totally dead to all idea of decency that she could ask why it should come to nothing, but mentally she put the question plainly. She had ceased crying now, and sat looking straight before her, her little plump tear-disfigured face a picture of misery and bitterness. Massey, in spite of his pity and remorse, half smiled at the childish look of woe. He laid his hand kindly on hers.

'Look up!' he said. 'I do not know my little friend with that woe-begone face.'

Pollie regarded him with wrath in her eyes.

'It is easy for you to laugh,' she said, 'and to say "Look up." You have behaved badly to me – shamefully – shamefully! and it is all you care.'

'Come, come!' he expostulated, drawing back. 'Not quite so fast, Pollie.'

'Shamefully! I will say it – I'm not afraid. And what do you intend to do now? What –'

'What I intend to,' he interrupted, speaking with more determination than he had yet shown, 'is to go to your father, now, at once, and to say to him that a mistake had been made – a misapprehension – what you will; that no engagement existed between us, that you had been frightened into saying it had been so by his anger, but that I, myself, am ready and anxious to take all the blame, and that you hope he will forgive the – the – well – deception. Of course, he won't be pleased. It will be disagreeable, rather; you have put me into an uncommonly awkward hole, but it will be all right, as far as you are concerned, as I have said, and by the time you get home, you will find –'

'I get home?' she repeated, more calmly than she had yet spoken. 'I shall not go home.'

'You won't go home! What do you mean?'

'I mean what I say. Of course I shall not go home. I would not face my father after you have told him that tale for a million golden sovereigns. I shall never go home any more – never.'

Massey was silent for a moment, experiencing an awful feeling of exasperation and helplessness.

'What is it that you want, Pollie?' he asked presently. 'I tell you plainly – I am sorry you make me say it so plainly – that I shall not marry, that I do not wish to be bound in any way. Do you want me to be engaged to you against my –' He was about to say 'will,' but stopped, and substituted 'better judgment.' 'You know the whole case. Tell me, under the circumstances, what better I can do than I propose. Mind you, I know that mine is the only way – the only straightforward and *decent* way out of the difficulty. But give me your idea, straight out, no beating about the bush! Let's know what it is that will satisfy you.'

'I have told you. I want you not to tell my father – only that. I want you to let things be, just for a time, as they are. I will tell my mother, I promise you I will, that there is no thought of our being married, and that you are anxious there should be no talk. The thing shall go no farther; nothing will be wanted of you or expected but just what you have always done. I will take an oath, if you don't believe me. It will not be so hard for you, I suppose, to be – to be civil to me for a little while longer? I never knew, till now, that you found it so hard! That is all I ask – a little time to let things right themselves, to let me put them straight, so that father is not angry with me, and I am not made a laughing-stock before everyone – I mean, of course, before my father and mother. You need not be afraid; I promise you that no one will interfere with you or annoy you about it. My people aren't at all anxious for me to marry you; that's the fact. It's a very different young man pa wants me to have; but I don't want to trouble you about that. Only, considering all your words and actions, James Massey, for months past, since ever we first met, and remembering what a different finish from this they might have led me to expect, I think you will admit it is not much I ask.'

She sighed bitterly as she concluded, looking away from him, her dreary eyes fixed on the roots of a neighbouring apple-tree.

Massey pondered a minute; having pondered, said to himself with forced resignation, 'There is no help for it,' and gave in – gave in with a sigh half of relief at an escape from the performance of a most unpleasant duty, half of apprehension of the consequences of his weakness. And yet he was not a particularly weak man, in spite of his failure now. Given an object which appeared to him desirable to attain unto, he had been used, all his life, to struggle with more or less persistency until it was gained. It was not for nothing that he would knock under! In dealing with men he was not apt to be soft nor easily set aside; but here was a woman, a girl, almost a child! It was not in his nature to be hard with such an one as this. Besides, had he not been to blame all along, and had he not always dimly known that in some way he would have to be punished? She had known no better in her innocent folly, so he told himself, but his own superior wisdom and greater experience ought to have taught him to protect a little unsophisticated girl such as this from herself.

'I suppose it will have to be as you say, then, Pollie,' he said presently; 'that is, for a time. But mind, if either your father or mother speaks to me, I shall give them the exact position. You understand that? And you will see that the affair is kept strictly between ourselves – eh?'

'Why should I want to talk of it more than you?' Pollie said. 'It will be all right.' And she gave a sigh of entire relief. If she had not been quite successful in what she had set herself to accomplish that morning, neither had she altogether failed. The blue eyes came back from the old apple stump to Massey's face, and the look of dreariness had quite departed from them. 'It will only be for a very short time,' she said, 'and I will try not to trouble you too much.' She was touching with that little air of humility, and Massey smiled upon her as he sprang to his feet.

'I shall put up with you,' he said. 'And now run along home, and let me go and earn my daily bread.'

CHAPTER XIII

How the Secret was Kept

'MOTHER,' Pollie began that day, when *tête-à-tête* with her parent, 'all that about James Massey and me had better not be talked of.'

'How d'ye mean?' Mrs Freeman asked. 'Them kind of affairs gen'rally do get talked about, I fancy – you can't help it, child, and I don't see that you need try to.' The good lady was, in fact, longing to spread the news, seeing more cause than ever for pride in her daughter since that daughter's engagement. Her husband might jeer and sneer and talk of the better things Pollie might have done with her cousin Arthur and his fine prospects, ready to her hand; but Mrs Freeman had seen and was quite able to appreciate the superiority of Mr Massey over her husband's nephew, paying London business and only-son-ship included. 'He is a perfect gentleman,' had been her words always in speaking of her neighbour, and her thorough acceptance of this fact had given her a certain awe of him, for to the ways of 'perfect gentlemen' she certainly had not been used. She did not, therefore, approve of this new-born maiden shyness of Pollie's which would lay an embargo upon her tongue. 'Why not talked about?' she asked. 'Most girls are proud of their lovers, Pollie, and I'm sure you've no call to be ashamed of yours!'

'All the same, ma; don't talk about it. If people find it out, as I dare say they will, why, let them, but don't you help them. James Massey says he detests the kind of fuss that people always make, and I know he'd go in an awful rage if anyone mentioned our engagement to him.'

'Why? do you mean I'm not to speak to the man about marryin' my own child?' her mother asked, putting down her sewing to stare at the girl. 'Like that, I don't see how everything is to be gone through with and arranged, and that! There'll have to be a lot o' talk, Pollie, with me and him and your father, too, before you can get married.'

'Married!' Pollie repeated scornfully. 'One would think I wanted to be married to-morrow! Why, I'm not twenty yet, and I know James Massey won't think about a wedding till I'm of age.' Pollie was rather pleased with this idea, which had come to her on the spur of the moment, and determined to make the most of it. 'I'm not to be married till I'm twenty-one,' she said, with emphasis.

Now, although it is certain that Mrs Freeman fondly loved her daughter, and had already shed many tears at the prospect of losing her, still, being truly feminine in mind, she experienced some disappointment at the news of this postponement. She went on with her work in silence for a minute, not liking to give her thought expression. Presently a knowing smile crept over her red and shining face.

'I fancy you won't find he'll be content to wait two years, Pollie,' she said. 'Young men in love aren't so fond of puttin' off. Why, there's lots marry as young as you. Look at your aunt Gosling there, with her first baby before she was nineteen. Let alone that, a long engagement do unsettle young people so, 'specially with the young man a neighbour, him always after you, neglectin' his business, now when he have two to work for instead of one, and farming not paying with the best attention. No, two years o' love-makin' is a serious matter, mark my words. I should be sorry for your sake if it was to be two years, Pollie.'

'Oh, well, it's early times to worry about all that,' Pollie said lightly. 'Just hint to my father, will you, not to speak to Massey about it till Massey likes to speak to him. I won't have him worried. Let him come and go as usual, and that's all.'

'You know your father 'on't do too much talkin',' Mrs Freeman said; 'not that I see the harm in having the thing over at once, nice and friendly, as I meant to have done this very evening.'

'You see, ma, James Massey isn't one to make a mistake. He is a perfect gentleman, as you know very well; and perhaps he knows better what is usual in such matters as these than either you or father. It is much better to abide by what he says, as I shall. We neither of us wish to get married yet, so why talk of it? Of course, if people find out we are engaged, as of course they will, why, we don't want to contradict them, that's all.'

Mrs Freeman did not by any means finish with the matter there, but by degrees she was lured on to talk over the other branches of the same subject, and Pollie found her mother more deeply interesting on that afternoon than she ever remembered to have done before. For, in spite of the two years' probation, she, being a hopeful and far-seeing woman, did not find it out of place to discuss the wedding with much interest and even in closest detail, holding out the most alluring prospect of what her father could be made to do for Pollie by way of trousseau, and discussing the probable marriage portion she might expect.

It was all very delightful to Pollie, this taking of the thing as a matter of course, and looking on the wedding as a settled thing. She quite meant, if she could manage it, one day to be James Massey's wife, and was quite happy for the present in pretending there was no doubt about it. She sat, curled up in her father's armchair, alone with her mother the whole of that spring afternoon, Dollie having been despatched with a servant to gather cowslips in the meadow, and gave herself up to the enjoyment of her own importance. She had often dreamed of playing the fine lady, in an endless succession of new dresses, in the pleasant Wood Farm rooms, of having this well-built, well-dressed, well-to-do young man for her own property in the eyes of the envious neighbourhood. She had gone to some lengths to make those dreams realities – surely they were going to be so now. She felt that things must go as she wished, as she listened to her mother's plans, lying coiled in the big chair, her yellow hair all ruffled and unthought of, her cheeks pink with excitement.

She had never been used to make a confidante of her mother, but she prattled to her unceasingly now of what she would do, and Massey would do, of what this person would say, and that.

'I don't think the Pearsons can try to snub me any more now,' she said complacently. 'James Massey is as good as they any day in the week. Why, his own sister is going to marry a parson, and he looks down upon him, that he does.'

In spite of Pollie's professed contempt for the cloth, this proposed alliance of Miss Massey was a source of much secret pride to her.

'I don't fancy Helen will like my engagement,' she continued, with a knowing nod of her head.

'Why, 'twon't be any business of hers, sure-ly!' Mrs Freeman cried indignantly. 'What have she to do with it, Pollie?'

'Oh, I don't know! You see, she's getting pretty old now not to be married, and I daresay they've thought about him for her. There's not so many chances hereabout.'

'She ain't much Massey's kind, I fancy,' the mother said contentedly; 'she ain't flesh and blood enough for him.'

And she looked up with some pleasure at Pollie, who was certainly looking very pretty that afternoon, in a fleshly, unrefined way.

'The fact is,' Pollie said vindictively, 'she's no one's kind; that's the whole truth; she's no one's kind! There isn't a man born that can put up with all that fad she runs on about, reclaiming the people, making friends of the poor (a nice lot to have more to do with than you can help!) and worrying after their children. If you can get her off those subjects, then she'll rave about books – and such books! – and music, or go in raptures over a weed or a flower, with half a dozen names for it at her finger's end. How can you expect a rational man to stand that? As for her looks, there's a kind of idea that she's a beauty, but did you ever hear anyone admire her? I've asked heaps of gentlemen, and they agree with me that she'd do very well for a statue, as far as that goes, but that's all. There's nothing in her – nothing! She's as slow – as slow as anything!'

Pollie was quite excited about Miss Smythe's shortcomings; the subject was one on which she could always wax eloquently bitter, for she had a vague, uncomfortable idea that Mr Massey had not been one of the many discriminating gentlemen who had taken her view of Miss Smythe's character and charms.

'Massey do seem to have been pretty often dropping in there, and the Vicar, he go to the Wood Farm a good bit,' said Mrs Freeman reflectively. 'I wonder if that is what it mean. She'll have a good bit of money of her own, too, if all they say is true, when that old aunt dies that they're always reckonin' on. 'Tis odd *that* ha'n't got her a husband before now.'

'Money's no good,' said Pollie, with superiority, 'when there's no liveliness and no "go" in you. That is what the men like.'

'They like it in a sweetheart, my dear, but not in a wife,' said Mrs Freeman oracularly, and proceeded to read her daughter a lecture on the advisability of her now at last consenting to put herself under her mother's tuition in matters of household usefulness. But at this point Pollie found the conversation to lose its charm, and soon she slipped out of her chair and left her mother to the enjoyment of her own counsels.

That evening at the Vicarage Mr Pearson was observed to be unusually cheerful. He ate his lukewarm dinner without a word of fault-finding, and even pressed tit-bits upon his wife in a pleasant marital fashion.

Miss Smythe, who was of an observant nature, and who knew the Vicar well, was quite prepared for the air of self-importance with which, as soon as they were alone, he announced that he had a piece of news to impart.

'I've something to tell you, Anna. Now, Helen, what is it?'

'Well, I hope for your credit's sake it's something good, Alfred,' Helen said. 'You look so terribly cheerful about it. Does it concern us personally?'

'Well, no. But it concerns our nearest neighbour.'

'Then,' said Mrs Pearson, with frigid indifference, 'I do not care what it is.'

'And I,' said Helen, 'know what it is.'

Mr Pearson opened his small blue eyes as wide as they would go, and stared at his sister-in-law. He was not too pleased at the prospect of his budget being forestalled.

'Since the thing was only settled last night, Helen, and since I am the first and only person out of the family who has been told of it, I don't exactly see how you gained your information.'

'And since you do know, you may as well say what it is,' said Mrs Pearson impatiently, having forgotten her indifference.

'Well, then, it is, Anna,' Helen said slowly, her face a little flushed, 'it is that Mr Massey is at last engaged to Miss Freeman. That is the news.'

And that was the news, and Mr Pearson was much put out at being thus robbed of the honour of being the first to tell it.

'Who told you about it, Helen?' he asked suspiciously. 'The woman assured me I was the first to hear it, and that the whole affair was to be kept secret for a time. I should like to know how you learnt it.'

'Why, Alfred, I could not help guessing. Have we not all seen it coming on for months – haven't you speculated about it yourself ever since Mr Massey first came to Hilby? Did not everyone see that Miss Freeman, at least, had made up her own mind from the very first?' Then she checked herself. 'I did not quite mean that,' she said. 'I do not mean to be uncharitable. Tell us about it, Alfred. Mrs Freeman seemed pleased, I suppose?'

'Pleased! Yes, that she is – pleased and proud too; there's no getting away from the woman,' said the Vicar, who had been quite as eager to listen as she to talk. 'She'd speak of nothing else. But it seems the thing is to be kept, in a measure, secret – nothing is to be said of it to Massey himself, Anna. He appears to have an objection, strange to say, to having the engagement spoken of yet. Pray bear this in mind, Anna.'

'I really do not know,' said Mrs Pearson, with dignity, 'why you should imagine me likely to transgress in the matter. She, Miss Freeman, is a person of whom I strongly disapprove, and for Mr Massey I have no feeling but the mildest toleration. I should not dream of alluding, in his hearing, to anything that concerned him so nearly as that.'

'Ah, there I do not agree with you,' Helen said. 'People generally expect such an important matter as this to be taken some notice of by their friends. I should have liked to congratulate Mr Massey myself, and I am disappointed that I may not do so.'

'Yes, you have an infatuation about him, as you have about all commonplace uninteresting people,' her sister said calmly. 'I have always noticed that this Mr Massey was another of your *protégés*, Helen.'

'What can you mean, Anna?' the girl cried, with an indignant look.

'I do not know what it is that you and Alfred see in him,' Mrs Pearson went on, heedless of the interruption. 'To me, I confess, he seems only a very mediocre specimen of his class. I have been willing to take your view of him, and have tried to discover his attraction. On several occasions I have endeavoured to interest him in intellectual subjects, and have addressed my conversation to him with the hope of drawing him out; but he is apparently incapable of even comprehending my remarks, and he is not enough of a gentleman to pretend the interest he does not feel, but lets his eyes, as well as his thoughts, wander away from me and my subject.'

Here Helen arose and carried her flushed face over to the window. She too, perhaps, had noticed those wandering eyes, and guessed at the errant thoughts.

'Oh, Massey's a good fellow in his way,' the Vicar said, with pompous condescension, and a timely recollection of the good table which Massey kept. 'I take it that he is a fair specimen, Anna, of the farmer of to-day. We do not go to them for intellect, my dear. Out of his place a bit, perhaps – they all are – and a little bit too – a – a – um – free and independent in his manner, but with no vices, and, as far as I can see, few bad habits. Smokes? Yes; he does smoke, too much, perhaps; and yes, I believe he drives into Gurton now and then for billiards. Still, if one do not altogether approve, it is nevertheless advisable to be neighbourly. I drop in upon him now and then – it is an advantage to him to see a good deal of me, and a clergyman should endeavour to keep on good terms with his parishioners, however – um – um – inferior to him they may be.'

'Anna,' Helen said, turning from the window, 'we ought to see more of that girl – Miss Freeman. We must try to like her better, and to be good friends with her; she will be our nearest neighbour. Don't you think, perhaps, we might like her a little if we really made a duty of it, and tried very hard?'

'That is a duty, Helen, I will leave you to fulfil. She is a person of whom I quite entirely disapprove. I expect no good of her in any relation of life, and I shall not be so insincere as to pretend to welcome her as a neighbour. You will, of course, please yourself in the matter, but I should say that any show of cordiality on your part would be a pure affectation.'

'Well, well,' interposed the Vicar. 'They are not married yet, Anna. Two years – did I tell you they are to wait two years? – will give you and Helen time to settle how it will be right to behave to them.'

Here Helen, catching sight of her little nephew at play in the garden, opened the French window and went out to join him.

'The fact is, Alfred,' Mrs Pearson said, looking after her sister, and dropping her voice to an unusually confidential tone, 'the fact is, I think we have seen too much of the young man. He is one likely to misconstrue your friendly advances, and to abuse the privilege of our acquaintance. He belongs, apparently, to that most dreadful class of young men who think themselves privileged to cast glances of admiration at every woman they see, and I have always felt that if he were not at a safe distance, he would become horribly familiar. I scarcely like to mention it, Alfred, but the way in which he watches Helen about has been most annoying to see. He, too evidently, does not know his place at all, nor understand the respect which is due to his clergyman's wife's sister.'

'Dear me!' said the Vicar, his blue eyes very round and staring. 'Now, I never observed anything of that kind, Anna, and I have not thought myself obtuse. Dear me! It never went further than that, I suppose? It would have been very unpleasant if he had made that sort of thing – um – um – obtrusive in any way; but just looking at her –there wasn't, after all, much harm in looking at her, eh? – women don't object to being looked at, my dear, and Helen is used to it. She is a fine girl,' he said, rather enjoying the unusual experience of his wife's confidences, and gazing after Helen where she walked with Perrie on the lawn; 'and a good girl, too, though somewhat opinionated. I often wonder that she has never found up a lover of her own.'

Mr Pearson had put his foot in it now, as he was pretty sure to do before long when left in unprotected enjoyment of his wife's society. She rose from the table in offended dignity.

'What a phrase!' she exclaimed. 'What a phrase! and to come from the lips of a man who ought to be a gentleman, and who is my husband! About my sister, too! I think you, at least, must have known, Alfred, that there are women with higher aims in life than the "finding up" of lovers.'

Meanwhile, Helen, all unconscious of the revelations of her sister, that one person of unswerving rectitude in the midst of an erring world, paced the garden paths with little Perrie, giving but a divided attention to his prattle, but holding his hand kindly in her own, and letting him lead her where he would. They carried food to the little chickens, and saw them safely shut up for the night; they walked down to the paddock-gate to inspect the few-days-old foal, trotting through the cowslips on its long ungainly legs after its mother; they wandered into the shrubbery, and the little fellow was hoisted on his auntie's shoulders to inspect the eggs in two or three birds' nests they knew of. She answered all his questions, and finally heard his prayers at her knee before he was sent off to bed, and all the time the news of Miss Freeman's engagement occupied almost solely her thoughts. What good girl of her age is above taking interest in the history of a love-making? The romance of this one was in the spring air to-night, Helen thought.

Presently, when Perrie was safely off to bed, and she still walked the garden paths in the sweet dusk, came Mr Pearson to join her. They went down the broad fir-bordered drive, side by side, and leant by the gate at the road, while the Vicar enjoyed the innocent cigarette forbidden him in or near the house, and there the question of Miss Freeman's marriage was discussed more openly than before the mistress of the house. Helen gradually learned all that Mrs Freeman had said on the subject, and heard her brother-in-law wax clumsily sarcastic over the ill-concealed exultation of that lady.

'And you aren't surprised, Helen?'

'Surprised? Well, I hardly know. Of course one was ready to hear it. And yet, after all, Alfred, in a way, I am surprised. Now, tell me, does he not strike you as being – well, too good for Miss Freeman? Oh, I know she is pretty, and perhaps quick and amusing; but – I must say it just once, and have done with it – I do think it an awful pity – there! He is as far superior to her as – as his own hunter to their ungroomed pony. He is! And it's a pity – a terrible pity! Why, what kind of wife can a girl such as that make to any man with a brain and a heart? She is too indolent to interest herself in one of his pursuits. She has not character enough to attract him for any length of time. There is no depth of feeling in her to respond to the love a man would, I suppose, want to feel for his wife. It's a pity – a terrible, terrible pity!'

'She is a vulgar little person,' the Vicar assented easily, throwing away the end of his cigarette. 'But I suppose he likes her, and it is not for us to judge, Helen. Aren't you a little uncharitable, my dear?'

'Perhaps I am,' she said. 'I do not know. Though, as a rule, I believe it is you and Anna who attack, I who defend. One must speak out one's thoughts sometimes, if one is not all humbug, and I will to-night, by way of change. Alfred, I think a great deal about the people I know. I like to understand them – I think I can, as a rule, feel of what they are capable; and I tell you that that little, frivolous, unsatisfactory girl is altogether incapable of appreciating one manly quality that he has.'

''Tis for her face, I suppose, he wants to marry her.'

'I will tell you another thing, while we are on the subject. He does not want to marry her at all. He can't; I am sure of it! Imagine a man tied to such a woman for all his life! In a little time,' she said, lowering her voice to solemnity, 'I should think he would *hate* her; should not you? And then what is to become of him? His life all spoilt – made barren by want of sympathy and encouragement – wasted to satisfy a vanity that is after all insatiable!'

Miss Smythe's uncharitable words crowded forth to-night with irrepressible force, so seldom did she give such thoughts vent. She kept herself usually so well under control, and she knew quite well that soon she would repent, and in a measure recall her words, but for the moment they must have way.

'Young men take their own course in these things, you know, Helen,' Mr Pearson said, not quite unimpressed by her earnestness. 'There is nothing to be done now. Had he asked my advice, or even mentioned the project to me, I might have pointed out –'

'Oh, but of course that is impossible,' Helen interrupted. 'He must take his chance. It is a pity all the same. I maintain that. And it is not his way; it is her way – a very different thing! In my experience, Alfred, it is not the young men who take their own way; it is the young women. A woman sets her mind on marrying a man, and if she be bold enough and persistent enough, why she marries him. That old idea about men following their own choice in such matters is exploded nowadays.'

'Well, well,' said Mr Pearson, meditative, and partly assenting, recalling, perhaps, certain passages in his own courtship. 'Well, well.'

And while he pondered, a white fox terrier going by on the road ran up, and stopped to investigate the two figures leaning against the gate.

'Mr Massey must be going past; that is his dog,' Helen said. 'Remember not to mention this thing to him, Alfred. I dare say it will turn out better than we expect. In any case, we must be neighbourly and kind to him and to her.'

There was nothing in Mr Massey's manner to-night, Helen thought, to indicate the freshly accepted lover. He even appeared less cheerful than usual, and there was a kind of constraint in his manner. He came in at the Vicar's invitation, and took several turns up and down the drive between that gentleman and his sister; and Mr Pearson was very effusive in his friendship, and smoked one of Massey's cigarettes as he walked, and put a few more in his pocket, at the other's suggestion, for use on a future occasion. Helen, too, was very sweet and gracious, relieved from all fear of misconception now, and unconsciously trying to make up to the young man for the bad opinion she had formed of his matrimonial prospects. She was the chief talker as they paced the garden in the gathering dusk, the Vicar subsiding into silence as the surest safeguard from dangerous subjects, and Massey himself having apparently few subjects to start. The stars were beginning to show overhead while they loitered there, and among the darkening shrubs on each side of the drive, pale jonquils and narcissi, that Helen loved, showed star-like at their feet.

'How sweet those things are!' Massey said, breaking a short silence. 'What are they? – lilies?'

Helen stooped, and gathered one or two with the night-dews on them, and put them into his hand.

'They are not exactly lilies,' she said with a smile, 'but as beautiful. Just now they are my favourite flowers. Should you like some bulbs? I can spare you some if you would. Have you carried out the plans you spoke of in your garden, Mr Massey? I have not yet been to see, but Alfred will bring me some day, soon.'

'When?' Mr Massey demanded, with somewhat startling abruptness. 'I have waited a long time. When will you come? To-morrow?'

Here the Vicar interposed, and stated that he was going to the Wood Farm on business in the morning. Mr Massey had been appointed the parson's warden, and in this capacity was always receiving visits on 'business,' which as regularly was postponed.

'Very well,' Helen said. 'Then Perrie and I will call for you when we think your affairs are over. I will bring you some roots of my spring flowers, Mr Massey, if you really care to have them.'

CHAPTER XIV

In the Wood Farm Garden

MASTER PEREGRINE PEARSON'S education was conducted by his mother in a somewhat fitful and uncertain manner, in a manner, also, which caused the young student great bewilderment and most abundant sorrow. The morning on which Helen had fixed to take him to the Wood Farm proved to be one of those, to him, grievous occasions on which Mrs Pearson's maternal instincts directed her attention to the unsatisfactory state of Perrie's studies, rather than to the instruction of the larger sphere which it was her vocation to enlighten.

It was a flushed and woebegone little face, turned to Helen, as she appeared in the cheerless nursery, where the mysteries and the miseries of learning were being unfolded, and asked for the child's release, which was promptly refused.

'Then let Perrie say his lessons to me,' his auntie said, pitying the trembling lip. 'Come, Perrie, where's that round O, old man?'

But Mrs Pearson would not on this occasion allow her authority to be usurped.

'Leave him to me, Helen. It is you who spoil him,' she said. 'I will have no more of it. He is a bad and backward boy.'

At this impressive alliteration the small culprit shed silent tears on his book, and Helen remarked apologetically that he was at present but young.

'He was old enough to know every letter of the alphabet but one –W – the last time I heard him –'

'A fortnight ago,' was mildly interposed.

'And to-day he tries to make me believe that W is the only letter he knows. I will listen to no excuse. It is all through obstinacy and a spirit of wickedness. He will stay with me this morning until his lesson is perfect and his frame of mind improved.'

So Helen had to turn her back on the little patient figure, whose wistful eyes followed her to the door, while he called out the wrong letters wearily to his incensed parent. She began to wish that she had not given her word last night to go to Mr Massey's house; she had an odd distaste to the mission which she could not quite account for, and she was positively ashamed of the feeling of shyness which came over her as she put out her hand to open the Wood Farm gate. She had brought with her a basket of bulbs and roots, and suddenly deter-mining that she would not go to the house, she walked about the pretty overgrown garden awhile, and then, no one appearing, set to work to put out the plants she had brought for that purpose.

Presently, the front door opening, the Vicar and Massey appeared on the step. She heard their voices, and saw that they were unaware of her presence, they pacing the gravel sweep in front of the house, she keeping at work on the border surrounding the bowling-green at the side.

'Miss Smythe has forgotten her promise,' she heard Massey say; and yet she did not get up and come forward to show herself, as would have been both right and reasonable, but knelt on the grass, pressing the mould firmly with her gauntleted hand round a freshly inserted root.

For once the old proverb was belied, and this fortunate eavesdropper listened to a favourable report of herself, for –

'She will come,' said the Vicar confidently. 'If Helen says she'll do a thing, you may always look upon it as done. She is a woman, Massey, whose word, in the lightest matter, do you see, is her bond. You can always depend upon Helen.'

And then Helen, still on her knees, lifted her head and laughed, and both men turned and saw her.

'Here I am, you see!' she said, and looked very lovely, with that blush and half-embarrassed smile upon her face as she arose and smilingly refused Mr Massey's eagerly offered hand.

'I am not in a condition to shake hands,' she said, showing the gauntlet, with the soil of the garden all clinging to it. 'I have been sticking in those roots you wished for, Mr Massey; I could not find a trowel.'

'Set you grubbing in a garden, and you are happy,' said her brother-in-law, with a good-natured but somewhat contemptuous laugh. 'I have just to see Massey's shepherd about that dog of mine, Helen; I'll be back for you in a few minutes.'

'Oh, but do wait, Alfred,' Helen cried eagerly; 'wait for one minute, and I will go with you.'

But Mr Pearson, who, like all idle men, never had a minute to spare, refused to wait. He could be back, he said, before she had looked round Massey's garden. She was looking after his retreating form with a rather blank expression, when he suddenly turned back, and approached them again with a particularly knowing smile upon his face.

'You'll be very careful,' he said to Helen in a stage-whisper; 'very careful not to mention to Massey about that engagement we heard of yesterday. It is very important that it should be kept secret until it is found out.'

Then, with a chuckle of delight over his facetiousness, he departed.

Helen flushed hotly with annoyance and distress. She began to speak at random of the garden and the plants. She had still some to set. Could Mr Massey find her a trowel? Glancing at him as she put this question, she saw a face, ordinarily ruddy and pleasant to view, now white and wrathful. She faltered a little at the sight. Alfred had been guilty of bad taste, perhaps of impertinence; but, after all, there had been nothing to account for such a look as Massey wore. He was silent for a moment, staring gloomily down upon the grass at his feet; then, without raising his eyes, and in a voice altered and constrained –

'Was that some joke, perhaps, that Mr Pearson intended?' he asked. 'Was it a pleasantry that I was meant to share?'

'I cannot say,' she said lightly. 'You must ask himself, if you think it worth your while. I do not pretend to interpret Alfred's jokes.'

She turned from him, and began digging energetically in the damp mould with her hands again.

'Here, do wait one minute,' he said, rousing himself; then, with an effort, 'I will get you what you want.'

In a minute he had returned, bringing with him a huge spade.

'It seems my garden tools are deficient,' he said gloomily. 'This is all I can find. Now show me where to dig for you.'

But Helen laughed and declined his assistance, sticking the few remaining roots in the earth with haste and slight ceremony. It was embarrassing, she found, to have that silent man at her side, with his dismal face and abstracted air. She grew uneasy and annoyed, and fervently wished herself away. She arose from her knees, and, as she pulled the soiled gloves from her hands, glanced unwillingly in his face.

'One would imagine you were intending to dig a grave,' she said, with a little unusual irritability of tone, 'what with the size of your spade, and what with the gloom of your aspect.'

'Miss Smythe, will you be so very good-natured as to tell me of whose engagement Mr Pearson spoke just now?'

'You heard him particularly caution me not to tell you,' with a smile.

'But it appeared to me that I myself was involved in the joke. If I have anything to do with it, I should like to understand. Was it by any possibility of *my* engagement he spoke?'

She hesitated a moment, the colour rushing to her face.

'That was it,' he said, 'I see.'

With the strength of sudden passion he flung the heavy spade from him; it fell crashing among the branches of a laurel across the bowling-green, and he moved a couple of steps, and stood in front of Miss Smythe.

'You have heard that I am going to marry – Miss Freeman – is that it?'

He spoke in a tone that was simply troubled, but which sounded angry in Helen's ears, and which she resented.

'That is certainly what we heard,' she said, proudly lifting her head. 'I am sorry that my brother should have mentioned it, as I believe the news was told to him in confidence, but –'

'And you believed it?' he interrupted; 'believed that I was going to take that girl for my wife?'

'Believed it? Of course – why not? I am very pleased to believe it, and to congratulate you, Mr Massey – I hope –'

'Hush – for God's sake! You, at least, should have known better.'

He looked at her for a moment – at her haughtily carried head, at the proud indifference of her delicate face, at the hands hanging lightly locked in front of her – then he put out both of his and grasped her wrists.

'Did you believe it?' he repeated hoarsely, and bent his head closer to look into Helen's eyes. 'You surely did not – because I love you – and because I think you know it.'

'Mr Massey!' she cried, and drew back with a startled movement; but he only tightened his hold of her wrists.

'I love you – I love you – I love you!' he said wildly. 'Ah, Helen! let me say it! I love you so, my dear! my dear!'

'You must forget to whom you speak. You can't know what you say.'

Her voice had a touch of scorn, in spite of the tremble in it; her face had grown white, but was yet proudly held.

'I forget? I think of no one but you, and what I have said now I could have said with equal truth months ago – the second time I saw you.'

'Your saying it now is an insult to me – an insult; and – and –'

'Go on,' he said, and dropped her hands. 'An insult! – and what?'

'And a wrong to some one else.'

'To Miss Freeman, of course, you mean – and you are mistaken; but we will take the "insult" first. What do you mean by an "insult"? The feeling I have for you could be no insult if you were a queen. If you were an angel in heaven, I could not reverence you more than I have done. Where is the insult?'

'Where!' she cried, 'in every word you speak. Don't you know that it is so? – in every moment you keep me here against my will. Let me go, Mr Massey – I will go! Be kind enough to let me pass.'

'No,' he said, keeping his position doggedly in front of her – 'not yet. We have got to have this thing out now; and you have still got to tell me where the insult lies. I swear I do not know. Is it in my having thought of you in this way, from the first time I saw you (as God is in heaven, I believe I did, and that you knew it); or is it that I have had the boldness to tell you of it now? Have I bungled so terribly over what I had to say that the manner of it has offended you, or am I personally so hateful to you as to make the matter an impertinence? Is it –'

'You cannot really want me to tell you,' she interrupted; 'but since you compel me, I will. I do not understand how your mind can be so perverted nor your ideas of honour so hopelessly astray! I will ask you one question – just one. When you say all this to me – all this so uncalled for and so unwelcome – have you forgotten that you are at this moment engaged to marry another woman? Do you take me for Miss Freeman herself, or for whom do you take me, that you dare to trouble me with such – such nonsense? How do you dare to do it?' she cried, her face hotly flushed, her voice raised. 'I don't know how you dare to entrap me here against my will, to keep me prisoner, to force me to listen to such folly. In any case such words coming to me from you would be most – most objectionable. I could not, I never could, have given you the slightest encouragement to speak them; they would have been a liberty. Under the present circumstances they are, what I have said, an insult to me – and to you, a disgrace!'

All that sweet face of hers showed nothing now but anger and hurt pride; her whole frame was filled with indignation and a bitter sense of injury. The sight of his sudden pallor brought to her, who was always so pitiful, no pity as yet. He had lowered her self-respect. How could it be possible that one should have so misunderstood? He was false and contemptible and presumptuous: she would hurt him if she could.

'You are very severe,' he said; 'too severe, perhaps. Wait, I will let you go in one minute – have a little more patience with me. I see quite well that what I say will make no difference with you – no difference that I should care about; but wait. You are desperately hard on me; but I don't know that I am surprised. I have never been very hopeful as to my fate at your hands. I have loved you for what you are yourself, never for what you were to me. I do not alter for a few hard words; but you are a little too severe. I am under no obligation to any other woman. There is not, nor ever was, the least likelihood that I should marry Miss Freeman. It is my misfortune – my terrible misfortune – that I am so offensive in your eyes; but I am not disgraced.'

He moved aside from her path; but Helen stood irresolute, looking at him with startled, doubting eyes.

'What is it that you mean?' she asked. 'Such a mistake as that could not have arisen! Mrs Freeman – her own mother – said that it was so, and that you are to be married in two years. I have no right – I do not wish to interfere; but surely, surely she could not have *invented* such a tale as that!'

'Perhaps some one invented it for her,' he said, with bitterness. 'It is easy to see you think I am telling you what is untrue. Certainly, your opinion of me is not flattering.'

'I do not understand,' she said; 'nor should I desire to do so only that if I had really been misinformed, I would ask your pardon for certain words I just now used. I dare say, in any case, I ought to do so; it is not for me to judge you. I want to be hard, as you say, on no one. Only, Mr Massey, your conduct all along has led every person who witnessed it to imagine that you were – were intending to marry Miss Freeman. I have heard it noticed for months past on all sides, and it is evident – whatever you may say to the contrary – that the poor girl considers herself engaged to you. I do not want to be impertinent or to seem to interfere, but is not that the case?'

'She knows, at any rate, that I do not mean to marry her,' he answered, a little sullenly. 'There is no doubt on that point, I assure you.' Then, suddenly firing: 'How can I marry her,' he cried, 'when I tell you I love you? Let me tell you how it is. There is not much that I mind telling; and if there were, it could not give you a worse impression of me than you seem to have already.'

Then, in a few words, and bearing as lightly on the absent girl as was possible, he related the – to him – unfortunate case.

'You see,' he finished, 'I am bound to her in no way. If it had been possible that you could have listened to me, I should have held my conscience free from any atom of blame to her; as it is, I look upon the thing as a matter of no importance, and I have simply told you because you seemed to question my word. And now will you allow that I have offered you no insult? If you do not, I cannot help it. It will make no difference, because what I feel for you is past your control and past mine. Oh, you need not be afraid – I shall not pester you; in all probability, you will never hear it mentioned again. But for all that, I shall love you, I think, while I breathe.'

'Ah, I hope not,' she said, with sudden humility; 'I am sure not! That would be a horrible misfortune for you.'

'Why? Why a misfortune? You seem to me the sweetest and the loveliest woman I have known. It would be my misfortune if I did not love you. You like to influence people for their good, do you not – to convert miserable wretches to bliss and to light? You have thrown away a fine opportunity in me. You might have made anything you liked of me; I should have asked for no greater delight than to please you; I have always longed to follow where you led. Even now you shall be a conscience to me; I will do, as far as I can, what you think to be right – I will – even in this matter of which I have told you. Tell me what to do, and I will do it.'

'How can I?' she asked sadly. 'I do not know what is right. It has always seemed to me a cruel thing to awaken in a person's breast a hope that you fail to fulfil. You may not have been wholly to blame, but those poor people – it sickens me to think of them. The mother was so pleased and proud, she told my brother all her plans; the girl – it is easy to see that she – she –'

'She what?' he asked, coming a step nearer as she hesitated.

'That she loves you,' she said, the hot colour rushing into her face.

Something in her aspect startled Massey.

'Helen,' he said quickly, 'Helen, tell me once more – swear it to me, that if all this had not been, it still would have made no difference to you – that you could still, under no possible combination of circumstances, have been my wife. Say that to me once again.'

'I could not,' she said, lifting candid sorrowful eyes to his face. 'Pray believe there never could have been a chance of that – pray, Mr Massey, never think of that again.'

'Very well,' he said, with a desperate effort to speak carelessly, 'then that is over! That means "good-bye" to most that I'm good for, and to all that I care about.'

'Just for the moment,' she said, anxious to comfort him now. 'Men recover so easily from that kind of attack, I have heard. Soon you will laugh at it all.'

'Shall I? I think not; I don't feel like laughing now, and I don't know that I want to recover. But I don't mean to trouble you, and I shall try to pull myself together, of course, by-and-by. I've a notion, though, that it will be uncommonly stiff for me. I dare say I shall run up to town for a bit – things'll have to take care of themselves down here for a while. I hate the place – the cursed place! After that, no doubt I shall be all right, as you say, and shall settle down if you wish me; and marry Miss Freeman, too, if you think I ought – what does it matter? That's all over! Look, here comes Mr Pearson through the meadow; shall you wait for him, or will you go out this way, by the drive-gate?'

'Oh, this way, please,' she said, brushing the tears away from her eyes, knowing well it was on their account that it had appeared to him advisable she should not show her face to her brother-in-law just then.

They turned together and walked quickly, and in silence, down the short drive; but when they reached the gate and she put out her hand in farewell, he could see that the tears had gathered again.

'Good-bye,' he said; 'I am sorry to have grieved you – there is really nothing for you to regret.'

'I do regret it,' she answered with a half-sob. 'It is horrible to me to have caused you such trouble! And I misjudged you, and said some things of which I am ashamed. Forgive me, and try to forget it all. You can if you will – you must – you must, for my sake.'

'For your sake!' he repeated huskily; 'I would die for your sake if you would let me!' and he wrung her hand and left her.

CHAPTER XV

Massey Turns his Back on his Troubles

MR FREEMAN thrust out that nether lip of his that night in a manner which Massey thought simply repulsive, but the significance of which was quite plain to his wife and daughters, when he heard of the young man's intention to leave home for a few weeks. He gave no other token of disapproval, but his household knew as well as though he had uttered his thoughts that he was displeased. He took his pipe alone into his confidence, paying it more than customary attention during the remainder of Massey's visit, sucking at it noisily, looking down his nose at it with staring blue eyes, apparently engrossed with its eccentricities. Something had gone wrong with its interior arrangements to-night; a mysterious 'ruttling and rattling,' as Mrs Freeman called the guttural sounds, were emitted up and down the length of the stem.

'Please yourself,' he said, with contemptuous brevity, when his visitor, at length addressing him directly, waited for a reply. 'Please yourself.'

'Why, of course I shall do that,' the other said, with some irritation. 'I wasn't asking you about my plans, man, but about my crops. You needn't answer, however, if to do so is any trouble. I spoke for the sake of speaking.'

'Can't you give a civil answer, pa, to a civil question?' Pollie asked angrily, and Mr Freeman was half afraid of his daughter's anger; if she was against him, her mother was against him too, and even Mr Freeman was not anxious to make foes of his own household.

'My opinion ain't of much importance that I know of,' he said slowly, taking the noisy pipe from his mouth, and inspecting it as if it had been an unknown implement, and he were deeply interested in its construction. 'I ha' only had to do wi' the crops o' them that stay at home and look after 'em, and give 'em a chance.' Then he looked up at his wife, and gave the chuckle that awoke quite dangerous feelings in Mr Massey's breast. 'Crops are like sweethearts, eh!' he went on. 'They both want looking after.'

'And when Mr Massey wants advice about his sweetheart, he'll come to you, pa, no doubt,' said Pollie quickly, noticing that Massey, who was not in his usual good temper to-night, had flushed angrily at her father's words.

'Perhaps Teddie'll look round for you too sometimes, sir,' ventured Mrs Freeman, desirous, as her daughter, to cast oil on the troubled waters. 'You won't be away for very long, for sure, and 'tis but natural you should wish to see your mother again. You are goin' home, of course?'

'I shall no doubt see her before my return, but I don't intend to stop long in London,' he answered. 'I am due at several places first –shall not, I dare say, stay long anywhere. At any rate I hope to be back before my crops, at least, go seriously wrong. If you'll just have an eye to the men, my boy, I shall be vastly obliged to you.'

He had risen to leave, and he put his hand kindly on the hobble-de-hoy's shoulder as he spoke. The boy blushed and fidgeted in his chair, uncertain how to receive such a familiarity.

'All right!' he said in his bashful croak, looking uneasily at his father the while; 'I'll do it. I haven't much time to spare, though.'

'And about your letters, and where you're to be written to?' demanded Mrs Freeman anxiously, as he shook hands with her.

But he was determined, apparently, to render no account of himself. 'I'll leave all necessary directions with my housekeeper about my letters,' he said carelessly. 'Pray do not you trouble. All that is easily arranged.'

Mrs Freeman looked in silent dismay at her daughter – this was indeed a new-fangled style of love-making, was her thought. The young man was coolly holding out his hand to the girl. 'Good-bye, then, for the present,' he said, with unusual indifference of tone. But Pollie was equal to most occasions, and never was known to lose an opportunity through undue shyness.

'I'll come down the garden with you,' she volunteered now; and while he made his brief adieus to the male portion of her family, she snatched a scarlet and white woollen abomination off a horsehair chair, and threw it over her head. Before they had reached the door, Mr Freeman, having loudly cleared his throat, and emphatically spat into the fire to call attention to his remarks, thus addressed his son:

'There's one thing you'll do, if you take my advice, boy; before you meddle wi' Massey's men, you'll have that drunken rascal, Moore, discharged.'

'My man Moore?' asked Massey, stopping and looking round quickly. 'Why, pray?'

'Because,' said Freeman, still addressing his son, 'I 'on't have you takin' the r'sponsibility of the management o' this here farm while that tipsy, dangerous blackguard's mixed up in it. Mind that, boy! He's at the bottom of all the deviltry that go on in the parish. If I'd ha' had my way, I'd ha' had him starve before he should ha' had a chance o' playin' 's games agin. Them that ha' taken him on'll have to rue it, and let 'em; only you let 'em be!'

Massey looked for a minute at the speaker, as if he would have enjoyed to translate his sentiments towards him into actions, but he turned from him to the son, who sat stolidly staring into the fire, and said quietly, 'I don't think I shall discharge any of my men just yet, Teddie, so I won't trouble you. Good-night once more.'

In less than ten minutes Pollie was back into the parlour, and although she had pulled the antimacassar well over her face, and although she kept well out of the light of the lamp, it was easy to see she had been crying.

'I'm going to bed – I'm tired,' she said, giving her mother her good-night kiss, making her usual peck at her father's cheek, and pulling her brother's hair by way of parting salute.

When she had reached her room, and was about to lock her door, fearing the intrusion of her too inquiring mother, she heard her father's voice outside call 'Pollie,' in what was meant to be a whisper.

'Well,' she cried sharply, being rather startled. 'What ever do you want?'

'Open the door a minute.'

She obeyed, but kept the door in her hand, showing her face and figure through a very small aperture. 'What is it?'

'I'd ha' done with that feller if I was you,' Mr Freeman said, chucking his head backwards to denote the direction taken by the departed Massey.

'What d'ye mean?' Pollie cried angrily. 'What ever d'ye mean, father?'

'What I say. I can't talk to your mother about it – what's the use of a hape of fuss? and she'd make a hape. But you take my advice, and ha' done with him. He ain't my sort, and never was – a poor conceited fool that thinks he's doin' us a favour to talk o' marryin' you! Have no more to say to him, d'ye hear?'

'I hear fast enough,' Pollie said. 'You should have made your objections before. It's too late now.'

'You try him! Tell him you've changed your mind. 'Twill be a good day's work for you and he,' grimly; 'he'll get over it.'

'But you forget that I haven't changed my mind. I am perfectly satisfied. What have you against him, pray?'

'He ain't my sort.'

'No, he ain't,' Pollie admitted with alacrity, but inelegance. 'Anyone can see that when they look at him, and hear it when he speaks. But he's not the less *my* sort for that, remember, pa. I don't put down a man for useless because he wears well-made clothes, or for conceited because he knows a little how to behave.'

'You are as big a fool as your mother,' her father said, with rough contempt. He had always been comfortably sure in his own mind that his wife had reached the lowest depth of ignorance. When he wished to make himself particularly unpleasant to his children, it invariably occurred to him to compare them to the maternal parent – the force of ignominy could no farther go. 'I try to give you a word of advice, and you begin rating at me. D—n it! does it matter to me? Marry him, if you like, and curse the day you did it.'

He began to move away, but Pollie, who had a spice of the virago in her composition, followed him on to the landing.

'I shall marry him fast enough,' she called out, 'and glad of the chance. Glad, glad, to get away from here!'

'Oh, I dessay!' he said ironically. 'Then look here, you fool! I'll give you another word of advice. If you mean to have him, keep him at home after his business, instead of lettin' him make an ass of himself all over the county – the Lord knows where. See that he don't dangle half his time after the parson's sister, too. There's another hint for you, d—n you!'

Pollie was so unprepared for this outburst that she quite forgot the usual necessity upon her to get the last word, and so, glaring angrily at her from his light protruding eyes, and with a scornful snort which was intended for a satiric laugh, Mr Freeman began to descend the stair, and as he went he vigorously cursed and swore to himself below his breath; while, for the remainder of that evening, which he spent with his wife and son, there dropped, at intervals, from his lips disconnected words which might seriously have offended ears more polite.

The next morning, as Mr Massey drove himself to the station, he came upon Teddie Freeman, waiting for him by the side of the road.

'I only wanted to tell you,' the boy said, as he pulled up, 'that I'll have an eye to things for you while you're away.'

'Oh, thank you,' Massey said; 'but if it is against your father's wish –'

'That's no matter! We never wait for what father wish when he's in one of his minds. I'll look round every day or so for you. Likely enough father will, too – there's no knowing. And here,' blushing uncomfortably, 'here's a letter from Pollie I was to give you.'

'I'm hanged if that boy isn't the best of the lot,' Massey said to himself presently, as, having thrust the letter into one of his pockets, he drove off. It was wonderful how distasteful the rest of the Freeman family had become to him within two days. For several months he had received their hospitality, and been happy within their walls, had cheerfully given and received proofs of friendship, had never dreamt of complaining of the man's boorishness nor of his wife's presumption. Suddenly this was all changed. Both had shown signs of an extra interest in his movements, of a right to question his proceedings, and both were hateful. Even the tenderness he had felt for Pollie had utterly vanished at the first hint of his having to call her his own, and the lively pleasure hitherto experienced in their frequent meetings had given way to a feeling of utter weariness when he contemplated, ever so remotely, the possibility of his having to pass his life with her.

He put off opening her letter until he should be in a more humane frame of mind, waiting, perhaps, for the little thrill of lazy amusement which he had been wont to experience at sight of the not infrequent, although generally uncalled-for, epistles from the same hand. No amusement, however, would come, either in anticipation or at the moment of deciphering the letter, which proved to be chiefly a reiteration of the reproaches she had heaped upon him last night for his cruelty in leaving her; there was, besides, a highly incoherent account of the wrath with which her father had visited her on the previous night. He had said dreadful things to her, being surprised, no doubt, that Mr Massey had not spoken to him about his daughter. It was all terrible, terrible! but she would not complain; she would bear anything that Mr Massey thought she ought to bear; she was getting used to trouble through him. She had made use freely throughout of terms endearment, and she signed herself his 'Loving Pollie.' 'I do not like your Christian name,' she had also said. 'James is ugly and formal, and Jim is ugly and vulgar; Jamie, however, has a better sound – I think I shall call you Jamie.'

This last observation rankled in Massey's mind to the temporary effacement of more serious troubles. This, at least, he resolved to kick against. His life had become worthless to him in those days, he thought – things had altogether gone wrong with him somehow – the pleasant unconsciousness of his days, the peaceful slumber of his nights, had left him for ever. The only thing which appeared to him just now to be in the least worth the trouble of living was denied him. Wearisome entanglements had entrapped him, from which he lacked the energy to free himself – his soul was fast bound in misery and iron; he could not get forth; but this was the one thing he could not bear.

'Do what else you like with me,' he wrote off to her before he slept; 'I don't want trouble to come to you or to anybody through me, and what you think is required of me with regard to your father I dare say I shall do when I come home; but for heaven's sake do not call me "Jamie."'

The month that Mr Massey took in which to save himself from getting drivelling and stupid in his disappointment and misery seemed a dreary age to impatient little Pollie, and was an offence and an unheard-of imprudence in the eyes of her parents, who vaguely believed him to be wasting his time and his patrimony in all kinds of riotous living and debauchery. 'A man that would give no address wasn't proud of his whereabouts,' Mr Freeman shrewdly said, and became so glum and black at the mention of the young man's name, that it came to be a tabooed one in his presence; and poor Pollie, who had at last gained the prestige of an acknowledged lover, was duller and less happy, perhaps, than she had ever been in her life before. For even to her mother she could rarely talk of him, that good lady being used, at the first approach to the subject, to relieve her mind of some of the astonishment and uneasiness which did at all times grievously oppress it.

However, in spite of the plan of secrecy, the affair had got wind, and the young lady found some solace for the uncertainty of her prospects and the general discomfort of her position at home in the interest and the gossip she excited abroad. The good people who advised her and joked her, and envied her good-looking lover, need never know of the pains and the indignities which had been suffered in securing him; she took great care they should not guess he was not wholly secured even yet. Besides, was he not? On all sides people talked of the coming marriage; the confidence of the public impressed Pollie – her faith grew as people talked.

Meanwhile with Mr Massey those four weeks passed in anything but the orgies with which they were credited at Hilby. He never gave much account of himself during that period, nor perhaps, after the lapse of a little while, could he have detailed clearly how his time was spent. Through most of it, in all probability, he did not find himself abjectly wretched; before it had fully expired he began to tire of his uselessness, to think he would be less restless, less sick of himself at home.

At his mother's house, which he visited a few days before his return, he found a second letter awaiting him from Miss Freeman. It was with a queer mixture of feelings he opened it, for a month had pretty well elapsed since he had had tidings from Hilby. He ran his eye hastily over the commencement, noting, by the way, that he was her 'Dearest James' (he had never taken the trouble to post her in the fact that, to his intimates, for all his life he had been 'Jim'), and quickly skimmed the profusely scrawled terms of endearment and longings for his return which occupied one page. 'And Teddie says you ought to be at home now,' the second commenced, 'for everything is getting to sixes and sevens for want of you. The men are dissatisfied, and want more wages, of course; that's nothing new, you'll say. No one is going to give it round here, because we did not "drop" when other people did in the winter – so Teddie says, for I know nothing about it, and don't want to; but I heard them saying there'd be a row with them, and that if they mean striking, they'll do it now soon, when the hay has to be cut – it's the time the beasts always pick. What a set they are! Father says they'd take your last shilling, and so they would gladly; they are brutes, and your man Moore is the worst – he is the ringleader, and why you put up with him no one can think. There was one of those agitators – don't you call them? – speaking at the next village last week, and this precious Moore went over, and, Ted says, beat the agitator hollow. Father is always saying he ought to starve in a ditch, and so he would if you gave him up; and why ever don't you? You should have been here the other night; we had a teetotal meeting. Teddie and I went, just for the fun, and Mrs Pearson actually asked us to take the pledge! I call it an insult. I said I would when I felt like getting drunk; she soon let me alone. But the fun of the thing was with this very man Moore. Helen Smythe (have you forgotten that he is her great pet?) made a dead set at him. I verily believe the lecturer was got down on purpose. The wife had washed him up and put him on a clean jacket, while Helen, we suppose, brushed his hair, for he was quite painful to look upon, he was so smart. Well, his appearance was all right, but he went to sleep directly the lecture began; and he snored above Helen's harmonium when she played the hymns, and Mr Styles, the teetotaller, was nowhere in the noise beside him. And the best of it was, they couldn't wake him when 'twas over. But at the last, when man, woman, and child had all refused to give up the delights of tipsiness and had gone giggling away, they somehow managed to rouse up Mr Moore; and between his wife, who of course knew all about it, and whom he hided, Teddie says, afterwards, for being such a fool, and Helen, who, in spite of her being years older than me, is as innocent as a baby, they got him to the table; and there, if Ted and I hadn't waited, he'd have had to sign the pledge, but out of very shame they dared not do it before us. When he fell for the second time into the inkstand, the Rev. Mr Styles took back the pen out of his hand, and said sorrowfully to Helen, "Dear friend, the man is intoxicated." At this Teddie and I roared, so we had to rush away; but no doubt Helen and the parson lot all stopped and wept together. How any woman can make herself such a fool! There's a tale that the whole village is laughing at her watching Moore into the inn at the time of his first breaking out after his last pledge. She watched him in, and stood at the door and listened to some men who dared him to drink, and called him a sneak and a coward, and things worse. After he'd stood as much as he could of it, he called for some beer, and had the mug in his hand, when in stalked Miss Helen – the room full of half-tipsy men was nothing to her – and haled him out. Did you ever know such a fool as the man must have been to go for her? The others were all laughing and cheering to see him with his beer; but Helen had got her stately air on; she was born for a queen, according to her own ideas. "Tom Moore," she said, "I want you. Come with me!" He hadn't even tasted his beer, too. How ever had she the heart? But he had to go! It's a kind of byword now in the village, "Tom Moore, I want you. Come with me." I can show you the whole scene when you come home. Did you know that the old aunt is dead that has been wanted to die for ten years past, and Mrs Pearson and her sisters have come in at last to the money they've been looking out for so long? She died the night you left, and the whole family is now more important and more unbearable than ever. 'Tisn't much of a property after all, father says, to have such a fuss made about it, and there's several to divide it amongst; but ever so little is attractive, we know, and so let's hope that Helen will at last find the lover she has waited for so long. I see great signs of the Hall people looking her up. The second son is at home again now; he is a wicked little wretch, and our pious Miss Smythe has always shown great anxiety to convert him. I wish she'd convert him from staring at me!' And so on and on the letter ran.

But Massey's heart seemed suddenly to contract with pain as he read these last few sentences. 'She won't do that,' he said, half aloud; 'I know that she could never do that!' But if it were his disbelief in Miss Smythe's power of converting Captain Back he was announcing, this history doth not say. After a time he turned back to the letter, and re-read all that part of it relating to Helen, carefully omitting, however, the disturbing introduction of Captain Back's name and of the girl's accession of fortune. When he had thoroughly mastered those parts which appeared to him most interesting, and had put the letter away in his pocket, he folded his arms on the table at which he sat, put down his head upon them, and let his thoughts run riot on a theme they loved. He clenched his hands and held his breath as he conjured up before his mental vision a scene which Pollie had, not very graphically, portrayed. But, unfortunately, the humorous side of the situation, which alone had been discerned by Pollie, did not present itself to him at all (he was so hopelessly deep in love that the thought of impropriety on Helen's part in thus obtruding herself, where women are neither wanted nor respected, did not for a moment occur to him); but he set his teeth hard and felt the blood rush to his face as he pictured her, fearless and unprotected, among that hostile irreverent crew. 'If I were an artist, I would paint her so,' he thought by-and-by; 'that pure proud face of hers among those grinning devils! – my darling! my darling! my angel among women!' and so on, moaning and sighing in weak and boyish fashion over the hardness of his case and the depth of his hopeless love.

A few days more, and he was at home again, and Pollie was happy in that as yet he made no effort to escape from his toils. She enlarged to her heart's content on the various subjects touched on in her letter; but had little new to add, except that Miss Smythe had that week left the Vicarage to stay with the young ladies of the Hall.

The family was in London now, and Helen had gone to finish the season with them.

CHAPTER XVI

The Strike

A MONTH has gone by since James Massey's return to Hilby, home, and duty. The hedges that were white with May then are sweet now with briar-roses and honeysuckle; the meadow-grass is half-way to the knee; the scent of the clover, in fields ready for the hay-cutting, is heavy on the summer air. June has come, and has brought with her much annoyance and unpleasantness to the tenant of the Wood Farm.

One evening, when Massey paid his labourers their weekly earnings, they had each, as they came one by one into his little office, quietly and in respectful terms, asked for an increase of wage.

'I wish I could have given the poor devils a shilling a week more,' their master said to himself, leaning back in his chair, when the last man had left him. 'If I had only myself to think of! But I gave my word to Freeman. After all, thirteen shillings a week isn't much of a sum; queer work to live and bring up big families on that screw! Freeman would cut them down to six shillings if he dared. I half wish I had not promised him. It's devilish hot for outdoor work at that pay.'

The little overcrowded room, in which Mr Massey contracted his business, kept his guns, his boots, his books, all the untidy numerous trappings of bachelor country-life, was close and stifling. He leant his head through the honeysuckle-bound lattice, and found to his surprise that the men had not dispersed, but were still hanging about the gateway at the back of the house. Several of them were listening to Moore, declaiming with much energy in the middle of the roadway; and several, leaning with their backs against just anything that afforded support, devoted their energies to nothing beyond the study of scientific lazing.

Massey drew his head in quickly, and executed for his own edification a long and noiseless whistle.

'That means mischief!' he said to himself. 'That fool Moore! I would have kept the fellow straight if I could.' Here a big sigh was breathed through the room, whether of grief for Moore's delinquencies or of sad remembrance of one other person, for whose sake the man was of more importance to the master than he, Moore, would have thought possible even for his own, need not be said.

'Please, sir, the men wish to speak to you,' said presently a servant, appearing at the door.

'Tell them to come in, then, one at a time,' said the master promptly; for he understood his men well enough to know that singly they would be reasonable and deferential – collectively, irrational and lamentably hostile. The men were unconsciously aware of this themselves, perhaps, for they would not risk a *tête-à-tête*. Then Massey arose, and went among them.

'Tom Moore, I want to speak to you,' he called, as he approached them; 'you others clear off home. I have said to you all I mean to say to-night. If you are not satisfied with me and my pay, go elsewhere; that is what I mean. I prefer you to stay with me, of course; but equally of course you will please yourselves. If you can get better wages, I shall not grumble at your leaving me; only don't throw yourselves out of work under the impression that I shall give way. I am no more likely to do it than that wall against which you are leaning. Good-night, my men!'

He waited in silence while the men, having looked at each other without expression, spat in an unemotional fashion on the ground, and having, with great apparent effort, slowly rolled their shoulders off the wall, at length, with much deliberation, sauntered off. When they were out of earshot, their master turned to the only one remaining – a dark, wiry, undersized man, with patches of scrubby iron-grey hair about his mouth and chin, having the effect of making his face look dirty rather than adorning it. He had bright, rather fierce eyes; and there was a general air of alertness about him, absent in his comrades.

'I only want to speak one word to you in warning, Tom Moore,' Massey said, standing bare-headed, his hands in his pockets, looking down upon the man: 'Do you pull up, my man, before it is too late! Mind you, I know quite well whom I have to thank for sullenness and dissatisfaction among my men. I have already put up with a good deal from you, for reasons with which you have nothing to do; but don't make a mistake, and go too far. At the first serious trouble with my men I pack you off home, and you never touch another shilling of mine! You know best if that is of much importance to you; if it is, why, I advise you to be careful. That is all.'

'I give you honest work for your money,' the man said quickly, his small, dark eyes blazing into the other's face.

'If you want to hear the truth, you are a dissatisfied, mischief-making hound! If I had consulted my own interests, I would have sent you to the right-about months ago.'

'Ah! why not?' the small man cried. 'Let my wife and children starve! What is it to you and the likes o' you, that murder women and child'en with cold and hunger, that grow rich while we that 'arn your money are dyin' for want, wi' our child'en's bellies goin' empty, that you may stuff and grow fat? Why not turn me orf? I wonder you aren't done it long before this.'

'I wonder I haven't; but I can't help thinking it's rather a good thing for you, do you know. Another good thing is that I don't mean to turn you off, if you'll exercise the commonest discretion. And – shut up, Moore! I want none of your rant, thank you; keep it for the public-house or the labourers' meeting, where your eloquence comes out so well. Ask your wife which has been her best friend – you that have beaten her, and have done your best to starve her, while you have spent your money – the devil knows how! – or I, that have at least kept her and her children in bread. And mind you, 'tisn't for your sake I have done this, my man – as far as you yourself are concerned, I have always considered the muddiest ditch too good for you – or even for your wife's sake, much as I pity her. I should think –' he said, suddenly breaking off, the blood rushing hotly to his face – 'I should think there is one face into which you, with all your insolent ignorance, will be ashamed to look. Do you know that it is through her that you have had a chance to become a man among men once more? – that she has interceded for you as angels – perhaps, I don't know – intercede for devils? that to the best of her ability, she, knowing so little how to deal with vermin such as you – she has thought for you, worked for you, prayed for you – great God! – and what is her reward – what is it to be? She tried to save you, soul and body, by keeping you away from that which ruined you; and you have damned them – soul and body – fifty times deep, by taking her name in derision into your filthy mouth, and by cursing and blaspheming to your vile companions over what was too holy for your lips to soil. I heard you!' he said, dropping his voice as if ashamed of the moment's excitement which had whitened his lips – 'I heard you – you did for yourself that day with me, my man!'

'You mean the teetotalling business!' said Moore, with an oath. Whatever else the little man was, he was no coward – he stood in not the slightest awe of his master. He gave a scornful laugh now, spat on the ground to emphasize his contempt, and drew the back of his hand across his mouth. 'I give that d–d consarn a trial,' he said; 'I did – my ole woman 'll tell ye – but d—! I'd sooner be dead. You with your gin, and your wine, and your drinks onlimited – you try it! – see if you wouldn't sooner be dead! Give it up for a single day – darn me! – and see how ye'd feel.'

'I'm not in the habit of making a beast of myself,' Massey said. 'Therefore there is no need for me to give it up. No one wants to deprive you or anyone else of drink while you drink in reason.'

'I give it a fair trial. I kep' my word while life was left in me – till my missus, she said, "Send for a drop of brandy," she said, "for the sake o' yer inside." And if I hadn't a took and sent, a dead man I should ha' bin! No one can't say I hain't gi'n it a fair trial – and to come baitin' and badgerin' a chap and a huntin' him up, and a watchin' of him night and day – d—n me! if 'tain't like to make a man worse an' he would be – and tha's why I up and spoke to the men. I ain't a word agin the young woman; she done her best, and done her duty; but when t'other come a pokin', and a pryin', and a sendin' a chap tracts, 'tis enough to turn the stomach o' the honestest man. I'm bad, I dessay, but I'm much about what I was born to, same as she is, and there ain't no help for neither of us to be no differs – on'y if I'm i' the bad way they make out, and there ain't no hope for me unless I give up what keep life in me, I 'on't give it up – I can't give it up – then – darn it – let me be!'

'With all my heart! Only remember that while you kept from the public-house – at whatever pain to yourself – you were a respectable man, doing your work intelligently and well. However you may have suffered, your wife and children prospered. Since you have gone back to your old ways, your children would starve if left to you. Your wife – how did she get that black eye, Moore? You stint the labour of your hands to work with your tongue, and it is only evil that you work. You have been very successful in agitating this parish and those around, I hear; look out that the result is not disastrous to you.'

'And you look out, Mr Massey,' the man said derisively, as his master turned away. 'What's an extra shillin' a week to you, rollin' in plenty wi' your d—d old uncle's savin's – pinched out o' us – at your back? Gin us what we ask on yer, before 'tis too late.'

'I should not give you a farthing extra now,' Massey said, stopping and looking back at him, 'to save you from the hanging you deserve. As to the other men, Mr Freeman and I have agreed as to what is reasonable, and we shall of course abide by our decision.'

'Him!' the man cried savagely. 'Him! A trumpery beggar! He's a fine 'un to agree with! He'll throw yer over as soon as look at yer; mark my words.' And with many more oaths – whether directed at himself or at Mr Freeman, Massey neither knew nor cared – Miss Smythe's interesting *protégé* took himself off.

The next morning when Dunn, the steward – who had worked on the farm man and boy for thirty years – came to call his master, he had a disturbing tale to tell.

'Five o'clock, sir,' he began as usual, knocking at the bedroom door loud enough to wake the dead.

'All right!' sleepily from within. 'Sort of morning?'

'Fine morning, sir.'

'All right! You know about everything, Dunn?' Dunn having taken orders as to this morning's operations overnight.

'Yes, sir.'

'All right!' And Massey shut his eyes upon the sunlight streaming in at his open window, and turned round on his pillow to resume his interrupted dreams. In vain! Another terrific knocking at his door. 'Well?' sharply, lifting up his head. ('What the devil does the fool want now?')

'Please, sir, there ain't none o' the men come to work.'

'None come? Why, what is it? Five o'clock? What makes them all late?'

'They aren't comin' not at all, sir.'

'Not coming!' Massey sat up in bed now, his sleepiness all gone. 'Indeed! No one here?'

'Only three boys, sir, and Solomon.'

'All right!' said Massey again. Then pulling himself together, 'Set the boys to feed the stock, and tell Solomon to look after the horses. I'll be down in ten minutes, Dunn.'

'Yes, sir.'

'He's a cool 'un,' Dunn said to himself as he stumped heavily downstairs, and he felt some mild astonishment, notwithstanding that he himself was a person to take things philosophically. 'Lord! how my old master would have swore!' he could not help reflecting.

But although Mr Massey displayed much outward calmness, it is certain that inwardly he was most seriously perplexed. His hay was waiting to be cut; he was to have begun that very day. 'It's a pretty mess!' he told himself, with much perplexity and apprehension, as he hurried over his toilet that morning. It hurt him, too – over and above the inconvenience and loss it would cause – that he should have got wrong with his men. He knew that he had been a good master to them; that his justice had ever been tempered with mercy. In case of sickness or trouble, in case of wrong-doing even, he had stood their friend. He had listened to Mr Freeman's account of the ingratitude and the viciousness of the race, and had heard him exult when, as pretty often happened, that gentleman had got the better of them in any matter. But although he had never attempted to alter his neighbour's feeling, he himself had not gone heartily with him, and had for his own part endeavoured honestly to secure his labourers' welfare, partly because it was his nature to be generous and kindly, partly that he did eagerly covet the approbation of one who was always the poor people's champion and friend. This catastrophe was therefore a great shock and an immense disappointment to him, besides being so disastrous in a more material way.

As soon as his early breakfast was finished, he started to drive down to Mr Freeman's, thinking, with some misgiving, that it would probably be anything but a pleasant time that he would have there.

'It'll all be put to the credit of that confounded Moore,' he said. 'Freeman'll show me how right he always was about him; and, confound him! he is so unbearable when he is right.'

'The men are at work again down to Freeman's,' Dunn said to him, standing at the horse's head and smoothing its mane as he spoke, while his master jumped into his dog-cart.

'Oh, have they come back?' Massey inquired, in a somewhat triumphant voice. 'I'm glad to hear some of them, at any rate, have come to their senses.'

'Yourn'll be back, sir, when you like, on the same terms,' the man said; 'and 'tis certain the hay must be seen to. Mr Freeman he gin the men what they asked; and it is better so 'an ruinin' hisself for sake of his word.'

'That'll do, Dunn. Let go his head. Are you dissatisfied with me and my pay, Dunn?'

'No, sir,' said Dunn, who as a matter of fact was not subject to the fluctuations of the other men's pay, and was very well off indeed; 'you ha' allus dealt fair by me, an' I'll deal fair by you.'

'That's right, my man,' the other said, restraining his fidgety horse and experiencing some comfort in even this amount of fidelity. 'Those that stick to me 'll come to no harm; but as for these other rascals, I wouldn't take one of them back now, not if he'd come for nothing. You understand that, Dunn? I shall manage all right, no doubt; but I'd sooner see every bit of hay rot on the ground than owe the gathering of it to them. And, Dunn, don't you take in that tale about Mr Freeman. We agreed together, and we shall stand together, of course. Stand away!' And Mr Massey was off, driving briskly through the sweet country roads that morning, with a mind too preoccupied to heed their sweetness. Although he had spoken so confidently to his man but now, he was far from feeling faith in his own words, and he knew quite well that it was more than probable his neighbour had thrown him overboard. 'It will be a contemptible trick,' he said to himself; 'but what can one expect?' Presently in a field close at hand he heard the pleasant click-clack of the mower at work, and, looking over the hedge, saw that at least some of Mr Freeman's labourers had returned to their allegiance and their hay-cutting. 'The beggar has sold me, sure enough,' Massey said, 'but I'll make him tell me so with his own lips; not that he has either grace or sense to be ashamed of such trickery.' He stood up in his cart and shouted to the men, 'Where is your master?' One of them pointed silently in the direction of the house, and Massey drove off to seek him there.

'I'll make it unpleasant for him, if I can,' the young man said, with tightened lips, as he pulled up at the Grange gate.

A lad came forward to take his horse, but knew nothing of his master (who, if the truth must be told, having seen Massey's approach, was hiding in his bedroom out of his visitor's way); and Massey having poked about the premises ineffectually, at last attacked the house. The servants could not tell where their mistress was, unless she was gathering gooseberries in the kitchen-garden; their master had been out since eight o'clock, and Miss Pollie was having breakfast in the dining-room.

'Breakfast!' Massey said to himself with some surprise, making his way towards his fiancée's locality. As he passed up the long passage leading from kitchen to dining-room, his ear was greeted with a shout of laughter, which subsided into an ill-suppressed titter before he reached the door. At the sound, Mr Massey recalled at once what had, in the worry of more personal matters, escaped his memory till now – the fact that the much-talked-of London cousin had been expected down the night before for his annual holiday, and it was at once apparent that it was for his benefit breakfast was kept about at such unseemly hours, and by his accustomed witticisms that Miss Pollie was in the act of being thus enlivened. Massey paused a moment at the door, hesitating in his present state of mind to enter. There was a noise as of two persons tearing round the room, of a chair being knocked over, of Pollie's shrill laughter. As he opened the door, unheard in the general commotion, the chase apparently ended, and Pollie took refuge in a corner. There she stood, exhausted with laughing and running, brandishing in her hand the hot teapot, with which effectual weapon she defended herself from the too near approach of a young man hovering by – a young man, short of stature and slight of build, on whose pale, unhealthy face pimples did more plentifully thrive than either whisker or moustache – a young man attired in dark trousers and a long, shiny, black frock-coat, whose feet were thrust into gorgeous slippers of violet and gold, and whose lank hair was adorned with smoking-cap and long tassel of the same colours.

'Oh, Arthur, let me go!' Pollie cried to him. 'As sure as I'm living, I'll pour the scalding water on to you if you come a step nearer!'

But before Arthur had time to reply they both became aware of the intruder, and Pollie blushed very much and looked at once exceedingly foolish and exceedingly pretty.

'Good-morning, Pollie,' Massey said gravely, and with no lightening of his gloomy face. 'You are merry this morning, it seems.'

'You frightened me out of my wits,' Pollie said with a little gasp. 'Arthur is so silly, he has made me quite out of breath.' Then, still holding the teapot, she looked from one to the other of the young men. 'Mr Gosling – Mr Massey,' she said, awkwardly introducing them.

Mr Gosling, whose vocation, apparently, it was to be funny on all occasions, put his hand up to the back of his neck and ducked his head in a spasmodic bow.

'I'm afraid I interrupted your – your breakfast,' Massey said, eyeing the young man with unconscious severity. 'Pollie, you were about to pour out your cousin's tea – pray go on. Does he prefer it straight from the pot without the usual medium of a cup? I came in to look for your father.'

'Father's been out this two hours,' Pollie said. 'We are late this morning, because Arthur didn't come till eleven o'clock last night, and he was tired.'

'Used to early hours, you see, sir,' Mr Gosling explained, with a knowing wink. 'Always in bed at home at eight o'clock. Mamma removes my candle punctually at half-past.'

'Pray don't be so stupid, Arthur,' Pollie said, making violent efforts not to giggle.

'There's been some difficulty with the men this morning, Pollie. Your father expected it, I think. Have you heard anything about it?'

'Oh yes, they struck – beasts! aren't they? Of course, with the hay about, father had to give in to them; but he'll be even with them yet, you'll see. Wait till the winter comes, when they're at his mercy! Are yours all right?'

'No; I didn't give in to mine.'

'Oh, but why not? Do!' Pollie cried, quite shocked. 'Why, what ever will you do else?'

'I don't quite know. I shall do without them, at any rate.'

'Well, pa isn't so foolish as that – to go and half ruin hisself just for his mind's sake!'

'Nor yet for his word's sake, it seems,' Massey said, somewhat bitterly. 'Perhaps you don't remember that it was at his request I refused to raise my men's wages a week or so ago, when they first asked for it. It was a kind of favour to him. I did not care much about it one way or the other; but we were to stick together – he and I! He might, at least, have let me know he meant to cave in so utterly.'

'Hanged if I would!' said Mr Gosling with spirit. 'Blame the hay! I'd see it rot before I'd knock under to such a set of beggars! Hang it all, a man must show a little pluck sometimes, even if it costs him money!'

'Oh, there's no accounting for father,' said Pollie, quite willing to deliver her parent up to justice now that she saw the weight of opinion was against him. 'He isn't like anybody else, you know.'

'Thank Heaven!' devoutly ejaculated Massey below his breath. 'I should like to have seen Mr Freeman, to hear him explain matters a bit,' he went on aloud; 'but I must wait no longer. I shall have to drive about all the morning, I suppose, to try to knock up hands. Perhaps you'll ask your father to make it convenient to see me this evening when I come in, Pollie.'

'Oh, James!' Pollie cried, noting the grimness of his tone. 'You surely aren't going to make a scene, and quarrel with pa?'

'What makes you fear I shall do that?'

'Oh, I know you're going to, James; and what ever shall I do then?'

The young man was standing leaning over an empty chair by the breakfast-table, and there was a certain air of unsmiling resolution about his aspect which was not very reassuring. Pollie was really anxious. She went and sat herself down in the chair, and put her hand on his arms, crossed over the back.

'James, promise me you won't get wrong with pa,' she begged.

Mr Massey slowly brought his eyes from their rapt gaze out of an opposite window to settle on her face.

'Here wait one minute,' said the London visitor, and with ostentatious hurry he sprang out of his seat at table and flew to the window. 'Pray do not consider me for the moment,' he said, waving his hand benevolently in their direction without turning his head. 'I am a nothing, a nonentity, a nought, a cipher! Pray go on! From this window I get a view of a most interesting creature, hitherto but imperfectly studied by me. It is – yes – I think I am correct in stating that it is a cow. I am engaged in improving many hitherto-neglected opportunities by a careful inspection of this truly exciting animal. Mr Massey – Pollie, my dear, bless you! carry on as if I was in London!'

By the time he had finished this speech, gazing conscientiously the while at the animal, Massey was by his side, holding out his hand.

'I will bid you good-morning, Mr Gosling,' he said gravely. 'I am rather hurried just now, and must ask you for your impressions of the bullock under inspection at some future time.'

'And so that's the young man, is it, Pollie?' Mr Gosling inquired of his cousin when they were again alone. 'And it's for *him* you won't give yours truly the cousinly kiss you have never denied him before. Is it bashfulness, now, or is it 'ortiness that he wouldn't give his girl a kiss with another fellow lookin' out of window? If it's bashfulness, I pity him – but these country bumpkins are all alike for it. You never see that lay up in town. If it's only 'ortiness – why, there's two can play at that game, and yours truly can be 'orty too.'

CHAPTER XVII

In the Hayfield

THE parish of Hilby, as the days went on, gleaned much enjoyment from the strike among Mr Massey's men, and gained also something of importance thereby.

It was the first time such an event had occurred in that village; it was something to find it could now hold its own in this respect against neighbouring parishes. The men themselves hung sullenly about at first, not knowing how to dispose of themselves in their unaccustomed idleness, too much out of gear even to work in their own gardens, and keeping themselves as much as possible out of tongue-reach of their wives, who, one and all, were antagonistic to the movement. But at the end of the first week, when the union delegate came down in state, and paid every man his money, publicly, on Hilby Green, a change came over the demeanour of both husbands and wives. The latter, for the most part too shrewd to approve – for was it not out of nature that Bill and Bob should receive money unearned by the sweat of their brow? – still, for the present, lost their ground of complaint, and bided their time; while the former, the heroes of the hour, were triumphant in every way.

A glowing account of this gallant resistance to oppression was given in the *Labourer's Friend*, the local union paper. The strikers were invited to Rockby, a neighbouring parish, to address the sufferers there – the down-trodden, broken-spirited, ill-advised sufferers, toiling at the wages these more valiant ones had refused. Tom Moore, among those who accepted this invitation, distinguished himself so well in his character of orator, and was so generously treated by sympathetic auditors, that he subsequently returned to Hilby in a state of helpless drunkenness, in which condition he managed to maintain himself for a very considerable time. The occasion grew so festive that some of the younger men, moved to adorn their persons in accordance with the joviality of their circumstances, trimmed their hats with ribbons, and tied coloured sashes about their persons, while one of musical tastes brought his concertina into operation, and played indefatigably 'The Blue Bells of Scotland,' with never a pause but for sleep and refreshment. One of the village innkeepers, who was also Mr Massey's blacksmith, was perforce inimical to the strike, but the other was so exceedingly friendly, and his house so well frequented at all hours, that it followed the money so easily earned was very easily spent. Many enjoyable hours were passed in the little sanded kitchen, reeking of beer and smoke, or on the bit of green, open to the road, by the side of the White Hart inn; but apparently the greatest satisfaction, after all, was to be derived from hanging over hedges and gates from whence their late master could be descried with the one or two men he could muster, and the two or three boys who were left to him at work in his fields.

The weather was very hot, the hay made quickly, and probably Mr Massey had never worked so much before in his life as he did during those few weeks when he learnt by experience the wide difference between master and man. Instead of riding into his hay-field in cool and comfortable attire, walking his horse two or three times over the field, shouting to a man to strew the hay again here, or calling for a wagon to be sent forward there, finding a little fault, giving a little encouragement, ordering a great deal of beer, here he was working as if for dear life, under the burning mid-day sun, his face and neck burnt to a copper colour in its beams, his coat and waistcoat thrown upon the fence, the handkerchief loosened at his throat, his hair clinging damp and matted to his head, his mouth and throat nearly always parched with thirst. No wonder he was a pleasing sight to his late servants. He took no notice as they leaned there, and he never gave them the gratification of seeing him anything but cheerful and good-tempered, however much the reverse of either he was feeling. On all sides it was said that the young man was a 'good-woolled 'un,' and it was put down to his credit that he never complained.

In the middle of the morning, Pollie, generally accompanied by Arthur, the cousin, would bring him some lunch, and the men would cease to see the fun of the spectacle, and would return to their public-house when that substantial and usually (thanks to the cousin) noisy meal began. In the evenings, too, Mr Massey's staff would be strongly augmented. Teddie Freeman would come and lend a hand, working for a couple of hours like ten men; the young man from the village shop would put in an appearance, as would also the friendly innkeeper and his blacksmith son. Be sure James Massey knew how to treat these good friends of his so as to retain their services; and to some of them it was, after all, a pleasant time. It was good fun to see Miss Pollie trying to use the 'toppling' machine; the young blacksmith did not complain, even although he had to stand idle while she made her futile efforts. The gent from London – he was a funny one, too – to see him giving out the beer was as good as a play. Altogether there were several in Hilby who would remember the strike at 'Massey's,' and those long, pleasant evenings, for some time to come.

The refreshing evening, however, is a long way off as yet; it is scarcely noon, and sultry hot. There is a storm coming before night, Massey thinks, and looks often anxiously towards the west, where the clouds are banking up. The hay is in splendid condition; he wants to get this field clear to-night. Several of his whilom labourers are, as usual, looking on, lounging against the gate or lying under the hedge; the smell of the malodorous, bad tobacco they are smoking cannot reach Massey where he works in the middle of the big, shadowless field, nor can their coarse remarks, nor their vacant laughter; but their presence is an offence to him, nevertheless, and he does not often turn his eyes in their direction. He is not aware, therefore, that a diversion has occurred for them – that himself and his exertions are not for the moment their first object of interest. They, still lazily lying and lounging about, have turned their heads to look down the road which curves a few hundred yards from them and leads to the Hall. A sound as of the hoofs of several horses in full gallop is heard, and presently turning the corner of the road, there appears a cavalcade of several ladies, a gentleman, and a groom.

'What, are they come back?' one of the men asks somewhat unnecessarily, seeing 'they' are before his eyes.

'Last night,' replies another, calmly expectorating, 'my missus was sent for up to the Hall to help the servants to-day.'

'Who's the t'other one? the woman behind with the captain?'

'What, ha' yer lost yer eyesight, Bill? The parson's sister, by the look on her. She ha' som'at better to do now that she ha' some money of 'r own to spend, than lookin' after the "parson's work."'

'She's lookin' after the capten's work now, I s'pose. 'Tan't much good none of us 'll have of her money, that have as good a right to it as she.'

'I'm derned if I'm going to wait here to be preached to by her,' one of them who had somewhat of an uneasy conscience said, moving off.

Miss Smythe's acquaintance with the class had been too deep for her to have been surprised even could she have heard these remarks, and her charity was too simply the result of love and pity for her to be in the least degree influenced by such injustice. The time for anger and sorrow that so little success was accorded to her honest efforts, that worse than nothing was always given back to her who most willingly bestowed her all, had passed away long ago. 'Blessed is he who expecteth little,' had unconsciously to herself been her motto for years. She looked sadly after the men who lounged off now at her approach, and nodded without a word to those still remaining, as she and her companions drew rein at the gate of the hayfield.

'He's getting on all right, you see,' Captain Back said to her, pointing with his whip to where the loaded wagon stood, and looking round at the half-carted field. 'Plenty of help he's found up, no doubt, without these lazy beggars' (in a louder tone this, and with a contemptuous glance at the two or three men smoking at his feet). 'Where is Massey, I wonder?' he went on; 'did you say you would like to speak to him?'

'I think I can see Mr Massey over there,' Helen said, flushing a little, and nodding her head towards the group by the wagon.

'Shall we go in, then? You girls,' to his sisters, 'had better ride on a bit; Miss Smythe and I will overtake you in a minute or so. Now then, my men, roll your lazy carcases out of the way, if you please, and let this lady pass. Open the gate, one of you – look sharp about it – and then go hang yourselves for useless cumberers of the earth, as you are.'

Helen laughed as the men, having sullenly obeyed, rode in.

'It's well your father is so generous with his soup-kitchen!' she said. 'There's not one of them who would not have said some rough things to you but for a timely remembrance of that.'

'Not before you, surely? I should look to you, who have been a sort of ministering angel among them, to protect me.'

She shook her head.

'What I have done has only made me unpopular. I have had hitherto, you must remember, only advice and no money to give away. Even you, you know, have not been so grateful as you might have been for my advice.'

'Oh, I have,' he said; 'you'll see a fine result some day if you will only concentrate your efforts. But there is something so decidedly discouraging in your benevolence – it is so aggravatingly universal – that is what I complain of. If I could once get myself to believe that you had any interest in my especial reformation, Helen, you'd find what a model young man I'd be.'

'But after all, I don't know that you are so very bad,' she said, laughing. 'You have a rather high opinion of yourself, certainly; but seeing you are of the male gender, I shall not expect to alter that. You are somewhat offensively contemptuous of the rest of the world, but I suppose you have something within which tells you you are superior to the rest of the world. You have a reprehensible propensity for attempting what you would call a flirtation in every quarter, whether encouraged or not, endeavouring to make conquests of women's tender hearts in every direction; but I don't know, after all, if you do much harm. Lastly, you have forgotten, for the fiftieth time, that to you my name is "Miss Smythe," and not "Helen." With these exceptions, I see nothing vicious in you.'

'Thank you! You think me a conceited ass, I know. Perhaps you might think me otherwise if you cared. I know you could make me better if you tried. And as to your name, I think of you as Helen, I dream of you as Helen, I will call you Helen a million times before I die.'

'Hush! we will settle all that afterwards. Do you know Mr Massey, or shall I introduce you?'

'I have spoken to him, I believe, but I don't see him here.'

'This is he,' said Helen, bowing towards a man who ceased his occupation of pitching hay at their approach. A man whose coloured shirt was open at the throat, and rolled up at the sleeves; whose face, and neck, and arms were bronzed by the sun; whose close-cut, curly hair clung damp and dishevelled to his forehead. He lifted the peaked linen cap he wore, and came a step or two forward.

'He is an uncommonly good-looking young fellow,' Captain Back said, looking with admiration at the strong well-built figure and noticing the carriage, he himself being a rather small man of particularly neat and trim appearance. 'He should throw over this concern and go into the army.'

Before Helen could answer this suggestion, she was leaning forward and holding out her hand to Mr Massey.

'I am not fit to touch you, Miss Smythe,' he said, glancing at his brown, work-soiled hand; but he put it forth and grasped hers nevertheless. Then Helen mentioned her companion's name, and the two men lifted caps to each other.

'I'd sooner kick that little conceited beggar than shake hands with him,' Massey said to himself, and the other no doubt congratulated himself warmly upon escaping such contact for his own well-cultivated fingers.

'You have been having an unpleasant time of it, Mr Massey,' he said. 'What a set these labourers are! An ungrateful, idle lot of rascals! What is it they would have, I wonder?'

'More money, I suppose,' Massey said. 'A want in which a good many of us can sympathize, unfortunately.' ('Does the fellow mean that for me, I wonder?' the hard-up little Captain asked himself uneasily.) 'Miss Smythe,' Massey went on, 'will tell you they are quite right to strive to improve their condition. They have her sympathy, I remember of old.'

The colour came to Helen's cheek.

'I have always thought they had some right on their side,' she said. 'No one took their part – they were obliged to make a stand for themselves. But, Mr Massey, I am very, very sorry that you should be the victim, and we came round now on purpose to tell you so. We only came back last night; I have not even been home yet, I wished so very much to say to you that I am – that everyone is – so sorry.'

'Thank you, you are very kind.'

'But surely some of your men have kept with you? Where's Moore?' she asked, looking round. 'Of course, Moore stayed with you?'

Massey pushed his cap to the back of his head, and brushed the damp air from his forehead.

'Moore is all right,' he said. 'Moore is in his proper place, you may be sure.'

'I am so glad that at least you have him!' with a sigh of relief. 'And are you getting on pretty well? Will it be much inconvenience – much loss to you?'

'Oh, I shall do very well. I have had to work tolerably hard, but I dare say that has been good for me. I don't regret it.'

'And you have had plenty of help,' Captain Back remarked. 'There are always volunteers in a case like this.'

'Yes. People have been wonderfully good. I wish they were more in number, certainly; but their zeal has been terrific.'

'I wish that I were a man that I could help you,' Helen said impulsively; then seeing a change pass over Massey's face, and feeling that Captain Back had turned to look at her, 'I have an enthusiasm for work, you know,' she explained, looking with heightened colour at the latter. 'I love it for its own sake; but to work to save such a gift as this,' waving her hand comprehensively round the hayfield, miserably conscious the while that she was talking rather high-flown nonsense, 'appears to me to be noble work.'

'I wish you could impart some of your views to my neighbours, to say nothing of my men, Miss Smythe,' Massey said. 'If I could fall in with one or two assistants holding your enthusiastic views, I should do well.'

'Perhaps I can,' she said, eagerly; 'I know one or two men who would, I think, come for my asking. I might help a little so, perhaps.'

'But pray do not trouble about it. Your time is no doubt very fully employed now, and the worst is pretty well over for me. I shall manage very well, I dare say.'

'Now, do not grudge Miss Smythe the right of going about doing good,' Captain Back said, his slow, refined tone a contrast to the brusqueness of the other man. 'It is her privilege to succour all distressed persons with whom she comes in contact. Her benevolence, as I have just told her, is too universal for my sympathy; still it is no doubt admirable. I shall take you round,' turning to her, 'to drum up recruits to-morrow, and I wish Mr Massey mayn't find himself embarrassed by the number we enlist.'

'I am coming home to the Vicarage immediately,' Helen said to Massey, paying no heed to her companion's speech. 'I shall like to see what I can do then, if you will let me.'

'What makes her so gracious to that sullen, ill-conditioned fellow?' Captain Back wondered to himself. He himself, who had been of late most devoted in his attention, who was her equal in birth and position, and whose admiration could have been no secret, had yet perceived no such humility in her bearing towards him. And while he thought this, and while with some surprise he watched Helen leaning forward in her saddle, and talking with flattering interest to the 'good-looking clod-hopper with the pitchfork,' as the little man mentally called Massey, a diversion was created by the appearance at the bottom of the field of Miss Freeman in her little pony car, bringing her cousin and the lunch.

'Hallo! Who are our friends on horseback?' Mr Gosling inquired. 'Here are some tip-tops, Pollie. Let's make ourselves scarce till they clear out.'

'That must be Captain Back!' cried Pollie, becoming excited. 'What ever can Captain Back be doing with James?'

'And who's the girl? A one-er, by Jove! whoever she is – looks the real thing, Poll – eh?'

'It can't be one of his sisters,' considered Pollie, intently gazing. 'Why, it must be – it is – Helen Smythe. And what's she poking in her nose here for, where she's not wanted? Come on, Arthur; let's drive up to them, and see what they'll do. James don't want her worrying here, I know.'

'Shouldn't object to her worryin' me, if she took a fancy to it; p'r'aps she will, when she sees me.' And assuming a comic air of self-complacency, Mr Gosling, by dint of much wrinkling and sneering, stuck an eye-glass into his eye, and crossed his arms across his little chest. To show his delight at freedom from the trammels of civilization, he had abandoned his 'stove-pipe' for an enormously big straw hat, which his cousin had adorned with a red ribbon, and in which she herself looked very bewitching when, as sometimes happened, they were moved, in the lightness of their hearts, to an exchange of head-gear; but he still retained the long-skirted, black frock-coat so dear to the city young man.

Pollie looked a little contemptuously at him, and declined to laugh at his face of assumed complacency.

'Why, you've seen Helen Smythe often enough,' she said, 'and I never heard you saw much in her to admire. You may make your mind quite easy that she'll take no notice of you. Why, look! she's got off her horse, and is coming to meet us. What mighty condescension! I've a great mind to drive straight past, up to James, as if I didn't see her.'

'I wouldn't do that. Bad form, Pollie. Here, stop, and let me get out. The young woman ain't quite my cut, Pollie; our styles don't "gee," I remember – though I'm hanged if she don't look deuced well in a habit.'

Miss Smythe bowed gravely to the incongruous figure which snatched at its hat of comic proportions as it passed, and then was at the side of the car.

'How do you do, Pollie? I would get down to speak to you, because I could not shout what I wanted to say from my horse, and with everyone looking on. I have not seen you since – since your engagement, you know; and I want to congratulate you, and to tell you how heartily you have my good wishes.'

'You are very good,' Pollie said, very cool as to speech, very warm as to face. 'Thank you.'

That her engagement, as it was called, should have the usual happy consummation had become a very remote possibility indeed to Pollie, and she had noticed, too, that her friends were becoming shy of mentioning the subject to her; she was quite aware that Helen's confident mention of the matter arose from her late absence and consequent inability to mark the course of events, and yet she was glad to have it so mentioned by her, and proud to feel that, at least in this woman's eyes, she could appear as James Massey's future wife.

'You will be our nearest neighbour, will you not?' Helen went on. 'We must try to be good friends. Will you let me see more of you than I have done? It will be pleasant, living so near, to be good friends. Mr Massey, you know, has been such a good neighbour. We all like having him there so much.'

'Yes,' Pollie said, sharply; 'neighbours are useful things sometimes, especially when you want to borrow of them.'

Helen only vaguely felt that this speech was meant to be unpleasant, knowing but little of the daily calls of Vicarage on Wood Farm for implements, men, and horses; but Pollie was triumphantly conscious of having scored one, and received much applause in her home circle when her 'hit' was reported.

'To borrow?' Helen repeated. 'Yours will be too perfect a household for need to borrow of us, Pollie, although you would be welcome to all we had.'

'I wasn't thinking of *my* housekeeping,' said Pollie quickly; 'I've never been used to shifts of that kind. You won't mind my moving on, Miss Smythe. James is generally looking out for his lunch by now.'

Helen walked by the side of the car, her habit thrown over her arm, and talked of where she had been and what she had done; she would not alter the friendliness of her manner for the other's ungracious reception. She had decided to make the best of the girl whom poor Mr Massey had to marry – it would be something done for him as well as for her, and she had an uneasy, undefined longing to compensate to him in some manner for something. For the rest, what were the moods of such a girl as Pollie Freeman to her – Helen Smythe?

And now Massey, anxious to keep her from contact with Mr Gosling, of whose companionship he was small-minded enough to be heartily ashamed, led up Helen's horse, but neither was Captain Back delighted with the jocose young man's society, and having an eye for a pretty, saucy face such as Pollie's, he also wheeled round and joined them.

'We are keeping you from your lunch, Mr Massey,' he said, and looked at Pollie, to whom Helen quietly introduced him.

'Bring forth the briny, Pollie,' cried Mr Gosling, approaching. 'Uncork the sparkling nectar!'

But his cousin was inattentive to his lively wit, being launched into a brilliant conversation with Captain Back, and having realized within the last minute one great ambition of her life. Captain Back laughed, and was amused; but while he chatted with her, and accepted the mug of home-brewed beer which Arthur had poured out, and which she passed up to him with the laughing injunction not to let Helen see – while he drank the beer and looked with looks of admiration at Miss Freeman – he had not forgotten his charge; he had an eye for her as well as Miss Pollie. He watched Massey put Helen on her horse, although he seemed to be noticing only the smiling face before him, and he broke off rather abruptly, in the midst of his praise of the home-brewed beer –

'Come, we must be off!' he said a little sharply to Helen. 'We are interrupting Mr Massey's lunch; and have you forgotten that the girls are waiting for us?'

'I am quite ready. Thank you, I think that will do nicely, Mr Massey. Good-bye, Pollie; I shall see you again before long.'

'And I have your permission to call for some more of that delicious beer, Miss Freeman? I shall not forget. Now, Helen.'

Miss Smythe blushed crimson at the sound of her name, and glancing involuntarily at Massey, saw that he had paled to the lips. He had lifted his head quickly, and snatched his hand from her horse's neck as though it had stung him. In a moment more he had dropped back a pace, had lifted his cap in silent farewell, and was watching them ride from his field.

'You waited too long for your lunch, and now you can't eat,' Pollie said soon afterwards, looking aggrievedly at him, while Mr Gosling devoured the sandwiches and hot buns unassisted.

'He makes up for it in his libations,' her cousin sagely remarked. 'Hold hard, old man! or you'll have to pass your afternoon like the classical bloke, asleep under your own hay-cocks.'

As they two rode off, 'What uncultivated cattle these farmers are!' said Captain Back. 'Really no lady should run the risk of contact with them. What is it in their business that makes such boors of them? This man now, you say he comes of respectable people, and he is himself an uncommonly fine-looking fellow, but he has no more manners than one of his own pigs, and is a presuming cad into the bargain.'

'What fellow?' asked Helen, quite pale as at an insult to herself, and with dangerously flashing eyes. 'Of whom are you speaking?'

'Of the fellow we have just left. If you will take my advice, Helen, you will keep out of that man's way. Mind I'm not speaking without my book – I have good reason for what I say.'

'And if you will take *my* advice,' Miss Smythe said, in a voice quite altered from its usual languid sweetness, 'you will never presume to speak to me in such terms of one of my friends – never again! More than that, Captain Back, if you ever dare – *dare* to call me by my Christian name again, I give you my solemn promise that I will never speak to you any more. I have asked you before to desist from this – it is most annoying to me – I cannot think how you can be guilty of such terribly bad taste. You knew that, before all those people, I could not rebuke you – it was – it was mean of you – and – and did you just now call another person presuming? Yours was the only piece of presumption I saw.'

'I beg your pardon. I am sorry that you are so angry, and I am sorry that you are so blind. Or is it that you are simply one of those who will not see?'

'I do not understand you,' she said quite honestly; 'but I don't know that I care to do so. Something has made you a little angry, too, has it not? because you are scarcely polite. You who would die, as I have always fancied, rather than not be polite! But pray do not let us quarrel; it would be too much trouble for either. For a change of subject, what did you think of Mr ——, the gentleman from London?'

'He is an awful beast – he made me ill; I observed that he looked with the eyes of affection at that pretty little girl. Poor child, I suppose she knows no better, and will have to put up with him for life – I pity her!'

'You need not. She is going to marry a totally different person. Look, here come your sisters.'

'Ah, yes. Who, then, is the little girl to marry?'

'The – what did you call him? – the presuming cad, the boor, the man with whom no lady must come in contact. She is going to marry Mr Massey. You see, he has an eye for a pretty face as well as other people.'

'To marry Massey?' asked the Captain, in a tone of surprise, and he looked rather intently at his companion, contracted his lips, and gave vent to a noiseless species of whistle; but he said nothing more. He said nothing, but he thought of a thing he had seen that morning – seen out of the corner of his eye, while he drained the foaming cup held to him by Miss Freeman, and rallied that young lady in his lightest vein. He had watched the same Mr Massey lift Miss Smythe with much care and science to her horse, and while she settled herself in her saddle he had noticed him lean forward, under pretence of tightening a strap, and had seen also that before he raised himself his lips had touched the folds of the blue-cloth habit lying so close to his face.

'So that is going to be the pretty little Freeman's fate?' he said, musingly, as they joined his sisters.

CHAPTER XVIII

Helen Intercedes

THANKS to the strenuous exertions of Miss Smythe and to the power of her eloquence, the staff of volunteers on the Wood Farm increased by two or three quickly on her return. Operations began to go on swimmingly there now, and the harassed master and his staff consequently ceased to be objects of such attraction to the disaffected hands. These last, as time went on, began to attend the public-house more, and Mr Massey's neighbourhood less; several of them went about with something of a gloomy look, and the gatherings by the roadside or in the inn kitchen at length assumed an air the reverse of festive in spite of the concertina's persistent strains and the ribbons still streaming from the shabby hats. The strike now wore an aspect less welcome than ever in the eyes of the anxious women, and to the men themselves the prospect began to be serious. They had done very well for the first two weeks, having received from the Labourers' Union a good portion of their weekly wages, but this had gradually become less and less, and some of the most despondent began to look ahead uneasily to the time when there would be none at all. Even now the wives and children came but poorly off, and the men, miserable in the altered state of affairs at home, driven to seek comfort where, in the imagination of their class, it can always be found, ran up long scores at the public-house, while their wives got into as much debt as was permitted to them at the village shop, and the children played about on half-rations.

From the position of heroes the strikers began to sink down into something very like that of pariahs. The parson thundered at them from his pulpit – not that this affected them much, they being never there to hear – and gave them the rough side of his tongue when they met. The shopkeeper looked askance at them, and began to be very chary of selling them two penn'orth of goods without the two-pence in advance. The class immediately above them triumphed in their down-fall, and openly prognosticated worse things to come. The labourers at work on the other farms, having at last perceived that the strike was not to be a success, did not hesitate in the plainest, least complimentary language to pronounce it the failure it was, while to each of the unfortunate men, the presence of his wife or his mother had become as the application of a blister to a raw place.

To only one among them had any good fortune come. Mr Tom Moore, by reason of his great flow of language and the enlarged intelligence of his ideas, was selected by that branch of the Labourers' Union to stump the county in their behalf. He was reported to be well paid for this post, and certainly was as well fitted for the honour as any worthless scamp in the county could be. Helen had been overwhelmed with sorrow and annoyance on hearing of this man's disaffection, as she did of course hear immediately on her return.

'What makes you trouble so much about it?' her sister asked her, being herself weary of the trivial subject. 'If it had not been Moore, it would have been some one else. It really has nothing whatever to do with you.'

'But, Anna, I can't help thinking that it has to do with me, unfortunately. You see, I asked Mr Massey to take this very man – to whom no one else would give work, you remember – and I believe – I am afraid he took him, against his better judgment, just to please me – because I asked him. Oh, how I wish I had not interfered!'

The tears would come in Helen's eyes as she thought of it. That he should have had yet more trouble through her!

'No doubt you wish that you had not interfered. Had you asked my advice at the time, I could have saved you all this unpleasantness; but you set always such undue value on your own judgement! In the first place, the man Moore was an ill-behaved, ill-conditioned person –'

'But he was starving,' Helen interrupted.

'And he deserved to starve. Had he not resisted all efforts made for his benefit?' Helen was silent, knowing too well that the unregenerate Moore had never taken kindly to the *Enlightener*, and other well-meaning works, showered on him by Mrs Pearson. 'Then why not let him alone? In the second place, Helen, I cannot help saying that if you had exercised any nice feeling at all in the matter, you must have been aware that this Mr Massey is the very last person in the world for *you* to stoop to ask any favour of.'

'Anna, how can you be so absurd?' the girl cried, with angry, crimson face. 'I don't know what you mean by such nonsense! I had asked Mr Selby on several occasions to give the man work, and should have asked Mr Freeman if he had been less of a bear.'

'You would have shown far more discretion in asking Mr Freeman, objectionable as that would have been. He would have refused you in the most boorish manner possible, of course; but this man does worse, infinitely – he takes him – to please you! It appears to me to be a piece of most insufferable presumption on his part, this trying to please you. I do not know what you think.'

'I don't think anything so mean and – and unworthy of myself as that, thank God!' Helen said, with hot indignation. She sprang up from her chair and crossed over to the window, standing there with her back to her sister. 'I should be ashamed – ashamed to have such thoughts!'

'Do not excite yourself unnecessarily, Helen,' the other said, with cold disapproval; all expression of feeling was 'vulgar' in Mrs Pearson's eyes, and she could hear by the change in the usually slow, sweet voice that Helen was moved. 'You surely are not so self-opinionated that you cannot bear a word of censure. Where your great mistake lies is in not having borne in mind, while dealing with the person of whom we speak, that he is no gentleman, is necessarily without gentlemanly instincts, and so misconstrues any advances that are made to him. I have known from the first, and I remember making the remark to Alfred, that Mr Massey was a man to be held at arm's length.'

A rather hysterical laugh came from the window.

'Alfred has found it useful to hold him closer than that, I think. You had better talk to Alfred, Anna, about asking favours of a man who is not a gentleman. A gentleman, indeed!' turning swiftly round and confronting her sister with wet and angry eyes. 'Who is a gentleman, pray? You had better tell me, that I do not disgrace myself by farther mistakes. Is Al—? is Captain Back? is that dressed-up, leering old Sir William Atmore, to whom you are anxious always that I should be gracious – staring into women's faces, and making them sick and ashamed? If Mr Massey is not such a gentleman as that, then has he something to thank God for! Anna, I am sick of this unworthy nonsense about "gentlemen"; I am weary of the twaddle of "position." A gentleman, I take it, is one who leads an honourable life in the sight of God and man, and his right "position" is the one he holds without shame and fills to the best of his ability.'

'Thank you, Helen, I can hear perfectly well; pray do not raise your voice. Your ideas on the subject have undergone a rather rapid change lately; but such cheap sentiment as you are talking is not likely to alter mine. However, we will not argue the question. You appear annoyed with me, I don't know why. You tell me that you asked a favour of this Mr Massey, and that you regret it. Then are you right to be angry simply because I regret it too?'

'Of course I was wrong to be angry,' Helen said, with a prompt humility whose expression came with a double charm from her proud lips.

With the same humbleness of spirit she had acknowledged to Pollie Freeman the grief she felt at the disastrous result of her own interference, and she had borne with characteristic patience the young lady's comments on her confession. It was not in the Freeman blood to be generous to a fallen foe, and the 'I told you so' formula was one they never scrupled to employ.

'Will you tell Mr Massey how sorry I am?' Helen asked her humbly. 'Tell him I feel as though I myself were the cause of all this trouble.'

'Well, you see,' said Pollie frankly, 'it all did come through Moore, they say, and Moore came through you, so to speak. James admits he always knew the man was no good; but at the time father and all of us tried our hardest to persuade him off taking the wretch – there's no turning James when his mind's made up! They tell me I shall have my hands full with a man as obstinate as that; but he's a soft heart with it all. Now, about this very thing – this horrid strike – he worries about it, you wouldn't believe how much! Don't you notice how harassed he looks now lately, and as moody as ever he can be? Not like the same man, I say: it's wonderful how he takes it to heart! And the wives of the men keep going to him, and crying and taking on, for they get next to nothing now from their precious union, and serve them well right! They want him – the women do – to say he'll take their husbands on again if they'll knock under. Of course he can't say he'll do this yet, and pa thinks he ought to throw the lot over – he can make shift without them now. He isn't one likely to give in himself, but it all worries him.'

'I'll see all those women,' Helen said eagerly; 'I can at least keep them from being troublesome to him.'

'Well, but don't you give them money, Miss Smythe, or help them in any way. You must be sure not to do that, you know – that would be only helping on the strike. The only way is to starve them back to their senses.'

'That may be justice to the men,' Helen demurred sadly; 'but it is terribly hard on the women and children.'

'But if you help the women and children, you help them, don't you see; and it must be done, Miss Smythe. If you really feel you are in any way answerable for the state of things, you owe it to all the farmers round to do your utmost to bring them right again. That's your plain duty, anyhow,' said Pollie with conviction; the path of duty on which others were to tread was always clear to Miss Freeman's mind.

The hay was safely stacked now, the busy time over, and still the men made no overtures; they still said to themselves and to their friends that they would see their own master and all the masters in England in the very warmest locality before they would knock under; but in spite of these protestations and the oaths by which they were accompanied, it was quite obvious to all concerned that the men could not hold out much longer.

'Something must be done!' Helen cried distressed, as she went from cottage to cottage, and witnessed the distress she dared not alleviate.

'Something must be done,' Mr Massey said uneasily noting the altered looks of his men as he passed them on his rounds. He always gave them 'good-morning' cheerily enough, and had been used to receive response more or less polite; but now, as he went by, he found his greeting received in silence, or would hear a curse ground out as he passed. Something must be done, and that speedily, and the sooner the affair came to a climax the better. With a view to this end, he sent to the tenant of every cottage on his farm a notice to quit at the end of the week, his men being in every case weekly tenants.

'That will bring them to their senses, if anything will,' he thought comfortably, looking on the proceeding simply as a ruse, not realizing the alarming reality it must seem to the other side.

'For God's sake, miss, speak to the master,' one miserable woman said to Helen that day. She had come down to the Vicarage, a baby in her arms, another small morsel of humanity tugging at her skirts. She flung herself into one of the kitchen chairs, and rocked herself backwards and forwards in tragic distress. 'Do the man mean us to die in a ditch when he ha' turned us out o' house and home?' she demanded fiercely; and then proceeded to apologize for herself and her 'forra'dness.' 'Excuse my a-settin' down, miss; the fact on't is I'm dead beat,' the tears rolling down her face. 'I stood at the wash-tub all yesterday, miss – I was forced to wring out the bits o' things – without a bit nor sup; and when I'd finished at night there weren't a morsel for me – not a morsel for me and my children – Lord help us! 'Tain't through no fault of mine; I ha' done to the best as far as I knew, and I never thort I should ha' come to this. I feel it hard – werry hard, I do. 'Tain't nothin' but the truth, miss; we all on us went wi' empty bellies to bed last night.'

'I believe you,' Helen said, setting to work to cut huge slices of bread-and-butter, which she handed round, tears of sympathy in her eyes. 'I am so truly sorry for you. But you have had something to eat this morning – you surely are not hungry now?'

'My neighbour gin us a half of a loaf, and I poured boiling water on to mak' it go farder; but 'twas as heavy as lead – she had a bad batch this week, poor critter! and 'twouldn't swell up much. That's all we ha' tasted since yes'day mornin' – my poor little uns and me!'

'But your husband?' Helen asked; she took the elder child on to her lap, bread-and-butter and all, smoothing its hair, cosseting it, in her pity oblivious of its dirt.

'I don't know what's come to my husband,' the woman said, in a quietly hopeless voice. 'I know he ain't like the same man to me. Seems as if, so long as he's full o' beer, wife and child'en may go. But he's only like his betters i' that. Who cares what's to come of such as us? Master here wants to see us all perishin' by the roadside – p'r'aps he'll be satisfied then.'

'Your master is not hard-hearted,' Helen said; 'I think, Mrs Brown, you must know that. Look how good he was to you when your husband broke his leg in the winter. You told me how for weeks his housekeeper sent Brown his dinner, and how it was Mr Massey who paid the doctor's bill. You must remember that all this dreadful trouble is none of his work. I know that he is distressed about you women and children, and would help you if he could.'

'Looks like it! to turn us out o' house and home i' this manner, to rot in a ditch or to go to the workus! and look you, Miss Ellen! sooner the ditch for me!' the woman cried with excitement, lifting her arm by way of emphasis. 'No workus for me nor none o' mine – mark my words! – I'll watch 'em all perish o' hunger first!'

'Oh, hush!' Helen said. 'Look, you frighten the child,' the little one on her lap gasping affrightedly over its bread-and-butter. It was so that 'mother' had lifted her hand this morning, and declaimed on the first receipt of that dreadful paper, and 'father' had sworn wild words, and had flung his boot at 'mother' – small wonder the poor dirty mite wept and hid its greasy face against Helen.

'I will see Mr Massey,' Helen said, 'if you think I can do some good. I do not quite know what it means, this notice for you to leave, but I am quite certain that he will never do what is harsh or unjust – certain of it!' Helen cried with a warm glow at her heart. Then, having visited, with predatory views, her sister's larder, on Mrs Brown's behalf, and having sent that lady somewhat comforted away, carrying the results in her not too clean red pocket-handkerchief, Helen put on her hat and went out.

'I may as well get this over before I begin to think I had better not see him, or to recollect I should never interfere,' she told herself, with some contempt. She did not go to Massey's house, but met him after a half-mile's walk coming towards her on the road which ran through his farm.

Helen began to blush and tremble at the sight of him. 'What a *fool* I am!' she said to herself angrily. 'Among them they have made me feel and look like an idiot.' She pulled herself together with an effort, and went forward without flinching.

Massey was now clothed and in his right mind, so to speak; his exertions in the hay-field being over, he had resumed the *rôle* of master, and no longer toiled madly in a state of semi-undress. It so happened that Helen had not spoken to him since the occasion of her introduction to him of Captain Back, and they both thought of that gentleman now, she with exasperation and a tingling of her blood, remembering a certain caution he had given her – Massey because the man, to his own rage and sorrow, was associated with her now in his and other people's minds.

He raised his hat to her in silence, and Helen noticed at once in his face the harassed look of which Pollie had spoken. He was older-looking, too, and surely thinner, she thought; that month's work in the heat of the sun had told upon him sadly, and Helen's tender heart began to melt with pity.

'I came to meet you, Mr Massey,' she began at once. 'I promised some of the women that I would see you. They are so bewildered, poor things, and so starved and wretched, and they do not understand about these notices you have sent them. I thought that if I saw you, you would tell me what they meant.'

'They mean pretty well what they say, I'm afraid,' he answered. 'You see, Miss Smythe, the cottages on my farm are for my own accommodation; they are to shelter my labourers. Now that these men have ceased to work for me, they must make way for new tenants, you understand. There is no other course open to me but to turn these people out.'

'Oh, dear!' Helen sighed, 'that is dreadful! I half hoped all along that you would tell me it was not so bad as it seemed.' A few months ago, how she would have opened the vials of her wrath to pour on the devoted head of any miscreant so obdurate as this! She had learnt now that she herself could be unwise in her indiscriminate benevolence, and had also unconsciously learnt to trust in the other's discretion. 'What will be done?' she went on. 'Mr Massey, if you could see the state of things that it is! They are starving – positively starving! – and I, who have money to help them, must stand by and see them starve, they tell me, for fear of prolonging the strike. I cannot do that,' she said, looking with pleading eyes in his face. 'I cannot see little children cry for food, and not give it to them. It may be awfully weak of me, but it is beyond my strength to do that.'

He saw her lip quiver, and for one happy instant Captain Back and Pollie were as though they had never been.

'You shall do what you like, of course,' he said, tenderly. 'Who is there that would wish to prevent you? But it is like this, do you see, Miss Smythe' – then in a few words he explained to her how it was hoped that this last misfortune of having to quit their homes would bring the men to reason – 'I am tired of it,' he said. 'I like to be on friendly terms with my men; they have behaved badly, and I dare say, if I cared much for my dignity, I should take the advice of all my friends and let them go to shipwreck; but I am not particularly dignified – and that would not be your advice, I know. I shall, I suppose, take them back when they ask me, only they must be quick about it, you understand – it must be done by the end of the week – or they go. That is pretty much what the notices mean.'

'I wish I might tell them that,' she said. 'May I?'

'Of course you may. Why not? That is, you may tell the wives – do not have anything to do with the men; they are brutalized, I think, by their own ignorance and indolence, and are quite unfit for women to encounter. Do you know, Miss Smythe, in spite of faithful efforts, I still do not admire, as I ought to do, your pet *protégé* the agricultural labourer? He seems to me an ungrateful, insensible brute enough – without knowledge to discriminate between good treatment and bad, or to know when he is well or ill-used. When he is at the height of good fortune, he grumbles consistently, and knows no limit to his greed; when reverses come as the certain effect of his own acts, he snarls and swears, neglects his wife and children, stupefies himself with beer while they starve, and heaps insults on his would-be benefactors. I think he is altogether a bad lot and an unprofitable subject – tolerable perhaps when he works, but altogether abominable when he loafs. By the way, how did you come? – past the White Hart?'

'Of course I did; I should not be here unless.'

'The men were there, I was thinking. You met with no un-pleasantness?'

'No, indeed. You are naturally incensed with them, I do not wonder; but they are not wholly bad even now – they would not molest me. I do not speak to them when they are in a body – union gives them a not altogether desirable strength – nor did I look at them as I passed, but I fancy that I heard Moore's voice. Is he with them again?'

'Yes; I heard that the rascal was back. He is come to take away his wife and children, I think. Out of evil cometh good, don't they say, Miss Smythe? One never-to-be-forgotten benefit arising from all this bother will be the removal of that brute.'

'You cannot think how I have reproached myself about him,' Helen said with a sigh. 'I remember how I made it almost impossible for you to refuse to take him. It has really been a great trouble to me, and I have felt myself responsible for all this that has followed. But I was so sure that he only wanted a chance to reform, and so anxious to get him the chance – one can hardly help hoping that there is some good in people, can one?'

'I suppose that you cannot,' he said, looking at her with a smile; 'let's hope you never may, but you must get cruelly disappointed very often, I should think. As for your having had anything to do with this trouble with my men, I grieve to say the thought never entered my head, or I should have borne all the inconvenience with much greater equanimity.'

'The thought has been a real grief to me, I assure you,' Helen said, hating herself that the blood had rushed to her face at his words. 'I have always felt that you and everyone must blame me in the matter.'

'At least you might have known that I should not,' he said, and then a pause ensued – a pause with which he was apparently content, but which Helen anxiously cudgelled her brain to break. It showed want of tact and want of taste on his part, she thought, to make that kind of speech to her, in that tone of voice – it was not generous, seeing that she had sought him of her own accord, and in such manner had shown her trust in his good sense and good understanding of her motives. It hurt her to think that the others – those wiseacres, had, after all, been right in one thing, that this man was better to be kept at arm's length by her, for the present at least. This train of thought naturally presented Captain Back to Helen's mental view; that she had better not speak of him, she knew by some curious intuition, but for all her struggles to avoid the subject, she could not steer quite clear of the dangerous topic when she did speak.

'You are not so busy as on the last time I saw you,' was all she could think of to say at length.

'Thank Heaven, no! The worst is over. By the way, Captain Back seems to be making a long stay; he is still at the Hall, I believe. His military duties are not onerous apparently.'

'He has sold out of his regiment, I believe. His father wishes to keep him at home. You see, the elder son is nearly always away, and poor Mr Back so much of an invalid, it is natural that he should like to have one of them with him.'

'Quite natural,' Massey said, knowing well that the young man's debts had been paid for the last time, on condition of his settling down and keeping out of harm's way. 'It is only right that a man should keep his sons about him if he likes; and this, I suppose, is a very affectionate family. Captain Back is glad to give up his own prospects for his father's wishes, no doubt.'

Helen thought of the perpetual quarrels and bickerings to which she had been a witness at Hilby Hall, and held her peace.

'And I suppose,' the other went on with hardly concealed bitterness, 'that he is as clever as well as amiable, and so very filial? He did not strike me, I confess, as having the kind of head to hold many brains, but it is, of course, for all that, a very good-looking head, in ladies' eyes.'

Helen smiled to herself, remembering the other's eulogiums on this man's appearance. 'I don't suppose Captain Back is very clever,' she said; 'he is not what might be called learned, perhaps, but he knows enough, he can talk,' smiling again, 'chatter even and be amusing. One is never dull at the Hall.'

'I should not have imagined that you would have cared for chatter.'

'Not for just anybody's chatter, nor for a continuance; but I find it agreeable, when you are obliged to talk to a person, to have that same person equal to the occasion, as it were; to have none of those terrible pauses coming in which in a *tête-à-tête* one so dreads.'

'All that depends. There might be cases in which those pauses, if rightly understood, would be eloquent. They might come, for instance, because a man had too much to say, rather than too little. Poverty of words need not always show a deficiency of ideas.'

Here, she deeming it wise not to reply, there ensued one of those very pauses she had characterised as terrible. Massey made no effort to shorten it – had he not just spoken in favour of such a pause? It lasted until they reached a gate which led across some meadows to the Wood Farm. Helen stopped and held out her hand.

'I will see you past the White Hart, if you will allow me,' he said. 'The men are still hanging about there.'

'But that is really unnecessary,' she eagerly said. 'They would not be uncivil to me, I am certain, and in any case I am capable of taking care of myself.'

'Nevertheless, for once give me the pleasure of thinking I am taking care of you,' he said, and moved on by her side.

'Miss Freeman seems to be really nervous about encountering the men,' she said, feeling it incumbent on her to mention that young lady's name. 'She was telling me so yesterday.'

'So she also tells me. It is a good thing that she has her cousin to look after her. He has not the appearance of a very able defender, but she seems to consider him eligible in every way.'

'He seems very good-natured,' Helen said, naturally picking upon the one point which had appeared to her to be in his favour.

'Oh, yes, I dare say. He laughs a good deal, and plays jokes, and makes puns, and generally skips about. I have no doubt that he is good-natured. On the whole, I don't know but that it would be preferable to be ill-natured, than to have the disastrous effect on one's fellow-creatures which that species of good-nature produces. Gosling's vivacity is his great point, but I for one should prefer him infinitely without his vivacity. That incessant play of spirits has, I am ashamed to confess, a perfectly maddening effect on me.' ('He is jealous!' said Helen to herself quickly and with considerable surprise.) 'The chatter which you have been upholding this morning would be a terrible infliction even to you, don't you think, if you were weary or out of spirits?'

With this a glimmering came to the girl that he had been, perhaps all along, thinking of Captain Back while he condemned the other lively young man.

They were opposite the White Hart now. Two or three men, with the now frayed and faded ribbons in their hats, were leaning against the door-post, a few more sitting or lying on the little bit of green at the side of the inn, while one great hobbledehoy – neither-boy nor man – was staggering about in the middle of the road, preparatory to starting on his homeward way. As Helen and her companion came up with him, an unusually frantic lurch – made probably in a heroic resolve to get out of his master's way – landed him straight in Helen's path.

'Hold up, you brute!' Massey said angrily, giving him at the same time a heave with his shoulder, which sent the unsteady youth reeling across the road. There was a horse-laugh from his comrades, and there came at the same instant a sharp cry of fright or pain from Helen.

'What was that?' Massey cried, startled. 'Was it a stone? Are you hurt?'

She had turned white, and was holding one arm in her hand, already moving forward.

'Not hurt,' she said. 'Only frightened for a moment. Something struck me. Oh, no, Mr Massey' – swiftly letting go her arm, to lay her hand on his coat-sleeve – 'oh, no; you must not go to them! Pray – pray do not! I – I am frightened! – you must not leave me!'

'Go on a little way,' he said peremptorily. 'I will overtake you in one minute.'

But she would not go on alone, and watched him cross the road to the group on the turf.

'Which of you men threw that stone?' he demanded, looking round upon them all. Not one of them spoke. 'Do you hear me?' he asked again. 'Who threw that stone?' Silence still; but one of the men slowly turned his head and looked behind him to a gate a few yards off, where a man stood quietly whistling to himself with his back to the rest. In an instant Massey was beside him. 'Oh, it's you, you cowardly beggar! is it?' he ground through his teeth. 'Then, for once in your life, take what you deserve!' Down came his heavy stick across Mr Moore's devoted back. A little cry, which none of them heard amid the whizzing of those fast-falling blows and the curses of the victim, came from Helen over the way. It was not until his stick broke in his hand that Mr. Massey's vengeance was satisfied. 'Thank your lucky stars, you black-hearted ruffian,' he panted, 'that your villainy has been cramped into a little body. But for your being such a helpless reptile as you are, I would have killed you!' Then flinging from him the remnant of his stick, he turned his back on the bruised and blaspheming orator; and striding past the men, still lounging in the same attitudes, with hardly a change in the expression of their faces (what is there in all creation, short of the suffering of their own personal wrongs and pains, startling enough to disturb the apathy of the average farm labourer?), Massey again reached Helen's side.

He put his hand on her arm, and led her in silence the few yards intervening between the inn and the entrance to a meadow-path leading to the back of the Vicarage. He was out of breath, his chest still heaving, and the expression of his face not yet quite good to see. Within the meadow-gate and well out of sight from the road, he stopped and looked at her, who was quite white, with tears of excitement on her cheek.

'You are sure you are not hurt?' he asked her, a little hoarsely. 'Quite sure? Show me exactly where the stone hit you – here?' touching her arm above the elbow and gently running his hand over the place. 'Does that hurt you?'

'No; it is nothing – I was startled!' with a little gasping sigh.

'You are not deceiving me? You look so pale.'

At the pitying anxious tone she, being quite upset, felt the tears rushing to her eyes again.

'Sit down for a moment on this bank,' he entreated anxiously. 'This has been horribly unpleasant for you, and I fear you are in pain.'

'No, indeed,' she protested, obeying him. 'It is nothing, really nothing! There will be, perhaps, a bruise; and that is all. But it was such a horrid sight – such a horrid, horrid sight!' shuddering, and putting her hand before her eyes. 'I shall never forget it – never!'

'I ought not to have chastised him before you,' he said contritely. 'Will you forgive me? The temptation was too strong. Do not fret about it; for heaven's sake, do not, Helen. He is not worth one of your tears – who is? It makes me mad to see you cry!'

But to speak to her in a voice unsteady with passion was not the surest way to stop the girl's tears nor to calm her perturbation. It seemed an age to him before Helen uncovered her eyes and controlled her voice to its usual quiet tone.

'Oh, what a terrible state of things it is!' she said sadly; at length, 'What will the end of it be? Mr Massey, I am greatly afraid you have only made matters worse. I wish – I wish that you had left Moore alone.'

'And when I look at you, I wish that I had killed him!' he said fiercely.

'Oh, hush!'

'Still there is one thing that must not be lost sight of in the matter. If I had given myself time to reflect on it, I mightn't have laid on so hard – might not have ruined my stick, perhaps; and that is, that the stone was not intended for you, but for me. That is something to Moore's credit. You see, there is some fatality about me where you are concerned. To-day I meant to protect you, for instance, and this has occurred. I shall begin to think that you are in the right to keep out of my way, as you have done lately – to shun me as if I were plague-stricken.'

'But, indeed, I have not done that,' she said, turning wet, startled eyes up to him, standing over her. 'I – that is, we – have not seen you often lately; but that has not been because I wished to shun you. You have not come in with Alfred, as usual; that has been all.'

'Has it been my doing, do you think? I hardly know. I only know I have not seen you, and that life is not worth having, to me, if I don't see you. I am sick of it – sick of everything; that is about the truth. If that rascal just now had knocked me over the head and finished me, I believe that I should have been distinctly thankful. Perhaps he'll send a bullet into me from behind a hedge yet. What do you think?' (He laughed as he asked this, although his misery was real enough to him just then, and his eyes were full of pain and trouble.) 'If he should – if he should finish me off, you'll know better than to regret it, after what I've told you; but I should be glad to have Moore hanged all the same – remember that!'

'Please do not jest about such horrible things,' she said, unable to repress a shudder. 'If you really believe Moore to be such a wicked, dangerous wretch, I think you terribly rash to treat him as you did just now.'

The idea of Moore's vengeance, which had been but a jest with him, had evidently taken hold on her imagination. A glimmer of joy came to him as he perceived this.

'But if I can jest,' he said, 'isn't it better for me? You ought not to grudge me such a wretched joke as that – you would not, if you knew how utterly miserable I am.'

He understood Helen's character sufficiently to be aware he was surer of her sympathy in speaking of his misery than of his love.

'I hope that you are jesting still,' she said, turning her face away from him.

'Good Heavens, no! That part is downright, dismal earnest. I am horribly miserable – you may believe me now. Would I whine like this if I could help it? I can't. I have done my utmost – I have fought against it – this feeling of wearisome disgust for everything and every person – but just one. It's all of no good. I would not have believed it of myself that I could suffer so. I am not a boy; I have thought that I have been in love with women before (how you will despise me for saying this!), and I have been cured in a week! How was I to know that this thing was to master me so? I did my best; I went away, you remember, and I was mad to get home, that I might be near you. I have tried hard work; I have tried keeping out of your way – it's all of no use; I am done for – for life, I suppose. I did not mean to tell you all this; it will do no good, I know.'

'It makes me very unhappy,' she said. 'It makes me wish heartily that you had never seen me.'

'Ah, even when I am at my worst now, I do not wish that. You see, I dare say, I take this thing, this misfortune of mine, to heart more than another man might, for I have never been used to ups and downs in my life; things have always gone pretty smoothly for me. I never remember to have wanted a thing badly before that I did not somehow manage to get (perhaps it was that I have not, till now, been presumptuous in my desires). I am in this matter like a spoiled child, don't you see, and I do really think that I shall break my heart because my moon is denied to me. I suppose it is selfish of me to trouble you with all this? God knows I don't want to make you unhappy, but you are always sweet and pitiful to those who are in suffering, and I have so little pride where you are concerned, that I should like you to pity me.'

'You want no one's pity,' she said softly. 'I know – I *know* that you will forget all this in a little time. If I were a man – strong mentally and physically, as you appear to me to be – I would never acknowledge that any feeling could get the better of me in such a fashion. You can conquer it if you will – think, it is only a sentiment, a fancy, a thing that does not really exist – no man who was worthy to live and to do a man's work in the world would spoil his life and his usefulness for an idea! it is nothing more. And you – you have other reasons; you have formed other ties; Miss Freeman –'

He interrupted her with a not very mirthful laugh. 'You are giving me the spoilt-child treatment,' he said. 'I long – long, my God in heaven! – for the moon, and you offer me the green cheese. No, Miss Smythe, there are no ties that I have formed. I am dishonest to no one else in giving all I have to give to you. Miss Freeman, as I told you before, chooses to say that I am engaged to her, but she exacts from me no attention, nor do I offer her any. She knows perfectly well that I shall never marry her, and is already, I hope, forming other plans for herself. Did you ever seriously imagine that I could have married her after dreaming of marrying you?'

'I do not know what I imagined,' she said in a troubled voice. 'I cannot help thinking that you might have married her if – if it had not been for me. I shall always think so – always!'

'I don't agree with you there,' he said, with a flicker of a smile around his mouth. 'But you see there has been you – and now I can take an oath that I shall not, even should she wish it, which I assure you she won't – I should knock out my own brains first. Pray do not trouble on her account. She is one of those intensely selfish persons (I say it with all respect; it is quite wise to be selfish in this world), who is sure to be all right. And do not trouble about me,' he went on, putting out his hands to help her to rise. 'This has come about through no fault of yours. You cannot help being lovely and lovable more than I can help seeing that you are so. And now good-bye. There is Perrie at the garden-gate looking for you.'

'You will go home by the fields?' she asked him, while he held her hand in farewell.

'Why?'

'Because I ask you to do so.'

'But tell me why?'

'Because I wish you, then. It is surely a very simple request to make.'

'You think that your friend Moore is waiting for me at the White Hart, intent on vengeance?'

'I think that my friend Moore is too bruised and broken to be ready for mischief again just yet, but all those men are there still, no doubt, and you have no stick now, remember.'

'You are thinking that they will stone me again, and that there will be no soft arm to save me.'

'I do not think any nonsense about "soft arms," but I hope that you will do as I ask you.'

'*Because* you ask me, I will,' he said. 'I wonder if you could ask me what I would not try to do!'

CHAPTER XIX

Mrs Pearson Speaks her Mind

THERE was quite a stir through Hilby at the news which soon permeated that somewhat stagnant parish, to the effect that Tom Moore had stoned Miss Smythe and had received condign punishment from the hands of Mr Massey. The tale gathered as it circulated, as tales still do in more enlightened spheres; and Massey, to his intense annoyance, came to be regarded as something of a hero by his neighbours, and had to suffer congratulations, satiric or otherwise, on his exploit; while Helen, represented as having escaped imminent peril, was compelled to hear allusions to the murderous attack and the gallant rescue from everyone she encountered. The Vicar was especially interested. He was a man obliged to speak of peace, and not himself particularly courageous, who had yet a lively sympathy with those who make themselves ready for war, and he now openly lamented to his wife and her sister that more mischief had not been done to Moore's person.

'The man was able to move the next day,' he complained aggrievedly; 'got himself and his wife away at daybreak. It is odd that Massey should not have punished him more when he had the chance. His stick broke? Yes, but he had his fists. A strong fellow like Massey could have pounded Moore into a jelly with his fists,' said the Vicar, always brave with other people's skins, and even doubling up his own big hands by way of illustration. 'Why, I remember when I was at college, a man there – low little cad he was! – insulted a friend of mine – Anderson – yes, that was his name – big, strong fellow; why, he could have shaken the life out of –'

'Do you remember that Perrie is present?' Mrs Pearson interrupted; 'I never find that your tales of college life are edifying, Alfred.'

'But did he shake the life out of him?' the small man inquired, his little face alight with interest. 'Did he, father?'

'Why, of course he did not,' Aunt Helen said. 'Mr Anderson was no doubt a very brave man, Perrie – brave enough to forgive the insult, and not to punish the man too small to defend himself.'

'Mr Massey punished Moore,' Perrie said, arguing the matter in his little head, 'and Moore is much littler than Mr Massey: would Mr Massey have been braverer to forgive him?'

'Mr Massey was very angry,' Helen explained gravely, 'more angry than it is good to be, Perrie; he –'

'I should think he could have shaked out his life if he had liked, shouldn't you, Aunt Helen? He is as strong as strong! I wouldn't be afraid with him, if a lion, or a bull, or a robber was to come. I'm glad he has not got that kind of braveness that that Mr Anderson had.'

'You see the result of the conversation to which that child lately has had to listen,' his mother said, including Mr Pearson and Helen in a glance of indignation. 'The brutal and unchristian manners of – of prize-fighters are becoming to him subjects of admiration.'

'You do not wish to put an end to the talk more than I do,' Helen said wearily; 'my life is becoming a burden to me through the everlasting theme.'

But although she did hate to hear the thing mentioned, and although Massey's conduct had been unchristian, and she, contrary to the degenerate Perrie, had no love for the display of brute strength, she did not the less think of the result of that morning's walk with Mr Massey. If truth must be told, it required a grand effort of determination on her part to get her thoughts to dwell on anything else. She had forgiven Moore, herself, instantly, and thought, in accordance with her strictly Scriptural upbringing, that she would have had Massey forgive him too; but the image of him in attitude of meek forgiveness of an injury done to herself would not present itself with any clearness to her mind, while the remembrance of him standing over those lounging figures on the grass, his form so strong and erect, his face so white and set, in his usually kindly eyes that look of passionate wrath – this memory was always present with her; and although she knew it was a proceeding which should have been condemned, that swift vengeance of his on an offender, she could not put from her some feeling of pride in his strength and of delight in his wrath.

Mr Massey's affairs altogether occupied a large portion of Helen's thoughts just now. A great deal that he had said while she sat on the meadow-bank that day had been of a nature to cause her much distress, but it had caused her a good deal of wonder too. Was it not wonderful – wonderful as well as unfortunate, that this thing should have befallen her – her, who had lived for twenty-three years her calm uneventful life, with never a romance of her own before to interest or disturb it? She could not cease to marvel at the strangeness of it all. And there was no doubt about the embarrassing reality. One could no longer pretend to question his earnestness or to suspect the stability of his passion, as she had half succeeded in doing after that first hasty declaration in the Wood Farm garden. What a pity that it must for ever be neglected and wasted – all that disinterested tenderness and passion! If he could but have felt it all for a woman that he might have eventually married, for instance, what a beautiful thing it would have been! There was not too much strong feeling such as that in the world, Helen thought, in her innocence, and told herself quite plainly that it could never come to her again.

She thought rather scornfully, too, of Captain Back's addresses –Captain Back, who had not given her a serious thought before she had become possessed of a little money, but of whose intentions since then there could be no mistake. It would be expected of her, however, that she should marry Captain Back, whose father had promised to provide suitably for him when he had finally settled down according to paternal wishes; all her friends would think it a suitable and satisfactory match, the world would approve of her choice, and Anna would be pleased.

Helen's mouth set itself firmly as she thought of it. 'Never,' she said to herself, lifting her head proudly – 'never!' A year ago she might have done it – who could tell? But now – never! If Mr Massey had failed to touch her heart, he had at least opened her eyes, and she recognised how a woman should be loved, although, at the same time, she fully comprehended that his love she could never in any case accept.

Had such a person as Pollie Freeman never existed, nor such a person as Captain Back – had she herself, to imagine such a case for a moment – loved him even, all question of marriage between them would still have been impossible. What would happen to Mrs Pearson, could such an alliance be thought of? What would become of her own fixed ideas on the subject of equal marriages? Was not she, with her shy sensitiveness, the person of all others to suffer most horribly in thus shocking her own and other people's cherished prejudices, by marrying a man beneath her in station (it was precisely because the difference was so small and ill-defined that Helen felt it must be marked with greater emphasis), who, beside, could not be in sympathy with her in one emotion natural to her heart – the traditions, tastes, and habits of whose life were of necessity so different from hers – who was in every way so opposed to the ideal man with whom, even though with him she could not desire marriage, she could yet find some pleasure in intercourse, some profit in association, to whom she could at least look up as to her intellectual superior?

With this man at her side, than whom, she acknowledged, she could have no more able protector, who was tender as a woman, besides, over her weakness or distress, who would, in his rashness, have had her sacrifice her prejudices and her convictions at his desire, with no serious thought of the lasting, the everlasting consequences to them both – how would it ever have been possible to enjoy the calm and holy happiness which was to her the only rational bliss of wedded life with him?

It was impossible. And yet what a grief his unhappiness was to her! Short of the one great sacrifice, there was nothing that she would not have given to restore his peace of mind. She had thought at first that Pollie might have comforted him – had so thought with a little contempt, perhaps – but that hope was dead; she would not have revived it for worlds. 'He deserves a better fate than that,' she told herself plainly now, and longed to hear that the doubtful tie between the two was really broken. It was not, indeed, a dignified position which Massey held with regard to Miss Freeman. Helen felt that strongly, and chafed at the feeling. On all sides now it was being said that 'poor Massey was going to be jilted.' Certain it is that every person who prophesied this calamity was more excited at the probability than 'poor Massey' himself.

'What the man can be thinking of to let the thing go on under his very nose in this fashion, is what I cannot understand,' the Vicar said; 'and why Freeman does not send the other horribly low person away is another mystery.'

'I said before that if Mr Massey wished to marry the girl he was unwise to keep her waiting,' Mrs Pearson said; 'but I have my own ideas on that subject, and consider that the man has behaved in the most dishonourable fashion.'

'Do you really think so?' the Vicar inquired. 'Dear me! But from what I can make out' (he had been quite busy and interested over his investigation), 'the other is really the best chance for the girl. This – this Gosling's father is a London tradesman, I hear, and this the only son – nothing like trade nowadays, Anna; there is no shutting our eyes to the fact. The mother, it is said, still favours Massey; our friend Freeman's wishes aren't so easy to come at. But Massey, himself, ought to insist on Gosling being sent off – that's how it appears to me; and I really think (you object to my interference with the parishioners, I know, Anna), I really think it is my – my – um – um – *duty* to give a word of advice to Massey on the subject. I shall not feel that I have acted a – a friendly part until I have done this. I shall merely say – point out to him that he is allowing himself to be put in a ridiculous position, and that it is time for him to – to assert himself in some way – that is if – if – in short, if he does not want to be made a fool of.'

'He would resent any word of that sort, terribly, from you,' Helen said in alarm. 'Anna, *don't* you think it would be most ill-judged of Alfred?'

'As far as Mr Massey's feelings are concerned, Helen,' her sister made answer loftily, 'I am really quite indifferent. I have told you that I consider him to be behaving dishonourably to the girl; and however much she may merit such treatment – forward, ill-bred little creature as she is! – his conduct is not to be excused, for he knew her character through the months in which I have heard Alfred say he pursued her. He is too evidently intending now to slip out of the consequences, in a manner both contemptible and cowardly.'

'Just so,' the Vicar said amicably, although that view of the question had certainly not presented itself to him before. 'Just so; and I think I ought to put it to Massey, don't you see, in that light, Anna. He may not fully have considered – I am sure that it is my duty to speak to him.'

'You will do nothing of the kind, Alfred. I will not have you approach the subject with him. I myself – if, on maturer consideration, I consider that a judicious word might be effective – I myself will speak.'

'To Mr Massey, Anna!' Helen asked, horror on her face.

'And why not to Mr Massey? Is he to be held sacred? Does he expect to avoid all unpleasant consequences of his behaviour? However, Helen, for your peace of mind, I may as well assure you that he is safe from me; the less communication I hold with that person, the more agreeable it will be to me for the future. I shall, if necessary, address myself to the Freemans in the matter.'

'It is to be hoped that you will think better of it,' Helen said. 'It is no concern of ours; and why do you not carry out the doctrine of non-interference you preach to Alfred?' Then her tone changed to one of pleading. 'What harm has Mr Massey ever done to us? He has been a pleasant neighbour – has he not, Alfred? – willing always to give, to lend, to do anything that you required of him. When the others have opposed, as they invariably do, any of your schemes, Anna, he – if he has not always approved – has at least held his peace. We have always felt that in everything he has been on our side, when hitherto we always, as you know well – for what reason I cannot say – stood alone. I think myself, Anna, that you ought to remember all this before you condemn so unhesitatingly – I do indeed. We in this house, Alfred, are not the ones, surely, to set an example of want of charity and of evil-speaking. You yourself have seemed to like Mr Massey, and to have sought his companionship; you should uphold him now if he is in need of a good word. He would stand by you – by any of us – without a thought of flinching, let things ever so dreadful be said against us; you know that he would, Alfred.'

'My dear,' Mrs Pearson said, on her face a smile the reverse of pleasant – a smile which made the blood rush to Helen's face, which made her almost wish that her tongue had been paralyzed before she had so spoken – 'my dear, Alfred knows as well as I that Mr Massey requires no other champion than you.'

'But she is right, in a measure,' the Vicar said uneasily. 'He is a sufficiently pleasant fellow, with – well, with all his faults – oh, I admit all his faults, Anna – and I confess that I have no desire for a rupture with Massey. He has been of use – ha – hum – that is to say, he has been agreeable to me. If you do not approve of him, Anna, we need not receive him in our house; but I see no objection to my – um – um – occasionally going to his.'

'That you will please yourself about,' his wife said indifferently; 'I have reasons which quite justify me in discountenancing his visits here. I am not speaking without reflection. I shall receive him no more.'

Helen was white with anger and surprise; it was with difficulty she controlled her voice to say calmly:

'That prohibition will not affect him much, fortunately. It is fully two months since he was in this house; he was never so cordially received – who is? – that he should much desire to come again; he will survive your determination, I think, Anna.'

'Helen,' said Mr Pearson, with heavy reproof, 'you forget yourself! When Massey has been here, he has been treated as – as an equal; he has received of my hospitality, he has eaten and drunk of – um – um –my best, he –'

'Oh, yes,' cried Helen, fairly roused and desperate now; 'and while you have impressed on his mind the honour done him, you have smoked his cigars, borrowed his horses, his guns – anything! while Anna has regaled him with plenty of cold shoulder, and has never been so happy as when she has decried him to me or to you, or to anybody who would listen.'

A pause of surprise and consternation followed this outburst; then:

'Are you aware, Helen,' Mrs Pearson asked slowly, 'of the construction which people are likely to put on your conduct and your words? I say nothing of the insult to me – I can forgive – but are you ignorant of what your attitude in this unpleasant matter implies? I would have spared you what now I think it will be better for you to learn at once. You must know, then, that your name is everywhere being coupled with this man's – it fills me with shame and disgust to say it – but so it is. This miserable disturbance of the other day has done you incalculable injury; your name, through it, has been in every mouth, and his most reprehensible conduct is put down as a – actually as a tribute to you.

'At that meeting which I attended yesterday in Gurton, the interest in the object of the assembly was, I assure you, quite secondary to the interest in the scandal (I am sorry for you, Helen, but I can call it nothing less) about you. No sooner had I finished reading my pamphlet than I was assailed with questions – some asking me if you were really engaged to this person; one vulgar woman presuming with a laugh that if you were not now, you would have to be before long, as an acknowledgement of Mr Massey's gallantry. Imagine what a humiliation this all is for me as well as you! No; let me finish now, Helen. You shall hear the whole, and then let us never recur to the subject. This miserable strike has been another means of coupling your names. While it lasted and it pleased Mr Massey to pretend to be obdurate, it was to "Miss Helen" that the people must come, and what you ask of him is done as a matter of course. Now that, I suppose, it is virtually over, it is "Miss

Helen" that has to be thanked for bringing about that desirable result. I am tempted to say, Helen, that it had better have gone on for ever, rather than that you should so have compromised yourself. And I am not alone in thinking thus. This tale has of course reached the Backs' ears, and Captain Back has had an interview with me on the subject.'

'And how dared he!' Helen interrupted, her dark eyes flashing in her pale face. 'How dared he be so impertinent? What business, Anna, is it of his?'

'Ah, that you know best, Helen; but I should say – if you give him the answer your conduct has led him to expect – I should say he has every right.'

'My conduct, Anna!' the girl cried. 'Do you remember to whom you are speaking? Alfred, do you think I have deserved that such things should be said to me?' But on turning to make her appeal, she saw nothing of her discreet brother-in-law but his empty chair. The reverend gentleman knew full well what a dangerous position to occupy is that of third between two women. 'To hear you speak,' the girl cried, with bitter indignation, 'one would think that I was a forward, shameless woman, a disgrace to my sex. There is no one living but my sister who would for one moment harbour such a thought.'

'I have no bad thought of you, Helen; I believe you, on the contrary, to have acted in pure guilelessness. It is not of your intention, but of your discretion, I complain. And, however angry you may be, I consider it my plain duty to show you, as I have ever done, in what I consider you to be wrong. Not that I hope much from my words, as I find that Captain Back has already exerted his influence without effect. He saw at once that this man was a thoroughly undesirable acquaintance for such a girl as you to possess – that he was one liable to encroach on any innocent encouragement you may have given him. I believe that all this he told you – surely his word should have had some weight. The Backs, remember, are a proud family; such a report about one who – about you must be offensive to them. At least you ought not to resent his anxiety.'

'But I do resent it!' Helen cried; 'I resent it bitterly. I will neither suffer his advice nor allow his interference. Oh, if he means to ask me to marry him, as I suppose he does, why does he not do it at once – get the thing over, like a man – and give me the chance of refusing him and being rid of him for ever?'

'You will hardly be so insane as to do that!'

'Will I not? You will see. Often and often I have wished lately that it might not be considered unmaidenly to refuse a man before he has offered himself. Perhaps, as it seems so well known that I cannot conduct myself with propriety, my doing this would not be thought remarkable or unpardonable.'

An angry red had risen to Mrs Pearson's face.

'Helen,' she said, 'if you do refuse Captain Back – if you do, I shall believe that what I have just told you people are saying – is true! The man himself – this ill-bred clownish farmer – will believe it too' (in her distress allowing herself the vulgar relief of calling names).

'He, at least, will never believe it!' Helen said, with a quick throb at her heart. 'Who has told you that he would even wish to believe it? You may make your mind quite easy about him, Anna, and you may set at rest the flattering curiosity of all your friends – I am not in the smallest danger of marrying Mr Massey. I am very unsatisfactory, no doubt, but I could never so forget what was due to you my sister, as to so irretrievably commit myself – to say nothing of the violence which would be done thereby to the feelings of the people at the Hall.' Then, after a moment's pause, and in a calmer voice, 'I cannot help people's tongues, remember, neither can he. Do you think he would not stop all this foolish babble if he could? What did he do more than any man in his place would have done? How could he tell the annoyance which would spring from it to me? There, I am defending him again, you see; but should I do it, Anna, if he were not attacked? Have I ever been silent when a word could be said for the absent? – why should it be a crime now? And what more have I done? If he were never spoken of to me, I should be glad – glad! Do I want to hear his name? But now lately it seems that nothing else can be talked of among us; and if I think the talk unjust, how can I hold my peace?'

A great deal more was said, both on this subject and that of the suitor at the Hall; and here, at least, Mrs Pearson found her sister, usually so tractable and easy to persuade where the strong wishes of others were concerned, immovable.

'I don't want to be married at all,' she declared. 'Oh, you mayn't believe it, but it is so. As I feel now, I believe that I shall choose to remain single all my life. I am not in love with matrimony. Yes, I may alter my mind, of course, and get married eventually as other women do – especially women with a little money; but to marry Captain Back, with his useless life, his empty talk, his pretty face – no! I would rather die!'

She had a way with her, when very much in earnest, of dropping her voice for emphasis, when others would have raised it. If poor Massey, who knew by heart every trick of the voice which was so sweet to him, could have heard that solemn declaration, his heart would have been lighter that night by a heavy load; and even Anna, from the sweet low tone of that 'I would rather die!' knew that she must in Captain Back's case abandon hope. Not that this would have caused Mrs Pearson annoyance at another time; it was not for an alliance with this especial man that she was so desirous, but she had just now been rendered anxious and seriously uneasy on her sister's account, and would have been glad to have seen her suitably settled and disposed of. The mind needed to be thoroughly at rest, untroubled, free from all domestic anxiety, which occupied itself in composing matter for the columns of the *Enlightener*; but it was now with difficulty that Mrs Pearson could succeed in attuning her thoughts to her literary labours. For the first time in her life she doubted her power over an inmate of her own house. She was afraid of Helen, and could not feel sure of her discretion. She knew well how soft and tractable the girl could be up to a certain point, and until now it had not been necessary to pass this same safe point; but Helen had now lately developed an inclination to think for herself, and a dangerous desire for independence of action, unbecoming and alarming in an unmarried girl; and for all her gentleness her sister knew that where Helen's conscience or her idea of right and justice were concerned, the girl could be firm and strong.

It was something of a relief to her, therefore, as well as a very great surprise, when Helen told her on the day following this conversation that she had been thinking it would be well for her to go away for a while. There had been a Miss Smythe, older by several years than Mrs Pearson, who had married, been widowed, and was now living abroad for the education of her children. To her, after many invitations refused, Helen, in the watches of the night, had decided to go. 'It will stop all this miserable talk,' she thought sadly; for she had been by no means unimpressed by what she had been told yesterday, and was quite alive to the undesirability of being so publicly discussed. She would thus escape from Captain Back, too, which would be even better than refusing him; while with regard to Mr Massey, the course appeared equally desirable. She had not forgotten what he had told her of the fruitlessness of his own flight in search of peace – that he had not rested until he had returned to her neighbourhood once more. She remembered this, and cried softly and quietly in the darkness, at the thought.

'I, too,' she sobbed, 'how shall I not long to come back to it all – to Perrie and my poor, and all the places and the people that I love – all – all – they are all here!' for the elder sister had been away so much as to be a stranger to her, and Helen was one who clung with a tender love to her surroundings, animate or inanimate. Still the decision was a relief to her mind; it was a cutting of the Gordian knot of her own difficulties, and it seemed to her the one thing that she could do to alleviate Mr Massey's trouble.

'I will go for a year at least,' she thought. 'I dare not tell myself that I must stay away longer; although, if I find that I can bear it, it shall be for ever.'

CHAPTER XX

Pollie is Off with her Old Love, etc.

MR GOSLING had three weeks' leave of absence, and he had stretched the three into five before he talked seriously of returning home. He could not make up his mind to abandon the delightful freedom of the country, he would say, throwing himself back in an armchair and looking ecstatically up at the ceiling, puffing the while at a cigarette which Pollie had made him, his inevitable smoking-cap on his head, his thumbs in his waistcoat-pockets. He would descant quite eloquently on the beauties of a country life from that safe vantage-ground; on the superiority of the air, poisoning the sitting-room with the fumes of his tobacco; on the freedom from restraint, crossing his feet in his tight patent boots; on the openness of the prospect, flourishing his cigarette at the four ill-papered walls. He was cheerful, as we have seen, in the hayfield, dispensing the lunch, and making jokes over the home-brewed beer; he was calmly stoical on a muck-heap, where Mr Freeman's mare, which he had ventured to mount without that gentleman's sanction or knowledge, had speedily de-posited him. He was not dismayed, outwardly, when challenged to shoot rooks with Teddie in the plantation, although provided with a weapon that 'kicked' and went off with an explosion surely unusual with guns; he was equal to the occasion, too, when ordered by Pollie to drive her in her little pony-car, on a wet day, into the market-town, although the animal, under his guidance, did certainly develop traits the reverse of reassuring. It had the queerest habit of jogging from one side to the other of the road, of pulling up quite unexpectedly to nibble grass, or to drink up a puddle; of turning suddenly round, at its own pleasure, to take them home again, and of going round in a quite bewildering fashion, when, in obedience to Pollie's sharp-voiced instruction, Mr Gosling pulled one rein tight to get it in the right direction again.

'It would look deuced queer up to those sort of games in the park,' he said afterwards, over the comfortable tea; but he was happy and good-natured through it all. He had never made so long a stay before, and Pollie knew that she would miss him dismally when he should be gone; while Mrs Freeman was always ready to laugh over his jokes, and her husband cut him slice after slice of ham in perfect amiability, feeling perhaps that matters were going as he wished.

Only with Mr Massey did the visitor not appear comfortably to 'hit it off.' Not that they were impolite to each other. Massey even felt a good deal of interest in the young fellow, who contrived to live so long in the Freeman atmosphere without suffering visibly from weariness. He did not always drop in at the Grange of evenings now, as had been his wont; but his presence or his absence mattered little in the gay circle of which Mr Gosling formed one, except that perhaps, during the half-hour of his appearance on the scene, the gay young man's liveliest sallies would be made. Comic songs were sung, conjuring tricks performed, imitations of popular actors given, even 'break-downs' danced. The other man would smoke his pipe in all but silence, addressing a word now and again to Mr Freeman, which met with response or not as the case might be, hugging up little sleepy Dollie against his breast, but not exerting himself after any fashion for her amusement. Sometimes the all-brilliant Mr Gosling would beckon the children away from him, and he, his thoughts far enough away from the present company and the stifling room redolent of hot grogs and dim with the smoke of several pipes, would, all unconscious, let her go, Dollie thus giving one more unneeded proof of the irresistible attractions of her accomplished cousin.

'I do think 'tis the contrast,' Pollie said once to her mother. 'There he sits like mum-chance, with never a smile on his face or a pleasant word to throw to you. I don't believe he even looks at – at anyone; or, if he does, he doesn't see them. Most likely he didn't as much as notice I had a new dress on at all to-night.'

'It must be that he's jealous, Pollie,' the mother conjectured, clinging still to her first admiration for Massey. 'You and Arthur do certainly make me laugh with your goings-on; but you ought to be more careful before Massey, you know.'

'Mother,' Pollie said solemnly, 'all is over between us. I am waiting until Arthur goes, to have a final break with him. It's no use talking; my mind is fully made up. James Massey's wife I won't be! Him, with his morose temper and sullen jealous ways, a nice life I should have! Yes, I know he used to be different; but, if he's so mighty particular he can't stand seeing me have a bit of nonsense with my own cousin, why what chance of happiness is there for me? Now, ma, what is the use of asking me if I shall marry Arthur. As if I could say that before I'm off with the other one! Do you think that would be honourable in me, now, to think about that yet?'

'One thing, Pollie, your father 'ud be pleased; I know that much,' her mother said. 'Hows'ever, I hope as you'll behave honourable to Massey all through – of course I do.'

Thus it will be seen that Miss Pollie's mind was pretty well made up, and although Mr Gosling's offer had not been entirely and unconditionally accepted when he left, he did not himself feel much uneasiness as to his cousin's ultimate decision. She, being bent on irreproachability in her love-affairs – in accordance with a plan she had laid out for herself – waylaid Mr Massey on his rounds one evening, as had been so frequently her custom some short time since.

'Why, Pollie, where is Mr Gosling?' he asked, as they shook hands. ''Tis not often one has the pleasure of seeing you alone, latterly.'

'If "one" means James Massey, I suppose "one" doesn't want.'

'Ah, that's unkind! Look what pleasant times we used to have together, you and I, till you threw me over for this London young man! Are you going to give me a treat this evening, or is that irrepressible cousin coming on after you soon?'

'And where were your thoughts last night, pray, when we were all talking of Arthur leaving us early this morning? He even asked you about the train he should go by. Shows what interest you feel in anything which concerns me, now.'

'And does it concern you so very much, Pollie? You used to be very happy without him; you'll get along all right again, don't you think? Now, I wish I could dance those break-downs for you, in which he so excels. I think my voice is about as good as his, for comic songs; but then, you see, I could not look so funny. He has not, by chance, left one of those nice shiny black coats behind him, has he? – that, and the smoking-cap you so kindly made me, might bring me a little nearer to the mark, perhaps.'

'Is that meant for wit?' inquired Pollie, very naturally incensed.

'For wit? – heaven forbid! I leave that to Mr Gosling. What awfully amusing puns he makes, by the way, Pollie! These London men do have the advantage of us country ones considerably, don't they?'

'Well, if you ask my candid opinion, I really think they do. They are more to be relied on, certainly. For instance, when they say they want to marry a girl, a good many of them mean it.'

'And don't we?' asked Massey, smiling. 'I'm ready to kill the man outright who has said anything so serious to you without meaning it, Pollie.'

'Then,' said Pollie, her voice trembling a little over the reproachful words, 'perhaps you'd better stop laughing at me, and – and look at home.'

'My dear,' he said gently, 'I am always looking there; and I am sick – sick to death of the prospect! I hoped you were come to give me something more cheerful to look at and think about. Where shall we go? When we last used to see much of each other, the hay was getting ready to cut; and now – how time flies, Pollie, when the London cousin is by! – the corn is nearly ripe. I should like you to come with me to see it; but you really are,' regarding her critically from a respectful distance – 'you really are such a terrific swell that I suppose I ought not to ask you. You do look awfully nice to-night, you know.'

'A lot you care how I look,' said Pollie, with affected disdain. 'Is that how you talk to Miss Smythe, perhaps?'

'Talk to whom!' with a swift alteration of look and tone apparent to the girl. 'What do you mean?'

'I mean what I say – why shouldn't I? Do you joke Helen Smythe about her new dresses when she has any, and compliment her when she looks smart?'

'No, I certainly do not,' he answered, with careful carelessness. 'I never remember to have joked Miss Smythe about anything; and now you mention it, I have never once seen her look "smart," as far as I can recollect.'

'Does she?' Pollie cried, astonished as well as pleased at this unexpected expression of her own idea. 'She's always a dowdy, I say. Even now that she has some money you never seem to notice her one time more than another, do you? There's never a bit of interest about how she'll look?'

'Not a bit. She's always about the same, isn't she?'

'You've heard that she's going away, of course?'

'Miss Smythe, do you mean?' turning sharply to look at the girl –'how going away? Going with the Backs again?'

'Oh dear, no – fancy your not knowing! The Backs are quite out of it. The Captain would not come forward, I suppose. No, she's going to Germany; she has a sister there – going for good, you know. And what ever will Hilby do without her! Do you actually mean they have not told you? I thought you were hand-in-glove with them!'

'I hear nothing about them,' he said irritably. 'Are we to stand here all night? If you won't come with me, I will walk towards home with you.'

Pollie turned and walked at his side.

'You needn't be so cross with me about it,' she said, glancing up at him. 'I can't help her going away. I suppose you know what people say about it – what has been dinned into my ears for this fortnight past?' She paused; but he neither looked nor answered. 'They say that she is in love with you, and that you are going to marry her.'

'Who is it that says that?' he asked angrily, stopping short. 'I should like to ram his teeth down his lying throat for him!' Then moving on, 'I beg your pardon,' he said, 'for losing my temper; but it is such an infernal lie!'

'You to lose your temper over it!' she said; 'and has it been pleasant to me, do you think? The report has put me in an awkward place enough, I should say, without your – your swearing at me, and going on in this kind of way. My friends have contradicted it left and right – they have all been most kind; but I'm sure I don't know if it's true or not. I know you've altered to me; you may be on Helen's side now, for all I can say.'

'We won't talk any more of Miss Smythe,' he said impatiently. 'I do hope that your friends, whatever they may find to say of me, will leave her name alone for the future. You and they can be perfectly assured that I am about as likely to be prime minister as to marry her. As to my altering, to you, I don't think so. You used to like to talk to me, and now you prefer to talk to some one else – that's about the difference; and that's on your side, you see.'

'And you know while you say it that it's not true,' she cried, turning on him quickly. 'You know which of you two, in my heart, I like best to be with.'

'I know which of us two you are likelier to be happy with,' he said gravely, noting a little catch in her voice which showed that the girl was really moved. 'Do not let us pretend to joke on this matter any more, Pollie. You are going to marry your cousin, are you not, my dear? I think that is what you came to tell me to-night. I was worse than a fool to laugh at him. I am sure that he is a good fellow, and he is awfully "gone" about you; it's easy to see. I believe that you will be happy with him, and from the bottom of my heart I hope you may.'

Pollie was struggling to keep from tears. Never in her short selfish life had she felt so weak, so dangerously full of sentiment as she did to-night. It had been only a farce, this engagement of hers – full speedily had she been compelled to realize that it could never be played out in sober reality; but a certain amount of pleasure and of pride had come to her in the performance of her part, hollow as it was. The act of renunciation was not pleasant. Mr Gosling was a substance of solid worth, and Massey was but a fleeting shadow; yet a horrible longing came to her now to forego her chance of the desirable reality, that she might grasp at the deceitful shade. At a word, at a look even, from the man by her side, she would have given her cousin the go-by. And Massey, on his part, with the weakness of mankind – with his own especial weakness, perhaps – felt a momentary revival of tenderness towards the girl who was about to release him from a serious entanglement – a dangerous longing to pet and make much of her, by way of showing his genuine relief, came over him.

'If I do marry him, I suppose I shall do very well,' she said, in a rather weary tone of voice – 'as well as other people. No one gets things as they wish in this world, they say, and I begin to think it's true. You've got to make the best of your fate, whatever it is, as you can't help it; and I don't intend to whine about mine. Not that I've settled he is to be my fate; but I suppose you've made up your mind we are done with each other, so I don't want to bother you with what concerns me.'

'But there could hardly be anything that could interest me more. I am your friend, remember, whatever happens – shall we make that a bargain? Tell me about yourself. Mr Gosling is coming back, of course?'

'If I ask him,' Pollie said in a dull voice, looking away.

'And of course you will ask him – what is there to prevent you?'

'Perhaps he thinks what a good many others think – that you might prevent me.'

'But, my dear, do not let him think that. I am one of those wise people, Pollie, who can recognize that their day is over – mine was over with you when Gosling came. I know that you will care a vast deal more for him than you ever could have done for me; and I am, I suppose, glad to know it – at any rate I ought to be.'

'If you know it, then, it's more than I do.'

'Hush!' he said, in some alarm. 'That is treason, and treason to a good fellow who is going to be your husband.'

After this he thought it advisable to refer no more to the state of Miss Freeman's affections; she was a young lady possessed of so little becoming reticence on the subject that it became for him a dangerous one.

'Tell me,' he said to her before they parted, 'is there anything you would like me to do about this affair, Pollie? I would do a great deal for you if I could. Have you told your father and mother? These arrangements are better settled off at once.'

'It is so kind of you to be anxious.'

'Now, do not speak in that tone of voice. Where's the good of being bitter to me now?'

'Then do not talk of helping to get me married to another man, and don't let me see how horridly glad you are about it. I will manage my own affairs without your troubling. And now I will say good-bye – that is what I came for; and that means good-bye to a lot of things – to everything.' Then she stood still and put out her hand. 'Good-bye!' she said, without looking at him.

'You do not mean that I am not to see you or speak to you?' he asked, overlooking her hand. 'This is not good-bye to our friendship, Pollie?'

Her eyes were full of tears, and she did not answer.

'No, I won't say good-bye to that,' he said. Then he paused for a moment, and her hand being taken by him, fell back to her side. Presently, bending down to her, he asked: 'Are you really engaged to Gosling yet, Pollie? – tell me – or is it only an event in the near future?'

'I am not engaged to him yet,' she whispered, with a trembling lip.

Then Massey put his arm about her for the last time, and stooped to kiss the sorrowful pretty face. 'Good-bye,' he said, hardly in the moment's folly knowing if he were glad or sorry. 'Good-bye to all the old folly, and the pleasant nonsense between us; but not good-bye, remember, to you, my dear.'

When he let her go and she turned and went away from him, Pollie was sobbing like a broken-hearted child; but Massey knew of old both that her grief was likely to be very transitory, and also that to attempt consolation was, for him, a dangerous experiment. So, with many pangs of pity and self-reproach, he suffered her to depart. More unpleasantness than delight had come to him from his association with her, and yet, according to the perversity of human nature, he felt that he was losing something of value to him, as he watched her on her solitary way. Her attachment to him had been the result of at least as much vanity as love, but it had been flattering nevertheless. He knew quite well that Gosling's chance would havc been but small should he himself have cared to whistle; and although for worlds he would not have kept her at his side, the remembrance that she would have preferred to be there was consoling.

Pollie, too, as she walked forlornly homeward, was more shaken in her self-esteem, more depressed, more nearly miserable than she had ever been before. She had gone in the pride of her spirit and in her smart attire, to carry the high hand, to tell her lukewarm lover that she had been mistaken in the state of her feeling for him, that she had altered her mind, that she gave him back his promise (conveniently oblivious of the fact that there had never been a promise). Instead, her strength had forsaken her at sight of him, and the perception of the fact that she had now to sever the slight connection between them had broken her courage, and made her weep like a child for his favour. She had shown him plainly that at a word she would have gone to him, and had waited for the word in vain. Her face was all blurred and disfigured with tears; when she reached home to hide it she ran up to her own room at once, locking the door upon herself and her grief. The poor child was not sufficiently accustomed to tears to shed them scientifically or with decent quiet, and for hours that night she lay on her face, and stifled her noisy childish sobbing with her pillow, that 'mother' should not hear. James Massey knew that her renunciation of him had not been perfectly voluntary, but she would have died rather than allow anyone else to suspect this; and so at last, with the good sense inherent in her where her own interests were concerned, she turned over and went to sleep, reflecting that some hours of peaceful slumber would be required to restore her cheeks and eyes to their normally clear condition.

In the morning, except that she was a bit paler than usual, there was nothing to tell the tale; and she blushed in a becoming manner, and looked very conscious, at sight of a letter in Mr Gosling's hand lying on her plate. She opened and read the missive while she ate her egg and toast, and was comforted thereby. It was soothing to her hurt vanity to find that at least this lover did not want to 'call off'; that, on the contrary, he wrote in a manner less flippant than his usual speech, begging her to hurry with her answer, and urging her to do at once what she had apparently promised him – viz., to give 'that sulky devil' (it was in such manner that he spoke of his harmless rival) the 'straight tip,' and to send him for ever about his business; hinting at a lovely ring in a certain jeweller's window, upon which he had fixed his affections, a ring so wide that it would reach up to a certain little knuckle, and quite plain – all the rage just now, none of your trumpery flash stones and rubbish – and which at a certain word from Hilby would be transferred from that jeweller's window to the dearest little hand in the world. Pollie smiled very brightly over the prospect of that ring. Her father looked up from his plate of cold meat to her conscious face.

'What! have you and Arthur put matters square?' he asked.

'I don't know, pa,' she answered, beginning to put away her letter. 'How do you mean, "square"?'

'Well, I thought by the time he'd been walkin' round you, down here, he'd ha' told you hisself what *his* idea o' "square" was. I don't want to interfere, mind ye, but I think there's been pretty nigh enough o' this shilly-shally. I give you my opinion, pretty plain once before, if you recollect; if you'd ha' taken my advice then, instead o' runnin' agin what common-sense must ha' told you was right, you'd ha' looked much less of a fool now.' Then Mr Freeman made, as his manner was, a sudden transition from apparent good temper to most serious wrath. 'One thing I *am* settled on,' he went on, with a thump of his fist on the table and a raised voice; 'whether you please to have this here man or not, I'm darned if I don't put a stop to the foolery with the t'other one! His hain't been the kind o' treatment to you I'll tol'rate a day longer – so you make your mind easy o' that score.'

'Why, William,' his wife said plaintively, 'how you du get yourself into rages all in a minute! Who ever would ha' thought of you puttin' on such parts like this all of a suddint!'

'You be blowed!' he said, turning his staring blue eyes on to the partner of his joys – perhaps it was a wickeder word than 'blowed' that he used.

'Let him alone, ma,' Pollie interposed, with indignant looks. She was not in the least afraid of her father, although it sometimes pleased her to pretend to stand in awe. 'If you think I am not responsible to manage my own affairs, I wonder you don't lock me up,' she said to him now, tauntingly.

'I'm —— if I don't, if you come any o' your sauce to me! D—d if I'll stand it from you or from anyone! D'ye think I'll have my own self or anyone in my house made a laughin'-stock of any longer for the pleasure of a tarnation prig like that – a conceited ass that you women ha' made a fool of till he don't know if he stand on his head or his heels! If you and your mother don't know when you're bein' laughed at I du; and d—d if I ha'n't stood it long enough!' He sent his plate into the middle of the table as he spoke, pushed his chair back noisily, and got up. 'My tongue ha' itched to tell him a bit o' my mind for a good time. I'll do it to-day, if I live!'

'Wait one minute, pa,' Pollie said rather hurriedly, for he had gone to the door as if to put his pleasing project into execution there and then. 'Before you go and see Mr Massey you'd better wait and see that some one else don't make a fool of himself, as you so politely put it. There's nothing between James Massey and me – nothing whatever. I made a mistake in thinking I could marry him; and I have told him so, and broken off my engagement.'

'Your engagement!' her father echoed, with slow scorn. 'A fine kind of a' engagement!' But he was somewhat appeased evidently, and came back to his place at the table, where, however, he sat and glared at the fine leg of cold boiled pork in front of him with a brow of thunder.

'Come, surely we ha' had enough o' them black looks, William!' Mrs Freeman pleaded. 'Pollie ha' done the right thing by Massey, and behaved straightfor'ard and honourable as a young girl should. We have nothin' to complain of now, and more have he –'

'D—— his complaints!' said Mr Freeman. 'I should like to catch him complainin' to me – I'd complain him! And now' – to his daughter – 'how about this next one? P'r'aps you'll tell me how you mean to act about him.'

'How nicely you ask for my confidence!' remarked Pollie, with withering sarcasm.

'And do let the girl be, William!' her mother said irritably; ''tis her that have got to be married, and not you. Surely you might trust her to take her own way!'

'You hold your tongue!' Mr Freeman commanded firmly. 'She had her own way about the t'other one, and a pretty mess she made of it. No; I'll ha' no more o' that wi' my girl – taking up first wi' this man and then wi' that. I don't hold wi' women o' that fashion. I'll know what she mean to do; and that she do, I'm d—d if she don't stick to – else out she goes from my house!'

'You don't make your house so pleasant that a person need be very sorry even then,' his daughter said in a tranquil tone of voice, as if she were simply stating an agreeable fact.

'Drop that!' he advised. 'You aren't quite a fool, I take it; although your mother have done her best with ye towards it. You know I don't often say much, and what I say I gen'ally mean; and I mean to know before I go out this morning if 'tis your wishes to marry this here man or not. Do as you like about it; there's things for and things against. Only recollect, what you say, that you abide by. Make that clear to yourself. Now, how is it to be?'

'As you are so pleasant about it,' said Miss Pollie pertly, 'I may as well tell you that I dare say I shall marry him. I fancy I shall write and tell him so to-day. As to all that about having to stick to it, why I pay no attention to that; if I change my mind, and find, as I have done once before, that it would not be for my happiness to marry him – why, I shan't marry him – that's all.'

Mr Freeman grunted as he rose from his chair again and prepared to leave the room.

'I take it you know pretty well what you're about,' he said, with rough approval. 'You aren't all fool, and know better than to play that game twice.'

And so at last the matter got itself settled. Mr Gosling was written to, and, it is to be hoped, made happy. Before the week's end, the plump third finger of Pollie's left hand was half hidden by the massive gold band with her own initials and Arthur's intertwined, in what that gentleman styled a 'whopping monogram'; and Miss Freeman was once more known as an engaged young woman – her engagement this time having apparently every prospect of a speedy and happy termination after the usual blissful fashion.

CHAPTER XXI

Sunday Afternoon at the Grange

THE transference of herself and her belongings to such a distance, and for such an uncertain length of time, was a matter which Helen found could not be quickly arranged. The date ultimately fixed for her departure was six weeks distant from the night on which it had occurred to her that it might be better for her to go. The announcement had been received by all her friends with much surprise, by many with real regret, by one with something like despair. The parishioners were unanimous in their sentiment of sorrow. Now that they were to lose it, they began to value that kind hand of hers which had always been ready – nay, anxious to help. Who was to look after them now, when their wives and children were ill – when they themselves were in trouble or out of work? Nothing would come from the Vicarage but sermons, and tracts, and unpalatable advice, when Miss Helen should be gone, they knew right well. Captain Back and the rest of his family were angered as well as grieved at the news. A good deal had been hoped from Helen's help and influence; and he had until now made comfortably sure of her as of a very pretty, if too 'goody-goody,' girl whom it might be convenient for him to make his wife – a girl who would hold her own in that pretty semi-languid manner of hers where he had difficulty in keeping his footing; who would put his father into a reasonable frame of mind with regard to the prospects of this expensive second son; who would, finally, in the matter of personal beauty, 'take the shine' out of most of those she came across. Captain Back, to Helen's dismay and his own discomfiture, managed to defeat one object – if only a minor one – of her flight.

Mr Massey sought no opportunity to enlighten her as to his views on the subject; therefore, although she felt a great deal of curiosity and even anxiety on the matter, she had no definite knowledge of what he thought. In the Vicarage itself, opinion was divided. Mrs Pearson, recognizing that Helen's removal was necessary, was consistent enough to bear without complaint the consequent disadvantages. Her husband was noisily distressed at losing an always good-tempered companion and a steady champion of his own. He had a shrewd suspicion that his own matrimonial curricle would not run so smoothly when Helen was no longer by to oil the wheels with her unfailing sympathy and her ready help. While Perrie was not to be consoled. She was the light of his little life, his Aunt Helen; the sun of his existence would have set –all his prospects would have clouded over – when she should have left him. He did not speak of his misery even to her, but bore his affliction in pathetic silence, slipping off her lap and out of the room if she attempted consolation. He had encountered Mr Massey once lately in his walks, and had been taken from his governess (a new acquisition since the improvement in the Vicarage exchequer) to sit on that gentleman's horse.

'When is she going, Perrie?' Massey had asked him, his arm thrown round the child to hold him safe. But sudden tears had been the only answer given, and the young man had sighed and gently patted the little sorrowful head.

'My poor little man! What is to become of you and of me?' he had groaned. 'I suppose she does not think of that, Perrie?'

As the time drew near for her departure, Helen felt that she could not love them enough – all these kind, simple people who so loved her – nor show them sufficient gratitude for their affectionate thoughts. The school children had clubbed their pennies together, and assisted by those elders who wished to have their names inscribed on the imposing cardboard where the titles of donors were to be given, had purchased for Miss Smythe's acceptance a monster Bible, which Helen, no doubt, valued, as she said, more than any present she had ever received, but which began to assume formidable proportions when its transference to Germany came under discussion. In return the children were regaled at such a 'treat' as had never been holden before within the annals of the school, where there was positively *no* stint as to jam and cake, and no limit to the fun, where there were handsome prizes distributed wholesale, in what Mrs Pearson considered a demoralising manner, falling indiscriminately to good and bad alike, till there was not a child in the school without some trophy to take away, hugged to its happy little heart.

And then, not content with the fatigue and the trouble and expense of this, as said her sister, Helen must take it into her head to entertain the grown people too. She would give a garden-party for her poor people, she declared, and stoutly maintaining that this was a brilliant idea, refused to listen to adverse criticism. Indeed, none of them cared to thwart her very much just now, and her way was easily won. She was to leave for London, where she intended to stay with some friends for a week or so before leaving England on the Wednesday, and this farewell entertainment she resolved should take place on her last evening at home – the Tuesday – and so it was finally settled.

'I wish that the Freemans had been at church this afternoon,' she said to Mrs Pearson as they left that edifice on what was to be her last Sunday at Hilby. 'I am going ask Pollie to help me on Tuesday evening.'

'Really, Helen, I think we can do without the kind of help she would give.'

'Perhaps so, but Pollie might feel hurt if I did not ask her, and I want to be on pleasant terms with everyone before I leave. And besides, I must bid her good-bye in any case, and I shall be so engaged that this seems to me my only chance of doing so. You will come down to the Grange with me, Anna? I do not really feel equal to the encounter with the entire Freeman family – unsupported and alone.'

There was one other person about her leave-taking from whom Helen had thought a great deal, although of this she could not speak to her sister, knowing well that her advice on the subject would be neither gentle nor palatable. It seemed that she could herself do nothing in this, yet surely – surely he would not let her go without one word of farewell. It seemed somehow, to Helen, that it would be an impossibility for her to leave so. She thought that the spirit of unrest which possessed her now, the uneasy fear that in her determination to leave her troubles behind, she had but been selfish and hard-hearted, inducing evil instead of good, the hopelessness with which she thought of her own future life, and the compunction laying hold on her when she tried to realize his, she thought that these would all leave her when once she had put her hand in his, and heard him say 'good-bye.' It would be a kind of absolution, she told herself; without it she could not depart in peace.

The Reverend Alfred, as of old, spent a good part of his days, and most of his evenings, at the Wood Farm, and there was little doubt that the impending change at the Vicarage was fully known to its inmate, but he had made no sign. Whether, in his general inability to conceal that which for divers reasons it were wiser to leave untold, Mr Pearson had communicated his wife's edict of banishment, Helen could not tell, and feared to ask, but certain it was that at the Vicarage, Mr Massey was seen no more. The Vicar might stay within upon wet evenings till he was weary of himself, and the rest were weary of him, but his neighbour came no more to while away the hours, with cigars for two, in the shabby library where alone smoking was allowed. The garden was at its loveliest in this August month, but Helen and Perrie, as they paced the walks, sweet with mignonette, and gay with a thousand flowers, were joined no more by one who, of old, had loved to linger there, in the gathering dusk, while Helen discoursed, in a jargon all her own, of the flowers, and the birds' songs, and the stars above them. Never a day passed that she did not hear his name – scarcely a day that she did not see him – in his fields, his dogs beside him, on horseback, or driving through the village. He would pull off his hat to her as he passed without a smile upon his face, and Helen would bow her head, with as much grace and apparent self-possession as if her heart had not stood still for a moment in her breast, while her limbs had suddenly threatened to fail her.

Mr Massey had entirely given up his attendance at church lately, at which Helen grieved in her innocently orthodox mind, praying that love for her might not have ruined him, body and soul; but on this especial Sunday he had broken through his later custom and had appeared in his pew for morning service. He sat where she could have seen him plainly by turning her head, and from whence, as several people knew, Pollie and Mrs Pearson among them, he had been accustomed to watch her every movement with quite unremitting attention; but after that one rapid glance, which showed him in his old place, Helen had looked no more, but had gone through her devotions with a more contented mind than she had known for many a day. Massey knelt and stood up and sat down without much appreciation of what his mechanical movements meant; but Helen prayed for him that day with such fervour as he could never have hoped to feel for himself; and the old harmonium forgot its wheezings and all those various complaints brought on by age and damp, and spoke under her fingers as it never surely would speak again when her place should be forsaken; and her voice in the singing seemed to one of the congregation to rise above the others, as sweet and as pure as the voice of those that cried 'Hosanna.'

But when the Vicarage party left the church, Mr Pearson pointed out Massey's lessening form disappearing with the Freeman family in the direction of their house. Mr Gosling was also of this party, having arrived the previous night on his first visit to his betrothed; and he was, at that very minute, if those lookers-on could but have told, giving a lively example of Mr Pearson's style of elocution.

'Not any more, my dear,' he was saying presently to his affianced – 'never again! Much as I'd do to please you, Pollie, I ain't going to spoil my dinner listening to that old buffer again. Give me a cushion and a night-gown – excuse the allusion, my dear – and pour two or three glasses of port wine into me, and I'm game to beat your vicar hollow; but I'll beat 'im at home, Pollie, and you shall sit in the easy-chair, my pretty, and be my only beloved brethren.'

Mrs Freeman laughed at what she caught of this, the lovers being a little in front, then glanced into the face of Massey by her side, with a sudden, womanly pity for the gravity, not to say gloom, depicted there.

'Won't you come home, and eat your bit of dinner with us, Mr Massey?' she asked. 'Do; we can make room for you always, you know, if you'll only come. It must be lonesome for you on a Sundays.'

Massey, however, declined the dinner with many thanks, subsequently engaging himself to go and take a 'glass o' wine' with the Freemans afterwards, 'just to show we are all comf'table, and no malice,' the kind woman said.

He was not, however, given to the consuming of heavy port in the middle of the day, and was not sorry, on his arrival, to be waylaid by Pollie in the hall, scolded in a whisper for coming late, told that 'pa,' having had his wine, was asleep in the dining-room, while 'ma' had just got hold of the newspaper, whose well-known somnolent effects rendered it wiser that she should be left undisturbed, and 'would he mind coming into the drawing-room to Arthur and me.'

Mr Massey hung up his hat in the hall, by the side of that glossy erection worn that morning by the gentleman whom the Grange now delighted to honour, and prepared to follow Miss Freeman. He put his hand lightly on hers as she was about to open the drawing-room door.

'You are sure I shan't be spoiling sport?' he whispered.

But Pollie gave a toss to her head (keeping her hand very quietly under his the while).

'We've said our say to each other, and Arthur 'on't mind you, you'll find,' she assured him.

Nor did Arthur, unless the presence of the other man incited him to greater display of amorousness; it certainly did not render him shy in the exercise of what he considered his rights.

The visitor sat and smoked his cigar, and heartily wished himself away. He looked out of the window at the overgrown, neglected garden, where a broken wooden horse of Dollie's lay lumbering in the path; he looked within at Pollie, who had pretended to love him the other day, now sharing an arm-chair with her future husband, and puffing at a cigarette between her lips. 'All the gyurls in town smoked,' Mr Gosling had assured him, and had farther propounded the theory that there was 'always room for an engaged couple in one chair'; and seeing the theory put in practice before his eyes, Massey had not been able to refute it, even had he cared. There was plenty of room apparently for these two, who were neither of them of imposing stature, and there they laid contentedly and devoid of shyness – he in his violet and gold smoking-cap and his inevitable, shiny black coat; she carefully posed, so that the innumerable little yellow curls should run no risk of disagreement, her tightly fitting pink gown disclosing a good bit of ankle, her smartly-shod plump feet dangling several inches from the floor.

Massey surveyed them both calmly for some minutes, seeing that they rather courted observation; then turned away his head in disgust. A horrible feeling of weariness was upon him, of sick distaste of himself and his surroundings. The room was full of smoke; for the Londoner, who was delicate and afraid of a breath of air, always insisted on closed windows. Massey rose to his feet, feeling faint and oppressed with wretchedness.

'I'll go outside for a bit, till your father awakes, Pollie,' he said. 'This room is so confoundedly close. I must get a breath of air.'

'Why, you do look bad!' Pollie cried, jumping up. 'Have a glass of wine, do. Never mind disturbing father. I'll get it.'

But Massey would not hear of this, and got himself outside into the pure air. Up and down the box-edged paths, between rows of broken-down hollyhocks and sunflowers that had fallen for want of a stake, he paced. It was a dull, hot, August day, with no stir in the air – oppressive and uncheering.

'A beast of a day!' Massey called it, pushing his hair from his hot brow, and looking about him discontentedly. 'A beast of a place! A beast of a life! I wish I had never been born! I wish I was dead! I wish we were all dead!'

‘Tum and dive dear Dollie a fwing,’ called a small voice at his knee; and a chubby hand was put out to drag him to an old apple-tree at the end of the garden, where dangled a rope on which a cushion was hung for Dollie’s pleasure.

‘I can’t come now, Dollie,’ pulling away his hand. ‘I’m tired to death – don’t bother!’

‘Tum on!’

‘Get out; I won’t. I hate the lot of you. Be off!’

‘You’re a ole beast if you hates dear Dollie. Dollie’ll kick ole beast!’ suiting the action to the word.

‘Now then, drop that!’ Massey laughed, warding off her attack with some very tender buffets on her soft person. ‘Go and kick one of your own size! Be off, and span into your cousin Arthur.’

‘He welly kind,’ Dollie said, stopping in her small efforts at chastisement; ‘he bring dear Dollie fweets.’

‘Does he? Then go you and kick his legs, and tell him I sent you.’

The child stood a moment, regarding him with deep surprise, then trotted off towards the house.

‘So dear Dollie will,’ she remarked threateningly.

Massey laughed to himself as he looked after her.

‘She’ll do it, safe enough,’ he said; ‘I may as well go and see the fun.’

He went to the drawing-room window and looked in. Pollie had soon grown tired of that tight fit in the easy-chair, when Massey was no longer by to watch her position with feelings perhaps of envy and longing. She was seated now at the piano, playing, amid many false chords, the air of the hymn they had sung that morning in church. She, however, flew up with alacrity at the sight of Massey’s face at the window, and quickly throwing it open, made him enter. Dollie, who had fortunately been waylaid on her journey hither, and diverted from her dangerous errand, did not appear.

‘Play something,’ Massey said presently, nodding towards the piano. It was a request Pollie had not often heard from his lips, Miss Freeman’s musical talents being of the most meagre description. Such as they were, however, she by no means hid in a napkin, being ready to strum away, after just a little pressing, at any moment. She had a vast accumulation of music; ‘gentlemen’ were always sending her ‘pieces,’ she said; and she would play off any amount of airs with a bass mostly of her own invention, and with small regard to the laws of harmony, or sing her songs in her untrained voice, in a manner quite satisfactory to herself, whatever might be the effect on other people. She sat down now, and began again on the hymn she had been trying over. ‘Art thou weary, art thou languid?’ she sang, then broke off to remark...’

‘How high Helen Smythe did sing this morning. I suppose she wanted to have it all to herself; and so she did pretty well. I heard her voice all through above the others. Didn’t you?’

Yes; Mr Massey had certainly heard the voice, but that hymn was one he rather liked.

'Go on and play it, Pollie. Never mind singing if you don't care to.'

'Oh, hang all about hymns,' cried Arthur impatiently. 'Had enough of them this morning.' Catch him in that blessed old edifice again! Wasn't fond of too much church at the best of times, but a bloomin' old barn like that didn't see him again! 'Why,' he demanded, 'could not that fat noodle the Vicar, and those two washed-out women who looked after him, make the service in this place more attractive? Hanged if there was a thing to look at but mouldy old walls, and a poor beggar of a bird that had got in by mistake, and afterwards most sensibly devoted all its energies to getting out again. Put a few flowers on the altar, why not? and light up a candle or two (tallow dips if they were too mean for wax, what did he care?), and stick a cross or two about, and you wouldn't know the place. Pitch that blamed old harmonium into the street, and start a decent organ; it would soon be seen if people would not go to church. Give us a comic song, Pollie; I've had enough for to-day of hymns. Try that thing I brought you down last night – all the go in town just now.'

It was a comic song of a rather low order which Pollie played, the words verging dangerously on the vulgar even, but there was a good deal of swing and go in the air, and the impressionable, irrepressible Arthur was soon joining in the chorus, waving his meerschaum pipe above his head, in time with the movement, and at last in the lightness of his heart springing to his feet, his sleek coat-tails flying behind him, he executed various wild gyrations, to the imminent peril of Pollie's unsteady little tables.

It was at this minute that Massey, leaning, cigar in mouth, against the chimney-piece, looking wearily away from the eccentric little man making such a fool of himself in the middle of the room, saw the drawing-room door open. There had been too much noise to distinguish any sound beyond that of the duet going on, and the performers were so pleasingly engaged themselves that they did not even become aware of visitors for fully half a minute after Massey had seen Mrs Pearson and her sister standing aghast in the doorway.

CHAPTER XXII

Mr Freeman is Unpleasant

THE appearance of these ladies was so thoroughly unexpected and so exceedingly perplexing that none of the three occupants of the room could sufficiently collect his or her wits to make the best of the untoward occurrence. Mr Massey, for what seemed to the visitors an unseemly length of time, still leant with his back to the mantelpiece, his cigar arrested halfway to his lips, an embodiment of astonishment and dismay. Mr Gosling, his capers cut unexpectedly short, finished his performances by knocking down a table and falling backward into a chair, where he lay, panting from his late exertions, but puffing vigorously at his nearly extinguished pipe, his eyes fixed in exaggerated unconsciousness on the ceiling. Pollie, at first thoroughly disconcerted, having pulled the music from the desk and loudly slammed the piano, was the first to recover herself, and was dragging forward a couple of chairs, and, with a burning face, suggesting that her visitors should be seated, before Massey had come to himself so far as to leave the friendly support of the mantelpiece and to fling the end of his cigar in among Pollie's fine shavings.

'Thank you, we will not sit down; we shall not interrupt you for long,' Mrs Pearson said frigidly to Pollie, calmly ignoring the others. 'We have but just left church, and a class is now awaiting us at home. I believe that Miss Smythe has something she wishes to say to you.'

Never had Mrs Pearson looked so uncompromisingly severe; never had her voice sounded less conciliatory; her lips were drawn tightly over her teeth; her eyes were gleaming – into what a polluted atmosphere had she not been ushered! It was of the moral pollution alone she thought at first; but soon the hot smoke-burdened air, forced itself unpleasantly on her notice; she put her handkerchief to her lips and coughed protestingly, a look of extremest disgust on her face.

Massey had held Helen's hand for a moment in his, and had looked with a deprecating glance into her face. 'What'll she think of me now, I wonder?' he sighed to himself, as he moved to throw up the window.

'Put down that cursed thing,' he whispered angrily to Mr Gosling as he passed, alluding to the brand-new meerschaum at which that young man was violently puffing.

'You mind your own business,' Arthur retorted with prompt resentment; but he did remove the obnoxious article from his lips, nevertheless; and having knocked the ashes into his hand, proceeded to rub up the beloved bowl with a red silk handkerchief. 'Hope my weed hasn't annoyed you ladies?' he said graciously as he proceeded with this operation. 'Not used to smoking, perhaps?'

Helen had gone over to the open window, against which Massey, too, stood. 'This is good-bye, then,' she had said to herself, and was half glad, half sorry. It was to Mrs Pearson that the task of replying to the 'odious' creature's remarks fell.

'I am not indeed used to it,' she said. 'The smell of smoke is extremely unpleasant to me.'

'Really now' (winking at Pollie with an air which said, 'Observe me; I am about to produce some fun!') 'the difference there's in the sex! There's some ladies of my acquaintance which enjoy the perfume of a pipe. Some of them even go so far as to take a cigarette themselves!'

'I do not doubt it,' said Mrs Pearson, stonily staring. 'There is no accounting for the depraved tastes of some women.'

'Oh, as to depraved – come, I say, isn't that too strong? That's prejudice, you know – sheer prejudice. You mustn't be so hard –prejudice's absurd in this enlightened age. Where's the harm of a cigarette?'

Here Pollie, for reasons of her own, hastened to change the subject, by remarking that they had expected a thunderstorm, but that it had apparently passed off.

'So sorry we could not avail ourselves of the privilege of afternoon church,' the irrepressible one put in again. 'Have been solacing ourselves with serious talk, haven't we, Pollie? and just as you, ma'am, and the other lady entered, we were about indulging in a h – h – ymn.'

Mrs Pearson, with a silent glance of disgust, turning a stiffly protesting back on the objectionable young man, called upon Helen to fulfil her errand quickly, reminding her that they had no time to spare, remaining herself apparently insensible to Mr Gosling's satiric entreaty that she should not hurry, and deaf to Pollie's tittering 'Hush!' Helen, thus adjured, soon explained the object of her visit.

'Will you come, Pollie?' she asked. 'I do hope that you will. Do you know it will be my last day at home for – for years, perhaps.' Massey turned and looked at her swiftly – such a dangerous tremor was in her voice. She went on – 'Everyone who can is coming to bid me good-bye; all the village people. We are going to have tea for them – for as many as can come – in the garden. Will you help me with them? I thought, perhaps, you would take a table for me. It will be so very kind.' Helen was almost abject in her desire to propitiate her little ungracious neighbour, before she went away.

'I don't know that I mind doing as much as that,' Pollie said with deliberation. 'That is, if it will be of any assistance.'

'It will, indeed! And after tea we shall want to have some games started to amuse the men – cricket, or some races.' Looking across at the athletic form of Mr Gosling: 'Perhaps you would help me there?'

'Happy,' said that gentleman urbanely, with a gracious duck of his head.

'But the men?' asked Pollie, who was always matter-of-fact, and often unpleasantly sensible. 'How are the men to be there, just in the beginning of harvest, too? They are at work till half-past nine at night, you know.'

'Oh dear, I hope that Mr Freeman will let them come,' sighed Helen, somewhat crest-fallen. 'I shall be so disappointed if they cannot all come. Mr Selby, I feel sure, will make no objection, and you will not, I know,' she said, turning to Massey, with an unconscious lowering of her voice.

At this moment the door opened, and Mr Freeman, all unconscious of visitors, put in his head to call his daughter to tea, and would, at sight of the 'Vicarage women,' as quickly have withdrawn it, but –

'Come in, pa,' cried Pollie; 'Miss Smythe has something to ask you. Now, Miss Smythe, ask pa yourself,' honestly thinking her parent was more likely to do the gracious thing if thus taken by surprise, than if given liberty to curse and swear on the subject in the bosom of his family. Besides, sometimes Mr

Freeman awoke from his Sunday siesta in a quite genial frame of mind; also, unfortunately, sometimes he didn't.

Helen hesitated nervously, having almost a fear of the man and his boorish ways; and Massey seeing the flush on her face, spoke for the first time.

'Miss Smythe wants all the men to go up to the Vicarage to-morrow evening,' he said. 'She was afraid you might object. But,' turning to her again, 'Mr Freeman will tell you that in harvest-time the men are our masters, Miss Smythe. They begin work when they like, and leave off when it pleases them. They will be only too glad to go to you, if you wish for them.'

'We would not have tea before seven if that would be more convenient to you,' Helen said, addressing the elder man, but turning from his unpromising countenance to Massey's face.

'Have it what time you like,' the one of them said to whom the pleasing of Helen was just then of more consequence than the ingathering of all the harvests in the world.

'Does your silence give consent, sir?' Mrs Pearson asked with dignified impatience of Mr Freeman.

'Consent!' he repeated, slowly pushing out his nether lip. 'Accordin' to our friend here, I ha' nothin' to do with it. If you was to reckon up what the takin' away o' fifteen men for three or four hours would be out of my pocket, you might be of a contrairy opinion.'

'At least,' said Mrs Pearson, mounting her hobby, 'there would be some advantage in keeping them for a few hours from the beer-shop. Your men were tipsy, and creating a disturbance in the village again, last night, Mr Freeman.'

'Dessay. And do you think I care where the devil they are, or what the devil they do, when they ha' finished my work? They may go to blazes for me when they ha' given me my money's worth.'

'And for that reason, Mr Freeman,' said Mrs Pearson, her head well up, defiance in her eyes – 'for that reason you are the most unpopular employer of labour in the county. Now, Helen!'

'Thank you, ma'am!' said Mr Freeman ironically, and he favoured the good lady for a full minute with a silent smile not pleasant to see. 'Thank you, ma'am! If you were as free wi' your money as you are wi' your twiddle-twaddle, you might be a more popular woman yourself.' Then he turned from her to Massey, standing with his hands thrust into his coat-pockets, the nails digging into the flesh. 'You and I ha' often had difference of opinion, young man,' he said slowly; 'we'll agree to differ once more, by your leave. I think I'll manage to keep my men at work in my harvest field on Thursday night.' With that and a threatening nod and glare round the assembled company, the pleasant master of the house walked from the room.

'You must not mind pa,' Pollie said, really ashamed and vexed as she shook hands with Helen. 'He'd been asleep, and got up his wrong side, I suppose.'

'Oh, pray do not trouble about it; I quite understand,' the other said, compassionating the girl. 'You will come all the same, Pollie? I have your promise?' Then she held out her hand to Massey. 'Shall I see you again,' she asked, 'or is this good-bye?'

He wrung her hand in his.

'Not good-bye,' he said, below his breath.

'Thank the Lord,' said Mr Freeman presently, busy over his ham and tea, 'the day is near at hand when all that kittle-cattle will be done with! To think that eighty pound o' my money – hard-earned and scraped together – go year by year to keep that weak, pappy idiot to talk his d—d trash from the pulpit, and them beggarly interferin' fools o' women to go pokin' their noses into people's houses and creatin' unpleasantness between master and men –'

'I do wish, William,' his wife remarked in her most aggrieved tone, 'I do wish you'd manage to keep a civil tongue in your own house, however you may feel. From what I can hear, a pretty sight you ha' been and made o' yourself just now. 'Tis one thing to say what you think behind people's backs, and another to out with it to their faces i' this manner. I ha' no patience wi' sech tempers!'

'Who d'ye think cares? Whoever don't like my ways, let 'em keep out o' my house. What the devil is it to me whether they're pleased or urnin? – or whether you are, for the matter o' that! They ha' never been here to put money into my pocket, as I remember, and hapes o' times to take it out. D—n 'em! let 'em keep out o' my way if they don't want the rough side o' my tongue!'

'Don't you fear they'll trouble you again,' said Pollie, bitterly. 'Who'd be fool enough to come near you if they could keep away? You aren't fit for decent women to be with, with your oaths and your swearing. No one but me and mother is forced to put up with that, remember.'

Mr Freeman laid down his knife and fork, and glared, speechless, at his daughter. Her mother trod on her foot under the table, to warn her to stop her tongue, and Arthur loyally threw himself into the *mêlée* to avert her father's wrath.

'You were a bit rough on the ladies, uncle,' he said good-humouredly; 'but it was aggravating – deuced aggravating!'

'D—n it!' Mr Freeman ejaculated, encouraged by this extenuation, 'I hate the whole bilin' of 'em, d'ye see, Arthur? The very name of a parson makes me sick. Why can't they be made to earn their livin' as other folks have to do and work for the money they're paid? Here's this lazy beggar here; pretty nigh three hundred pounds a-year o' the country's money goes into his pocket – for what? For standin' up twice on a Sunday and makin' a fool of himself in public, and for twaddlin' round the rest o' the week from one house to another, settin' folk by th' ears!'

'There must be parsons – eh, uncle?' Arthur inquired in his airy voice.

'Then, if there must, I'm —— if I want 'em! But if there must, let's have a different sort o' man to this; and let's ha' th' power o' yurning' rid on him when we like.'

'Why, you're for separating Church and State, uncle!' Arthur said, tilting back his chair. 'Dear, dear, where are your Tory principles?'

'D—n all principles!' said the farmer comprehensively, as he rose from the table. 'We should be a deal better off in such times as these if we acted with a view to common-sense without no hamperin' o' principles!'

'Uncle's a revolutionist, aunt!' Arthur said, turning to Mrs Freeman, as her husband left the room. 'He's positively dangerous!'

'He gets a perfect bear,' Pollie said crossly. 'There'll be no putting up with pa soon. All that rubbish about parsons! I don't like 'em particularly either, I admit; but then I've got to listen to 'em – he hasn't! What does it signify to him?'

'All the same, you do seem to get a horrid lot o' duffers down in the country; there's no common error habout that. In town, you see, they have to be here and there, or they get no one into their churches. Some o' the fellows in big parishes, – poverty and badness all round 'em, don't ye know – work like niggers, devilish ill-paid and ill-fed niggers, too! But enough of parsons. Pollie, my dear, your old flame seems to be sufferin' from blues pretty well. Hang the fellow, his temper was pretty well unbearable this afternoon. If it hadn't been that I was supreme myself just then, I'd half a mind to punch his head.'

'Why iver didn't he stay and take's tea like a Christian?' Mrs Freeman grumbled. 'I don't think it looks well, after all that's come and gone, for him to be yurning' his back where he used to be at home. And don't you get quarrelling with him, Arthur. You ha' got the best o' the bargain, remember; and 'll have to keep your tongue still for a time, when he's by.'

'But all that's devilish hard sometimes,' said Arthur, as though he were thirsting for the other's blood. 'I don't want to hit a fellow when he's as down as he is; but, hang it, there's a limit to all forbearance, as he'll have to learn to his cost some day or other.'

Pollie laughed not quite pleasantly, looking her cousin over with some significance. 'I think I should let him alone if I were you,' she said. 'Come on, let's go out for a turn; it's cool and pleasant by now.'

CHAPTER XXIII

Farewell!

THE next day was a busy one for Helen; she had so many last arrangements to make, so many treasures she could not bring herself to part from, to pack up, so many directions to give for the morrow's entertainment. Perrie trotted about all day at her side, Mrs Pearson, who had accorded him a holiday for the occasion, having judiciously ensconced herself in her own room, that her mind might not be distracted by the general tumult.

It is evening now; his auntie has seen the melancholy little boy to bed herself, by way of superlative treat; has sat by his side, his hand in hers while she has sung him to sleep; has kissed and left him, and further has, the drawing-room being close and depressing on this lovely August night, strolled again on to the lawn, where the tables are already placed for the tea to-morrow, and is now leaning over the light iron railing which divides that part of the grounds from the paddock, watching the rising of a big full moon. The daylight has not faded yet; it is a glorious evening – warm and still – hardly a breath of stirs; the leaves on the trees do not even rustle; the mignonette, which sows itself, unchecked, year by year in the Vicarage garden, sends out a strong sweet perfume; some owls, which make their home in a tree in the shrubbery, make loud wheezings in the stillness, and a bat swoops and flies unpleasantly close to Helen's dusky hair. She starts back nervously from the creature, and faces round to see Mr Massey coming towards her across the lawn. The bat has really alarmed her, apparently, for her face is quite pale as she puts out her hand.

'The servant told me that you were in the drawing-room,' he said. 'When I found it empty, and caught sight of your white dress on the lawn, I ventured to follow.'

'Have you seen Mr Pearson or my sister?' wondering how he had been permitted to escape.

'No, oh no! I will not disturb them to-night. I only asked for you. I wanted only to see you.'

Helen was silent, thinking that this simple and guileless process to gain that end would probably bring down wrath on both their devoted heads by-and-by.

'What a lovely night it is!' she said presently. 'But you are a late visitor; have you been busy until now in the harvest field?'

'I have not been near it to-day. I have passed my time in hanging about your usual haunts and vainly looking for you.'

'For me?' in a not too well-acted tone of surprise, and with a blush that the light was still good enough to make visible.

'And when you did not come, I did what I should have done before if I had not been a fool – came here and found you.'

'I have been very hard at work all day. I had no idea how many belongings I possessed until I came to pack them up, nor how much that I was fond of until I had to contemplate bidding it all good-bye.'

'Ah! I am come to bid you good-bye.' They had moved as they talked beyond the range of the drawing-room window, to where a clump of shrubs hid them from view, and had there stopped again by the lawn fencing. Helen looked at her companion as he thus quietly announced the object of his visit;

he was leaning against the railing and calmly contemplating the beautiful rising moon; there was nothing of agitation in either his look or tone, nor of tragedy in his bearing; but Helen, as she glanced and glanced away, suddenly felt that to say farewell to him here, alone in this silent garden, with that glorifying light shining on him, and on all the beloved surroundings that she was so soon to leave, perhaps for ever, was a task beyond her strength. 'My nerve is all gone,' she thought. 'I should break down, and then what would he not think? Oh, I cannot – I cannot to-night! In the broad light of day and with other people near, it would be easy enough – very easy; here and now it is impossible.'

'I am come to say "good-bye,"' he repeated, turning to look at her as she continued silent. 'Miss Smythe, you must teach me how to do it. I have been wondering how it would get done all day, and for weeks past. I haven't found out yet.'

'It is simple enough – sometimes,' she said, looking away, wondering the while if she could advise him to defer this particular leave-taking for the sobering, sensible daylight, for the salutary support of numbers.

'Sometimes? Yes. Because of most of one's acquaintances one is glad to see the backs, but when it comes to parting, perhaps for ever, with all one most cares for on earth, it isn't quite so simple, do you think? That is what you are expecting me to do?' he went on in a low, dispassionate voice, still leaning carelessly in the light of the moon. 'It is easy, you say, of course. You would put out your hand, and say sweetly, "Good-bye, Mr Massey," and would turn your back and go away quite cheerfully, and the thing would be done. But how about me? You don't think of that, I suppose. What is to become of me when the hope, and the peace, and the light have died out of my life? Tell me that. Oh, I know well enough it is no new thing; the tale has been told before, and men don't always get the women they want to marry for their wives, but either my feeling for you is stronger than other men experience, or I am a greater coward than the general run of unlucky lovers; I don't know which it may be, but I do know I can't take leave calmly of everything that is dear to me in life – I can't say good-bye to my one hope of happiness – the only happiness I'd lift up a finger to get for myself – for ever – I can't do it – I have tried, but I haven't strength for it. I can't.' Here he paused, looked at her, turned away his head. 'And I won't,' he finished very quietly.

'What do you propose to do?' Helen asked, trying vainly to steady her voice. 'I do not understand. You must not talk so at random, Mr Massey; this must be all done with – forgotten –'

'Hush!' he interrupted; 'that is all so useless, Helen. Do not let us go back; don't let us waste our time over these old conventionalities with which you used to put me off months ago. "It would soon be over." "I should forget." What's the use of all that between you and me now? I suppose it is as certain, as that we stand here a living, breathing man and woman, that I love you with all the strength which God has given me, and that you love me – not at all. That is agreed between us, at any rate?' He had risen upright, and was facing her now. 'You acknowledge so much, Helen?'

She was silent. It might be a true statement; but it was such a cold-blooded and horrible way of putting the fact, that it was almost a shock to her.

'At least answer me,' he urged. 'Is not that about the state of the case?'

'No,' she said slowly; 'I do not think it is.'

'You do not! How do you mean? – you do not disbelieve in my love for you, surely?'

How could she pretend to such want of faith? – she who knew that secretly, but with her whole heart she had believed in it from the very first!

'Tell me, Helen!'

Reluctantly she sighed forth that she did not doubt his sincerity.

'Then when I say that you have not an atom of love for me, is there exaggeration there?'

Perhaps there was; but Helen knew that she dared not admit it. If his unfortunate passion for her were so impossible to kill in circumstances so little conducive to its existence, how alarmingly vigorous might it not become if she only dared to tell him that, although she would certainly never be his wife, and although she could never – *never* care for him in the measure he desired, there was yet in her heart a great tenderness for him; that although she must at all cost decline his embarrassing affection, it did still fill her heart with gratitude, and even seem to her at some wild moments the most priceless gift that had come into her life. All this, however, were best kept to herself; so –'

'Have it your own way,' she said wearily, as he repeated his question.

'God knows it isn't my way,' he said quickly. 'I would give half the years of my life for a different answer, I swear. My way! Listen to me; I have thought this thing over night and day – night and day, till my brain has been crazed and my heart sick; and on one thing I am resolved. I will not cut myself off from all hope. When I say good-bye to you, presently, it may be for ever; but I won't believe it – I cannot, I dare not! Why are you leaving Hilby and everyone you care for? You need not tell me. I know, of course; it is to get away from me.'

'No,' she interrupted; 'do not say that! I will not deny that you had something to do with my resolution; but it was not to – to "get away" from you. You – you say it as if there were something distasteful to me in your presence; and – and there is not! But, under the circumstances, it seemed to me better; better for you, at least, that I should go.'

'I believe that that is what you thought. I know that others are always first with you; but, Helen, it is a mistake, and a useless sacrifice. I should not cease to love you and to long for you if you were at the end of the world. You won't get rid of me by going to Germany; and that is what I want to tell you. When I have existed here as long as may be possible to me, without a sight of your face or chance of hearing your voice or of touching your hand, I shall go to where I may get the chance again. You cannot prevent me; for I shall be desperate, and shall not stop to think of what you might wish. And who knows, you may be, by that time, so home-sick that you may welcome even the sight of me. I shall try to believe that you will, at any rate.'

She was silent.

'Tell me what you think of that plan,' he said presently. And when she did not speak, 'Are you angry with me? Helen, I will do nothing against your wish if I can help it; but give me leave then; let me do as I have said – not now, not yet for months, perhaps – but let me look forward to it some day!'

'Oh, how can you ask me to allow anything so mad – so miserably, miserably mad as that? Where would be the use of all this that I am doing? But I am tired – tired of trying to do for the best. If you will not think for yourself – if you won't care to spare yourself pain and mortification, think for me, then. Unpleasantness and trouble have come to me through you; and – and words have been said which have been hard for me to bear –'

'You mean by your sister? I know,' he interrupted quickly.

'All this would increase a hundredfold, if you were to do this that you suggest. Everyone – *everyone* would believe that you were not acting unencouraged, and I should have the blame – I, who have never been used till now to have my conduct called in question. How are you to leave your home and your business to follow me without giving rise to talk most – most injurious to me?'

'Ah! that is Mrs Pearson speaking now, and not you at all. And, Helen, too often you let her speak instead of you. Look here! She does not like me, I know, and she looks down upon and despises me, and you – you see me a bit with her eyes too. I know that it is so. She, naturally enough, would like you to marry a better fellow than I am, better in position and every way. Well, I think you ought myself; God knows you are good enough and fair enough to be a queen; but then you are not the sort of woman to think that of yourself, to let your own ambition, as it were, stand in the way of a man's happiness, only that you have been so imbued with other people's ideas that I suppose you have never ventured to put before you, even as a possibility, that you could be my wife. Is that not so? Oh, Helen! how is it that such a tender-hearted woman as you can be so hard? Why must I be the one person in the whole world to whom you can be so pitiless? If there were anyone else for whom you cared it would be different; I would not say one word; but there isn't. Do you think I should not know? Why did you not marry Back here? I always knew you'd never do it – I knew it even when I was madly jealous of him – but you contemplated the possibility of such a thing, did you not? and you dare not say I am not more to you than he, more likely to make you happy – better to be trusted. Then why – why have you never given me the ghost of a chance? Why? Tell me!'

'I have always known it was an impossibility,' she said, sadly.

'But why? Only tell me why! I don't believe that I am vainer than other men, but I see no reason why it should be impossible. If you will only think it over once again, Helen, amid different surroundings, away from the influences which have moved you here –'

'Indeed I have not been influenced.'

'Not consciously, perhaps; but, Helen – tell me, then – why impossible? It is not that you so dislike me? Tell me so much.'

'No, oh no.'

'You even like me a little, perhaps?'

'I like you very much, but –'

'Wait one minute. Suppose you heard that I were about to marry some other woman – well, do you see anything in me, do you know anything of me, that would render me, in your opinion, unlikely to make that other woman happy?'

In an instant Helen had settled in her mind that that 'other woman,' for whom there would be no unsuitability in such a marriage, would be a very happy woman indeed.

'No,' she said cordially; she was sure that he was kind, and good, and true.

'Then why should you, who are so soft and pitiful to the rest of the world, be so hard to me, so resolute that I shall know no happiness in my life, when you could give it with one word from your lips? Helen,' he went on, his excitement rising, 'I shall believe that I shall hear that word yet. No, do not speak; I must believe it if I am to leave you now. And, Helen, I shall come to you in a few months' time, perhaps sooner – who knows how long I can keep away? And you – I know that you will be glad to see me, a home figure in a strange land – and my luck will have turned at last!'

'Oh, hush! I dare not let you believe that,' Helen was beginning sorrowfully, when the sound of the drawing-room window, pushed sharply up, fell on their ears, and the voice of Mrs Pearson calling 'Helen!' sounded across the lawn.

Massey put his hand on the girl's arm, and drew her further within the shelter of the shrubs.

'I must go,' she said nervously, looking with hurried entreaty into his face, whitened and beautified by the moonlight. 'Let me go!'

'Hush! one moment.' He held her by both arms and looked at her intently. 'Helen, say good-bye to me!'

'I can't! I must go,' she whispered, beginning to shake and quiver in his grasp. 'There is Anna calling me again; Mr Massey, you must not keep me now – pray do not! You will come to-morrow night, do –

'And take farewell of you in a crowd? No! Unless,' speaking low and quickly, and tightening his hold of her arms – 'unless you will give me some hope to come for – Helen, can you not? are you sure? Yes, I will come – Helen, let me come! Whisper one word to me, my dearest, and say that I may come!' He was looking eagerly into the moonlit troubled eyes raised to his, and his voice trembled with a last desperate hope.

'Helen!' cried the voice once more, nearer now, and with a well-known asperity of tone – Mrs Pearson was apparently seeking her sister in the garden.

Helen started as if from a momentary dream. 'No, do not come,' she whispered; 'I could say nothing different to you; indeed – indeed, I could not! It is best to say good-bye at once – I am sure it is. Oh, do not be angry with me – do not! I cannot – cannot – cannot!' Then with a supreme effort she steadied her dangerously trembling voice, and turned away her eyes from him. 'Good-bye!' she said – 'good-bye!'

'Good-bye!' he echoed. 'Lift up your head; let me see your face again.'

'Hark! here comes Anna!' – lifting a startled, listening face to his. 'She will be so – so angry with you. Oh, Mr Massey, let me go!'

He raised his eyes for a moment, saw Mrs Pearson's form approaching the friendly shrubs, and knew that his time was short.

'Good-bye,' he repeated in a husky, altered voice, looking down to two tear-dimmed, appealing eyes; then swiftly bent his head, and with one passionate kiss on a helplessly quivering mouth, at length made his farewell. In an instant more he had vaulted the iron railings, and was making his way across the paddock to the road.

That same night, as Helen, an hour before her usual time for retiring, passed through Perrie's room on her way to her own, she found the child sobbing in his sleep. He awoke at her pitying touch and started up in bed.

'Is that you, Aunt Helen?' he asked. 'I thought you was gone away, and all my flowers was dead, and my bird were flown away.'

'Instead of which, darling, here I am as large as life, not thinking of leaving you yet – not for a whole beautiful day and a half; and your canary is as snug as possible in its cage, for I have just been to look at it; and the flowers – It is a lovely moonlit night, Perrie; let me carry you to the window to look at the flowers.'

The child held in her arms looked out for a minute at the silvered motionless trees, at the glorified tranquil garden; then the tears crept down his face again.

'Take me away,' he whispered; 'I don't like it – it looks so awful sad.'

'You funny little boy! It is not sad. The moon loves the flowers, Perrie; she is come down to have a good look at them to-night.'

'Then if she loves them, why don't they get married?'

'Married? – who?'

'The moon, you know; Miss Armytage says' (Miss Armytage was the new governess) 'that people marry because they love each other dearly – best of any one on earth. I know, because I asked her why they did it. I wish I was old enough to marry you, Aunt Helen; I love you the best on earth, I know.'

'Hush! Perrie, I will not have you say that; you forget dear papa and mamma.'

'I love you better than them, a lot – I do.'

'Then I won't have you say it, Perrie. It would vex them very much if they knew. You must never tell anyone such nonsense as that, you silly little boy.'

'But I have. I told Mr Massey, and he didn't scold me and call me "silly"; he –'

'How came you to tell him anything about it?'

'Oh, one day he was ridin' me on his horse in front of him, and I was tellin' him how you and me had been diggin' my garden, and how you was goin' to buy me a pony some day; and he asked me if you was good to me, and I said "Yes"; and "Who did I love best in all the world?" then he said, and I said, "My aunt Helen," and – and "Yes, and so did he," he said; and he squeezed me ever so hard, like you do now, and he never scolded me a bit, and – what are you cryin' for, Aunt Helen? There ain't nothin' for you to cry for, 'cause you don't want to go away unless you like.'

But Perrie's reasoning could only stay his auntie's tears till he was safely in bed and asleep again. When she was in the solitude of her own room, they broke forth unrestrainedly. Somehow those simple words from Perrie's lips had loosed the floods, and there was no stemming them. The child had only repeated what she had known for months, what she had heard a dozen times from Massey's own mouth; but, apart from the passion with which they had been spoken before, in the pathetic childish voice they seemed to strike her with a different sense – to represent a fact, somehow, that was more stubborn than she had been willing to believe it hitherto.

She lay and sobbed and tossed for hours, dressed as she was, upon her bed, thinking over Perrie's innocent words and Massey's farewell, flushing and trembling at the remembrance of that alarming kiss – the first from a lover's lips which Helen had ever received – that bold and passionate kiss which had shamed and frightened but had not angered her.

'How can I be angry with him?' she asked of herself, knowing well that it was her duty to have been shocked and indignant. 'Has he not enough to bear through me, and do I want to give him pain? Would I not comfort him and make him happy if it were possible?'

And then she remembered that he would not admit the impossibility, and held her breath for a moment at the surprise of a new thought. Suppose it were possible – suppose, for a moment, she were to be false to her own ideas, to the whole tenor of her previous thoughts, to her predetermined line of conduct; false to her sister beside, careless of her prejudices and of the hopes which had been formed for her own future; forgetful of the position which she was bound to uphold, and of which she had been taught to think so much – suppose that she were daring enough to risk the disappointment and the anger of those about her, and rash enough to give up everything for the love of this one man – suppose that all this could be done, would she be glad, would she willingly make the sacrifice, if it were one, for his sake – would it be well for him, and would she run any reasonable chance of happiness herself by so doing? Her heart beat quickly as she tried to imagine how it would be with her, if it were allowable, to do all this – if she dared promise to be his wife! She thought of his joy and his unbounded love, and of how all the difficulty and doubt would at once vanish from her course; how she might then stay among those she loved, herself the constant companion and delight of a man with whom she could be content to live. For it was so. 'If I might have done it, if it had only been possible, I know that I should have been happy – so happy!' she said, and cried softly again, her face to the pillow, to think it had not been possible, and that it was over now – over for good!

She should see him no more – no more! 'I wish he could know,' she thought – 'could know how well I like him; how thoroughly I trust him; how I hate – I hate to give him pain! He thinks that I despise him, as Anna does; that I have not sense or heart to know how good and true he is.'

For a moment she almost determined to write to him, to tell him something of this. But he would not understand, she decided sadly; all that being so, how could he be made to respect the obstacles intervening? They were not such as he would understand or care for. To a man – to such a man as he, they would be as nothing! And, looking at them from his point of view, these formidable impediments did all at once appear as mere phantoms in the path.

What, after all, would it signify – they two being all in all to each other – that Anna might be disappointed in her ambition for her pretty sister; that her friends might be surprised or might laugh; that he himself was different in each single condition from such a man as she had thought she would marry – different in position, in manner of look and speech, in all the habits of his life? What would it all signify, he would say, since she – well, loved him? 'And what, after all,' the girl asked herself, after hours of anxious thought – 'what, after all, did it signify?'

The daylight was creeping into her room before she arrived at the startling conclusion that the obstacles in the way of her future and of Massey's were as nothing – ought to be as nothing – if they loved each other; that it would be wicked and cowardly to allow such formless fancies to cheat him of his happiness, and her perhaps of her peace; that she ought no longer to allow her own pride and her sister's prejudice to stand in the light of another's welfare. Then her tired thoughts refused to work again over the old vexed question, but busied themselves instead about what Mr Massey would do and say supposing that she could ever bring herself to tell him that she had changed her mind.

Helen blushed to the roots of her hair at the alarming contingencies conjured up, and tried to give her mind to less agitating imaginations; but all in vain, and she fell asleep at last, with a smile upon her lips. Fell asleep, and dreamt that it was imperative that she and Mr Massey should be married before the villagers came to tea on the morrow; that she and he were waiting behind the shrubs on the lawn for the service to commence; that Mr Pearson refusing to don his surplice for the occasion, it had to be hurriedly adjusted on the small shoulders of Mr Tom Moore, who forthwith made them man and wife without further delay, standing with his back to the iron railing in lieu of the altar. Her husband had his arms about her, and had repeated that vehement kiss of overnight before she awoke from an ecstasy of joy and delight, all exaggerated in her dream, to battle through once more with her doubts and difficulties.

But a new ally had arisen for unconscious Mr Massey in Helen's tender conscience. Was what she had been doing right? she now asked herself; and when once she had thoroughly convinced herself that it had not been right, that she had been wrong in ruthlessly determining to put aside all question of his happiness for the sake of some foolish frivolous vanities of her own and other people – when once she had fully arrived at this conclusion, then Helen was decided, and no earthly power could have turned her. If it were right to marry him she would marry him, although all the world should be against her! She was quite resolved at last – no terror of Anna, in wrath or disappointment, would deter her now; there was no natural shrinking from the unmaidenly task of calling a dismissed lover back to her side – it was *right*, therefore it should be done. There was no longer any doubt in her as to the matter of her duty, although the manner of its performance still continued to trouble her.

There was much expected of her on that last morning of her sojourn, but Helen only lounged about in unusual idleness. What should she do? Supposing she were to leave Hilby and then to write to him, how would that be? It would be an extra and unnecessary day or two of suffering for him, and Helen had become anxious over his suffering. Besides, where was the use of her journey, seeing that she had thus made up her mind to frustrate the very purpose for which it had been undertaken, and what was the good of the preparations about which she ought to be so busy? It was not until the afternoon of that long, strange, exciting day, that she sought out little Perrie, standing silently, watching the adjustment of forms and chairs adown the long tables on the lawn, his hands in his small pockets, himself an embodiment of youthful and patient disconsolateness.

'Perrie,' she asked, 'will you do something for me now at once, and all alone?'

'Yes, Aunt Helen.'

'Will you run over to – to Mr Massey's for me, and take this note? Look, I put it in your pocket, and you keep your hand upon it, so; for it would be horrible if it were lost! and give it to him, into his own hands, before you come away. Will you, Perrie, darling?'

'Yes, Aunt Helen. What does the note say? because he'll want to know, you know.'

'He will find out for himself. And Perrie, if nurse or Miss Armytage or even *any*one calls to you, don't you stop, but run straight on.'

'But if Mr Massey's wild bull runs after me, that one with the clankin' chain – ?' Perrie asked with dilated eyes, being such a wee person and not at all courageous. 'What'll I do then?'

'You'll know it won't hurt you, Perrie. Nothing of his would hurt you or me,' she assured him, with firm but foolish faith. 'Run, darling, quick.'

So Perrie trotted off; to encounter dangers known and unknown, to skirt round that blood-red terrible bull, with the chain in its awful nose, to climb, with legs all too short, a five-barred gate which refused to open, to run, all unconscious, into a drain fresh opened in the meadow, and to be called upon, apparently, to deliver up his very life at the call of an inquiring and much-enraged turkey, who, at Mr Massey's door, swept his wings on to the ground, threw back his head, and swelled his indignant throat at the trembling little intruder. Through all those perilous ways the poor mite conveyed the note safely, keeping his hand on it in his small breeches' pocket, and never relinquishing his hold till he had safely deposited it in Mr Massey's keeping.

CHAPTER XXIV

Poor Anna!

'YOU really must ask Miss Helen,' Mrs Pearson said, turning sharply upon the servant who had been perforce driven to seek her mistress more than once for instructions; 'you see that I am engaged, and cannot be perpetually interrupted in this manner. Where *is* Miss Helen?'

Whereupon the servant replied that she believed the young lady to be dressing, for she was shut in her room and had been there for some time, and that they were waiting below stairs to lay the tables on the lawn, and that there were several things they wanted to be told before they could begin.

Mrs Pearson arose with a gesture of impatience and pushed her writing materials from her.

'I will send down Miss Helen,' she said, and set out to seek her sister.

She found her in her bedroom, in the midst of trunks packed and unpacked, the chairs, and drawers, and table loaded with things still to be put away.

'What are you doing here, Helen? Why,' looking round with surprise and disapproval, 'you were as forward as this yesterday! What have you been doing with yourself? I have been interrupted repeatedly to-day – called upon to give instructions, first to one and then to another, upon matters of which I really knew nothing; and I would not disturb you, as I imagined you were busy here. But you have done nothing – positively nothing!'

'I have not been in my room for very long, I think,' Helen said uncertainly, beginning hurriedly to fold some ribbons and laces that lay against her hand. 'I was in the garden this morning, was I not? I am so sorry they disturbed you, Anna.'

'I am not used to be left in peace for long,' the other said complainingly; and then, noticing the girl's flushed face and trembling fingers, she put on a cheerier, kinder voice, thinking – 'She is going to break down over leaving us, after all.' 'Come, I will help you,' she said. 'You will not have much time in the morning, remember.' She moved to the bed, and began awkwardly enough to fold a delicate-looking robe of soft muslin and lace which lay there. 'This ought not to be crushed, Helen; tell me where to put it.'

'Oh, do not trouble about it, Anna. I laid that dress out, thinking I would wear it to-night.'

'To-night!' Mrs Pearson echoed in surprise. 'Why, Helen, how absurd! Your dark silk, which you will travel in to-morrow, will be all that is necessary for to-night, and much more suitable.'

'I do not think so. I do not like myself in that dark silk. I will wear that one, Anna.'

'Really, Helen, I did think you had too good taste to do anything so out of character with the occasion, and too little vanity to care to do it.'

'But I don't think it is a sign of vanity to want to look nicely sometimes. All the poor things who are coming will be in their best; they would not be pleased to see me in that ill-becoming old dark silk.'

'And pray shall you expect me to array myself at all festively for the occasion?'

'I think it would be very nice of you; but you will please yourself, of course.'

Mrs Pearson stood and silently regarded the dress for a moment before she dropped it from her arms to the bed. It was odd that the vanity excusable in less fair women, but conspicuously absent from her composition hitherto, should have begun to show itself in Helen at last!

'If anyone were coming,' she said to herself, looking across at the girl, 'I could have understood it. You have asked no one but the Freeman people, have you, Helen?' she inquired aloud. 'There is no one coming from the Hall?' – with a swift hope that perhaps the little discomfited Captain might be expected.

'I hope not, devoutly,' the girl said. 'What a bore it would all be to them! Besides, I suppose they are offended past reconciliation. Not one of them has been near me since – for weeks.'

'At that you cannot wonder or complain.'

'Indeed I do not! I think, after all, I will leave these things until the morning, Anna. I will get up an hour earlier to pack them – if I go.'

'*If* you go! What do you mean, Helen – *if* you go?'

Miss Smythe looked at her sister for a moment as if about to explain; but the elder lady's face was anxious and sharply discouraging; the words she meant to speak died on Helen's lips. She turned aside to the toilet-table, beginning to unbind the long braid of her hair.

'If you go!' repeated Mrs Pearson, coming nearer. 'It is rather too late in the day, Helen, to begin to talk of "ifs"!'

'Nothing is certain in this world, Anna,' the other said weakly. 'We ought never to make too sure. I might – might die to-night, you know; or break my leg, or – or change my mind. Are you,' with a quaver in her voice – 'are you so dreadfully anxious to be rid of me?'

Mrs Pearson, leaning forward, tried to get a peep into her sister's face, but this was quite effectually veiled now by the dusky rippling hair.

'I do not suppose that you are in earnest when you ask that question, Helen; but I do not approve of trifling, as you know, and I will answer you as though you were. Yes, I am anxious to be rid of you, or, rather, anxious that you should leave. You know that, for my own comfort, I would keep you with me always; but with due regard to – to other matters, I am convinced that it is for your welfare to go, and I therefore refrain from selfish lamentation over a most wise decision.'

Helen sighed heavily as she brushed her hair. 'I am not sure that the decision was so wise!' she said softly. 'I am glad that it is not irrevocable; I –'

'It is irrevocable now,' Mrs Pearson said with incisive sharpness. 'How could you hesitate now? Could you be capable of such weakness, I should be ashamed to think that you were my sister. Fortunately such inconsistency is out of your power. All our arrangements are made, past the possibility of alteration. I admit that I think it, as you no doubt do, a hard and bitter thing that you should be driven from your home for such a cause; but it has come to this, that, for the comfort and credit of all concerned, it is necessary for either you or – or that other person to leave the parish; and he, of course, is far too ignorant of what would be acceptable to consent to obliterate himself.'

'But, Anna –'

'Wait. Of course you had the remedy in your hands. Had you married Archibald Back, all such unpleasantness could have been avoided; but you chose to throw away your chance there, and – and may you never regret having done so!'

'I know quite well that I shall never regret it. But, Anna, there is something I must speak to you about – something I ought to tell you –'

'There is no time now, Helen,' instinctively shrinking from what she had to hear. 'I will help you with your packing to-morrow; we can talk then.'

'Do stay, Anna. What I have to say must be said at once.'

At this moment scurrying little feet were heard mounting the stairs; and then Perrie's small pipe outside, calling excitedly, 'Aunt Helen!'

'Run away, Perrie!' she cried, starting up from the dressing-table and hurrying to the door, in her eagerness to prevent his entrance –'run away, and get dressed for tea, dearest.'

'Yes, I will,' he panted. 'But Aunt Helen, let me come in! I have took care of a letter here for you, and I am to give it d'reckly. The bull did run at me, Aunt Helen; he was awful fierce. And Mr Massey, he's coming to-night; and that ole turkey, he is in a drefful rage; and...'

By this time Mrs Pearson had approached the door and confronted her son.

'What are you talking about?' she inquired, looking down at him with her severest glance. 'Where have you been?'

Perrie dropped sail at the unexpected sight of his mother, and looked for protection to his auntie, standing speechless and beautifully ashamed, her hair about her shoulders.

'I took care of your note, Aunt Helen; and I'm to give this to you d'reckly,' reaching up an envelope to her and then edging off from the door. She took the letter in a hand that trembled visibly, but did not attempt to open it.

'Stop, Perrie!' his mother commanded. (The colour had flamed into her face, her voice shook her little son to his innermost recesses.) 'No, do not look at your aunt; look at me. Where have you been?'

'Let the child go, Anna,' her sister said beseechingly. 'I want to tell you everything myself; indeed I do. I have been trying to find courage all day, but I cannot bear to vex you. Run, Perrie, darling!'

But Perrie knew better than to move from beneath his mother's awful gaze.

'Where have you been?' she repeated, as though not hearing her sister's entreaty. 'I insist on your telling me instantly.'

'I jus' went to Mr Massey's.'

'What for?'

'To take a note from me, Anna. Oh, why will you not hear me? I am dreadfully unhappy until you listen to me.' She put her hand gently on the little boy's head, turned him from the room, and shut the door.

'Anna, you are blaming me. I knew you would; but only hear me first.'

'No!' said Mrs Pearson with decision. She was very red, her face and neck being now of one universal flame-colour, but she was majestic, too. She turned to quit the room. 'I will leave you to your letter,' she said.

'Anna!'

'I care for no explanation. Nothing will do away with the shameful fact that you have stooped to deceive me, seducing my own child to abet you; that you have carried on a clandestine correspondence with this – this man, that – But I will waste no further words; let me go!'

But Helen was too quick for her, and stood with her back to the door, barring her sister's exit.

A beautiful obstacle, could the other woman have used her eyes just then to see it – in her loose dressing-gown, with her falling curly hair, her face white, with little quivers of emotion thrilling over it, her eyes big and pleading, with tears in their dark depths.

'You shall not leave me so,' she panted. 'I knew – I knew how grieved you would be, but do not, oh, do not be too hard to me, Anna. You know that I love you – have I ever offended you before? I cannot, cannot bear it!'

'Tell me then for how long has this gone on? When did you begin to write to this man? To think, great Heaven! that you could stoop so low! you, my sister!'

'Anna, believe me, never until this day – never! Nor has he to me. You might have seen every word that I said, "would he come to-night; that I should be happy if he came." Indeed that was all.'

'And he – he has simply written an answer to that,' nodding as she spoke to the letter crushed in the girl's hand, and modulating her voice from its harshest tone. She was beginning to breathe a trifle more freely, to think things might not be so bad after all as she had feared.

'Is that what he has written about?'

'I suppose so,' but as she glanced down at the letter her heart gave a great throb, and the tell-tale blood flooded face and neck; she longed, yet feared to know what fateful words were written on that bit of paper. Mrs Pearson's heart sank again at the sight.

'Read it and see,' she said curtly, watching the beautiful face.

Slowly and with shaking fingers the seal was broken. There were but two lines, Mrs Pearson could make out as much as that, and once more her spirit revived. Helen, with her tender sinless conscience, was so apt to magnify small faults. All this trepidation *might* arise simply from an exaggerated notion of her boldness in writing to the offensive man.

Helen stared stupidly for a full minute at the hurried blotted lines, which had been written with a hand as shaking as her own, before she could grasp the meaning of the words, although there was certainly no ambiguity about them.

'I will come, my dearest, my love, my wife!' ran the single sentence. No signature even. Who could remember the conventionalities of letter-writing in the first delirium of a wild, unlooked-for joy?

When the black, unmeaning lines had ceased to dance before Helen's eyes, and the letters at length had settled themselves into their rightful places, and she had read the answer to her invitation, she crushed the bit of paper again in her fingers, and looked up vaguely, all the beautiful colour fading from her face.

'His wife!' she said to herself. It was very serious. For the moment she forgot the presence of her sister, gazing out with some awe and trepidation at the future before her.

'Does he say that he will come?' Mrs Pearson asked with grim irony, watching her.

'Yes; he is coming.'

'And is that all?'

'Oh, Anna, no! Dear, do not be angry with me. I have tried to act for the best – do believe that I have tried at least. But what could I do? He' – with a sob – 'he loves me so.'

'You knew that before,' the sister said, in harsh tones; she looked at the girl with hard cold eyes: full well she knew that the worst had come.

'For a long time you have known as much as that, and others too, unfortunately; he made no secret; I imagined it was for that – for this degrading love of his – for his unmanly pursuit of you, that you were leaving.'

'You must not say such things of him! I will not hear them! But you are angry, Anna; I shall not need to leave you now; say that you will not be sorry to keep me near you.'

'What – what has possessed you to act in such mad fashion? We have been deceived in you, Helen, whom we trusted and believed in – we have been made fools of, and the laughing-stock of the county – now, will you tell me for what? I know what you are about to say – I guess the shameful answer; but tell me with your own lips, lest I may have wronged you in my thoughts, as, pray heaven, I may!'

'I will tell you,' the girl said, lifting her head; the cruel words began to rouse her pride – she was not one to humble herself in vain. 'I am not ashamed of what I have done – never think that for one moment! I am grieved to the heart to grieve you, but neither grieved nor ashamed for myself. I am going, I suppose, to marry Mr Massey. That is what you expected me to say, is it not?'

'You suppose? Do you not know your own intention? or dare you not tell me? Have you already promised to be this man's wife? If not, Helen – if you are only thinking of so pledging yourself – for God's sake, pause!' Her voice was shaking, her form trembling; she laid her hand on the bedstead for support. Helen could but see that she was terribly in earnest – that this thing which had been done was to her a fearful thing. 'Think, think what you would lose by such a marriage –your position in society! – you, who in your own way are so proud! – your friends – for the loss of the one involves that of the other – the love and approbation of those nearest to you: your own peace of mind – for must not your whole life be embittered by the thought of what you deliberately threw away for the gratification of this man's selfish fancy? No; wait, Helen! I am not carried away by my anger, deeply incensed as I feel; this is too sadly serious a matter for simply wrathful words; it is a calamity! – a calamity requiring our most earnest endeavours, our prayerful efforts to avert. Do not speak until I have done. Think, as I have said, what you lose. And what do you gain? A husband – great heaven! that I should use the word of him to you! Do you not shudder – shudder, Helen, at the sound? – a husband of whom all your life you must be ashamed!'

'Ashamed!' the other interrupted indignantly. 'Why? Why ashamed?' She had flung herself into the one easy chair her room contained, and lay with her head turned from the speaker, and that short, first love-letter of hers held tightly against her breast. It had one merit in being so short, that at a glance she had learnt it by heart: 'My dearest, my love, my wife, I will come!' Not many more battles would she have to fight alone!

'Of whom you must always be ashamed,' Mrs Pearson went on, unheeding the indignant protest; 'who will not understand one refinement of your nature, or any high instinct you may possess. You gain him, certainly – a man you understand as little as he understands you. What do you know of him? Simply that he has had the impertinence to fall in love with your face – in his admiration of anything nobler, I do not believe; he has not discrimination enough to divine that you are not of the common herd – and by means of this vulgar passion of his, he has surrounded himself with a kind of halo through which you see nothing clearly. How will you endure his coarse endearments? Picture him, Helen, with the right to caress you – a man such as he, without one gentlemanly instinct! How dare you risk it? –how can you bear the thought? But, bad as his love is, what will his neglect be when he shall have tired of you, as men do tire of what they cannot understand – when he leaves you for his pipe, and his glass, and his low companions – you, with your position, and your talent, and your beauty? That he will surely do this, you know of yourself. Look around you where you will, upon the men of his stamp, and see if I do not speak truth. Well, you gain him and you gain his friends – the companionship of the Freemans, for instance, and that of the girl who jilted him, and you live in a closer atmosphere and a lower region – you, who had such high ideas of what to do with your life, whose dream it was to make the world a purer place – you will suffer yourself without a struggle to be dragged down – you will glory in allowing yourself to be defiled! Helen,' moving before the girl and throwing out her arms in a fashion quite tragic, and all unlike her usual self-contained deportment, 'Helen, tell me that it is not too late – that you will consider well before you commit such a moral and social suicide as this!'

The excitement which agitated her sister had all left Helen.

'I am sure that you believe yourself in what you have been saying,' she said calmly; 'but it is in reality so wide of the truth, so thoroughly – forgive my saying it – ridiculous, that it does not influence me one bit.'

'Have you given your promise? Tell me that?' the other demanded impatiently, with again that tragic flinging out of her hands.

'I will tell you how it is; I am anxious to do so if you will but let me speak; and then, Anna, do believe me, it will be useless for you to say any more.'

Then in a few words she explained how the asking Mr Massey to the Vicarage to-night was tantamount, considering what had gone before, to a promise to marry him; and how the answer which he had sent had shown that he comprehended this.

'Even if I believed in the awful fate with which you threaten me, Anna, I could not, I would not, draw back now! I have given rise to hopes I would die rather than disappoint. I should feel myself unfit to live could I be so treacherous and so false! Pray do not say more to me; try to believe that my mind is made up; that the thing is now irrevocable, and that I am content with my lot.'

Of course, a great deal more was said – entreaties, warnings, threats even – Helen listened to them all almost unmoved. Her indecision was all over; nothing could shake her now.

'You dare not tell me that you are happy,' her sister said at length. 'You are expecting this man for the first time as your promised husband; I will not believe but that the thought must fill you with horror and confusion. You cannot look at me and say that you are happy.'

'Happy!' Helen repeated (she had risen from her chair now, and she crossed to the dressing-glass, beginning to twist her hair about her head – 'happy, you want to know? Upon my life, I cannot say! You are angry with me; and I know that I have been wrong and foolish in much that I have done. I should have known my mind before, and should have given his wishes more consideration; and I should have been more open with you. Everything is strange, and a little bit terrifying. No, I don't suppose I am happy, yet – but in a little time, when he has been, and when the newness of the thing has worn off – I have a strong suspicion, do you know, that I shall be.'

Mrs Pearson was standing behind her sister as she said this; but she caught in the glass the reflection of her face, no longer veiled with hair – of her face with a very becoming flush upon it; and as the girl avowed her belief in her future happiness with her detestable lover, there was apparent a momentary trembling at the corners of her mouth which showed that a smile was hovering there. The sight incensed the looker-on more than the telling of her unprecedented folly had done – that she could blush and smile with such a fate before her! It was with a feeling of bitter rage that poor Anna turned away, fully recognising at last her own impotence and the uselessness of further speech.

'Be friends with me before you go,' Helen pleaded. 'We have been so much to each other, I can never – never be happy if you mean to quarrel with me. Forgive me, dear; say that you will before you go!'

'You know me too well to fear that I shall quarrel,' the sister said in an icy voice. 'I am not the person to indulge in vulgar brawls with those of my own household. But, Helen, you have chosen your own path; it is widely apart from mine. There can be no sympathy, no friendship, worthy the name, from this time forth, between you and me. I forgive you; but I can never forget that you have lived beneath my roof, and have deceived me. You have abused the confidence I placed in you; you have lowered yourself – yes, to the very dust; and in doing that you have lowered me!' She walked to the door. 'Before I go,' she said, with her hand on the lock, 'I shall be glad to learn if you still intend to start on your journey in the morning. It will be advisable for me to know so much of your plans.'

'I shall go to London, of course. They are expecting me; but I do not know – I should think I shall not go to Germany now,' Helen said doubtfully (thinking, 'He will not let me'). 'Anna, you will let me come back in a little time. You are very hard to me; but I do love you all so much: say that you will be glad to have me back.'

'While I have a home, my sister shall never want for one,' the virtuous woman said coldly; but would make no further concessions.

Helen, left alone, shed a few tears over her sister's hardness, as she sat before her glass. To be loved by those about her was one of the primary necessities of her being: the prospect of Anna's lasting displeasure was very grievous to her. 'No, certainly I am not happy yet, she told herself, remembering her sister's inquiry, 'How is it possible that I should be happy while she is so unkind?' And then she did think, with some alarm, of several things her sister had presented to her imagination; for as the time drew near, a great shrinking from the first interview with her husband that was to be did certainly distress her. Hitherto their intercourse had been divided into two epochs. During the first he had loved and pursued her, and she had been occupied in shunning him and defending herself; during the second he had kept himself from her presence, and had been by turns gloomy and desperate when they had chanced to meet, while she had pitied and grieved over him in her tender heart. In these two phases she had known and had learnt to like him well. How would it be with him in his new condition of accepted lover, and what would be expected from her?

Helen's cheek glowed hotly as she thought of it. It was alarming – terribly alarming! She thought she would have postponed the meeting now *sine die*, had it been in her power so to do. For all that, she did not shudder in just the manner Anna had predicted over those probable caresses; only her heart beat quickly and her face flushed. She remembered that kiss in the garden last night. 'Ah, how Anna would have despised her had she known! Did Alfred ever kiss Anna so?' Helen wondered, gazing unconsciously at her own reflection in the glass, her elbows on the toilet-table, her face propped on her two hands; she looked, till that lurking smile about the corners of her mouth surprised her as it had angered her sister; then she dropped her face into her arms. 'No, in all her life, Anna had never been kissed as he had kissed her – poor Anna!' was sighed through the room, that hot face pressed upon two soft comforting arms. Then, with a start at the sound, Helen arose, and put on that pretty cream-coloured dress, the wearing of which Anna had so deprecated.

CHAPTER XXV

Helen's Garden Party

'IT was an intensely aggravating thing,' Pollie declared.

She was feeling deeply injured, and consequently a little irritable, and good-natured little Mr Gosling was snapped at a good bit by his *fiancée*, while his puns and his well-intentioned jokes were passed over in contemptuous silence. It was of no use for him to assure her that she looked very well indeed that evening, to repeat to her that black silk was always 'the thing,' wherever it was worn, giving its wearer a 'genteel' appearance under all circumstances. Pollie refused to be comforted. She felt herself to be a dowdy – how could she be amiable or happy?

'You never know how to have these people,' she complained, alluding to Mrs Pearson and sister. 'They ask you to dine, and you go in a smart-looking dress, and find them sober as judges in plain dark gowns, making you feel a fool in your finery; while now, to-day – when I'd half a mind to put on my blue, and even mother would have had me, but I said "No, they're all bound to be dowdies, and 'll only stare at my gown," and so I came in this and my quietest hat – now, look at Helen Smythe!'

Mr Gosling did look at her obediently; truth to say, he had been looking at her a great deal, but he knew better than to say to Pollie what a pleasing object he found her.

'That costume of hers is very inexpensive,' he said with authority, being well up in the subject of ladies' dress, and able to give Pollie the correct name and the price per yard of the filmy material of which Helen's dress was composed. 'This silk of yours cost double – you bet!'

'I should like it in a colour,' Pollie said, somewhat mollified by this consideration. 'I should not fancy myself in whites or cream-colours, as Helen is so fond of dressing. If I could get it in blue or pink, Arthur? What do you say – do you think I can?'

'Wait till you're up in town. Where's the use of dressin' down here in this beastly hole? We'll fig you out there at half the expense; and there'll be several to look at you, too, when you're done.'

'It's so good of you to come, Pollie. Thank you a thousand times!' Helen now said, coming up to shake hands. She had been slowly making her way to them, as they talked, through groups of awkward visitors. 'I think that nearly all are here now; and will you take this table, and make tea for them? You will find it tiring work, but perhaps' – with a smile at him – 'Mr Gosling will help you.'

'Happy!' declared Mr Gosling, and could add no more just then; her beauty and her smile together had impeded his usual fluency. 'By Jove! you know,' he remarked injudiciously to his betrothed, 'she is an out-and-outer, that woman! There's no common error about her; she's the right form, and no mistake!'

'I didn't know you admired those lanky, dark-haired girls,' Pollie said contemptuously. 'You always said she was not your style.'

'Nor is she, of course,' he admitted quickly, looking tenderly at the little flaxen-haired creature by his side.

'And there's no "go" in her, remember; she's no company. You try her with some of your jokes, for instance; she wouldn't know what you meant. There's no being free and easy where she is, either; it's a perpetual state of P's and Q's, don't you know, Arthur? – enough to tire you to death with being proper. Look at her now, shaking hands with those people as they come in – look! actually with Downes the miller, and Mrs Turner from the little shop! – and she eaten up with pride! I call that downright affectation, don't you? But she always makes me wild. I won't look at her. Here are the people sitting down; we may as well go to our table. Come along!'

There were three tables set about on the lawn – long, well-filled tables, with cut flowers and plants prettily arranged down their length. Mrs Pearson presided at one. Her face had regained its usual rather florid colouring, but was very stern and discouraging in appearance; it was curious to see how the people with one accord made a rush for the other two tables, shunning the unfestive figure at the head of hers. Her husband stood at her side, evidently on duty, and doing his best to look as calm as she. Helen had had just a word with him, thinking it better to do so before her guests arrived. He had been watching her with portentous gravity ever since he emerged from an interview with his wife, and Helen easily divined that he had been made acquainted with the sum and substance of her offending.

'Alfred, Mr Massey is coming to-night,' she said to him, looking calmly in his face. 'Anna has told you, I suppose, that I have asked him.'

'She has told me – yes. But – hum – ha – Helen, I prefer not to enter upon the subject with you!' He was acting under instructions in this, she knew well; her sister was wiser than to leave her husband to his own discretion in any matter. 'It is far too serious for us to discuss now in this time or place.'

'I do not intend to discuss it at all,' Helen said. 'I merely wanted to say that he is coming – to remind you that his house has been open to you at any and every hour of the day, and to tell you that I expect you to show hospitality to him.'

'You expect! Is that a proper and respectful tone in which to address me, Helen? Is that the way – hum – ha –'

His sister-in-law interrupted him, laying her hand upon his sleeve.

'Alfred, are *you* going to turn against me?' she asked. 'I thought that you, at least, would have stood by us, and been our friend. You have always been so good to me; and you like him, do you not? Shall you not be glad to have me always near you, and to keep him for your friend? And, Alfred, be sure that if you will be on our side, we will always be on yours.' She pressed his arm as she said this, and lowered her voice somewhat. To him and to her the words appeared to have a certain significance. 'You will have two homes instead of one, Alfred – be good to me!'

Mr Pearson, who was sometimes cruelly accused of being soft in his head, was pretty well known also to be soft in his heart, and it melted at Helen's pleading. And it was not alone that his heart was tender. Although not a man of brilliant parts, he had a tolerably keen scent for what was for his own advantage; and pleasant visions did arise before him of a home in which he might always be welcome, where a pipe was not a forbidden luxury nor a glass of wine regarded in the light of a sin, where a man might speak his thoughts without certainty of contradiction, where snubbing was an unknown. Intuitively he recognised the *régime* which would flourish under the influence of Helen's sweet courtesy, and roseate possibilities began to dawn upon his mental horizon. He only shook his head at his sister-in-law, and moved away from her caressing hand; but she knew well that he was won, and was more at ease in consequence. 'It would have been so awkward for Mr Massey to be treated universally to cold shoulder,' she thought.

She was more at ease, but still uncomfortably nervous. The tea-cups rattled in her unsteady hand, and once or twice she forgot, with results lamentable to the table-cloth, to turn the tap of the urn behind which she sat. Her voice rang out excitedly above the chatter around her, as she talked to the old people on either side, or gave her directions to young Downes, the miller's son, who had appointed himself her aide-de-camp, and was assiduously distributing cups of tea and ham sandwiches at her direction.

'You be right glad to be gettin' away from us, Miss Helen,' said an old man, an especial favourite of her own, who sat at her right hand. 'Tha's how 'tis wi' the young folks; 'tis anythin' for a change, wi' never a thort if 'tis for better or worse, or wha's to become o' we tha's left.'

'Now that is cruel of you, Nobbs,' she said, with kindly reproach; 'how can you say that I wish to leave you! I never thought that you could be so unkind.'

'I don't find no fault,' he said hurriedly, putting out an old brown hand to touch hers – 'no fault! But there's some on us as'll miss ye badly, Miss Helen – 'tis nat'ral we should feel it more nor you. I'm right glad ye're cheerful – there, that I be! And yer look well, that yer do – yer look well!'

Old Nobbs lifted up a handsome head with long grey locks and a patriarchal beard, and looked askance at her out of a pair of sad blue eyes, with a queer sidelong movement of his body, to be accounted for from the fact that his back was crippled, bending itself nearly horizontally above his rickety legs when he stood upon his feet. Poor Mr Nobbs! his 'back was bad and his legs were queer,' and he had been deformed since an accident in early youth; and perhaps it was for this sad reason that his love for beauty in others struck one as being so pathetic as well as so unusual in one of his class.

While Helen was speaking to him she became aware that Mr Massey was on the scene. She would not look round – could not, it seemed – but she noticed that one or two heads were lifted as to survey a new arrival; and presently she heard her brother-in-law's voice from somewhere in the background saying stiffly:

'Oh – hum – ha – how do you do, Massey?'

The long tea-table seemed to rise up and come at Helen, the faces down its length bobbed and rolled, but only for a minute; by the time the new-comer had received Mrs Pearson's most awe-inspiring bow, and had responded to her iciest 'good-evening,' the earth was steady about her again. Presently two figures were standing at her side; but she was busy with the urn just then – how could she look up?

'Helen, here is Mr Massey,' one of them said, and Helen put out a hand quite calmly, although she still steadfastly regarded the tea-urn, and said 'Good evening – how do you do?' in her languidest, most indifferent voice.

It was all over – that dreaded ordeal! To the uninitiated it must have appeared a very frigid meeting, the lady saying so little, the gentleman speaking never a word, only holding a slim cool hand in his, with a grasp of which they two alone were conscious.

Mr Pearson took himself off, in obedience to orders, to assist his wife, leaving Massey standing by Helen's side, a dreadfully embarrassing presence to her. Once more the urn ran over, the cups received unequal allowance of sugar, or none at all.

'Dear, dear! Miss Helen, what a waste o' tea!' old Nobbs said, to whom tea was the one luxury of his life. He put out his cup to catch the precious stream.

'Oh, it is this stupid urn again!' Helen said. 'I cannot think what is wrong with it to-night.'

Then Massey, saying, 'Allow me,' leant over her chair and turned the tap. 'How is that? I think that is the best way to manage it, don't you?' he asked, and laughed, a little nervously, perhaps, and the ice was broken.

'Do you mind being useful?' Helen said to him, with only a suspicion of a tremor in her voice. 'And will you carry round the bread and butter? They have eaten all the beef-patties and the sausage-rolls, and the sandwiches. I think the bread and butter comes next.'

He obeyed her, and returned presently on the other side of the table with an emptied dish.

'What am I to do now?' he asked.

'Take round another,' she said promptly. But to this he demurred.

'You do not think of the exertion, or of their digestion. They ought to wait a bit; and mayn't I sit down?'

Old Nobbs, who was as courteous as a prince, began to shuffle his crippled body higher up the form.

'Sit here, sir – sit here,' he said. ''Tain't fit that you should wait on us!'

'Oh, that's right enough!' sitting down. 'How are you, Nobbs? But I've been standing about all day; I shall be ready to start off again in a minute. That young Downes is quite indefatigable; with what a grace he holds the bread-and-butter dish! I don't think I'll try to rival him. Let me attend to the urn for you instead. I believe that I have a really wonderful method with urns, and shall not quite invariably forget to turn the tap!' As he spoke, he again put a stop to its overflowing. Helen laughed and blushed.

'She look well, sir,' old Nobbs said – 'Miss Helen look well to-night!'

'She does indeed, Nobbs; very well!'

The old man lowered his voice to a hoarse whisper, more audible than his usual tone: 'She's a rare un for looks, sir, Miss Helen; there ain't her ekal nowheres hereabout!'

Helen blushed crimson. 'Oh, do go and carry round the cake!' she implored. 'There are so many people with nothing to eat. I do wish you would go!'

'Very well.'

'But you don't go!'

'I am wondering if you know who I am!'

'Who you are?'

'Yes. Who am I?'

'Have you neglected that, to a wise man, most important of all maxims, "Know thyself"? You are Mr Massey, of the Wood Farm, are you not?'

'Now, I cannot imagine how you guessed all that! You have never once looked to see.'

'Do hand round the cake!'

'I will when you have satisfied yourself as to my identity.' Then he bent over her, under pretence of taking a cup from her hand. 'Helen, look at me!' he whispered.

Reluctantly she lifted two soft shy eyes to his, and for a moment met his adoring gaze; then, with a sigh of utter content, he turned away, carrying that cup of tea, he knew not where.

'Here, Massey!' called a voice from another table; 'got any tipple there to spare? Our lot's exhausted – not another infernal drop to be squeezed out of the kettle!' Then, for the first time becoming aware of the propinquity of Pollie and her lover, Massey went over to them and shook hands effusively.

'You have been doing duty at Helen's table!' Pollie said. 'Can't you slip away now, and come and have a chat with us? Did you ever see anything like the way these people eat? It makes me sick – hogs they are! There's one man here – that wolfish-looking creature, half-way down the table; he's half an idiot, you know – he puts his hand into the dishes and grabs at the things, and stuffs them into his mouth; it's disgusting!'

'Poor devil!' Massey said compassionately; 'he's half-starved as a rule. Perhaps you and I should not think so much of the etiquette of the table if we were famishing – eh? He doesn't have full pay because he's a bit soft, you see; and there are about a score children, I think. Very likely he hasn't broken his fast before to-day!'

'Then I wish he'd break it where I hadn't to watch the process. It makes me sick!' the girl said, turning away her eyes. 'How are you getting on at your table? Rather slow, I expect. Arthur – where's Arthur? there he is – has been making the people roar! It's wonderful how popular he makes himself. I say, isn't Helen terrific? I wonder what she took the trouble to dress herself up within an inch of her life to-night for! Is it to captivate the labourers, or Arthur, or you, I wonder?

'Is she dressed up? Then you may depend it is for me!' Massey said, in a tone of calm conviction, moving off; and Pollie laughed with enjoyment at the joke.

'What is the name of that old lady, the tenth from you?' he asked of Helen presently.

'That is old Mrs Skelton. What of her?'

'Only that I forbid you to make any more tea for old Mrs Skelton, or to offer her further refreshment of any kind or description throughout the evening. You hear? – under penalty of my very severe displeasure. Do you know how heavy that will be? Are you very much impressed?'

'I don't feel particularly frightened. What has the poor old soul done to you?'

'The "poor old soul" is an ungrateful old wretch. She complained of that last cup of tea, that very one I took her after you – you looked at me. She said she warn't asked to drink sech in 'er own house, and she wouldn't do it here. She said, too, that there was nothin' but fat in the samwidges, and that the butter was rank as rank.'

Helen laughed. 'Is that all? Why shouldn't the poor old thing grumble? – it is the one pleasure in which she can afford to indulge. Once, when I knew that her house was very bare, I carried her down a big basket with materials, as I thought, for a good meal. There was tea, and milk, and bread and butter, and meat. I set them all out on her table, and delighted in the treat they would be to her. She looked the things over, sniffed at the meat, tasted the butter, weighed the parcel of tea in her hand. "And now you haven't brought no sugar," she said. It was the one weak spot in my arrangements. You see, I drink my own tea without sugar, and I had forgotten that she mightn't.'

'I should like to have the making of her tea for her.'

'Oh, nonsense! After all, I may have forgotten her sugar again, you know. Do you mind asking her to send her cup back?'

'Yes; I mind very much.'

'But will you do it?'

'I shall have to think it over. In the first place, it is much pleasanter to me to sit still here, where I can hear, and speak to, and look at you – although you do show such anxiety to be rid of me, and are particular, to downright incivility, never to look in my face. I am sure that old Nobbs here has observed it; he is always trying to get a look at your eyes himself. In the next, I don't know that I ought to allow you to humble yourself in such unresisting fashion to Mrs Skelton and her crew. It would be all very well if we others might expect humility from you, too; but I have a strong notion that you will never be humble to me, for instance. Shall you?' He was leaning on the table, his head not very far from hers; poor old Nobbs quite excluded from the sight of the face he loved to look at, by the young man's broad shoulders.

A smile flickered round the corners of Helen's mouth, but she did not look at him nor answer.

'Are you going to be humble to me?' he repeated. 'Shall you care if I am pleased or teased? Will you ever want to conciliate me as you do Mrs Skelton?'

'In the matter of sugar for your tea?' she laughed, with one swift, shy glance into his face.

'Do not laugh,' he said, his dark face alight with love and joy. 'You will have to make my tea, you know.' Then he dropped his voice a little, and bent his head nearer hers. 'By heaven! when I think of it all, I wonder I don't go mad for joy!' he whispered, suppressed passion in his voice; then sprang up hurriedly. 'Now for Mrs Skelton's sugar!' he said.

By the time that long tea was over – the invigorating beverage diluted down to warm water *au naturel*, the rows of dishes emptied, even the crumbs brushed from the table-cloths by means of pocket-handkerchiefs into horny palms, and from thence popped into capacious and rapacious mouths – Helen was at her ease again. She had got over that tremendous difficulty of meeting Mr Massey's eyes; she could hear him speak unexpectedly at her side, or from behind her chair, without experiencing a shock throughout her system; and when she could succeed in driving him temporarily away from her – a matter requiring some address – she could even take pleasure in watching his strong, well-knit figure moving about the lawn. She regarded the two men attentively, as, on one occasion, he stood side by side with her brother-in-law; and she noticed, as she had never done before, how oddly Mr Pearson's head was shaped, and that either his shoulders stooped, or the cut of his coat was to blame. She saw that his legs were too short for his body, and that his sleeves were too long for his arms. His hair wanted cutting too, certainly, Helen decided, glancing from the lank locks which stuck out at the Vicar's ears, to her lover's close-cropped curly head. He was not handsome or distinguished-looking, perhaps; but certainly, in the matter of personal appearance, she would never want to feel ashamed of her husband.

'You must not stay always with me,' she said to him, when, grace having been said and sung in most impressive manner, the company dispersed and betook themselves to the sports provided for their entertainment in the paddock adjoining the lawn, or wandered in disconsolate groups about the spacious kitchen-garden, or stood in hopeless awkwardness on the lawn, not knowing how to dispose of themselves. 'It really does not look well to do so; it is hindering me, and making yourself useless.'

'I have no ambition to be useful, unless to you. Helen, can't you come away from all this, and let me speak to you? There are things that I am dying to say to you.'

'You certainly must not say anything to-night, that you cannot say in public.'

'Not to-night?' in a tone of angry dismay. 'But I will!'

'You must learn to be patient,' she said with a provoking smile, beginning to move away from him. 'It is really a most useful lesson, and one we all need to be taught, sooner or later. Go and talk to Miss Freeman. She has been looking at us for some time. All kinds of imaginings will possess her little head if you do not leave me, sometimes.'

'Do I care what possesses her head?' he asked a little savagely; but being left alone, he moved in the indicated direction.

'All alone, Pollie? Where is Mr Gosling?'

'Oh, he's working like a stag over there in the paddock, setting them to cricket (much he knows of it himself, too!), and trying to get the unfortunate wretches to be happy. The fact of it is, it's a great mistake keeping them here at all. Now that they've eaten all there is to eat, what is there they care for? Let them go home, where they wish they were, and where I know I wish I was too.'

'Well, why do they stop?' Massey asked, who for reasons of his own was inclined to Pollie's opinion. 'There's no fun in that half-hearted cricket – look at the ghastliness of that feeble attempt at football! Can't you manage to impart to some of the more intelligent that they'd better make themselves scarce? It would look graceful in them to retire now, I do think.'

'Yes, and you could come home with us, and we would all have a pleasant evening together.'

'I don't fancy I'll go home with you, Pollie. You don't want me now.'

Unfeignedly thankful he was to know that she no longer wanted him; but somehow in the girl's ears the words had a mournful sound, for a little bit of Pollie's heart as well as all her vanity had been engaged in that old pretence at love-making.

'I shall always want you,' she said, with some warmth. 'Arthur can't ever make any difference to the welcome you'll always get from me, don't you fear that! I shall not forget those pleasant times we used to have together, before he came and put an end to everything.' (It was so that it pleased Miss Freeman to think that her romance with Mr Massey had been ended.)

'You are very kind, Pollie – you always were a kind little thing; but what's over is done with, you know, and had best be put away and forgotten.' If he could but have blotted out the stupid vulgar folly from his own mind, and from Helen's, how thankful he would have been!

'Ah, it's not so easy to forget,' Pollie demurred, not averse to the excitement of a flirtation, if she could but revive one, even though she were engaged. 'It's not easy to me at least. Do you know that I have shed rivers of tears over all that's come and gone, if it is done with! I cry about it at night sometimes, still.'

'You foolish child!' he said, somewhat uncomfortably. 'It was only a stupid folly, at the best, that was never worth a tear. Laugh at it instead, Pollie – that would be so much wiser. What a good-tempered fellow young Gosling is!' (Massey himself was content with all the world just then.) 'You are a lucky girl! I believe that he will suit you splendidly. I suppose he is never dull nor quiet, is he?'

'Not he!' discontentedly. 'I get tired of his pranks and his jokes sometimes. I dare say I shan't mind it all when I get up to London, where things are livelier; but down here you're so dull that it makes you savage to see people always in such spirits.'

'And you, of course, are going to be no end of a swell up in London, Pollie?'

'Oh! as to that, pretty fair, I suppose. The old people want us to live over the shop for a while, but I'll see them at Jericho first! That isn't exactly what I have been brought up to, I fancy; and Arthur, with his prospects, too! He's going to look out for a little villa somewhere Islington way, where he can take the 'bus and I can run up easily to town for a day's shopping, or to get to the theatre. That's one thing I *am* glad I'm going to be married for – that I can always go to the theatres. When there's anything on you want to see, James, you must come up and pay us a visit.' She added this with a slight air of patronage. The thought of that villa residence always lifted Pollie's imagination. 'We shall always be glad to see you.'

Massey thanked her, and was silent for a moment, picturing his lovely princess – his Helen – in that suburban dwelling, the guest of Mr Gosling and little foolish, ill-behaved Pollie.

'I'll go and speak to Gosling,' he said presently, and leaped the iron rails into the paddock.

'Are you a cricketer?' the little man asked of him. 'Then come and take a turn here. I'm not a hand at the game, or I'd go in; these fellows would think a lot of having a swell in with them, but my chest' (thumping that narrow contraction) 'my chest says no.'

'Then I wouldn't gainsay my chest,' the other man said, looking at him kindly, 'you must take care of yourself now, old fellow, or I suppose Miss Freeman will take care of you – eh?'

'Bless you, yes! Pollie'll look after me. I'm in good hands, Massey; she's sharp – sharp as a needle. Like 'em to have their wits about 'em, don't you? see through a nine inch wall, she can!'

'She's a capital girl,' Massey said heartily. 'She's a little bit bored to-night, though; would like to be getting home, she said.'

'Dare say! The same would also suit yours truly, down to the ground.'

'Then why do you stay?' Massey inquired, anxious to make a 'clean sweep' of the lot.

'What are you to do when a woman asks you for your help? Miss Smythe seems to have set her heart on having my assistance, so between her and Pollie I'm pretty well in a fix, d'ye see? – one wants me to go, the other hopes I'll stay. Between you and me, Massey,' lowering his voice mysteriously, 'she is such a devilish handsome girl that I'm hanged if it's easy to resist her. She knocked me clean out of time to-night, as I'm a living sinner she did! Jove! if they gave that girl a season up in town her fortune'd be made and no mistake. She'd cut the lot out, I tell ye! They'd be nowhere, sir, nowhere. Look at her there, coming over the green with my young lady – a trifle tall per'aps for my taste – but there's all kinds to suit. Pollie says there's no "go" in her, but who wants any "go" in a woman that can move like that? By heaven, it's a sight! She mayn't be larky or amusin' naythur, but you catch her smilin' into your face and saying she's "happy to find you've come, and she hopes you'll stop and help her while you can." Catch her at that, and I'm blest if you don't feel it all down your spinal marrow.'

Massey laughed uncomfortably. 'You are enthusiastic, Gosling,' he said.

'All that is between you and me, old fellow. A man of the world knows better than to praise one woman to another; you understand!' An expressive wink here occurred to quicken the other's comprehension.

'You admire her, Massey?'

'Miss Smythe? Well, I do. Look here; can't you start some races? You are good at all those sort of things. I have some shillings and half-crowns in my pocket on purpose. Can't you say to them that now they are to run some races *to finish with?* Make them understand that part of the bargain. For God's sake let's clear them off, Gosling!' (Then, seeing that Miss Smythe had left Pollie, and was for a minute alone, he was over the railing and by her side in a moment.) 'I have been very good, and they are going to run races for prizes I have offered. Now, may I come with you?' he asked breathlessly.

'*Certainly* not!' stopping by the drawing-room window with her hand on the raised sash.

'Where are you going?'

'I am going to see Perrie to bed.'

'And why should you? Is it right for you to put everyone before me? – are you fair?'

'I fear not,' sighing; 'for it seems to me I have put you before everyone else.' Then she slipped through the window into the house, and disappeared from his sight.

'Oh, here you are!' the Vicar cried, appearing suddenly before him as he leant, disconsolate, by the side of that open window. 'Don't you feel the air growing chilly? I have persuaded Mrs Pearson to go indoors; she is such a martyr to neuralgic pains that, if her presence is missed, it will no doubt be put down to the right cause. Do you – hum – ha – happen to have a cigar about you, Massey? Thanks. Let us get away from the vicinity of the house; the scent of tobacco in any form is objectionable to my wife, as I dare say you are aware.'

Together they strolled once or twice up and down the length of the gravel-drive, Massey thinking his own thoughts while he enjoyed his cigar, apparently listening the while to the Vicar's speculations on his harvest profits and minute descriptions of the condition of his own handful of corn – a handful, by the way, which he had never yet comprehended was not universally of more importance than was the produce of all the rest of England's broad acres. They stopped at the gate at the bottom of the drive; and while one of them, still prosing on, gazed up meditatively at the one star appearing overhead in the yet clear sky, the other turned his back impatiently and looked towards the house, by whose jealous walls his own particular star was obscured just then.

'And what's all this between you and Helen?' the Vicar asked presently, in an indulgent tone, as though he were speaking to a foolish child whom he did not intend quite to overwhelm, but at whose awe and trepidation he was not surprised.

'What is it that you have heard is between us?' the other said cautiously, not knowing how far Helen might like her brother-in-law to be trusted.

'Well, I have heard a hint – not a particularly pleasant one, I am compelled to say. We looked forward to different things for her, widely different! She is a girl who ought to have made a good marriage; but I hear you have asked her to settle down here with us for the rest of her life.'

'Oh, as to that,' Massey said calmly, 'I do not want her to settle here! It does not signify to me where it is, so long – I shall take her where she likes best to go. I am not tied to Hilby!'

Then the Vicar took alarm.

'But, my dear fellow,' he said, 'why not at Hilby? And you are tied. Helen is fond of the place; and is – hum – ha – useful, very useful here; and we shall be all together, and – and so on. I cannot perceive why you should want to get away!'

'It shall be as she likes,' the other repeated. 'I do not care; only,' rousing himself to speak with more animation – 'only if things are made uncomfortable for Helen, I shall certainly –'

'But they won't be,' impressively. 'Why should they? Look here, Massey. Mrs Pearson is disappointed; naturally so – eh? – hum – ha. I don't say but that it is natural. You see, a tenant-farmer isn't exactly the kind of – eh? – you understand me. What the girl can be thinking of! Well, well! that isn't quite what I was going to say! But Mrs Pearson is, to say the truth, disappointed; and not, perhaps – well, cordial. But you must not mind that, nor think anything of it.'

'Oh, I don't,' Massey said serenely, flicking the ash off his cigar. 'I don't, I assure you.'

'And she'll come round,' her husband went on. 'She'll come round in time, I have no doubt, and if she doesn't,' here he came to an abrupt pause, and lowered his voice, 'if she doesn't, why, it won't want to make any difference to you or Helen, Massey.'

'No, oh no, I don't think it will,' Massey said, politely reassuring him. 'And now will you show me where is the nursery, Mr Pearson,' they having neared the house again by now. 'I want to go up to say good-night to Perrie.'

'What! going in?' the Vicar cried with some disappointment. He had meant to chide, and to forgive, and had thought in return for his urbanity to be taken into the young man's confidence, and to have been the recipient of his plans, and his hopes, and his fears. 'The nursery, oh!' It was in rather a crestfallen manner that he pointed out the direction of that apartment, and then he turned away to find up the miller's luckless son, with whose respectful ears he solaced himself for the rest of the evening.

CHAPTER XXVI

Helen and – Jim!

PERRIE PEARSON's nursery was a bare and cheerless room, not much approved by him, who had not possessed brothers or sisters, nor had ever been allowed the companionship of other children to make merry with there.

It was here that he now daily sobbed through dreary tasks presided over by Miss Armytage; it was here that he was always banished by his mother when in disgrace or trouble, and it was here that Helen had found him this evening, sitting on the floor, his head leaning against the window-guard, looking out drearily upon the scene on the lawn below.

'Aunt Helen will undress her dear little boy for a treat,' she had said, her heart yearning over the sad little mortal. And, having got him ready for bed, she had wrapped a flannel gown around him, and sat herself down in a low chair by the window, the child in her lap.

'I thank God I am not leaving him for long,' she thought to herself, pressing his little form against her. 'The thought of him sitting here, desolate and lonely, would have haunted me for always.'

'You must let me go now, Perrie, darling,' she had presently whispered to him. 'Auntie will come to you again before you sleep,' and then the door had opened, and James Massey had come in.

It was growing dusk in the melancholy nursery, although still light outside, and the child struggled into a sitting posture on Helen's knees, and tried to make out who his visitor might be.

'I come to bid you good-night, Perrie. How is it you did not come out to see the fun to-night?'

'I wasn't let,' Perrie explained with a pathetic catch in his breath, which had come from much sobbing.

'Poor little man! Who wouldn't let you? Why was it?'

'Never mind now,' Aunt Helen said. 'We don't want to talk about sad things. Perrie, Mr Massey will have to sit on your tall chair – fancy that! There is no other here. Won't he look a funny big baby?'

Perrie laughed a little hysterically at this. 'He can have my little stool,' he said; 'it's under the table.'

Mr Massey declared that that was far better and more sociable, fishing it out, and seating himself – his knees nearly up to his chin – near the low chair in the window. 'Why, you've had the best of it up here, Perrie! Sit up! Look at that funny Mr Gosling setting them to run races. It's capital sport to have Mr Gosling to look at – from a distance!'

'I should have liked to have comed to the tea,' the poor mite said, without turning his head to the window. 'I should have liked some of they jam rolls! It was jus' because I took you Aunt Helen's letter,' he said, his small heart swelling at the remembrance of his wrongs. 'There weren't no harm in it, 'cause Aunt Helen telled me.'

'Is that really why he is being punished?' Massey asked, addressing Helen for the first time. She nodded her head in acquiescence – a flash of anger in her eye.

'By Heaven! what a shame!'

'Hush! not before the child.'

'Aunt Helen telled me to go,' the little grieved voice went on, the heavy eyes on his visitor's face, secure of his sympathy and championship. 'There weren't no harm, and that ole bull was awful savage, an' he came smellin' at me an' growlin' an' wantin' me to go back home, but I wouldn't, because my Aunt Helen had telled me to be a brave boy.'

'And so you are,' Massey said, leaning forward and coaxing his hair – 'so you are! and it's a shame – a wicked shame – to punish you! Never you mind, Perrie, you are the best little man in the world, and you shall have that pony I told you about at once. I'll go and see after it my own self to-morrow. What do you think of that?'

Perrie sat bolt upright now, his cheeks flushed, his eyes shining.

'Won't that cost you an awful lot o' money?' he asked.

'Never mind about the money. Do you know,' sinking his voice, 'that there was in that letter you brought me, so bravely, in spite of the bull, a treasure worth more than all the money in the world. It's only fair that you should have a share in my good fortune.'

'But it is for the carrying of that very letter he is being punished – it is hardly judicious to reward him for the same thing, is it?' Helen objected, in a not quite steady voice.

'Tell Aunt Helen that there is a time in one's life when one ought not to be expected to be judicious.'

'But why did my Aunt Helen give that treasure to you, if it was worth such a 'normous lot?'

'Ah! why? Why did you, Aunt Helen?' He had got himself off that uncomfortable stool now, and was kneeling by her side with one hand on the boy's shoulder, and the other resting along the back of her chair. 'Why did you give me all that? I am not worthy of it!' he said, 'but, – as God is my witness – with my whole life I will love and cherish it!'

Then his voice broke, and he bent his head till it rested on her hand, clasped round the little boy.

'What does Mr Massey do so for? Why do you cry, Aunt Helen?' the child asked, looking up with wonder at her wet eyes and quivering lips.

'Hush!' she whispered, and put out a trembling, timid hand, and touched with a caressing gesture the bowed-down dark head. But as he felt the gentle touch, the young man with a sob threw up his head, and flung his arms about her neck, and drew her lips to his.

Ah! how Anna would have shuddered, could she but have seen! Anna's sister did not shudder, but she wondered at herself somewhat. Was this really Helen Smythe? Was that only James Massey? Could it be that she had meant to leave this man on the morrow – for ever? –this man whose kisses she was suffering upon her mouth – in whose arms now she lay without one struggle to escape? How sweet it was to be loved like this – how sweet! Would Anna have shuddered? Ah, but then Anna had never known! Poor Anna!

Perrie had slipped off her knee, and was standing in his scarlet flannel gown, watching the unusual behaviour of his two friends, with an expression of great interest, but hardly of so much surprise as the occasion undoubtedly warranted. He often and often kissed his auntie himself, Mr Massey was a stronger person than he, and he kissed stronger, that was all that Perrie thought of it. When he had looked on in silence long enough, he interrupted that wild flow of whispered, incoherent words which was being poured into Helen's ear, by a loud yawn.

'The child!' she cried reproachfully, starting up; for once she had forgotten him.

Massey kept one arm about her, and with the other pulled the child to him.

'Will you give Aunt Helen to me, Perrie?'

'No!' very promptly. 'What for?'

'Because I want her badly. You shall have the pony instead, you know.'

'But that won't make up for my Aunt Helen. You love her, awful much, too, don't you?'

'Awful much!'

'Does my auntie love you?'

'I don't know. She hasn't told me. I'm afraid to ask her – you ask her, Perrie.'

'Do you, Aunt Helen?'

Silence.

'Do you hear?' Massey asked, looking down at the face on his breast. 'You've got to answer.'

'Perrie,' she said, 'when two people love each other the best of all the world, what was that Miss Armytage said they did!'

'They got married,' Perrie said with promptitude.

'And so they did!' Massey cried with a triumphant laugh, and declared also that Perrie Pearson was the brightest little boy in all England.

And now Helen would be kept no longer, but would carry off her nephew to bed; and when she had lifted him in her arms and he had bidden good-night to Mr Massey, he hid his face against her neck, and began quietly to cry in the old-fashioned, unobtrusive manner that was peculiar to him. Helen had seen too many of his tears for the same reason, to doubt the cause.

'Now, Perrie, I won't have you do that!' she said firmly.

'Oh dear me!' he sobbed, 'my Aunt Helen is going away from me to-morrow!'

'But your Aunt Helen will soon be back,' she assured him, 'and you will have your pony, and –'

'And you are not going away?' from Massey.

'Indeed I am; I have made every arrangement.'

'But you shall not! I cannot spare you for a day – an hour! What are you talking about? I will not let you go.'

'All the same, I am going,' she said, and nodding defiance at him, disappeared with the child.

Half an hour later, when Helen reappeared below, she went to the piano and played some dance music. A waltz first – the people flocked together outside the drawing-room window and listened – a polka; one daring young man – Massey's shepherd, put his arm about the waist of a pretty well-dressed girl – the daughter of a keeper at the Hall, and was soon turning round with her on the short grass, to his own and her entire satisfaction. One or two more couples, gathering courage from their example, joined in. Those standing round criticised and applauded. Pollie Freeman and Mr Gosling, worn out by their respective exertions, were sitting on the couch in the bow window, watching the performance.

'Do you know any country dances, Miss Smythe?' Pollie asked, and Helen, without speaking, changed the tune, and, as if by magic, there were twenty couples toeing and heeling, turning, twisting, prancing to their own serious satisfaction.

Helen played on and on, the same dozen bars over and over again, till her fingers ached, till she could hardly see Massey's face as he leant against the piano, in the gathering dusk, till Pollie and Mr Gosling, with lingering backward looks at the two heads so close together over the music, had crept away, till the moon had begun to shine on the untiring dancers, and to send some silvery illumining rays into the long, dismal drawing-room.

Presently Mr Pearson, putting his head in at the window, suggested 'God save the Queen,' and in a quarter of an hour more Helen's *fête* was over, and the Vicarage grounds lay once more solemn and peaceful, under the beautifying moonlight.

'Say good-night to me outside,' Massey said, and led her to the group of fir-trees beneath whose shelter he had pleaded to her an age ago – last night!

'It must be good-bye as well as good-night,' the girl said. 'I start to-morrow, you know.'

'It is simply monstrous!' he cried impatiently. 'You only say it to torment me. I will not have you go.'

But it was to be only for a short time, she assured him, and explained how she had thought it better to let Anna get over her first grievance in the absence of the offender.

'And, besides, my friends in London are expecting me. I could not – would not disappoint them.'

'It is cruel to me!'

'If you say one word more – ! How dare you complain? I will go to Germany, after all. What is there to stop me?'

'There is my wish, which is going to be your law. What have you to say to that? Do you not know that you will have to obey me?'

'I know that I shall not begin to obey you yet.'

'Yet! That means that you intend to be obedient by-and-by – soon? Ah! my dear, my dear! I do not believe that I shall be a very hard master. When I remember, Helen, that only last night – last night! – I thought that I had said good-bye to you for ever! I sat for hours trying to knock into my head that you were lost to me, that I should see your face no more – great God! how wretched I was! – but I was half dazed with my misery, I suppose, for I could not get myself to understand it – to believe in it. My instinct was right, you see. I don't believe I could have left you last night, only that all the time I felt that it was impossible that we were to be really parted – that I should not, after all, be called on to bear trouble that was too heavy for me – that I could not bear. Something tells me the same of to-morrow. I don't believe that I can let you go. Helen, for all that I could not quite despair, I have had a horrible time – a horrible time! I have sometimes hated myself and every creature on God's earth that looked at me, or spoke to me, but you. I have wanted you to know how hideously I suffered; but you could not have understood – you would have despised me for being so helplessly weak. You would not? – sure? my darling! And you won't leave me, Helen; or if you must, you will fix a day, now very soon, when I may fetch you back?'

With the arrangements finally made, he had every reason to be content, although, of course, he upheld the privilege of his sex and grumbled still; and 'Mind, I won't promise I don't come before you give me leave,' he said. 'I will keep away while I can – I don't know how long that may be. No, I won't be reasonable; it's the very last thing I intend to be – it's utterly ridiculous of you to suppose that I should be reasonable – to-night! Must you go in, now? Why? Your sister is in bed, and the Vicar over his pipe in the library, and no one wants you but me – not a creature! – and you are mine, and I am not going to part with what is my very own. Must you really go? Think of the long hours in which I shall sit lonely thinking of you! Last night it was misery that kept me awake – to-night I shall not sleep for joy. You will be the death of me yet, Helen. Well, then, before you go, say something sweet to me, my Helen, my love! give me something to comfort me while you are away.'

'What can I say to you?'

'Tell me at least that you are not unhappy – stand so that the moonlight falls on your face. There! Now look at me and tell me.'

'I am not unhappy,' she whispered, with a shy smile up at him that admitted so much more than her words.

'And you love me?'

'You say so.'

'Helen, tell me in so many words. Look at me, and say, "I love you, Jim."'

'I love you –'

'Go on.'

'I can't,' she declared. 'Mr Massey, I shall have to be married to you years! years! before I can call you –'

'What?'

'Jim! Jim, we must keep that a close secret between us that you are – Jim; Anna must never, *never* know: I think I like you well enough to bear it, but she – in her worst horror she never dreamt of you as being anything worse than James!'

'For Heaven's sake don't let us waste time over Anna to-night! You have not satisfied me yet. Say that to me once more.'

'And is not that waste of time, to make me say to you twice what you know already?'

'What do I know?'

'That I am happy, and that I love you – Jim!'

After that, how could he let her go? The night was an hour older, the moon riding high in the heavens, showing even through the closed blinds in Anna's room, assisting her aggrieved thoughts and her neuralgia to keep her awake and tossing on her restless bed, looking in at Mr Pearson, nodding, half asleep, over his pipe in the library, in darkness, but for her rays – for Helen had never come in to light his lamp, and no one else came forward to perform that office for him – shining full on Perrie's slumbers, showing the pathetic, old-fashioned face, all alight and glorified in the divine radiance; turning the rambling Vicarage garden into a scene as solemn and as beautiful as a dream of heaven, before Mr Massey could tear himself away from the presence that was a joy incarnate to him – from the face that shone for him in the moonlight as pure and as lovely as an angel's.